"SIR, MORE HOSTILES," GUNNY SAID INTO HIS HEADSET. THERE WAS AN UNMISTAKABLE URGENCY IN THE PLATOON SERGEANT'S VOICE.

"Where?"

"South of us. Out of nowhere, eight large military trucks came roaring across the desert. They've stopped approximately four hundred yards from our position. There are soldiers pouring from them. From what I see, it appears to be at least a company-size unit. Three enemy mortar teams are heading off to set up their tubes. The rest are running toward us."

"Roger, Gunny. Reinforcements are still a couple of minutes out. Can you hold your position until they arrive?"

"Negative, sir. We're outnumbered ten-to-one. With what I see coming this way, we'll be overwhelmed before help can reach us . . ."

PRAISE FOR

THE RED LINE

"[An] intense and gripping debut thriller."

—*Library Journal* (starred review)

"*The Red Line* is a smart, timely military thriller from a promising new author." —The Real Book Spy

TITLES BY WALT GRAGG

The Red Line
The Chosen One

THE
CHOSEN
ONE

WALT GRAGG

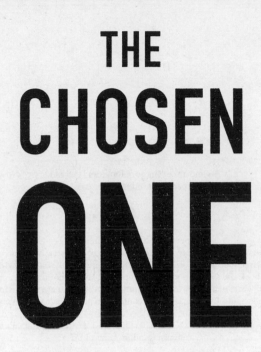

BERKLEY
NEW YORK

BERKLEY
An imprint of Penguin Random House LLC
penguinrandomhouse.com

Copyright © 2019 by Walter Gragg

Library of Congress Cataloging-in-Publication Data

Names: Gragg, Walt, author.
Title: The chosen one / Walt Gragg.
Description: First edition. | New York: Berkley, 2019.
Identifiers: LCCN 2019020180 | ISBN 9781984806338 (paperback) |
ISBN 9781984806345 (ebook)
Subjects: | BISAC: FICTION / Suspense. | FICTION / War & Military. | FICTION /
Action & Adventure. | GSAFD: Adventure fiction.
Classification: LCC PS3607.R3326 C48 2019 | DDC 813/.6—dc23
LC record available at https://lccn.loc.gov/2019020180

First Edition: November 2019

Printed in the United States of America
1   3   5   7   9   10   8   6   4   2

Cover photo by CollaborationjS/Arcangel
Cover design by Pete Garceau
Book design by Alison Cnockaert

To my children, Janet, Paul, Brian, and Jackie,
for all your help and support along the way

ACKNOWLEDGMENTS

Once more I wish to thank my legendary editor, Tom Colgan, and my incredible agent, Liza Fleissig, for their loyalty, hard work, dedication, and belief in *The Chosen One*. Without their efforts, my dream would likely have died long ago.

And a very special thanks to former Marine CH-46 pilot Chuck Wright for his immeasurable assistance and insight in making the Marine Corps portions of the book come alive. Semper fi.

1

Life is but an illusion. Scarcely more than a whispered dream.

3:04 A.M., OCTOBER 17
3RD PLATOON, BRAVO COMPANY,
2ND RECONNAISSANCE BATTALION, 2ND MARINE DIVISION
USS *WHITAKER*
OFF THE COAST OF EGYPT

Leaning against the cramped ship's railing, Marine First Lieutenant Samuel Erickson stared out at the black Mediterranean Sea. The surging ocean's waters, an aftereffect of yesterday evening's storm, crashed against the weathered ship's venerable hull.

To the north, having arrived within the hour, the ghostly silhouettes of the hushed naval armada stretched to the horizon. In front of Erickson, a sliver of a new moon and a dozen distant stars struggled to peek through the storm-swept clouds in the western sky. In the distance, a solitary flash of lightning waltzed upon the menacing heavens. The frightful sound of rolling thunder reached across the perilous waters. Its riotous discord assailed the night.

To the south, for hundreds of miles untold, the interminable artillery duels and flaming wreckage from three weeks of unyielding combat painted the fearsome skyline in vividly striking hues of red and yellow. Brilliant, death-filled flashes of man-made lightning went on without pause, its remorseless dance unending. The battle's hellish thunder consumed the North African desert.

None could have envisioned how quickly things had deteriorated.

Or how dire they would become. And with the aircraft carrier battle groups not yet present, the Americans weren't ready. It, however, no longer mattered. With the sunrise barely four hours away, they were out of time. For the Marine division it was now or never. Open a second front in the next few hours or Cairo would fall to the Chosen One's fanatics before the coming day's end. By this time tomorrow, his relentless armored divisions would be crossing the Sinai and nearing Jerusalem.

Deep in thoughts of past and future, the lieutenant heard none of the frenzied activity around him as Marines and sailors alike rushed to their positions on the troop transport. Erickson and the twenty-two men of his reconnaissance platoon pressed in close to the undulating rail. Like their leader, each carried a heavy pack. Each cradled a weapon in his arms.

Next to the lieutenant, the platoon radio operator, Corporal Hamilton Smith, quietly spoke with the flotilla command ship anchored a mile away. The awaited moment was almost here. It wouldn't be long before the order was given. When it was, Erickson's platoon would head for their Zodiac boats. After a wild dash to the beckoning coast, the platoon's stealthy entry onto the spanning desert would commence. Soon, in the dark of night, he'd be the initial American to set foot upon the treacherous shoreline. One hundred miles behind enemy lines he would lead his men onto the warm sands of Egypt. And he would hope for the best.

Even though the vast majority of the Pan-Arabs' massive army presently were involved in the brutal assaults upon Cairo and Alexandria, there were still ample forces lurking in western Egypt. Who or what the recon platoon might encounter once they reached the immense wastelands, the platoon leader hadn't a clue.

After a minute, maybe two, Smith's hand grasped his shoulder. Erickson turned to look into the solemn face of the young Marine.

"Time to shove off, sir." The radioman's voice was scarcely a whisper.

A pair of Zodiacs, each capable of transporting up to fifteen men, sat waiting. The loading of the small platoon would soon begin. Standing with
Gunnery Sergeant James Fife, his veteran platoon sergeant, Erickson
watched as the coxswain in each craft made his final preparations. Behind
their boats, three Humvees were being positioned on a large hovercraft.
The first two carried .50-caliber machine guns, the third TOW antitank
missiles. Each of the vehicles was fully armed and ready for battle.

"The men all set, Gunny?" Erickson asked.

"Ready as they can be, sir," was the reply.

"I know we haven't had much time to prepare for this, but given
the situation, there really was no choice but to go now."

"Yes, sir. The men understand. I've no doubt the platoon will do fine."

Silently, the earnest Americans began loading onto the rubber
boats. As they did, Erickson glanced toward the hovercraft and the
thirty Marines standing nearby.

"What about Sergeant Joyce's and Sergeant Davies's squads?"

With Erickson's highly decorated unit designated to handle the
division's most dangerous reconnaissance assignments, for the past
year the platoon had been reinforced with two infantry squads and an
antitank fire team. They would be the first to respond should the
scouts find themselves facing a situation beyond their capabilities. After twelve months together, Erickson considered the reinforcements to
be as much a part of the platoon as his recon teams.

"I spoke with both along with Corporal Whitehurst just before we
went topside, sir," Fife said. "They'll start loading the moment we
shove off. If we run into trouble, they'll launch immediately. With the
speed that hovercraft can maintain, they should reach us in slightly
more than five minutes."

"Let's hope this assignment turns out to be routine and we don't
need to call them in."

"Yes, sir. Is the initial wave of amtracs still scheduled to hit the beach within the hour?"

"Unless something unforeseeable happens, that's the plan. First two battalions in sixty, with a company of M-1 tanks a few minutes behind. If things go as scheduled, the majority of the division should be ashore before sunrise."

The last of the recon platoon's Marines had scrambled into the two craft. All that remained were the platoon's leaders. Erickson stepped onto the first Zodiac. Fife entered the second.

"Welcome aboard, Lieutenant," the coxswain said from his perch in front of the ninety-horsepower outboard motor at the back of the swift rubber boat.

"Like to say I'm happy to be here, Chief," Erickson replied. "But for some reason my mother continues to insist I not tell lies."

"Yes, sir, I know the feeling. I can think of quite a few places I'd rather be at this moment."

"Well, don't sweat it too much. After all, you're going into battle with the best damn platoon in the entire division."

Erickson's comment was no idle boast. His was the highest-rated unit in the entire nineteen-thousand-person division. Still, a casual glance wouldn't have explained why. On the surface there appeared to be little setting them apart from most Marine platoons. Many of Erickson's men had yet to reach their twentieth birthdays. And in their short lives none had distinguished himself in the slightest prior to becoming a Marine.

The team leaders were combat veterans and more than competent. But so were their counterparts in countless scores of 2nd Division platoons. Their battle-hardened platoon sergeant was as tough as the unrelenting Sahara winds and as smart as they came. Nonetheless, he was little different from fifty other platoon sergeants within the division. There was, however, one defining quality that placed Erickson's unit above all the others. The single feature separating 3rd Platoon from the rest was the six-foot two-inch, dark-haired, blue-eyed lieutenant who led them.

From the moment ten-year-old Sam was told his father had died in an unmerciful clash in the torturous mountains of a distant land, he'd wanted only one thing—to honor his memory and become a Marine. He'd eagerly arrived at boot camp on the day following his high school graduation. For three years he'd toiled without complaint as an enlisted man. But his abilities had been too strong, his intellect too great, his handsome face and captivating smile too memorable, for him to ever remain in obscurity. He'd soon risen up the ranks, being meritoriously promoted to sergeant. That, however, wasn't the end of things for Erickson.

Each year, an exceptional handful of enlisted sailors and Marines are selected for entrance into the Naval Academy. After three years of service, he'd joined them.

At Annapolis, he'd continued to shine, eventually graduating third in a fiercely competitive class. So prestigious a performance opened a world of possibilities. His efforts merited further educational opportunities and the best of assignments for the remainder of his career. Nevertheless, newly appointed 2nd Lieutenant Samuel Erickson would hear none of it. Instead, he requested an assignment with a combat unit, returning to the sole thing he truly wished to do.

It had only taken a couple of years for the highly skilled Erickson to be promoted to first lieutenant. With this promotion and his reconnaissance training complete, he'd spent the past two years in charge of 3rd Platoon.

Because he had been one of them, his empathy for his men was great. Even so, he understood that someday an exceptionally dangerous, soul-stealing moment like this would be upon them. So he'd pushed them harder and demanded more than any platoon leader within the division. Still, his concern for his Marines was genuine and because of it his platoon's loyalty absolute.

The platoon leader took a final look at those in his Zodiac and the one behind it.

"Let's get the show started, Chief," he directed the coxswain.

The sleek black boats were soon rocketing across the brooding waters. The mission was right on schedule. Three miles away, the barbarous North African landscape awaited. Despite the far distant battles' unceasing fireworks, not a hint of light or movement, nor the slightest sound, could be detected on the stretching shore.

In scant minutes, they would arrive.

2

E rickson leaped into the pounding surf. He struggled onto the wide sands. His platoon was right behind him.

Having disgorged their human cargo, both Zodiacs edged away from the coastline. They would retreat a safe distance into the swirling seas. Each would settle close enough to swoop in and evacuate the platoon should the situation call for it, but far enough away to not be susceptible to enemy rifles.

The Marines paused, crouching on the beach to get their bearings and determine if anything seemed amiss. Nothing out of the ordinary appeared—no unanticipated sounds or movements greeted them. Using hand signals, the platoon leader motioned for the three recon teams to start toward their objectives. Their rifles at the ready, night-vision equipment in place, the somber six-man teams responded.

With his best man in the lead, Staff Sergeant Laird's team headed east along the crashing surf. Anxious and wary, they would go out a half mile to scout the water's edge before heading inland to evaluate any potential threats looming in the unending desert. The Americans were exceptionally alert, as yet uncertain of their surroundings. With every tentative step, their keen senses assessed the dark, sinister world around them. In such a hostile environment all understood their next breath could be their last.

Staff Sergeant Charles's team headed west, their mission identical. Sergeant Merker's Marines moved south, directly inland.

The platoon's five remaining men stayed on the beach waiting for Merker's force to create some distance between them before edging forward. They would follow the scout team partway as it moved deeper into the Sahara. Two hundred yards from the water's edge, they'd set up their command post on the small bluffs where the measured beach met the unending vistas of the tedious desert. A few blades of parched grass were the only indications of where the mixing sands met. From the coastline, the beach gradually rose fifteen to twenty feet to create the slight hilltop where the first of the dry grasses lay.

It took less than two minutes for Merker's men to reach the rise and head down its far side. It felt significantly longer for those waiting near the angry tides. As Merker's team disappeared, the time had come for the command element to move. Erickson came up from his crouch and headed inland. The others followed.

"Sergeant Ingram, when we reach the top, set up your machine gun in the middle of our defenses," Erickson whispered.

"Will do, sir."

"Corporal Smith, stick with me every second. I've got to have the radio where I can get to it without delay."

"Just try to get away from me, sir," the likable corporal from the tough streets of central Los Angeles said.

"Petty Officer Bright, stay by Gunny's side so he can provide supporting fire should we have wounded needing attention," Erickson directed the platoon's corpsman.

"Yes, sir."

It wasn't long before Erickson and Fife were lying on the crest surveying the staid world around them. From their position they could see the three teams moving toward their objectives. Each had covered a quarter mile, halfway to their initial goal.

While the command group watched the trio's progress, Hamilton Smith was on the radio with the invasion task force. He looked over at the lieutenant. "First wave of amtracs will launch in a few minutes, sir. Twelve M-1s are being loaded onto hovercraft as we speak. Tanks should be here within ten minutes of the amtracs."

"Thanks, Corporal. Let them know that so far things are going as planned. No sign of anyone or anything near the beach."

Without responding, Smith spoke into the radio once again.

The relentless minutes slowly passed as the cautious Americans reached the boundaries of their search areas. A half mile inland, Merker's team set up a small defensive position directly in front of the center of the mile-wide landing zone. Laird and Charles finished their treks along the pounding waves and turned south, heading into the Sahara. Without incident, the torturous moments, one after the next, plodded on. Things couldn't be proceeding any better. At least that's how it appeared.

The situation, however, was about to change.

It was Laird's scouts who first heard, and then moments later saw, the approaching enemy.

The Pan-Arabs were coming up a desert draw that until this moment had masked their presence from the recon team. There could be no mistaking what was headed their way. A significant force crammed in the rear of a lengthy line of battered pickup trucks was churning across the inhospitable sands. So far, the roving patrol had yet to spot the Marines. Even so, the struggling formation was moving directly toward them.

"Sir, we've got company!" Laird's senior radio operator exclaimed.

"Where and how many?" Erickson replied.

"They're less than a thousand yards away, coming up that big ravine south-by-southeast of us. Got to be at least a dozen small trucks, each carrying a number of men. Must be sixty of them, possibly more. Most are holding rifles, with some RPGs mixed in. Wouldn't be surprised if they've also got a few machine guns and possibly a mortar team or two. What are your orders, sir?"

The threat was far too real. Unless the enemy changed course or the recon team took evasive action, there was no way the Pan-Arabs wouldn't spot Laird's men.

With so many in the approaching force, the lieutenant had little choice. "All three teams are to fall back on my location. We'll consolidate our rifles and call for help. Is that understood? Avoid detection at any cost and fall back on my position immediately."

After each team leader gave an affirmative response, Erickson turned to Hamilton Smith. "Tell Joyce and Davies to launch without delay."

As the teams scurried toward the rise, the combat-experienced Erickson began plotting the potential engagement. He would use the two things the Americans had going for them—the black of night and the element of surprise—to his advantage. Before they could respond, he would hit the oncoming intruders with everything he had.

The platoon's members soon arrived. Erickson turned toward Laird. "How far away is the enemy patrol?"

"Six hundred yards or so, sir. They should be leaving the gully soon and heading onto the open desert. As we watched their movements, they didn't seem to be in a hurry. The trucks appeared to be going less than ten miles an hour as they pushed through the deep sands."

"Were there any indications they'd spotted you?"

"No, sir, we were extremely careful to make sure that didn't happen."

"Good. With as slow as they're moving, we've ample time to set up a nice little trap. Given the time of night and the fact they're so far behind their own lines, the chances of them being prepared for what's about to hit them are pretty slim. With any luck they won't even realize we're here until they're right on top of us. By then it will be too late."

Still unaware, the quarry came on. Erickson had been correct in his assessment. After far too many nights patrolling the same tired stretch without the slightest incident, the approaching force had become lackadaisical and more than a bit bored. Little did they know what awaited.

The ambush was set. The motionless Marines lay in a straight line facing southeast with the machine gun in the middle and the three Americans with grenade launchers attached to their M-16s dispersed throughout the force.

"Don't fire until I give the command," Erickson ordered. "Best thing that could happen would be for them to pass without ever realizing we're here."

But luck wasn't with the hidden Marines. The roving patrol was headed straight for the furtive onslaught. Relentlessly, the ill-prepared prey came on, drawing closer and closer to the deadly trap. Barely one hundred yards separated them from an all-consuming tempest. The stilled Marines, hiding in the darkness, selected their targets from among the approaching line. The apathetic Pan-Arabs were about to pay dearly for their mistake.

"Open fire!" Erickson screamed.

In less than an instant, machine-gun bullets, accompanied by nineteen spitting rifles, ripped through the foreboding night. Lines of vivid tracers roared toward their ill-destined foe. Almost as one, all three grenade launchers fired. In seconds, a trio of lethal explosions tore through the black void. Each swiftly reloaded the tubes on the front of their rifles and launched a second grenade. The platoon of highly skilled marksmen brought a raging firestorm down around their overwhelmed opponents' heads. In a handful of seconds, four crushed trucks were ablaze. Five . . . ten . . . fifteen souls were gone without ever realizing what had hit them. More would soon follow.

The horrific screams of the wounded and dying filled a dispassionate world.

Unprepared and confused, the floundering patrol's response was slow and disjointed. Erickson's platoon didn't hesitate, hitting the stricken ones with everything they had. Those in the front of the convoy had no chance. Before they could leap from the rear of the dilapidated trucks, they were devoured.

The staggering survivors turned their vehicles and ran toward the open sands. The Americans cut them down in great numbers. In the end only a single truck, its assailed engine releasing a steady stream of gray smoke, and a fortunate handful of soldiers would escape the malignant encounter.

It was over almost before it began. As the scant survivors disappeared, Erickson ordered his men to cease fire. He took a quick look around, quite satisfied with the result. More than fifty Libyans lay dead or dying. The scouts had survived nearly unharmed. Two wounded, neither seriously, was all they had suffered in the uneven struggle. The lieutenant understood, however, that with their foe now aware of their presence, they couldn't let down their guard.

"Gunny, Joyce and Davies squads should be here in the next couple of minutes. Can you handle things here while I head back to the beach to get them organized?"

"Absolutely, sir."

"Corporal Smith, let the task force know what has happened, then I want you on me."

Erickson took a final look around, leaped to his feet, and ran toward the fuming waters. He would be waiting when the hovercraft arrived.

Other than the distant cries of their severely wounded rivals, the meager elevation went quiet once again. This time, however, the lull would be short-lived. Their hand forced, the Americans no longer had surprise on their side. And things would soon be growing worse. As he stood on the beach waiting for the hovercraft to reach them, Erickson had no idea of how quickly that would happen.

"Sir, more hostiles," Gunny said into his headset. There was an unmistakable urgency in the platoon sergeant's voice.

"Where?"

"South of us. Out of nowhere, eight large military trucks came roaring across the desert. They've stopped approximately four hundred yards from our position. There are soldiers pouring from them. From what I see, it appears to be at least a company-size unit. Three enemy mortar teams are heading off to set up their tubes. The rest are running toward us."

Whether the new arrivals had been backup for the first group of marauders or happened to be passing through the area as the fierce onslaught began, the Marines hadn't a clue. Yet unexpectedly the daunting numbers the platoon faced had more than tripled.

"Roger, Gunny. Reinforcements are still a couple of minutes out. Can you hold your position until they arrive?"

"Negative, sir. We're outnumbered ten-to-one. With what I see coming this way, we'll be overwhelmed before help can reach us. It's not ideal, but our best hope might be to pull back and dig in on the beach. Request permission to withdraw the men and retreat toward the shoreline to buy us some time."

Erickson had complete faith in his platoon sergeant's judgment. "I sure hate to give up the high ground, Gunny. But do what you need to do."

3

With only the flickering flames from the destroyed trucks to guide them in the blossoming battle with the Americans, up and down the beach the Pan-Arabs were shooting in every direction. The resolute lieutenant could see the streaking gunfire. The ghastly images appeared to be coming right for him. He could sense the bullets striking all around the settling hovercraft. He could hear the lurid sounds of a seeking death whizzing past. A pair of mortar rounds exploded on his left. Deadly shell fragments ripped through the horrific night. Erickson's agile mind registered that he was picking up movement everywhere he looked on the dunes above the beleaguered platoon. For the moment, there was no time to worry about such things. The reinforcements had to get ashore. If they failed to do so, it wouldn't be long before the mortars found the landing craft's range and destroyed them all with a single blow.

"Go! Go! Go!" he yelled while furiously waving his arm.

The lead Humvee, with its four-man fire team, roared out of the opening. Toward the rear of the vehicle, Sergeant Joyce was positioned behind the .50-caliber machine gun. The moment the tires splashed in the knee-deep waters, the combat-ready squad leader pulled the trigger. The first of many five-shell bursts was expelled from the imposing gun's barrel. Corporal Johnson's Humvee was right behind. The second vehicle's machine gun was soon firing.

"Concentrate your efforts on the low bluffs where the beach meets the desert!" the lieutenant screamed at the passing crews. "That's where most of the firing's coming from."

The initial Humvee hurried down the nightmarish seashore to the left. Johnson's felt its way along the fierce waves on the right. They'd go out a short distance to hold the flanks and keep their opponent from getting behind the Marines as they attempted to reclaim the high ground. While they raced along the perilous water's edge, each gunner focused on the small rise. Both came under extreme fire.

The final Humvee roared down the ramp and headed onto the thick sands. Corporal Whitehurst stood next to its TOW missile tube. A short distance from the landing craft, Whitehurst ordered his team to stop. His driver remained behind the steering wheel with the engine idling. Despite the mounting attention the stationary vehicle was receiving, Whitehurst stayed in his position just to the left of the anti-tank missile. He was ready to launch a TOW at the first sign of enemy armor. His 7.62-caliber machine gunner leaped from the front passenger seat. Using the Humvee for protection, he took up a supporting position. On the other side of the vehicle, the team's final member slid from the rear seat and began shooting his M-16.

The moment Whitehurst's Humvee cleared the ramp, the remaining fire teams scurried to escape the murderous confines of the motionless craft. Beneath a withering onslaught from the Chosen One's defenders, they rushed in every direction.

When he reached the end of the ramp and was poised to leap into the frenetic tides, a first of the Americans went down beneath the grievous assault. The lance corporal tumbled into the unsettled ocean at the edge of the craft. His mortal wound was so shockingly sudden and totally lethal that the dead Marine uttered not a sound. Those behind him in their mad dash for the beseeching sands were splattered with flying fragments of fractured skull and shattered brain cells. A half dozen stumbled over their dead comrade and fell into the spiraling currents. Spewing salt water and obscenities, they struggled to their feet. Each of the fallen Marines fought to regain his senses. A widening pool of blood trailed from the floating body. Pushed by the angry currents, it wafted toward the shoreline. While he stood thigh-deep in the churning waters, a faint ring of red formed on Erickson's pant leg.

Struck in the side by a burst of automatic gunfire, another Marine dropped in the ardent sea. The impacting bullets had penetrated his fleeing frame a fraction of an inch above the protection of his body armor. With great effort, he pulled himself to the violent ocean's edge before the final labored breaths deserted him. The attackers were beginning to find the range.

The scattering squads exited the idling craft and dashed for the windswept shore. Twenty yards inland, the lead elements started digging in alongside the recon platoon. On the right, a third and fourth running figure went down. Neither had reached solid ground. The first, his kneecap crushed by an AK-47's bullet, dragged himself onto the sands. The second moved not at all. His flowing blood soon added to the growing crimson foam tugging at the bitter waters. The incessant firing on both sides intensified. The enemy barrage zeroed in on the landing zone. Without warning, a whistling mortar round exploded in the center of one of Sergeant Joyce's fire teams. Four fresh-faced reinforcements were added to the ever-expanding rolls of those who hadn't survived to witness the coming day.

Radioman Smith rejoined Erickson. "Everyone's ashore, Lieutenant," Smith said.

"Good. Let's get out of this damn water and find some shelter so we can figure out exactly what we're up against."

"I'm with you, sir."

Erickson banged on the side of the craft. The ramp slowly rose while the anxious sailors worked to free their rebellious charge from the sandbar's clutches. The moment it was clear of the restricting sands, it whirled about and raced back toward the fleet.

An additional mortar round exploded in the bloody tides near where the fleeing hovercraft had rested. At incredible speed, menacing fragments flew in every direction. As he fought to reach the fragile shore, the overpowering force of the explosion knocked Erickson to his knees. A sharp-edged sliver searched out the platoon's leader. It sliced through his fatigue jacket and bored into his exposed flesh. The serrated metal embedded itself deep within the well-developed biceps on his left arm. Searing pain leaped into his startled brain. The stunned lieutenant fell face forward into the briny sea. Beneath his pack he fought with all he had to find his footing. The relentless tides tugged at his floundering form. The strong currents started pulling him toward the ocean's depths. Hamilton Smith grabbed the embattled lieutenant and dragged him to his feet. Fresh blood ran down Erickson's arm from the malicious rip in his shirtsleeve.

"You okay, sir?"

Erickson glanced at the torn sleeve. The intense anguish wasn't subsiding in the slightest.

Nevertheless, for the moment there was nothing he could do.

"I'll live," he said. "Let's get out of here while we still can."

Beneath their antagonists' riotous assault, Erickson sprinted forward past the line of dug-in Marines. He dove headfirst into a small depression. Smith threw himself down next to him.

James Fife raced up carrying the handful of satchel charges brought by the newly arriving squads. He joined Erickson and Smith. Sergeant Merker and one of his scouts leapfrogged forward. They took up defensive positions in front of the platoon's leaders.

"What're our losses so far?" Erickson asked Fife.

"At least six to eight of Joyce and Davies's men. Three of ours including Staff Sergeant Laird. But it's going to go a hell of a lot higher if we don't get off this stinkin' beach real soon."

"Still confident we're up against a company of infantry?"

"Yes, sir. From what I saw when they arrived, that remains my best guess."

Erickson poked his head up from the sands. There was no letup in the onslaught. "Are we strong enough to take them out and regain control of the beachhead?"

"I'd bet next month's paycheck on it, sir. Despite the fierceness of their attack, we really did catch them by surprise. There isn't much cohesiveness to their efforts. They seem quite confused and have had no time to fortify their positions. If we hit them with everything we've got, we should be able to take back the high ground. We'll no doubt suffer additional losses, but it'll be far worse if we stay where we are."

"Then let's get this done," Erickson responded. He keyed his headset, allowing him to communicate directly with every man in the platoon. "Okay, enough of this crap. Before the first of the amtracs arrives we need to regain control of the landing zone. Corporal Whitehurst, you and your Humvee are to remain here. The rest of you are to spread out until you connect up with Joyce and Johnson. Once you've done that, your team is to move forward on its own initiative until your grenade launcher can accurately hit that rise. Lay down a barrage at the point in front of you where the grasses begin. Give it everything you've got. Saturate the entire area with grenades then make a frontal assault on the enemy defenses. Are there any questions about what each of you is to do?" He paused, waiting for a response. His query was met with silence. "All right, then, let's take back this beach!"

The platoon moved into action. It wasn't long before each leapfrogging team's grenade launcher was within range. The eight surviving Americans armed with launchers loaded a stubby grenade canister into the tube below the barrel on the front of his rifle. Each pulled the tube back, locking the grenade in place. From this distance it would take a high-arching shot to lob the destructive ordnance onto the far bluffs. But the Marines had long hours of practice. And they were deadly in their abilities to put their virulent munitions in the center of the targeted area. Even in the severe pressures of what for many was their initial combat, they wouldn't miss.

A first reached forward and pulled his savage launcher's trigger. Others soon joined in. The soaring armaments sailed through the night. In rapid succession, one explosion followed the next. A hideous end rained down in fragmenting torrents upon the Pan-Arab lines. The proficient Americans reloaded, firing again and again.

The hellish anguish of their dying adversaries' cries punctured the fearful gloom. The abject agony of their suffering pierced the blustery darkness. On this soulless night, many of his believers would be going to the Chosen One's paradise. Beneath the Marines' fierce actions, the rifle fire from the wavering dunes dwindled until it was hardly more than a trickle. It took little time for huge holes to appear in their beset foes' defenses.

The Americans saw their opening. They charged straight for the disjointed remnants of their ravaged adversary. The slaughter was on. On the small crest, the apt platoon eliminated their opponent with ruthless intensity. While the diminishing fight continued, the command group rushed to the vista. They threw themselves into the strewed grasses.

"How much time before the amtracs reach us, Gunny?"

Fife peered at his watch. "Twenty minutes or so, sir."

"I calculate our losses at more than a dozen dead and half that many wounded."

"Sounds about right. Gonna grow further if we don't eliminate those damn mortars."

The pair lay on the hilltop and waited. They knew it was only a matter of time before the mortar teams fired again and revealed their location.

A few seconds later another whistling salvo screamed into the squall-swept skies.

"You spot 'em, Platoon Sergeant?"

"Yep. Three flashes in that gully about a quarter mile southwest of here."

"That's what I got. They're in range of Corporal Johnson's .50-caliber, aren't they?"

"Sure looks that way, sir. I'd say they're about five hundred yards south of Johnson's Humvee. And he rarely misses at that distance."

"Then let's give Corporal Johnson a little target practice and finish off the final obstacle in securing this beach." The lieutenant keyed his headset once more. "Johnson, the mortar teams are in a gully about five hundred yards south of you. Drive up to the crest, find 'em, and kill 'em. When you're done, return to your original position defending the flank."

Johnson's response was simple and straightforward. "They're as good as dead, sir."

And the battle-tested Marine was true to his word. In less than two minutes, all nine members of the mortar teams had been eliminated and the Humvee was back in its original location, ready to protect the right.

On the far left, the platoon continued to engage the final elements of the dissipating defenders. Yet with the destruction of the Pan-Arab mortars, the last of the serious threats had been destroyed without suffering further casualties.

In a modest depression a few feet in front of the platoon's leaders lay the twisted bodies of two of the Chosen One's mortally wounded disciples. Hamilton Smith crawled forward to verify both were dead. Their opponents' lifeless corpses were covered by the folds of their headdresses and masked by the night's onerous mantle. His rifle ready, Smith lifted the dressing from the face of the first. He stared at the inert image. The corporal pulled the night-vision equipment from his eyes to take a closer look. A puzzled expression appeared on his features. A bolt of recognition swept through him. Even in the weighty darkness, there was no denying what he'd uncovered. He dropped the silk cloth back onto the blood-creased body. Smith slid over to the second silent form. Once more he lifted the thin covering to view the motionless enemy. After a brief examination of the contorted shape, he let the cloth slip from between his fingers.

"Damn, Lieutenant," he said. "I don't believe it. They're both women." Farther down the small slope, devastated figures, gripped in death, were haphazardly strewed about. Their clothing was identical to those Smith had inspected. "It looks like they're all women, sir."

Erickson and Fife edged forward. The lieutenant raised the red-streaked cloth covering the first defeated soldier's face. It took only a cursory glance to confirm Smith was right.

"We've been fighting a company of women," Erickson said.

"So what?" Fife replied. "In the past few minutes those women have cost some damn fine Marines their lives. I don't care who we've been fighting—men, women, children, little green invaders from outer space. At this point, it doesn't matter."

"This one can't be over fifteen," Smith said.

Erickson let the cloth drop back onto the girl's sightless eyes. He looked at Hamilton Smith. "Gunny's right. It doesn't matter."

Just then, one of the jumbled figures on the backside of the rise stood up. She threw down her rifle and raised her hands into the air. The teenage girl had hidden among the dead in hopes of somehow escaping the anguish-filled destiny that had befallen her friends. She'd seen an opportunity to live and embraced it. The young Algerian figured her best chance of surviving was by surrendering to the Americans above her on the ridge.

"Looks like at least one of the Chosen One's followers isn't all that eager to enter the next world this morning," Fife said.

"Motion for her to come up," Erickson responded.

The platoon sergeant signaled with the barrel of his rifle for the terrified girl to start toward them. She took a first tentative step. A flash of gunfire rang out. Her fatally wounded figure sank to the ground and moved no more. Death seized another victim.

The startled Marines dove for cover. Each searched for who had
fired the shots. Yet none could identify the source of the assault. Unexpectedly, a perverse figure popped up from his hiding place behind
a rocky outcropping forty yards away. The turbaned image turned and
ran toward the desert. He hadn't gone far before Fife cut him down
with a quick spray from his M-16.

"That was no woman," Smith said.

"Goddamn company political officer," the platoon sergeant said.
"I'd stake my life on it. One of the Chosen One's religious fanatics. I'd
heard rumors he was placing them behind his lines to kill anyone who
tried to surrender." He paused, taking a quick look around. "The more
of those sons-a-bitches we kill, the better I'll feel."

Two more masked forms leaped up from behind a not-so-distant
dune. This time they were women. Both fired a handful of wild shots
toward the crest. With rifles in hand, they turned and ran toward the
open Sahara. Erickson brought up his rifle, aimed, and squeezed
the trigger. His gunfire echoed throughout the night. The retreating
images went down in a tangled heap. The sullen lieutenant dropped
the weapon from his shoulder. It was obvious he wasn't pleased with
the distasteful action that had been forced upon him.

"You had to do it, sir," Fife said. "Don't kill them now, they might
kill one of us later."

"I know. But that doesn't make it any easier. Send Sergeant Merker's team down to search those dunes in front of us and all the dirty
little places where the enemy could still be hiding. Let's make sure
there are no more of the Chosen One's friends waiting to surprise us."

Merker's scouts began scouring the area in front of the platoon's position. While they did, the small-arms fire ended as Joyce's squad eliminated the final pockets of resistance.

With Petty Officer Bright taking care of the platoon's wounded,
there was nothing the corpsman could do for any of the Arab girls who

were still breathing. Given the enemy's extreme indoctrination, few would have accepted help from the infidels even if offered. Most were severely wounded. Yet they did their best to suffer in silence, praying through the intense pain for the end to come. In little more than minutes, without medical attention, the majority would bleed out.

After the raucous battle, the near silence was deafening. For ten minutes the dark world around the Americans was almost serene. Yet to no one's surprise, the quiet wouldn't last.

4

Gunny peered at the distant desert. "Sir, there's more company on the way." The anxiousness in his voice was unmistakable.

"What? Where?"

Fife raised his arm and pointed toward the endless void. "South-by-southwest, cloud of dust about three miles out. Four tanks headed this direction in one hell of a hurry."

"Aw shit, get Whitehurst's team up here. As fast as those things are moving, they'll be here in five or six minutes."

The platoon sergeant keyed his headset.

Erickson watched as the rushing giants continued to approach the depleted platoon's lines.

In seconds, the Humvee armed with antitank missiles roared up the sandy slope and stopped next to the platoon leader's position. Their furious opponent was closing fast.

"What do we have, sir?" Whitehurst asked.

"South-by-southwest, a platoon of tanks headed toward us."

It only took a moment for the corporal to identify the approaching threat. "I've got them. From their silhouettes looks like American-made M-60s." Whitehurst immediately understood the immense danger the Marines faced. His mounting concerns matched those of the platoon's leaders. Yet even with the dire turn of events, he was too well trained and too confident in his abilities to panic. And the last thing he wanted was to further alarm the others. So he pushed aside any self-doubt and did his best to sound poised and professional. He knew his words wouldn't fool Erickson or Fife, but hoped they would calm his fire team and keep them focused on the task ahead. "TOWs will handle 'em just fine. Dinkins, grab the replacement missiles. These guys are not yet in range. But that won't last much longer. Half mile, maybe a bit more, and the TOWs can reach them. Unfortunately, their main gun will also be able to reach us. We've got to reload and fire as rapidly as possible. Our six missiles will be more than enough to eliminate them. All we need is time."

Whitehurst began tracking the spectral forms. He soon located the leader in his crosshairs. As it grew nearer the corporal followed the feverish M-60 to get a feel for its range and speed.

"Smith, inform the task force that four tanks are about to attack," Erickson directed.

The corporal started speaking into the radio.

"Wait!" Fife said.

The radioman stopped in mid-sentence. He stared at Fife, unsure of what to do.

"We've got much bigger problems than a platoon of tanks," Gunny said. "Look beyond them. There's an immense curtain of sand a few miles back that appears to go on forever."

Those on the modest hilltop focused their attention on the platoon sergeant's latest discovery. The strange image, giving every appearance of a savage Sahara sandstorm, also was coming their way.

But it wasn't a sandstorm.

A startled Erickson was the first to recognize what it was they were viewing. "Give me the handset." The radioman handed it to him. "Sierra-Victor, this is Bravo-Three-Six."

"Go ahead, Bravo-Three-Six."

"Sierra-Victor, four M-60s are three miles out and closing with our position. We've also identified a far more serious problem. The forward elements of a Pan-Arab armored division are five miles behind them. Like the M-60s, they're headed this way at a high rate of speed. Be aware there may be additional divisions approaching that we've not yet identified. How do you wish us to proceed?"

The threat was undeniable. Three hundred tanks, an equal number of armored personnel carriers, thousands of zealous soldiers, untold artillery pieces, bristling air defense missiles, and scores of supporting equipment were flying across the desert intent on destroying the Americans. They had significantly more firepower than the Marine division, on its own, could muster. If not stopped, their lead units would reach the landing zone in twenty minutes.

"Wait one, Bravo-Three-Six."

It felt like forever as the lieutenant lay holding the handset while the division leadership conferred. Finally a new voice came on. Erickson instantly recognized it was the division commander.

"Bravo-Three-Six, you are to proceed with the initial plan," the general said. "We are landing here, we are landing now. We've been ordered to establish a second front before the sun peeks over the horizon. And the 2nd Marine Division will damn sure do everything in its power to ensure that happens. No matter how challenging this becomes, no matter what obstacles we face, there is no other option if we're going to keep this potential planet-consuming holy war from erupting further."

"Understood, sir."

"We're launching a dozen Hornets to blunt the enemy attack. The aircraft carriers are still one hundred miles out so it will take eight to ten minutes to launch the aircraft and have them reach the coast. In addition, every destroyer in the task force is aligning to unleash their five-inch guns. The estimate for that to occur is the same as the fighters. Eight to ten minutes before we're ready to go. If that doesn't hold the sorry bastards until we can get our forces ashore, I don't know what will."

"Yes, sir. But what about the four tanks closing with my position? They'll be here in less than four minutes. Unless stopped they'll reach the beach just prior to the first wave landing. The amtracs won't stand a chance against such firepower. The tanks will rip them to shreds."

"Understood. Be aware we've nothing that can reach you in time. So there's no other option I'm afraid. For our plan to succeed we need you to take out those tanks. Can you do that, Lieutenant?"

"Sir, with a single antitank Humvee we'll need some luck. But we do have enough missiles to handle a force that size. We're tracking them right now and are seconds away from releasing a first TOW."

"Good. No matter what the cost, take them out. The landing depends on it."

"All right, here we go," Whitehurst said.

After a quick glance to ensure no one was within the backfiring canister's lethal discharge, the corporal released the first of his potent missiles. The noxious TOW burst from the firing tube. Trailing a thin fiber-optic cable behind it, the measuring slayer skimmed across the lifeless desert in pursuit of the targeted M-60. While it did, its fins popped out and a light came on in its tail. The approaching tanks continued on their determined way toward the Americans. Not one had the slightest notion that a hideous assailant was on the wing, ready to claim the first of them.

Whitehurst made a handful of adjustments to the menacing missile's flight. In seconds, the TOW's nose struck home. A mighty explosion rocked the callous morning. The dying M-60's crushing fireball reached high into the heavens. Within its flaming walls, four frantic beings instantly were consumed by the all-devouring blaze.

The remaining leviathans didn't hesitate. Without pause, they continued their fervent charge toward the American defenses. The horrid shadows came on, their shrilly creaking treads growing louder with every passing second.

Whitehurst reached for a replacement TOW to reload the firing tube. It would take at least a half minute to prepare for the next launch. For the next thirty seconds, the platoon would be at the mercy of the sordid tanks.

The lunging ogres were, however, too far away to open fire with their machine guns. And unlike the more sophisticated American M-1 tanks, they didn't have fully integrated shoot-on-the-move capabilities. Each would have to come to a stop before its crew could target its foe and unleash its main cannon against the Marines. The Pan-Arabs decided to continue their maniacal rush. At thirty miles an hour, a frightful end was coming to claim the battered platoon.

Whitehurst was up and ready. He selected his next victim. Once more a TOW leaped from the fiery container to seek and destroy. Straight and steady the searching missile ripped across the tedious landscape at incredible speed. It relentlessly closed with the surging formation. The corporal made the final adjustments to its destructive flight. The injurious armament struck home. Another thunderous blast swept through the crisp night. A second fifty-ton beast's roaring funeral pyre was added to the grisly bonfires near the coastline.

Yet the surviving armor wasn't dissuaded. They were a mile out and closing fast. Both had pinpointed the location of the murderous attack. The M-60 on the right raced toward the American lines. The other suddenly stopped. The halting tank's crew started feeding in the firing coordinates for the Humvee's position.

When he finished loading his third missile, Whitehurst looked up at their forceful adversaries. There was no mistaking that the barrel of the motionless M-60's powerful cannon was elevating.

"Get the hell away from here!" he screamed. "He's about to fire. If I don't beat him to the draw, this place will erupt in about ten seconds."

The command element and the three members of Whitehurst's fire team raced for cover. The TOW operator stood his ground. The unflinching Marine pushed back his mounting fears. He shoved aside the bile welling within him and forced his attention onto acquiring his prize. Even with a target as easy as this one, he had to confirm the hulking brute was securely within his sights. If he released his deadly missile too soon and missed, there'd be no chance of preparing another TOW before their fearsome opponent consumed him.

Whitehurst took a deep breath and fired. Bursting from the missile tube, the next resolved killer rushed across the smoke-clogged landscape toward the stationary tank. For the highly proficient corporal the destructive mission was almost routine. As long as he remained focused, there was scant possibility his quest would fail. His eyes grew wide as the irrepressible ordnance neared its goal. A final, slight correction of the TOW's frenzied flight was all that remained and a third life-stealing transgressor would be no more.

At the last possible moment, unaware that an unspeakable end was reaching out to claim them, the Pan-Arab crew fired. Whitehurst saw the unmistakable flash as the tank discharged its huge main gun. He knew it was too late. He had to stay with his TOW to make sure his dauntless missile found its victim. There was nothing he could do to save himself. His only hope was that the Pan-Arab crew's aim was poor. Whitehurst peered through his scope, watching his baneful executioner race toward its objective. The last adjustment was made. It brought the approaching TOW dead center onto the massive form. The morbid machine was about to suffer a horrifying result. Hades's fires would soon be upon still more of the Chosen One's followers. The massive cannon shell and crushing missile reached their tantalizing targets at the exact same instant.

Neither had missed.

In a thunderous roar, the vanquished tank exploded. Its crippled remains soon burned. Engulfing flames billowed forth over a wide area, further illuminating the predawn battle.

An infinite fraction later, the M-60's ruinous power fell upon the small combat vehicle. The impact of the striking munitions sent the devastated Humvee's twisted wreckage sailing into the malicious night. Burning pieces of its ragged frame poured down upon the ridge like the dying essence of a well-orchestrated Fourth of July display.

The instant the last of the falling embers touched the lifeless ground, the lieutenant and his platoon sergeant ran through the smoldering sands toward the scattered ruins. Hamilton Smith was right behind. There wasn't enough of the ravished Humvee to identify. In one swift blow, the platoon's armored defenses had disappeared. Whitehurst was gone, his body vaporized. The minute fragments of his fragile flesh were dispatched to the four winds by the enormous explosion. A few bits of singed cloth were all that remained. Like far too many on this appalling morning, his wife and family would never have the honor of burying him. His young children would not be granted the opportunity to say their final good-byes. Their fading memories of their heroic father would soon be lost to the persistent passage of time.

The stark violence of the perverse battlefield confounded them all. A dreadful reality sank deep within the defenders. The anguished screams of the wounded. The unearthly silence of the dead. A surreal horror surrounded them. It threatened to swallow whole the struggling men. And the reviling events were far from over.

The stunned lieutenant looked upon the wide desert. He fought to control his torrential emotions. And his disavowing wits. The final assassin roared forward, intent on finishing its conquering task.

"What do we do now?" Erickson asked as he turned toward his platoon sergeant. "How do we stop that last M-60?"

Fife stared at the growling beast as it flew toward the American lines. The all-consuming worry on his face was undeniable. He had no answer.

Three hundred yards distant the assured assassin identified the spot for which he'd been searching. He churned to a stop on the highest elevation for miles around. From here, he'd be able to attack anything on the beach or in the nearby waters. The platoon's survivors dove for whatever protection they could find. But there was little to be found. The tank's deadly pair of machine guns started firing, strafing the entire length of the ridge. The violator's spirited guns zeroed in on the thin line of widely scattered Marines. Ever so methodically, the vindictive killer's turret turned from right to left and back again as it concentrated its ardent fire upon the small rise. The steady assault from the unmerciful attacker went on without pause. This time it was the swelling ranks of dying and wounded Americans that filled the blood-creased desert.

With an endless chorus of crushing rounds smashing into the acidic world around them, the overcome Marines attempted to respond. But the lethal dragon was too far away and its thick plating much too imposing to conquer with their individual weapons. Without Whitehurst's armor-razing TOWs, there was little they could do to defend against so ravenous an intruder.

The vile assailant's turret halted. Its main gun lowered until the target was squarely within its sights. The stirring enemy fired. The repressive cannon's ear-shattering thunder consumed the North African coast. A mighty explosion tore apart Johnson's Humvee. His fire team vanished from the battlefield. The despairing Marines were outgunned.

"We can't just lie here while he takes his time and finishes us off. We've got to do something," Erickson yelled over the sounds of the slaughter. He glanced behind him. "The first wave's just outside the breakwaters."

Transporting an entire battalion containing more than nine hundred Marines, a wide line of AAVs—assault amphibious vehicles, or "amtracs" as the Marines called them—was pushing through the rough waters toward the coastline. A second wave was right behind. Each of the twenty-nine-ton armored vehicles carried a crew of four and twenty-one Marines. When they reached the beach the plan was for the tracked vehicles to come ashore and carry their passengers farther inland.

Their thin armor and modest weapons were no match for a tank.

Having not yet spotted those in the water, the leering image continued its highly accurate fire toward the little mesa. Without pause, its murderous guns spit death upon Erickson's Marines. The platoon's fleeting numbers were swiftly disappearing.

Another Marine, somewhere on the far left, screamed in agony when struck by multiple machine-gun bullets from the flailing M-60.

A feeling of helplessness sunk deep within them all.

5

How long before the Hornets get here, sir?" Gunny asked.

"Five minutes, possibly more."

"The amtracs will reach the beach in two. Given three unfettered minutes, that tank could destroy a dozen or more before the first Hornet shows up and takes him out. That's at least three hundred men, sir."

The frantic lieutenant had no answers. He'd promised the division commander he would eliminate the tanks. But he'd failed. And because of it hundreds would die.

Lying next to the platoon leader, his nose buried in the sand, Hamilton Smith had seen the horrid carnage. He'd heard the conversation between the platoon's leaders. He took a quick glance to his left and right. The dead and dying were everywhere.

"I can't let this happen," Smith said, his voice little more than a whisper. "I just can't . . . I've lost too many friends on this damn beach this morning. I refuse to do nothing while the rest of them are killed and countless others are slaughtered. Along with those in the amtracs, what's left of this platoon is going to survive."

Without Erickson or Fife noticing, he slipped off the radio and grabbed a satchel charge. Before either could react, the radioman was on his feet, running toward the relentless slayer.

"Smith, don't!" Erickson screamed. "You haven't got a chance."

Yet the platoon radio operator no longer cared. Through the strafing fields of machine-gun fire the young Marine raced straight for the demanding armor.

Unfortunately, his determined efforts wouldn't get far before the full force of the Chosen One's vassals fell upon him. At the exact instant of Smith's ill-conceived charge, their rampaging guns were nearing the center of the ridge. The primal firing was much too intense for the sole American to overcome.

He'd barely covered seventy-five yards when a slamming bullet from the tank commander's .50-caliber machine gun struck his rib cage, breaking his stride and knocking him off his feet. It was a glancing blow, and for the moment it saved him from an instant death from the potent shell. His body armor slowed the powerful projectile, but it was no match for so significant a weapon. The forceful round bored through the vest and tore into the meager existence within its false womb.

The lone Marine staggered and fell upon the unforgiving ground. A nasty pain gripped him, tearing at his side. It felt as if an enraged scorpion had stung him in the center of his right ribs. He stared at the hole in his uniform. Blood poured from the mocking wound. Even so, the fixated corporal didn't waver. A single bullet, even one this destructive, wasn't going to stop him. That tank was going to be destroyed. Its perverse crew was going to find their promised paradise this morning. He would see to that. It would take much more than a searing scorpion's sting to dissuade him from finishing his perilous task. He ducked his head, fighting to catch his breath, and waited for the M-60's turret to move past his position. The moment it did, he was on his feet again, running as fast as his faltering legs would carry him toward the corrupt form. More than two hundred yards of open ground remained between the stoic Marine and the beseeching target.

Satchel charge in hand, the grave figure sprinted across the lifeless ground as rapidly as his tattered body would allow. A lengthening trail of blood marked his path. With steadfast conviction, second by second, the grim Marine cut the distance by half.

The exacting M-60 finished its slow sweep to the east. The unrelenting turret turned back toward the west. The machine gun's crippling streams neared the center of the line once again.

While he ran, Smith reached for the munition's detonator. He willed his distressed body forward. His assailed lungs burned. His mind cried out in anguish. The nasty scorpion stung him over and again. Despite the agony, he pressed on. The squalid objective was getting nearer with each moment. With every grappling stride the ground passed beneath his feet. It wouldn't be much longer until he reached his prize.

Fifty yards to go. Smith gave it everything he had.

The tank's gunner spotted the lone Marine. He refocused his machine gun on the running American. The approaching heretic was squarely within his sights. The rushing figure was scarcely twenty-five yards away when the Chosen One's devotee opened fire. A line of 7.62mm bullets ripped into the struggling form. This time his damaged body armor stopped a significant portion of the smaller-caliber shells. But it couldn't defeat them all. A pair of seeking shells dug deep within the startled corporal's chest.

The crushing blow staggered him. He dropped to his knees and crumpled to the hard ground. He could feel his shattered heart pounding in his throat. With every halting beat, he could sense the life spurting from his mangled body. A river of red flowed onto the macabre landscape.

The latest threat defeated, the cocksure crewman returned to firing at the handful of surviving Marines on the western portion of the battlefield.

For an instant, Smith felt nothing. And then the devastation arrived, ripping apart his battered soul. Each languishing breath from his bullet-shattered lungs was filled with inescapable suffering. In disbelief, he stared at the warm, sticky blood. Despite his tender age, he refused to fool himself in the slightest. He understood his suffocating wounds were fatal. He realized he was going to die.

Anger overwhelmed all conscious thought. That spirit-encompassing rage turned into herculean certainty. No matter what it took, no matter how great his misery, he wouldn't fail. That tank was going to die with him.

With superhuman effort Smith pulled himself to his feet. The bubbling pool on the front of his shirt was expanding by the second. The precious streams of life-sustaining liquid that dropped onto the pitiless ground went on without pause. His distorted mind screamed from the unending angst. The wounded Marine felt death's shadow growing near. It threatened to overpower him. He stared into the abyss. His life's final, wretched moments would soon be consumed on the distressing sands of this foreign land. Yet it no longer mattered. If his end was to occur in this forsaken place, he was determined to drag the Pan-Arabs into the farthest depths of hell with him. He was going to save the remaining men of 3rd Platoon. He was going to save the arriving battalions.

The staggering corporal dragged himself toward the M-60. Every fleeting movement was laced with unimaginable terror. Each suffering second threatened to be his last. Twenty-five yards was agonizingly cut to fifteen. Fifteen became ten. With halting strides and endless stumbles, ten painfully dropped to five. The tempting tank was close. The inviting beacon called to him.

Nevertheless, his trembling legs could carry him no farther. His quivering knees buckled. He fell a final time upon the blowing sands. For what seemed an eternity, the dying American lay unmoving just a few arm lengths from his considerable quarry. The M-60's incessant firing went on without pause. Still Smith refused to give in. He stirred, fighting with all he had to reach his fading existence's final objective.

He tried again to stand. But it was no use. He didn't have the strength to regain his footing.

The vicious scorpion had grown to immense proportions.

Erickson watched the woeful scene, convinced the radioman's heroic effort had come up short. He stared helplessly as the platoon's last chance began to dissipate. He was certain it was over. He was convinced the dying Marine had failed.

Hamilton Smith's tenacious life was nearly spent. His impending passing was perilously close. He could sense its crushing presence. Yet despite the severity of his wounds and his all-encompassing distress, he remained unwilling to accept defeat. On his belly, his grief-stricken face pressed against the ground, he slowly pulled himself toward his objective. With his final, halting breaths he dragged his dispirited body across the unending desert. Inch by inch, the dying American neared his lasting goal.

The short ordeal felt like a journey of a thousand frightful miles. With each plaintive endeavor he drew closer. Four feet, three feet, two . . . He looked up, the severe pain on his swollen features forever seizing him, and realized his horrid mission was at its end. One more lunge and he'd touch cold steel. With his last measure of strength he pulled himself forward. The instant he reached the obscene image he turned back toward the crest and smiled an ironic smile. Calmness came over him, settling in his eyes. The martyred Marine set off the detonator.

In a mighty explosion, he vanished. The tank's assaulted frame erupted. Its crushed metal workings spilled forth upon the sterile land. Rabid flames licked at its vanquished sides. It wouldn't be long before the ravaging fires reached its ample ammunition. The hatches on the top of the M-60 flew open. Its four crewmen scrambled for safety. A dozen determined rifles opened fire upon the Pan-Arabs. The fleeing enemy was ripped apart. None would reach the beckoning ground. Moments later, the scorching blaze found the tank's huge shells. A feral blast tore the M-60 apart.

The platoon's dazed survivors looked out upon the austere plateau. Four defeated tanks were brightly burning. The smoldering pieces of a pair of crushed Humvees added to the demonic display. Except for an occasional secondary explosion and the haunting pleas of the platoon's wounded, the coming morning went quiet once more.

The first AAVs churned out of the water. Scores would follow. A few minutes later, the soaring Hornets appeared, ready to take the fight to their foe. The crippling naval broadsides began. In the distance, the shuddering land yawed and bowed with every furious strike.

The platoon's losses were severe. Yet the stark reality of what had occurred hadn't fully sunk in. There'd be plenty of time later to reflect and grieve. For the moment, there was only one thing the survivors understood—they'd won. The devastated wastelands would soon belong to the Americans. And the battle-scarred lieutenant and his tough platoon sergeant allowed for the briefest of congratulatory moments.

Fife looked at Erickson. "Well, sir, looks like we did it. The history books are going to say that on this day, despite unbelievable odds, the Marines landed in North Africa."

"Yep, Gunny, I'd say the Chosen One's had far better days than this one's going to be."

6

A t precisely midnight on the fourteenth of May 1948 a male child was born in Aynorian, one of the poorest villages in the unending wastelands of southern Algeria. The birth had been a difficult one and the frail newborn scarcely made it through the ordeal. The midwives did what they could. Even so, each held little hope for the struggling infant's survival.

Much to the delight of all concerned, however, the baby lived to see the coming of the next day's sun. And as the first twenty-four hours of his flickering life neared their conclusion his illiterate peasant parents anointed him with the name Muhammad Mourad. With each passing hour, the tiny infant fought to fill his striving lungs with enough sustaining breath to reach out for another sunrise. The surprisingly resilient child found strength in the nourishment of his mother's bosom, and the desperate battle to overcome his fate went on through the critical days that followed. In the spirit of a true warrior, hour by hour, day by day, he held on to the tenuous life Allah had granted him. In a few weeks, the crisis threatening his meager existence ended and the child took his place in the world of mortal man.

Mankind took no notice whatsoever of his birth.

The days and months slowly passed. A frail infant became a frail child. Muhammad was small for his age and quite fragile. His early years were marked by continual abuse and unceasing torture from the children of his backward village. By the age of six his life outside the protection of his meager home had become a living hell. The cruelty the Aynorian children displayed toward the weakest among them knew no bounds.

Yet each evening inside the walls of his threadbare dwelling, he found respite from the unremitting desert's scorching heat and the children's evil deeds. For in his home waited his devoted parents. At the end of the day he'd make his way to the place he loved. There his doting mother caressed his soiled brow and wiped away the child's endless tears. Nestled in her protective arms, with the setting of the sun, Muhammad would find his peace. Wrapped in her tender embrace he'd revel in the tranquillity he desperately craved. During the remainder of his years, he would equate the coming sunset with the exquisite paradise he felt in her arms. Every day for the rest of his life the ritual would be the same. When the piercing rays began to fade he'd stop whatever he was doing. While he watched the disappearing sun, his mind would fill with comforting thoughts of the modest place where unconditional love had waited to greet him.

His father's love took quite a different form from that of his mother. Yet it was no less strong. A fanatically religious man and a stern disciplinarian, he showed his concern for his only child by forcing the boy to face the multitude of problems the world had heaped upon him. Rather than protecting him from the terrible deeds of the village children, he taught him to fight back. He instilled in his son the fires of righteous indignation. Despite the plaintive pleas of the child's mother, his father refused to let him hide away from the countless troubles facing him outside the family's door.

He would return each evening, his body bruised and battered, his face filthy, his nose bloodied. Nevertheless, the next day his father would shove the reluctant child out into the brutal world once more. It was a harsh life. But his father understood Muhammad's only chance of enduring would come through learning to use the gifts Allah had graciously bestowed upon him. And in many ways his God had been truly generous. For Muhammad Mourad had been given an exceedingly strong intellect far beyond any seen in the isolated outpost since well before his father's lifetime.

Along with his quick wit came an orator's tongue and the cunning of a cornered lion. Even at this early age, his father realized it was his astonishing mind, not his meager body that would help the child find his way through this bitter existence. By his seventh birthday, the remarkable boy was amazing the elders in the mosque with his grasp of the tenets of the Quran. And with his ability to outfox and outthink them, in the dirty alleyways where the children played, he was continually astounding his bigger, tougher opponents. Even so, he returned home on many an evening with blood on his tattered clothing and bruises on his anguished soul. More and more, however, the child was beginning to comprehend his place in this difficult world. And the boy grew to love his father with all of his being for what he'd done to show him the way.

Unfortunately, within months of the passing of his seventh birthday, Muhammad's father would be gone forever from his life. For the 1950s found his country in the depths of a fearsome whirlwind beyond anyone's control. A savage tumult was reaching out to change the lives of the people in even the remotest of locales.

A scourge was upon the land. A reviled pestilence that had to be eradicated. Riding on the hot Sahara winds, a fervent call to arms swept across the barren desert. Along with nearly all of the men of Aynorian, Muhammad's father answered the revolution's siren song. Algeria had to be freed from the clutches of decadent French colonialism. Each man knew the only way such an event would occur was by the spilling of the blood of both the innocent and the guilty. So with no training and few weapons the men of the distant oasis marched north across the arid land to join in the great battle for liberation. Too young to comprehend the earth-shattering events unfolding around him, Muhammad watched his father go. Every day for the next nine months, from sunup to sundown, the boy waited on the edge of Aynorian for the first sign of his return.

Late one afternoon, as the sweltering North African sun sank over the low mountains, Muhammad spotted a rider approaching from the north. The child rushed back into the village to alert the elders. By the time the stranger arrived the entire population had gathered on the edge of the small town. His horse was nearly dead from exhaustion. Nonetheless, the news the rider carried was far too important to spare the animal the torturous trip. Out of breath, he dismounted and faced the anxious crowd. With him he carried the word of a great battle in the north. It was an evil word well beyond any of the villagers' comprehension.

Where the desert meets the sea there'd been a fierce clash with the enemies of Islam. The blood of victor and vanquished alike had flowed like a raging river onto the shifting sands. The losses were great. Thousands had died. The men of Aynorian had been among them. There was little chance the brave fighters from the humble village would ever return to their homes.

Muhammad's father had fallen in the struggle. While leading an assault against heavily fortified positions, he'd died a martyr's death at the end of a French bayonet. It would be the boy's first encounter with jihad—Allah's holy war. Yet it certainly wouldn't be his last.

The entire citizenry reeled beneath the crippling blow of the horseman's news. The finality of death, however, was well beyond the understanding of a boy of nearly eight, even if he was the brightest lad in the village. So with the next day's dawn, he went back to the northern edge of Aynorian to wait for his father's return. For many weeks he continued his hopeless vigil, his pleading eyes glued on the distant horizon while he prayed for his father's figure to appear on the interminable Sahara.

His mother was beside herself at the loss of the man to whom she'd dedicated her existence. In the passing of a handful of months, consumed by grief, she withdrew into the tormented world within her mind and lapsed into an uncommunicative stupor. Her arms no longer welcomed the child. Even so, Muhammad continued to provide his undying support to the woman who'd given him life. Day after day, the small boy watched her relentless slide into oblivion. Her failure to respond to his continued attempts to comfort her wounded him more deeply than the terrible scars caused by his father's death. The agony of her husband's demise had stolen away what coherent thought remained within her. And there was nothing her helpless son could do to end the nightmare that consumed every moment of his life.

One morning, six months after the loss of his father, Muhammad awoke to find an empty house. His mother was nowhere to be seen. Muhammad's frantic search of the desolate village failed to find any trace of her. Even at his age, he knew there was only one plausible explanation for her disappearance. She'd wandered off into the remorseless desert.

There was nothing anyone could do. The elders made every effort to find her. But too few able-bodied men remained in the desolate hamlet to conduct a proper search. And Aynorian was too poor to have any vehicles to aid them. She'd been gone for most of the night. Her head start was far too great to overcome. In a short time the unforgiving sands devoured her.

Her remains would never be found.

The boy was alone now. Alone in a hostile world appearing to have no room for him. In the lonely years that followed, Muhammad lived on the edge of starvation. Each day, the angel of death looked upon the trifling figure. Muhammad bravely returned the angel's stare and fought to overcome his desperate situation. He scavenged what he could, but with most of its men dead the impoverished outpost had little with which to nourish the abandoned youngster.

It would be quite some time before the forsaken youth would find the smallest traces of solace in his father's brave deeds. Eventually, however, he did receive a measure of comfort in his death. For his sacrifice hadn't been in vain. It had been a long, harrowing fight filled with unspeakable cruelty on both sides. Yet finally the end had come.

Shortly after Muhammad's fourteenth birthday word came that his countrymen had expelled the despicable oppressors. Algeria was freed from its shackles.

Even so, in his mother's senseless passing the orphaned boy could find no peace.

Muhammad's hatred for the hostile world outside the insignificant crossroads consumed every ounce of his being. A fire found its way to burn in his dark eyes. It was an indomitable flame that would remain there for the rest of his life.

And then the first miracle occurred.

Like an apparition, his uncle Sallah, long reported dead in the Great War for Independence, appeared in the barren desert north of Aynorian. Captured by the infidels, Sallah had lived for many years behind rusting barbed wire. With the freeing of their homeland had come the freeing of the French chains holding thousands of prisoners of war. Sallah had survived the mighty struggle. And by Allah's grace, he had endured the difficult journey on foot across the expansive sands. Of the scores of determined men who'd marched out of the meager oasis seven years earlier, he'd be the only one to find his way home.

Before the war, Uncle Sallah had been the most important man in Aynorian. Owner of the modest marketplace, he'd been Aynorian's sole link with the outside world. Prior to the conflict, Muhammad's uncle had been the only person in Aynorian to have ever ventured farther than fifty miles from their secluded desert home. And with the exception of the clerics in the mosque, the lone resident who could read and write.

As custom demanded, Sallah took in his starving nephew. Muhammad was given a job in his uncle's shops, a roof over his head, and three solid meals a day. For the first time in his life, his continued existence was no longer in question. Sallah's house was three times the size of Muhammad's parents'. Even though Aynorian had no electricity or running water, his uncle's home appeared palatial to the boy.

The unassuming teenager lacked for nothing. Except love. Not that Muhammad was abused or treated harshly, for he was not. Yet with his own children's needs to care for, and his shops to run, Sallah didn't have the time to grow to love his nephew. He was quite fond of him, but the attention Muhammad needed to overcome the severe scars that had crusted upon his crushed spirit simply wasn't available.

Like the boy's father, his uncle was a harsh taskmaster and a highly devout man. Muhammad's religious fervor grew even stronger under Sallah's firm guidance. The inquiring youth took to spending every free minute in the mosque. He loved nothing more than listening to the clerics read from the Quran and hearing them share their ideas of the true path to paradise. He reveled in the encouragement the clerics gave him in expressing his own views on the teachings of the Prophet. More and more, the holy ones praised the stunning boy's religious performance.

His father had burst with pride at the child's ample abilities. It didn't take long for Uncle Sallah to begin sharing those immense feelings for Muhammad's accomplishments. By the end of the clever teenager's first year in his house, Sallah and the clerics had reached full accord on what must be done with the incredible lad. As he neared his fifteenth birthday, Sallah approached with news that would forever change the direction of Muhammad's life.

"Boy, do you like your life here in our village?" Sallah asked.

"Yes, Uncle."

"And do you like your life in my home?"

"Very much so, Uncle."

"Will you obey my wishes?"

"I always have."

"Will you leave my home if I so order?"

Muhammad hesitated. "Uncle . . . I don't understand. Have I done something which has offended you?"

"Oh no, Muhammad, you haven't offended me in the slightest. But you didn't answer my question. For the good of Aynorian, will you leave my home?"

"If that is what you wish, Uncle," the dejected figure responded.

"Muhammad, you're a special child. In the past months, I've had many discussions with the clerics. And we're in complete agreement. Your talents can't be wasted. Aynorian needs your help."

"You know I wouldn't hesitate to make whatever sacrifices are necessary for our village. I'd gladly forfeit my life for Allah and my people."

"Then you must leave Aynorian. Go north to the great city. Go to Algiers. Go and learn how to read and write. Go and study the ways of modern man. And when you're finished, return and lead this secluded place out of its backwardness."

Muhammad was staggered by his uncle's edict. Algiers. In his entire life he'd never been more than ten miles from the time-forsaken settlement. To travel for many days on such a quest was beyond the boy's comprehension. The concept of leaving Aynorian and entering into so foreign an environment had never before crossed his mind. His uncle might as well have announced he was about to travel to the far side of the moon.

"Uncle, I . . . I don't know what to say."

"There's nothing for you to say. Allah has chosen this path for you, and you've no choice but to follow it wherever it leads."

Muhammad realized any further protest would be beneath the stringent principles his father and uncle had worked so hard to instill in him. His baffling destiny was sealed. To fight against it was a useless gesture. Nevertheless, his answer was a reluctant one.

"Yes, Uncle. It will be as you wish."

"The arrangements have been made. You'll depart at the end of the month and go north with the caravan that brings supplies to Aynorian."

"As you desire, my uncle."

"You'll attend the holy school in Algiers. You'll study hard. And when you're through discovering the world outside of ours, you'll return to show our people the way."

As his uncle had decreed, Muhammad left the modest gathering at the end of the month. It would be three difficult years before he'd see Aynorian again.

One chapter had closed in his life. And another had opened.

7

To say Muhammad struggled in his new surroundings would be an understatement. The world outside the high walls of the holy school terrified him. Algiers and its million and a half inhabitants overwhelmed his sensibilities. For a boy of fifteen who'd never before seen an automobile, the strange things waiting beyond the stout fences were incomprehensible.

To hide from his horrific dreams, he threw himself into his studies. At the rigorous Islamic preparatory school, the training and disciplining of his remarkable mind soon took form. Though he'd had no previous education, he quickly grasped the rudimentary elements of mathematics and Arabic. Despite the vigorous protests of the most radical of the country's clerics, geography, French, and English also were included in the school's studies. Even so, there wouldn't be a minute of education in the sciences. Science was banned from the program as heresy, as many of its principles were in unyielding conflict with the teachings of the Quran. And such contradictory information could never be tolerated.

Though most of his classmates had been at the school for many years prior to his arrival, it wasn't long before Muhammad was head

and shoulders above the rest. Once again, it was in his religious training that the extraordinary youngster astounded his teachers. This was
a child capable of grasping the most subtle of fundamentalist concepts.
The precepts of holy war were as natural to him as if he'd written the
sacred passages himself. Muhammad's tutors were soon singing his
praises to the elders in Algiers's grand mosque. Despite his sheltered
upbringing and lack of experience with even the most rudimentary
rules of living in the existing society, this was a youth with remarkable
religious gifts.

His instructors recognized he just might be the honored person
who'd grow up to lead the revolt against the secular government that
had seized power in the new Arab nation. The small boy was held out
to his classmates as a shining example for all to emulate. The painfully
shy Muhammad accepted the mounting praise with abject humility.

In the dark dormitory where fifty students slept in each cramped
room, the favorable attention given him by the rigid clerics didn't go
unnoticed. The other students didn't take kindly to being upstaged by
the insignificant outsider from the remote desert. Within days of his
arrival, the first assault upon the talented newcomer occurred. Each
night, for months without end, the beatings would begin anew. The brutality of the grim dormitory became a central part of the solitary teenager's life. This time there'd be no mother to wipe his furrowed brow
and soothe his wounds. There'd be no arms reaching out to comfort
him. Still his father had prepared him well for the harshness of others.
Muhammad took the fierce beatings without the slightest whimper.
Never once would the tears welling inside him appear upon his face.

He wouldn't give the others the satisfaction of knowing their abid-
ing torture was tearing away what little remained of his battered
psyche. So he internalized the pain, hiding behind a stoic façade of
callous indifference. Once again, he was totally alone.

Slowly his classmates recognized the true modesty of the timid
newcomer. And they began to realize having the brilliant Muhammad
as an ally when their schoolwork grew overwhelming was quite a wise

decision to make. Bit by bit, the beatings decreased until they stopped altogether.

Acceptance of him finally arrived. Nevertheless, in three long years he'd never make a lasting friendship among them. For he was far too different to ever fit in.

During his difficult days in Algiers his life also would be devoid of even the briefest of female contact. His was a male-dominated realm and no woman had ever dared to enter the sanctity of the frightening school's foreboding walls.

On rare occasions the students would leave the compound to venture into the center of the city. Yet Muhammad's fear of what waited on the other side of the wrought-iron gates was far too great for him to overcome. Despite the encouragement of his classmates, for the first year of his stay in Algiers, he remained locked away in this cloistered kingdom.

If it hadn't been for his teachers' insistence that he accompany them on a visit to Algiers's grand mosque, he might never have left the sheltering safety of the school yard. The exulting teachers had been ordered by the highest of the clergy to bring Muhammad to them. The time had come for an intense examination of the extravagant claims they'd made of the teenager's phenomenal religious capacities. Such a summons couldn't be refused.

At sixteen he made his initial appearance in the central mosque. Filled with idealism and innocence, his answers amazed the Quran's most learned scholars. The shy country boy understood neither the significance of the inquisition nor the results of his extraordinary responses.

For the first time in his life, the elders whispered the sacred name. After watching his incredible performance each cleric was certain the Mahdi—the Chosen One—the one who'd unite Islam and guide them in their conquest of the world, had revealed himself to them. Word of the reticent teenager's exploits spread throughout the Middle East.

From that moment on, he had no choice but to leave the concealing compound on a weekly basis to attend prayers in the mosque. Once these regular visits into the heart of Algiers became routine, he even allowed himself an occasional nonreligious foray into the bazaar. His aversion to the city abated, though each venture outside the school's austere surroundings remained full of uneasiness. He soon realized it would always be this way. For this wasn't his world. And he knew that would never change.

Muhammad never forgot his diffident past. Not a day went by when he didn't long to return to the tiny oasis of his birth. At the end of his third year at the ancient seminary he decided there was nothing further within its somber gray halls needing to be learned. He'd mastered his studies with ease. The time had come to fulfill his promise to his uncle. Filled with knowledge, he'd go back to Aynorian.

Leaving, however, wasn't going to be as simple as that. On a sweltering summer day, the eighteen-year-old student approached the headmaster to inform him of his decision to return home. The naive teenager was shocked at the furor his announcement created. Students his age were embarking every week, and no one appeared to take the slightest notice of their departures.

Nevertheless, this time it was different. For this young man was special. His panicked teachers were at a loss. He couldn't go back to his difficult life in the endless desert when the entire Middle East was waiting for him to guide them in their virtuous battle to destroy the nonbelievers and lead the world toward its judgment day.

For fourteen hundred years the prophecy had remained unfulfilled. Islam had yet to complete its conquest. Each day two billion voices prayed for Allah to give them a sign. Each evening they searched the heavens for the Mahdi's arrival. At last their prayers had been answered. The devout clerics recognized the greatness within the demure boy. Their guide, the Chosen One, had shown himself. The time had come for Islam to conquer. The time had come for the world to end.

And what happened? The unpretentious youth announced he wanted to go home to his meager village. The clerics' dreams of Arab greatness were shattered by a simple statement from the innocent teen. For days without end they reasoned with him. They begged, they pleaded, they cajoled. Yet when they were through, there was nothing they could do to change Muhammad's mind. Unfortunately, there was only one person who failed to recognize the greatness the humble boy carried within him. And that person was the boy himself.

He could recite the holy passages with ease. He understood the significance of the prophecy of the Mahdi's arrival. Like them he prayed for the Chosen One's appearance. To suddenly discover the sainted scholars believed he was that righteous warrior was beyond his understanding.

Until now Muhammad had valued their wisdom without question. But their pronouncement of his singular importance was too much for the quiet lad to bear. The more they praised his coming greatness, the more he wished to escape their confusing world. He needed a place to hide from their forthright glare.

Despite their fervent wails and endless protests, he gathered his scant belongings, joined a caravan, and traveled to Aynorian.

Back home, he couldn't have been happier. He threw himself into his work in Uncle Sallah's shops. He returned with the intention of living out the remainder of his years in the obscurity of the unassuming outpost. After his struggles in Algiers, Muhammad's desires were to never again venture into the bewildering world beyond the horizon. Yet despite his plans, he wouldn't be in Aynorian for long. He couldn't know it, but in two months an even greater adventure awaited.

It was obvious to Sallah his charge had learned many lessons. His knowledge of Arabic and mathematics was impressive. His French and English were without flaw. His uncle was extremely proud of the young man who'd come home to help his village. Still it was soon apparent that the anxious teenager hadn't mastered the primary lesson he'd been sent to Algiers to learn.

One day, as he worked in the shops, his uncle approached. "Muhammad."

From the look on Sallah's face, he could see something was wrong. "Yes, Uncle."

"You've failed me, Muhammad."

"Failed you? I don't understand. I labor from sunup to sundown to please you. In what way have I failed you?"

"You've failed to learn the one thing I sent you to Algiers to learn."

"Uncle, I toiled over my books for hours without end. My teachers heaped nothing but praise upon my efforts. I learned everything there was for them to teach me."

"But you didn't learn what I sent you there to explore. Once more, you'll go back into the outside world. This time you'll stay until this lesson is mastered."

"Please, Uncle, no. I'll not return to Algiers. There's nothing left in their books for me to discover."

"You're wrong, my nephew. While you were in Algiers you learned much from your books and the clerics. But what's written in the pages of books wasn't the real reason I sent you. It was something else entirely. In Algiers you acquired no knowledge of the things mattering most to our people. You failed to learn anything about what you were sent there to acquire. If this place is going to survive and someday prosper, we must comprehend how those outside of Aynorian view the world. And of all those here, only you have the ability to secure understanding of such things."

"Please, Uncle, I love my life in Aynorian. Please don't make me return to Algiers. It's not a place I wish to ever see again."

"I've heard your words, Muhammad. And I agree with your assessment. There's nothing left for you in Algiers. You'll not return there."

"Thank you, Uncle."

"Instead, you'll go to the university in France."

8

Forced to live among the hated infidels, Muhammad was confounded by the complexities of Marseille. This time there'd be no high walls to hide behind. He'd have to survive in the midst of his enemy. All the exceptionally poor Algerian could afford was a cold-water walk-up near the busy docks. It was located in the most dangerous part of the city. The area around his pitiful apartment teemed with ruthless thieves and heartless murderers. It was a treacherous place for even a seasoned traveler. Each morning, filled with dread, he'd venture forth to walk across town to the university. Each night, after studying in the library until well after dark, he'd return to his sparsely furnished flat. Every minute, Muhammad was terrified. He lived in continual fear of a revolting world of which he didn't wish to be a part.

The hours spent at the university were no better. It wasn't the work that bothered him. His studies were scarcely more challenging than those he'd faced in Algiers. It was the heretics' strange rules that were beyond his reasoning. He couldn't believe his eyes on the first day of classes when a young woman dared to sit at the desk next to his. Sharing a classroom with female students overwhelmed his sensibilities.

Such a thing broke every tenet of his religious teachings. And the scandalous dress of the French women was worse than that of the most obvious of harlots. The astonished desert dweller couldn't cope in this alien existence. Sullen and depressed, he withdrew into himself even further. Months passed. He grew so morose he'd no desire to leave his wretched bed. But his uncle's orders couldn't be disobeyed. So day after day he arose and headed for the university. There was a scowl upon his face. And an all-consuming anger burning deep within his heart.

The late 1960s were a turbulent time. In the world of the Arab, such was especially true. They blamed the West for the miseries that had befallen them. The birth of the modern terrorist movement was beginning to make its sadistic mark upon the planet. After their defeat by the Israelis in 1967, many Arab leaders announced the time had come for holy war. To carry out their jihadist intentions they recruited Arab-born university students throughout the Western world. Muhammad was an easy target for those whose agenda of violence needed willing foot soldiers. It wasn't long before he was approached. It didn't take many attempts to convince the naive Algerian to enlist in their noble cause.

The faction he joined was small and poorly organized. The motley band of misfits gave themselves the impressive name of the Martyrs' Brigade. Its self-proclaimed leader was a student from Syria no older than Muhammad. The cell leader did nothing more than spout clichéd venom against the West and chain-smoke French cigarettes. For half a year, their clandestine meetings served no purpose. Yet finally, their courage gathered, they drew up their first incendiary plot.

The five of them would place a homemade bomb at a bus stop near the Israeli consulate. None of the amateur terrorists, however, had any experience with explosives. It took them a month to create a crude explosive device. Muhammad was elected to put it beneath the bench.

On a busy Tuesday morning the nervous little Algerian approached the bus stop. As usual, the buses were running late. An annoyed group of men, women, and children was gathered at the intersection. Muhammad stood at the edge of the crowd for a few minutes. When he spied an approaching bus, he placed the package beneath the bench and turned away. The cell leader pressed the electronic detonator.

Nothing happened.

A few months later they tried again. A different plan, a different location, and another defective bomb. Their ineptness frustrated them all. There was strong talk of disbanding the cell. Still this was holy war and they weren't going to be denied their victory over the nonbelievers.

Near the end of Muhammad's sophomore year, they tried once more. One of them placed a bomb on a bustling street. He walked around the corner. The cell leader pushed the detonator. Six people, including two small children, were killed in the blast.

Muhammad's career as a fledgling terrorist had entered a new phase. The group began planning their next mission. It wouldn't be long before the heretics would feel their wrath once more. The first taste of blood was fresh on Muhammad's lips. He'd finally gained a small measure of retribution for the deaths of his parents. He wanted even more.

One evening, while he studied at a poorly lit table in the university's nearly deserted library, a sweet voice spoke to him in perfect Arabic. "Is this seat taken?"

He looked up with a start. Standing there was the most attractive woman he'd ever seen. She was dressed in an expensive Western-style outfit. Her face contained a light brush of makeup. Her lips were painted in the Western way. If not for her raven hair and enchanting dark eyes, she easily could've been mistaken for a woman of the infidels. Yet there could be no denying. This girl was Arab. A beautiful North African girl of nineteen.

The second miracle of Muhammad's life was about to begin.

9

What?" Muhammad said.

"I said, is this seat taken?"

He scanned the empty tables throughout the cavernous room. The small Algerian looked up at her with a confused expression.

"Aw... aw... no," he said. "No, it's not." He could feel his cheeks turning red.

"May I?" the stranger asked. She motioned to the chair across from him.

Without waiting for an answer, the enchanting girl sat down. Muhammad stared at her in complete astonishment. She raised her delicate hands and placed them beneath her chin. For fifteen long seconds the young woman searched the sun-weathered features of his gaunt face. He fidgeted in his chair, waiting for her rapt inquiry to end. By the time her examination was over, her dark eyes had filled with a thousand questions. Muhammad had no idea what to think. The painfully shy Saharan had never before been approached in such a manner. He'd no experience in dealing with women. And until this moment, no desire to learn how to do so.

She reached out her hand to shake his in the Western manner. Muhammad was taken aback by her continuing boldness. Not once had he known an Arab woman who'd make contact with a man in such a way. Unable to think of any other response, he reached out a quivering hand and shook hers in return.

"My name's Sharif Bahrami," she said.

"I'm Muhammad Mourad."

"I know who you are. I've been watching you for many months."

Once more the fetching woman's brazenness sprang forth in her words. He was at a loss to explain why he was letting the unusual scene happen.

"We shouldn't be talking in this manner," he said. "I don't know where you learned to act in such ways, but I was raised to honor Allah. Where I come from such contact between a man and a woman is highly improper."

"I was born and raised in Cairo. And I too was taught to believe with all my heart in the one true God. But I don't understand how our talking is in any way wrong. We're fellow students at this great university. Why shouldn't we sit together and exchange ideas?"

"I'm sorry, that's just not my way."

Sharif, however, wasn't going to let the ancient protocols deter her. She was the epitome of the modern North African woman. And her curiosity over the whispered rumors she'd heard about the reserved little man had gotten the better of her. She ignored his protests.

"You're the Mahdi, aren't you?"

"Some have called me that," he said.

"Then, I'm puzzled. If you're the Chosen One, why are you letting them make such a fool of you?"

"Letting who make a fool of me?"

"The handlers of those with whom you've become involved," Sharif answered.

"I'm certain I've no idea what you're talking about."

"You're a poor liar, Muhammad Mourad. Obviously you've little practice at it. You know exactly what I'm talking about. I'm talking about your involvement with the Martyrs' Brigade. I'm talking about your actions in last month's killing of six innocent people in Marseille's central square."

"Woman, you forget yourself. Jihad's been called. If you love Allah as much as you claim, you understand the significance of such an order. With holy war, there are no longer any innocents. There are only those who follow the righteous path to obtaining paradise, and those who do not. The Quran's teachings are clear. Those who fail to heed its sacred words, Arab and outsider alike, must be eliminated so Islam can claim its proper place as the world's honored religion."

"What you say is true. But I'll wager you're so unaware you think those so-called friends of yours are carrying out these attacks on their own. I'll bet you don't even realize who's pulling the strings behind that sorry group of which you've become an integral part."

"It doesn't matter."

"So I guess you'll die next week like the Syrian puppet you are. Because that's where the orders are coming from."

"Die? What makes you think I'm about to die?"

She looked into his eyes. "You're such a fool. The plans for your death are under way as we speak. To tell you the truth, I don't even know why I'm bothering with you." Sharif rose from the chair. "Go ahead and die for Syria."

"Wait." He motioned for her to sit back down. "I'm a devout warrior for Islam. If I should die fighting in our chaste cause, it won't be to serve Syria, it'll be in the service of Allah. And in my death I'll find paradise. As a martyr of the jihad the Prophet's promise will be fulfilled and I'll instantly find my way to the wondrous place reserved for all who give their lives in our noble struggle."

"I agree with you on one thing. Whether it's for Allah, or for Syria, you will die. And quite soon. The orders have arrived from Damascus. Next week, you'll enter a crowded city bus. There'll be thirty pounds of high explosives beneath your jacket. At precisely the right moment a radio signal will be sent to the bomb's timing mechanism. In an instant, many lives will end. Yours, of course, will be one of them."

"How do you know of these things, woman? They've told me nothing of such plans."

"They will. They're waiting until the last possible moment so you'll not have time to think before you step onto that bus. They're afraid if they give the backward Algerian an instant to reflect, he'll lose his nerve and fail them."

"Why would they think that? I'm a proud soldier in Allah's blessed war. I'd eagerly give my life in the service of the jihad. How could they think I'd fail them?"

"Because despite their brave talk none of them would ever make such a sacrifice."

Surprise spread across his features. He looked into her shimmering eyes. The truth of what she was saying was there for him to see. Even so, he didn't understand why the unfamiliar girl had risked the obvious danger involved in approaching him with such news.

"Why are you telling me these things?" Muhammad asked. "Why should you care one way or another what becomes of a poor boy from the distant deserts?"

"Because if you're really the Mahdi, Allah put you here for a glorious purpose. If what they say about you is true, then you're here to master the planet for Islam. You're here to guide us through this world's coming end. So going against Allah's wishes and blowing yourself up in a suicide attack won't carry you to paradise. It would be the greatest sin you could commit. To ignore his plan for your life is unthinkable. The consequences of such a dire act would be beyond comprehension. Despite my acceptance of many of the Western ways, I too am a fervent believer. Once I stumbled across their dirty little plot, I knew I had to do everything within my power to stop them. You can't throw your life away. You'll not be permitted to violate Allah's command. I'll see to that. You'll not be allowed to destroy yourself to serve the betrayers of our God."

"How could you think I'd ever violate the will of Allah? My life, my every breath, is spent in learning how to serve him with all my being."

"Then serve him."

"How?"

"Tomorrow you'll tell the Syrian puppets you're leaving the Martyrs' Brigade."

"What if they won't let me go?"

"You leave them to me. If they refuse to free you, then by sunset each will find himself in French chains. They'll be on their way to spending their lives behind bars."

"You've the power to do so?"

"When your father's one of the richest men in Egypt, you've the power to do most anything."

Muhammad glanced at the clock at the far end of the room. It had grown quite late. The library was minutes from closing.

"Then tomorrow," he said, "I'll trust in Allah's wisdom and find a new path to paradise. For now, I'd best be on my way. It's a long walk home, and I've grown quite tired."

"There's no need to walk. My car's right outside. I'd gladly drive you."

Once again, an astonished look came to his emaciated face. "Such would be impossible. It's bad enough I chose to speak with you. To let you drive me to my home would be unthinkable."

"Nonsense. Now gather your books and let's get out of here. There's a wonderful Turkish café nearby that serves the most delicious coffees. We'll stop on the way and have a cup and maybe a few pastries to celebrate our meeting. So far, tonight's discussion's been much too serious. You'll find I'm a lot of fun once you get to know me. Come on, I want to see if I've got what it takes to make the Mahdi laugh."

Muhammad shook his head in exasperation. "Impossible. Just impossible. Even if accompanying you weren't a violation of everything I've spent my life learning, I'm an extremely poor man. There's no money in my life for Turkish coffee."

"Well, there's more than enough in my father's life. So stop arguing and let's go."

"Understand this, woman, you're wasting your time with such outrageous offers. I'll not ride in your car. And I'm certainly not going to a restaurant with you to laugh and eat pastries. Now if you'd excuse me, it really is a long way home."

He got up and headed for the door.

Two hours later a sparkling Mercedes pulled up in front of the rundown apartment building where Muhammad lived. He quickly said his good-byes and got out of the car.

Sharif waved as she sped away.

He stood on the crumbling sidewalk, watching her disappear into the night. There was a smile on the desert descendant's face that engulfed him. Sharif had been right. The coffee and pastries had been wonderful. And for the first time, Muhammad had found someone with the ability to make him laugh.

The Mahdi was head over heels in love.

From that night on they were inseparable. Within days they'd grown to be fast friends.

And much to her surprise, within weeks Sharif found herself as deeply in love with the uncommon Algerian as he was with her.

For Muhammad those early hours and passing weeks were the most wonderful, and the most frustrating, of his life. Tradition called for him to end the relationship. But he couldn't stand the idea of spending a single day where he didn't see her marvelous face or join in her boisterous laughter.

Thoughts of her stole his every waking moment. Sharif's radiant smile filled his being and devoured his consciousness, causing his heart to soar. For the first time in his life, Muhammad's sleep wasn't filled with the essence-stealing images of his tortured past. Sharif's sweet smile had forced the terrifying visions from him and replaced them with a peace he'd never believed existed. His hatred for the non-believers remained. Yet the fierce fires burning in his eyes were soon joined by a new look. A look of complete contentment. A look of love for Sharif.

Through Sharif, Muhammad experienced the ways of modern man. With her help, his uncle was getting his wish. Nevertheless, even in Sharif's arms, his resentment of the Western world would never completely die. For the distrust he held for those who'd caused his parents' deaths was too strong to ever overcome.

Muhammad's time in France was rushing past. During his senior year word came that the health of his uncle was failing. The lengthy period entombed as a French prisoner had taken a greater toll on Sallah than anyone suspected. In a matter of months, he would begin the pious journey to his honored place in the next world. The moment was approaching when Muhammad would be called upon to lead his struggling village. While his strength ebbed, Sallah insisted his nephew finish his final semester of school. Even so, Muhammad knew the instant his examinations were complete he'd pack his insignificant possessions and return to his faraway home.

With each disappearing hour, his time with Sharif was slipping away. Weeks faded. Months flew by. Spring arrived. In two months Muhammad would leave France. Sharif was appalled by his apparent indifference. She was certain of his love for her. Yet she was becoming just as assured that eight weeks from now he was going to walk out of her life forever.

Late one evening, while they studied in their secluded corner of the library, she could contain herself no longer. She slammed her book upon the table. An echoing clamor resounded throughout the cavernous room. He looked up with a startled expression upon his face.

"Muhammad Mourad," she said, "are you ever going to ask me to marry you?"

His eyes were emotionless. "It's not possible, Sharif. I've got responsibilities that cannot be ignored. My village needs me. And where

I go isn't for you. My sparse homeland is quite poor. We've none of the things you so enjoy. There's not one automobile, or even electricity or running water. I could never ask you to accompany me to such a place. Life there's far too difficult."

"In case you haven't noticed, I'm not some wilting flower. I can take care of myself."

"But it would mean living in the old ways. You'd have to dress in the traditional manner. There'd be no more of your pretty clothes and Western makeup."

"Such things do not matter if we can spend our lives together. Even so, you must promise me that while we're married, you won't get involved with the kinds of people you were associating with when we first met. You must promise as long as we're husband and wife you'll love Allah with all your heart. And in all other things you'll practice moderation."

"Such is a promise I can surely make."

"Then I shall be your wife."

10

Sharif's adjustment to the primitive conditions of the squalid village went far better than any had anticipated. Not that everything in those first days was idyllic. There were many instances in the unrelenting monotony of her mundane existence when she longed for a bit of the world's excitement. In the early years, the dreariness of her situation often made her wish for Cairo or Marseille or Algiers or anywhere but Aynorian. Still she complained not at all. And in the darkest moments, when she felt she could no longer go on, she wrapped herself in her husband's love and went out to meet the new dawn.

She threw away her Western clothing and destroyed all remembrances of her previous life. Wrapped in traditional Arab dress, she appeared to be the most dutiful of wives. Outside their home she was careful to act in the manner expected of a subservient woman. The Mahdi's image demanded such a role. She played her part so well no one ever suspected her life was anything more than what they saw.

Inside the walls of their sheltering home, however, where prying eyes couldn't see, she was the old Sharif. She was once again her husband's equal. When they were alone, their relationship was as it had been in Marseille. He adored her all the more for it. Muhammad needed her support now more than ever. And Sharif was eager to give it. Leading the destitute oasis was a substantial responsibility to place upon his narrow shoulders. But like his wife, he too performed his role with never the slightest complaint.

Without Sharif's assistance, so bitter a reality, so challenging a task, might have overwhelmed him. Yet with her, he arose each morning with a broad smile upon his face. She could sense his every mood. She could read his every thought. When his confidence waned, she was there to support him. Not once did she fail. Her advice was sound and filled with encouragement. When he faced a difficult world, it was her counsel he treasured above all others. And it wasn't just in her assistance to Muhammad that she shined. In many ways, Sharif was the best thing to ever happen to Aynorian. For her money could do much to ease the strain of the isolated people's plight.

Six months after her arrival she surprised her husband with enough trucks to support the distant dwelling place for many years to come. No longer would Muhammad's people be dependent upon the whims of the caravan to sustain their harsh reality.

By the end of her third year as one of them, the massive generators were in place and the miracle of electricity flowed into each unpretentious home. A few months later the precious gift of running water became a way of life in Aynorian. Slowly but surely, Sharif was dragging the backward desert people into the twentieth century. In her lifetime, the village changed more than it had in its previous thousand years.

With her immense wealth she could've insisted upon a gleaming palace for a home. In the mistaken belief it'd make her happy, her husband encouraged her to do so. Sharif, nonetheless, wouldn't hear of it. Instead, she built an unassuming but comfortable house not far from his uncle's shops. After Sallah's death, the unimposing exchanges were now Muhammad's. And he slaved long hours to ensure his humble establishments met the needs of his people.

For their tenth anniversary Sharif astonished the entire region by building the grandest mosque ever seen on the shifting sands of the mighty Sahara. It wasn't long before pilgrims from all corners of North Africa were arriving to worship, and to hear the Mahdi speak. His sermons were a thing of beauty. His love for Allah filled each flowing phrase he spoke. Every visitor left Aynorian with a passion for Islam beyond any they'd previously experienced.

Muhammad's fame swept across the Middle East. From Iran to Morocco they spoke in reverent tones of the Chosen One. Despite the hardship involved in such journeys, by his thirty-fifth year the cry of the people to hear his words was so great he'd no choice but to begin traveling throughout the Muslim world.

In the finest of modern cities, and the meekest of communities, the Mahdi appeared. Wherever he went, great multitudes gathered to hear the sacred passages. He preached of his devotion to his creator. He described the paradise awaiting the true believers. He told them of the need to return to living in the simple ways of the Prophet. He spoke of the Quran's promise to Islam. It was apparent from his powerful oratory that he believed the time would soon come to vanquish the non-believers and control the dying planet.

His religious fervor was there for everyone to see. Still he kept the promise he'd made to Sharif. He loved his God with all his being. In every other thing, however, he practiced moderation. He'd little interest in politics, for he understood his reward would never be of this world. Simply by the words he spoke, he became one of the leaders of the fundamentalist order gaining strength throughout the land. That movement lived by a single tenet. It believed the governments of the Islamic countries should be ruled by those who followed a strict interpretation of the Quran. Even while fervently expressing such tenets, Muhammad spoke against those advocating violence and the overthrow of the secular governments. Instead he preached of love and patience.

He knew when the time was right Allah would find a way to

destroy those who stood in the way of the prophecy. Islam would prevail in his lifetime. And by the grace of God he was destined to play a major role in the chosen religion's conquest and the planet's coming end.

The adulation the Mahdi received from the masses didn't go unnoticed by the rulers of the West and the moderate Middle East nations. The lurid fires in his dark eyes made the Arab leaders quite uncomfortable. Despite Muhammad's peaceful message, at its core the fundamentalist cause called for the elimination of each of their governments by whatever means was necessary. North Africa's rulers knew this was a man who needed to be watched.

The modest personage scarcely noticed the rapt attention friend and enemy alike were giving him. At the end of each trek he wanted nothing more than to return to Sharif and care for the needs of his people.

Shortly after one of his distant ventures, while he and Sharif were preparing for bed, they began a ritual that would go on for the rest of their time together. Muhammad suddenly stopped what he was doing and looked at her with a puzzled expression upon his face.

"Is something troubling you, my husband?" she asked.

"There truly is. It just came to me that my life is reaching its middle years and I've done nothing of consequence. If I'm the Mahdi, when will Allah show me the time has come for Islam's mastery? How will I know what my role will be?"

"When the time is right, my love, you'll know. Now come to bed."

Night after night his questions remained the same. And her answer was always, "When the time is right, my love, you'll know."

The years passed. The pair's passion was as strong as it had been in those idyllic days in Marseille. Even with her efforts to modernize the insular village, life in Aynorian was still difficult. Yet for Muhammad and Sharif their existence was nearly perfect. The only thing missing was a child. They'd tried to conceive from the first moments of their marriage. Nevertheless, their God hadn't blessed them with a birth. When they reached their fortieth birthdays, both had to reluctantly accept that there appeared to be little hope for an heir. They'd been married for eighteen years. And time was running out. In the early days, they'd continually spoken of their desire for a child. Now neither mentioned it at all. Their lot appeared to be sealed.

Yet much to their surprise, Allah graciously granted their one remaining wish.

It would be a boy. In honor of his great-uncle, they named the little one Sallah. The infant grew into a healthy, strong toddler. He quickly became the center of his doting father's world. Muhammad's love for his precocious offspring was without measure. By the age of three, the child was accompanying his father on his numerous tours of the Middle East. Sallah's attentive parents had never been happier. The bright-eyed boy was everything to them.

Muhammad continued to preach of a need for the Quran to dictate the principles of the people's lives and the rules of their governments. And each night he asked his wife the same questions he'd been asking for years. Yet no sign came to tell them the time of the Mahdi had arrived.

By the 1990s, Algeria had once again become a land in turmoil. As in many Arab countries, the moderate government was under extreme pressure to convert the country to a strict form of religious rule simi lar to that in Iran and Afghanistan. The Algerian government steadfastly refused. So the fundamentalist party took to the streets to rally support for a new Islamic nation. What they couldn't convince their government to willingly do, they'd do themselves. In 1992, as the Algerian parliamentary elections neared, it was apparent the extremists would be victorious. The people had decided an exacting Islamic regime would be taking power in Algiers. A nation based solely upon the teachings of the Quran would soon emerge in North Africa. Muhammad had played no direct role in the political victory, but in his speeches his pleasure with the results was clear for all to see.

Such a radical government wasn't what the majority of the troubled planet wished for Algeria. They feared its intemperate teachings would soon spread across the deserts of North Africa. And from there consume the Islamic world. So, with support from the moderate Middle East nations and the leadership of the West, the Algerian army voided the coming elections and seized control of the country.

The people rebelled. Civil war was a real possibility. The military leaders cracked down upon the determined dissidents. Nevertheless, the unrest prevailed. The resistance grew. The new government's response was entirely predictable. The time had come to end the threat posed by those who advocated an extreme Islamic state. A secret tribunal, acting in absentia, ordered the deaths of the country's religious leaders.

Their first target would be Muhammad Mourad.

Late on a quiet summer day shortly after Sallah's fifth birthday, an armored convoy was spotted in the limitless desert north of the dusty crossroads. While he worked in his shops, Muhammad took little notice. The passing of a military formation wasn't an everyday event in Aynorian. Still it had happened before. The villagers showed a mild interest in the unexpected appearance, but soon returned to their daily chores.

The powerful force stopped a few miles from the oasis. Fifty French-made tanks and self-propelled howitzers gathered in a long, straight line. Each prepared to fire. The order was given. An abysmal symphony, filled with riotous result, filled the cloudless heavens. The hellish sound roared in every direction, its fury infinite. The first massive volley obliterated the center of the unassuming settlement. Muhammad's shops were reduced to refuse.

Beneath the shattered stone, the unconscious form of the Mahdi lay.

Panicked villagers raced from their homes in a desperate attempt to escape the precipitous events all around them. Sharif grabbed Sallah and hurried for the door. She would, however, be a fraction too late. A second volley screamed through the hazy afternoon. Fifty explosive rounds rained down once more. A huge shell landed in the middle of the couple's humble home. In a blinding flash, Sharif's and Sallah's lives ended.

A third and fourth volley were all it took to finish leveling what remained of the ancient outpost. Not a stone still stood.

A second order was given. Armored personnel carriers raced toward Aynorian. At the edge of town soldiers poured from the tracked vehicles. The army began a systematic search of the narrow streets. Fleeing men, women, and children were gunned down without a passing thought.

No quarter was given the terrified desert inhabitants. No mercy was shown. The few villagers they found who survived the attack were gathered up and taken to where the great mosque had stood. A single bullet ended each life.

The slaughter took less than fifteen minutes. At its end, twelve hundred peaceful people had perished. A remote desert dwelling that had survived for more than a millennium was no more. The ferocious column re-formed and headed north. Not a soldier had been injured in the siege.

Behind them, hidden beneath two feet of crumbling mortar, the battered form of the Mahdi lay. By the grace of Allah, he'd survived the furious onslaught.

It would be well after dark before Muhammad would regain his senses and dig himself out of the man-made tomb. With blood seeping from his innumerable wounds, he dragged himself to what remained of his home. Near where the front door had stood, he found his wife and son. He pulled their lifeless bodies from the rubble and fell to the ground next to them.

Tears poured down his anguished face. His grief flowed like a raging river for well into the night. With the coming of the next day's sun he got his first good look at what had happened to the people and place he adored. He could count on one hand those fortunate enough to have somehow survived. Anger soon replaced his tears. The government's brutality couldn't be ignored. Such terrible acts had to be avenged. The Quran demanded retribution for the senseless slaughter of his people. While his wife lived, he'd promised moderation. But she lived no more.

The time for moderation was over. The time for wondering when Allah would call upon him was past. As the sun rose high on that terrible morning and he held the crushed remains of Sharif and Sallah to him, he knew with absolute clarity what was planned for the remainder of his life. He would take to the high mountains and gather the true believers to him. There he'd spend the coming years preparing for the great battles to follow.

Sharif told him he'd know when the moment was here. The moment was now.

On that day, in the ashes of his smoldering birthplace, the Chosen One arose.

11

Tony Watson sat behind the anchor desk. From the control booth a voice said, "Okay, Tony, in five . . . four . . . three . . . two . . . one . . ." Watson's charming face appeared in millions of homes throughout the United States. The program's theme music played. As the stirring melody faded, the news anchor looked up and smiled.

"Good evening, I'm Tony Watson, and you're watching *Seven Days*. Tonight, as events unfold in the Pan-Arab War, we're presenting a story that initially aired on this program earlier this summer. *Seven Days* is dedicating the first part of the hour to ABC Middle East correspondent Lauren Wells's exclusive interview with 'the Chosen One,' Muhammad Mourad. Whether or not you saw our original airing, this is one you won't want to miss.

"But before we begin Lauren's fascinating interview, let's take a look at events in the war-torn Middle East. Throughout the day, Iraqi and Iranian forces pushed deeper into Kuwait and Saudi Arabia. With night beginning to fall, elements of the 1st Cavalry Division beat back a series of attacks near the Saudi city of Sakakah. Air Force fighters and naval aircraft from the carriers *Theodore Roosevelt* and *George*

Washington performed nearly one thousand sorties over Iraqi and Iranian positions. The round-the-clock bombing of critical military targets in and around Baghdad and Tehran entered its third week.

"In Cairo, fierce house-to-house fighting by Egyptian army units supported by a United States Special Forces contingent continued. In the fourth day of their assault upon the capital city's sprawling suburbs, the Chosen One's army pushed closer to the heart of the metropolis of eighteen million. At sunset, Pan-Arab forces were in full control of Giza and had reached the western banks of the Nile. White House and Pentagon officials refused to speculate on how much longer Cairo could hold out against such overwhelming odds.

"In the day's brightest news, the Pentagon announced that a successful amphibious landing by the 2nd Marine Division occurred this morning approximately one hundred miles northwest of Cairo. Despite heavy losses from repeated Pan-Arab counterattacks, the Marines were able to gain a secure foothold on the North African coast. At the moment, the Marine division is pushing farther into Egypt in an attempt to sever the Chosen One's supply lines and cut off reinforcements.

"Lauren Wells is on the ground with the Marine expeditionary force. At the end of tonight's program she'll be providing our nationwide audience with an up-to-the-minute report on the situation at the landing site.

"That's the latest from the battle fronts. Should events warrant, we'll interrupt our broadcast of Lauren's interview with Muhammad Mourad to bring you any breaking news."

Watson paused as the tape of the August show started running. On the video, the *Seven Days* set reappeared. An extremely attractive woman in a navy-blue business suit sat next to him.

The charming figure, who had scarcely reached her thirties, had a pleasing smile upon her face.

There was a look of confident determination starting at the corners of her mouth and reaching into her radiant eyes. It was that self-assured expression, bordering on the ruthless, that separated Wells from her rivals in this fiercely competitive business. Despite her age, in the tough world of television journalism she'd already reached the highest pinnacles of success. The highly popular, absolutely fearless Wells was head and shoulders above her peers. And no matter what it took, the tough-minded reporter planned to keep it that way.

If the public had been aware of the events of her fiercely challenging childhood, they would have admired her even more. In one way she was similar to Sam Erickson. For both had lost their fathers. In Wells's case, however, his passing hadn't been something to take even the briefest pause to mourn. His death had been a relief to her and her mother. For the smiling man an approving world perceived had been nothing like the monster who lurked behind closed doors.

Her immensely successful father had two completely different façades. The prosperous, personable individual the public saw. And the severely alcoholic, harshly violent one who released his fury upon his wife and daughter behind his spacious mansion's sheltering walls. The continual abuse, both physical and emotional, had been extreme. Even the slightest transgression, real or perceived, would send him into a rage. Nothing his beautiful wife and accomplished daughter did was ever good enough. The number of times they'd arrived at emergency rooms with black eyes, bruises, and broken bones was more than either could count.

From Lauren's earliest years, her mother had attempted to protect her. Yet all that had wrought was further anguish and suffering for the desperate pair. In the early years, her mother had reported her husband's extreme violence. Unfortunately, he had every politician in the state in his pocket. And her desperate pleas had gone unanswered. The records of the infinite calls for assistance, and every incident report she'd ever filed, had somehow disappeared.

She'd attempted to take her daughter and run away on numerous occasions, but with his limitless resources he'd found each hiding place in a matter of days. The malevolence committed against them upon their return had been unspeakable. More than once he'd made it clear that should she attempt to divorce him, he'd make sure she never saw her daughter again.

Such a demeaning, coerced existence would have crushed most children. It, however, had had the opposite effect on Lauren. With an exceptionally strong inner core, she'd refused to allow her father's cruelty to destroy her. Each horrid event had made her more determined.

Eventually, both she and her mother watched as he drank himself into an early grave.

The haggard women finally had been freed from the ghastly horror. A few months later, Lauren set out for college with profound goals and vivid memories imprinted upon her brain. The severe scars ran deep. Even so, she resolved to make herself into the absolute best she could be. And so far, her plan was proceeding exactly as she hoped.

"Good evening," Watson said on the tape. "Tonight, in an exclusive interview, America gets its first look at Muhammad Mourad, ruler of the Pan-Arab Federation. Our guest is ABC's chief Middle East correspondent, Lauren Wells." He turned to look at the auburn-haired newswoman sitting next to him. "Good evening, Lauren. Welcome back to *Seven Days*."

"Good evening, Tony. It's great to be here. I'm always thrilled when the opportunity arises to appear on your show."

"I'm told you've something quite special to share tonight."

"I believe I do. This interview was truly one of a kind."

"It's my understanding you're the only reporter ever to interview the powerful Arab leader."

"That's correct. After months of delicate negotiations, Mourad's government notified me a week ago that the meeting had been granted. Last Thursday I arrived in Algiers. My cameraman and I were whisked straight from the airport to a waiting caravan of four-wheel-drive vehicles. For most of a blistering day and well into a torturous night, we drove south across the unending Sahara and up into the high mountains near the Libyan border. Under cover of darkness, we were taken to see the man the Islamic world calls the Chosen One."

"Before we show our audience your interview," Watson said, "I'm certain everyone would be interested in hearing your impression of him. You've interacted with many of the world's most influential people. What was it about Mourad that made your discussion with him so unique, so different from the rest?"

"Tony, this was one I'll remember for the rest of my life. Muhammad Mourad's remarkable. Very gracious, very kind, and quite patient even when I asked some really difficult questions. Easily the most humble political leader I've ever encountered. Even though he was obviously ill at ease with the idea of being interviewed, he did everything in his power to make us feel we were his honored guests. As our viewers will see, his English is impeccable. He's one of the most brilliant people I've ever met. He's also one of the most physically unimposing men I've ever seen. He can't be over five feet tall. And I doubt he weighs more than one hundred pounds. Beneath his scraggly beard, his aging cheeks are sunken and weathered. His skin has little vitality and an odd sort of sickly hue. But there's something if you ever meet him you'll never forget."

"What's that?"

"It's his eyes, Tony. There's something haunting in those eyes of his. There's an anger, and at the same time a sadness his dark eyes can't conceal. As for the ground rules, there were no conditions attached by Mourad's government and no limits on what I could ask. The questions were entirely mine and his answers are unedited."

"Well, with that as an introduction, let's get to the actual interview."

A recording of Wells's meeting with the Chosen One began to run. The picture showed a nondescript room with peeling plaster walls. There was no furniture to be seen. Muhammad Mourad sat cross-legged on the floor. She had expected to find him wearing flowing Arab robes or a clownish military uniform. Instead, she found a simple man dressed in peasant's clothing. Three of his followers, also modestly dressed, sat on his right. Wearing a scarf, and clothing that covered all exposed skin, she was seated to his left.

"Mr. Mourad, first I wish to thank you for giving me the opportunity to conduct this interview."

"It's my pleasure, Miss Wells. I get too few chances to practice my English these days."

"I know the entire world is greatly interested in what you have to say. It's my understanding this is the first interview you've ever granted to a non-Arab journalist. So I'm certain there's much our viewers would like to know."

"Actually, Miss Wells, this is my first interview with anyone."

"Oh, I hadn't realized that. Why then did you pick me to conduct it?"

"Because my people saw your work and were impressed with your fairness and integrity."

"You've never watched any of my interviews yourself?"

"In my entire life, I've never seen anything on television. When I lived in France as a university student they had such things. But I didn't have the time or inclination to look at them."

"Since you, as you just mentioned, were a student in France, you've obviously had some contact with the world outside North Africa."

"Aw, Miss Wells, that was so many years ago. I'm certain I remember little of what I saw. The one thing I'll always remember, however, is it was the place where I met my sweet wife."

"That was something I definitely wished to ask you about, sir. Let's talk about your wife, if you don't mind. From what I've been able to gather, it was her death that started you down the path to where you are today. Can you tell me about her?"

"Sharif was a remarkable woman. For twenty-four years we were husband and wife. We had a wonderful life together. We lived in the small village in the southern desert where I'd been born. One day, after the military seized power, a large armored column appeared. No one had any idea why they were there. The next thing I knew, they opened fire with their cannons. The shelling didn't stop until the entire settlement had been destroyed. Over twelve hundred people lost their lives in a matter of minutes. Only a handful of villagers survived the attack. By the grace of Allah, I was one of them. But he chose not to spare my wife and five-year-old son."

"I'm so sorry to hear that."

"Please don't unduly concern yourself with my loss. The sainted people of my village, my wife and son included, now live in paradise with all of the martyrs."

"But I still don't understand. Why did the military attack your home?"

"Because they were afraid of me."

"Afraid of you? Why were they afraid of you?"

"Because I'm the Mahdi . . . the Guided One . . . the Chosen One. At the time the Algerian people wished to create a government based upon the teachings of the Quran. But the secular government and the Western powers resisted the idea of a fundamentalist Islamic state in North Africa. So the army canceled the election and seized power. Although I'd never been directly involved in politics, they knew I supported the Islamic party. It wasn't long thereafter they sent their soldiers to kill me and destroy my people."

"But you killed them instead."

"Yes, I killed them. It took many years after I declared holy war to create a people's army strong enough to defeat the blasphemers in Algiers. But with Allah's guidance, we were victorious. And a true nation of Islam was formed."

"That brings me to a rather controversial issue, Mr. Mourad. I hope you're not going to be offended by my broaching the subject."

"As we agreed, you're free to ask anything you wish."

"Your campaign to overthrow the military government, in the early years, contained some of the most violent acts of terrorism the world's ever witnessed. At least in the West, we had a great deal of difficulty understanding how a man, especially a man whose own wife and child had been murdered, could base much of his campaign on entering sleeping towns and indiscriminately slitting the throats of innocent men, women, and children. You've never denied your involvement in the slaughter of over one hundred thousand of your countrymen. These were people just like you. How could you do such a thing?"

"I'm afraid you're only partially correct in your assumptions, Miss Wells. I won't deny I was the one who gave the orders to kill those people. But they weren't as innocent as you've claimed. When jihad's begun, there's no longer room for innocent people. You either accept the call to arms or become an enemy of Islam. Those people were given a choice. When they refused to join our cause, we'd no other course from the one we took. They'd made their decision, and the Quran called for prompt punishment for all sinners. I realize such a consequence is beyond your limited understanding of our ways. Still the people who forfeited their lives knew what their refusal to join us would bring."

"But the horror of what you were doing. The terror you put people through."

"Terror's one of Allah's warriors' greatest weapons. Terror's always been a part of any holy war."

"So after the death of your wife and son it took nearly twenty years, but eventually your army defeated the Algerian military. Reporters who covered your triumphant arrival in Algiers said justice for the losers was swift and brutal. From what I've heard, beheadings in Algiers's central square became a daily occurrence. They said the streets ran red with blood."

"Justice is always swift for the losers, Ms. Wells. And life itself is brutal. You need to understand, such bloodshed could have been avoided if only the military had accepted the people's will and turned the government over to the appointed Islamic officials."

"Mr. Mourad, there's a personal question which bothered me during every minute of the long, difficult ride from Algiers. If you're the ruler of the majority of Arab North Africa, why do you live way up here in the mountains so far from everything? It's just so desolate. Why don't you live in Algiers?"

"Because I learned long ago that I don't care for cities. The desert's always been my home and this is where I wish to be. The clerics in Algiers can manage the day-to-day affairs of our federation. And we're in constant contact on those issues needing my personal attention."

"Okay, so it's many years after your wife's death, and you've conquered Algeria. Is it at that point you began calling yourself the Prophet?"

He stared at her with a dazed look upon his face. His surprise was evident in his answer.

"Prophet? I'm no prophet. Where did you get such an idea?"

"But that's what everyone in the Western press has called you for years."

"Then the Western press is mistaken. I'm no prophet. For the followers of Islam, the last true Prophet lived fifteen hundred years ago. He was the final messenger. There'll never be another."

"But you said earlier you were the Chosen One."

"I'm the Mahdi. But that doesn't make me a prophet. I'm the one who Allah, in his infinite wisdom, has selected to destroy the nonbelievers. I'm the one the prophecy foretold would arrive to lead Islam in its conquest of the world and to prepare the pious for the end of time."

"When you use the term 'nonbelievers,' who exactly are you talking about?"

"All those who don't worship the one true God."

"So when you say you'll destroy all nonbelievers, am I correct in my understanding of what that means? Since we worship the same God, the term 'nonbelievers' doesn't include Christians?"

"No, Miss Wells. Christians are also considered nonbelievers by those who love the sacred teachings of the Quran."

"But from what you just said, how can that be? We also worship the same God. The God Islam worships."

"But Christians don't recognize Allah's Prophet Muhammad as their own. And they fail to heed the righteous tenets of the Quran. By doing so they've guaranteed their destruction at the hands of the faithful. It's not just Christians, Miss Wells. Unbelievers also include all non-Islamic religions and those Arabs whose belief in Islam isn't as it should be."

"So as the Chosen One, you believe one of your roles is to destroy Arab countries who don't conform to your tenets?"

"That would be correct."

"Which nations are those?"

"Egypt, Morocco, Jordan, Saudi Arabia, Kuwait, to name a few. Their leaders must change their ways and heed the sacred words before it's too late. Islam cannot begin its conquest of the outside world until the Middle East is united under our banner."

"Is that the reason you conquered Libya, Tunisia, and the Sudan?"

"I conquered no one, Miss Wells. The people of Libya, Tunisia, and the Sudan were eager to join us in creating the world's first purely Islamic republic. The Pan-Arab Federation exists because of the wishes of the people of North Africa, not because of some alleged conquest. The majority of the Egyptian people also wish to join us. But their corrupt leadership usurped power from the duly elected Islamic officials."

"There's a belief, Mr. Mourad, that you're planning on invading Egypt in the near future. Are you willing, on American television with millions of people watching, to deny such rumors?"

"As we speak, Egypt is in the throes of a great unrest. The virtuous are battling for control of that great nation. I'm confident Allah will see to it truth prevails."

"Many suspect you're behind the Egyptian uprising. The methods being used by the Egyptian rebels are quite similar to those you employed in most of your victories."

"Nonsense, Miss Wells. The lovers of Islam in Egypt are leading the journey to their country's salvation. My assistance isn't necessary.

They know the path that must be followed to find their way to paradise. They don't need my help to learn such things. It's there for the devout to see in the hallowed passages of the Quran."

"Sir, that may be. But you still haven't answered my question. The United States has a mutual defense pact with the Egyptian government. We've promised to defend that country from any outside attack. I'm positive the American people want to hear your response. Whether or not our soldiers are going to find themselves fighting in the Middle East once more is an issue on everyone's mind. Are you, or are you not, planning on invading Egypt?"

"My soldiers are stationed on the Egyptian border solely to ensure their civil war doesn't spill over onto our soil."

"So you claim you've placed a million soldiers on the border for your own protection."

"I claim nothing, Miss Wells. But your answer's correct."

"And you have no intention of invading Egypt?"

"For what purpose?"

"You tell me, Mr. Mourad."

"There's nothing to tell."

"Since you brought it up, sir, let's talk about your military."

"If you wish."

"At the present time, how many soldiers do you have?"

"One never really knows. Ours is a people's army, and its numbers are constantly changing."

"Okay, then, if you had to estimate, how many soldiers are serving in your army today?"

"Today?"

"Yes, sir, at this very moment."

"I'd have to guess."

"Then guess if you must, Mr. Mourad."

"A guess? Oh, somewhere around three million."

"Your army has three million men?"

"No, Miss Wells. Not all who serve Allah are men. Many of our warriors are women. The Quran allows for such. And as I said, the numbers are of little significance. They vary from day to day. This is a reverent cause. If necessary, I'm confident we could put ten million fighters in the field in a matter of days."

"Did I hear you correctly, sir, you said ten million? Certainly you don't have weapons for ten million soldiers?"

"No, not nearly so many. But as Arab nations who've dared to stand up to the West in the past have discovered, the number of weapons isn't as important as the quality of those weapons and the training of those who hold them in their hands. In that respect, Allah has blessed my people, for the governments we've replaced had very modern weaponry. And since my rise to power we've been able to obtain many first-rate arms on the open market. The countries of the world have been eager to sell us their goods. In a few short years, my army and air forces have grown into some of the most powerful on the planet. Our oil money has purchased the best American, British, French, Chinese, and Russian armaments money could buy. And we've hired highly skilled instructors from across the globe to teach us how to use them. Each of my followers from ages ten to sixty has received a minimum of six weeks of military training. Still, to claim to have weapons for ten million would be a lie. Should the time come we won't need so great a number. Many would enter into battle without weapons. They'd take them from those who'd fallen and begin their own martyr's journey to paradise." He paused and looked toward his followers. It was obvious he'd tired of the discussion. "Now, I'm quite sorry, but unless you've a question that must absolutely be asked, I'm afraid I must take my leave of you. There are always important matters needing my attention and so little time with which to deal with them."

"I understand completely, sir. Before I go, I want to thank you for your hospitality and for giving me the opportunity to ask these questions. I hope we meet again quite soon."

"You're entirely welcome, Miss Wells. Although I cannot imagine how we'd ever have an opportunity to speak again."

She stood to leave. The tape ended. A picture of Tony Watson sitting alone at the anchor desk returned to the screen. "There you have it, ladies and gentlemen. As you know, two months after this interview, Mourad's army invaded Egypt. Iran and Iraq attacked Saudi Arabia and Kuwait. War rages throughout the Middle East. A brutal war that's already cost untold American lives and threatens to send the world spiraling into chaos. Stay tuned. After these messages, we'll have the latest from Lauren Wells, live from Egypt with the Marine expeditionary force."

12

Watson took a deep breath and collected his thoughts. Now would come the most difficult portion of the program. In minutes, he'd be live with Lauren Wells. Her report from the battlefront would make or break this evening's show.

From the control room the voice boomed, "Tony, we've got the telephone hookup with Lauren. We still have thirty seconds. Want to check things out before we go back on the air?"

"Sure, Ben, patch her through."

"Okay, Tony, she's on the line."

"Lauren, are you there?"

"I'm here, Tony."

"Everything set on your end?" Watson asked.

"Seems to be. At the moment, the winds are blowing really hard. And there's a lot of dirt and smoke flying around. A live picture from here's definitely out of the question. But the mobile telephone link appears to be working fine. Let's hope it stays that way."

"Yeah, let's. Look, Lauren, since we just got word we'd be doing

this minutes before the show went on the air, I don't have a set of prepared questions. We'll have to play it by ear."

"That's okay. I only found out an hour ago I'd been cleared to go
ashore. Had to call in lots of favors to get off that ship. So I really
haven't had much time to prepare myself. Don't worry, though, it'll
go fine."

"Okay, Tony," the voice said, "in five . . . four . . . three . . . two . . .
one . . ."

Watson's smiling face returned to America's homes. Once more,
the show's blaring music played. As it disappeared he said, "We're
back, and as promised, Lauren Wells has joined us from the battle
zone. Good evening, Lauren."

A file photograph of her standing in an unidentified Arab city appeared on the screen.

"Good evening, Tony. I'm reporting tonight from the beaches of
northern Egypt. So far, the military's only allowed a single pool reporter to come ashore. Having drawn the short straw, that reporter's
me. I hope everyone understands for security reasons I'm not allowed
to give the exact location of the Marine landing or the precise American battle plans."

"Of course. What can you tell us about what's happened so far?
What's going on at the moment?"

"It's nearly five a.m. here. Since before yesterday's sunrise the Marines have been reaching this beachhead. At the moment, elements of
the 2nd Marine Division continue to come ashore. If asked to make an
estimate, I'd say approximately seventeen thousand of the division's
nineteen thousand men and women are on the ground and in position
to battle the Chosen One's army. Right now, with the exception of the
distant rumble of artillery, things are fairly calm. They certainly
weren't that way earlier."

"How so, Lauren?"

"From our vantage point on the deck of the cruiser *Thomas Fine*,

the entire press corps had a front-row seat for the fierce battle that occurred to take and hold this landing zone. It was quite a sight."

"Lauren, I know all of America wants to hear about what transpired. What can you tell us about the Marine assault?"

"From what I've pieced together, we had hoped to catch Mourad's
army by surprise. For that reason, a small reconnaissance unit was
sent ashore to check things out. They soon ran into trouble and were
reinforced by a couple of infantry squads."

"How many Marines would that be?"

"Normally around twenty or so in a reconnaissance platoon. Thirteen in each infantry squad. An hour after the recon teams landed,
two battalions in amphibious vehicles joined them. Since that time,
additional battalions have steadily reached the coastline and entered
into battle."

"From what we've heard from the Pentagon, obviously the plan
succeeded."

"Not without a vicious struggle. The initial unit ran into a large
enemy force and a number of tanks. An entire Pan-Arab armored division was right behind them. At that point, an immense naval and air
attack was unleashed to hold the fanatics while we built up our numbers and began fighting our way both south and east. If you'd seen it,
you'd have sworn nothing could survive such an unrelenting barrage
as the ships and aircraft laid down. But somehow many of Mourad's
followers did. Throughout the day, I'm aware of at least four enemy
counterattacks of division-level strength or larger. Many of the furious
clashes included mass suicide charges. The last of those occurred not
more than five hours ago some distance from here. Despite the overwhelming numbers against them, the Marines have so far withstood
every attack."

"The Pentagon announced a few hours ago that there'd been significant loss of life on both sides. Can you confirm that, Lauren?"

"American casualties have been quite heavy. With each determined assault, the death toll mounts. I know firsthand such reports

are true. Here on the beach, near my broadcast position, green body bags are laid out in long rows. It's an eerie sight as I watch them fluttering in the strong winds. But our losses are nothing compared to those suffered by the enemy. You can't walk fifty feet in the desert without stumbling over the rotting corpse of one of the Chosen One's soldiers. And in every direction you look, burning Pan-Arab armored vehicles fill the horizon. Word from the aircraft carriers is our pilots are reporting endless trails of ravaged tanks. The smoke from these massive fires is so thick it threatens to suffocate everyone."

"Lauren, are you saying our military's projecting the tide's turned, and we'll soon defeat Mourad's army? After nothing but gloom and doom for the past three weeks, I know our viewers would be thrilled to hear such news."

"That's not at all what I'm saying, Tony. In fact, my sources are telling me quite the opposite. The Chosen One's promise of paradise is fueling his disciples far beyond anything anyone had projected. Today's struggles didn't even faze them. And that's not likely to change soon. This thing still has a long way to go before the killing will finally stop. Exactly how or when it will end, and who will emerge victorious, is a question no one can answer with any certainty. We've had our first good day of the war. But that's all the Marine landings amount to. For three weeks the Chosen One's had his way. Nothing's come close to slowing his advances. Now today, for the first time, he's suffered a setback in the deserts of northern Egypt. Still it's just a single defeat. We shouldn't fool ourselves into thinking we've won this war. If anything, the situation in Cairo's even more desperate than it was yesterday."

"From what you've heard, is the military saying Cairo's going to fall?"

"No one seems to know. By sunrise there will be nineteen thousand Marines on the shores of Egypt. I've heard unsubstantiated rumors that in three to five days, the 1st Marine Division will join them. That'll give us thirty-eight thousand lightly armed Americans against three million of the enemy. With yesterday's arrival of the aircraft carriers we've garnered a modicum of control of the skies. And we're continuing our efforts to bring American-stateside and Europe-based units to the battlefields. The French and English are doing the same. Even so, prior to now, the extent of our support for the Egyptians was the recent appearance in Cairo of eleven hundred Green Berets. Everyone needs to understand the desperateness of the situation and the limits on what we can do."

"Those are very sobering thoughts, Lauren."

"This is a very sobering place, Tony."

"I'm sure our audience understands there are limits on what you can tell us about the tactical situation. But if you could give us a feel for what you believe will happen next with the Marines, I'm certain it would be greatly appreciated."

"I can add nothing from any official sources. All have cited security reasons in declining to answer any questions. Throughout the day rumors have circulated about what comes next. But anything further I say is strictly conjecture."

"And what would that be?"

"Again I want to warn our audience to take what I'm about to tell them for what it's worth. This is just my opinion based upon the wild speculation of my fellow members of the press corps. It appears the basic idea's in two parts. The first is well under way. It involves around six thousand Marines moving west until they reach the Libyan-Egyptian border. They'll attempt to destroy any resistance they encounter along the way. Once there, the Marines will dig in and set up fortified defensive positions. In a few days, a regiment from the 1st Marine Division will land and hurry to join them. The purpose of this part of the invasion is to block the millions of reinforcements Mourad has waiting in Libya, Tunisia, and Algeria. Then, with his supply lines severed and most of his forces outside of Egypt cut off, the next portion of the plan will apply pressure to the Mahdi's forces in Egypt."

"What have you heard about the second part?" Watson asked.

"Nice and simple. Take the remaining elements of the 2nd Marine Division and push southeast to engage as many of the Chosen One's divisions as they can to take some pressure off the Egyptian capital. If nothing else, they hope to buy everyone a few days of valuable time. When the 1st Marine Division arrives, its regiments will rush in to reinforce whatever's left of the 2nd Division."

"Certainly, Lauren, even with relentless air support, thirty-eight thousand Marines don't expect to defeat an army of three million."

"Tony, some pretty high-up sources have hinted such a goal's almost laughable. There's just not enough firepower in these divisions to do that. The Marines have always been a light, highly trained fighting force based upon mobility and the quality of its members. They don't have the resources to destroy the vast armored force Mourad's assembled. My God, Tony, a Marine division's only got a few dozen tanks supported by some Stryker armored cars and Humvees. Even with what's been destroyed in the past three weeks, intelligence estimates show Mourad's army with nearly nine thousand tanks. It would take at least two or three of our best army divisions with their hundreds of M-1 tanks and Bradley Fighting Vehicles to engage and eliminate such a huge quantity of armor."

"So why did we send in the Marines? Why not one of our army divisions?"

"I can't give our audience a definite answer. But I've got a pretty good guess."

"What would that be?"

"We don't have the logistical capabilities to move an army division here quickly enough to keep Cairo from falling. Putting the Marines on planes to Italy and getting them onto ships to cross the Mediterranean's going to happen much quicker than loading hundreds of tanks in the United States and sailing them here. Remember, during Desert Storm it took us three months to build up our forces to the point where we felt strong enough to invade. And that was a single war against one Arab nation. This time we've got two war zones on our hands. And we've had less than three weeks. It's already been confirmed that the initial movement of our armored units who've arrived in the Middle East has been in support of the growing battles against Iraq and Iran. So at the moment I don't think we've got anything but the two Marine divisions available to attack the Chosen One. In a week or two, I wouldn't be surprised to find British or French or American armored vehicles rumbling through these deserts, annihilating anything in their path. But for now, it's up to the men of the 2nd Marine Division to stand up to the enemy tanks. The Marines are here to buy time. To harass and destroy. To give Cairo and the world a fighting chance."

"With those somber thoughts," Watson said, "I'm afraid we've run out of time. Thank you, Lauren, for your insights."

"Thank you, Tony."

Her picture disappeared from the screen.

Watson looked into the camera and said, "This has been another edition of *Seven Days*, America's fastest-growing weekly news and information program. Next week our guests will be . . ."

In the lifeless desert of northern Egypt, Wells handed the telephone receiver to her cameraman, Chuck Mendes. He began disassembling the mobile satellite equipment.

"Hurry it up, Chuck," she said. "There's an interview I'm dying to get before the rest of the press corps comes ashore."

13

The exhausted lieutenant knelt in the desolate sands. He tied a final toe tag and zipped up the body bag. That was all of them, the last of the platoon they could find enough fractured pieces of to place in the windblown green bags. He arose from the gruesome task and wandered across the invasion-cluttered beach toward nothing in particular. He could go no farther. He didn't have the strength to take another step.

Erickson slumped upon the shifting dunes. He propped himself against an empty ammunition crate and pulled at his exhausted eyes. Weariness overwhelmed him. With much effort, he removed the tattered remains of his fatigue shirt. The once-sterile bandages on his left arm were streaked with red. The wound had reopened. A trickle of blood oozed down his upper arm and dripped upon the ground. His arm throbbed. Beads of sweat gathered upon his filthy face and tugged at the corners of his parched mouth. He sat motionless, watching the steady stream of men and equipment coming ashore.

The platoon had done it. With their lives, they'd given the Americans a fighting chance to forestall the conquest of Egypt. They'd given the West an opportunity to defeat the Pan-Arabs and save the planet from erupting in an all-consuming war.

At the moment, however, such realities were of little comfort to the battered platoon leader. He turned to stare at the long rows of fluttering bags. He knew in a few hours the chaplains and escort officers would begin the grim process of ringing the doorbells of his brave men's families. The young wives, most with babes in arm, would learn the awful truth. The anxious parents, pain etched upon their tormented features, would never recover from the unbearable grief that soon would arrive upon their doorsteps. He understood from firsthand experience what that devastating event would feel like. He hung his head in an ever-mounting sorrow. His grief crawled deep within him and wrapped itself around his anguished soul. Lost in thought, he didn't notice the pair approaching.

"Lieutenant Samuel Erickson?" Wells asked.

The platoon leader looked up with a start. He couldn't form the words to answer.

"You're Lieutenant Erickson, aren't you?" she said.

"Yes, I'm Erickson." He made no attempt to get to his feet.

"I'm Lauren Wells from ABC."

"I know who you are," he said.

"Mind if I ask you some questions?"

He scarcely had the ability to respond. His answer was barely audible. "Actually, ma'am, I do mind."

"I'm sorry, what?" she said.

"To tell you the truth, I'm not in much of a mood for talking. Maybe some other time."

Wells, however, had never before taken no for an answer. And she wasn't about to start. She ignored his response and gave her cameraman the signal to begin rolling tape.

"You're the one who led the invasion yesterday, aren't you?"

"Yes. It was my platoon that came ashore first."

"I watched the whole thing from my ship. Had a front-row seat for everything. It was quite a show you put on."

There was a dazed look in Erickson's eyes. He didn't respond.

"Tell me what happened," she said.

"What do you mean what happened? What do you think happened? The Pan-Arabs were everywhere. We killed them. They killed us. We won. There's nothing more to say."

"How many were there?"

"We ran into a large roving patrol, followed by a company of infantry, and then four tanks."

"Company of infantry. That would be what? Two hundred enemy soldiers?"

"Counting those in the patrol we killed, body count was two-sixty-two last I heard."

"And how many men did you have?" she asked.

"With the infantry squads that reinforced us there were fifty-three."

"So fifty-three Americans killed over two hundred enemy soldiers and destroyed four tanks."

"Many were women," Erickson said.

"What?"

"They were women. Young girls really. Some were fourteen, fifteen years old. We killed them all. If you don't believe me you can see for yourself. Most of their bodies are still out there in the desert."

It was Wells's turn to be stunned. She quickly recovered. "What about the tanks?" she said. "What can you tell me about the tanks?"

"They were American-made M-60s. Showed up after we battled the women. Cost me most of my men. But somehow we defeated them. To tell you the truth, it's all one big nightmare I can't sort out at the moment. I haven't slept in two days and I'm real confused about most of it right now."

"That's okay. Can you tell us what happens next for you and your platoon?"

"What platoon? Even counting the reinforcements, I've barely enough men left to form a squad. Most are over there"—Erickson gestured toward the body bags—"or out on the hospital ship. The rest we couldn't even identify."

"Tell me about your men. What were they like?"

"What's to tell? They were no different than any other platoon. Most were in their late teens or early twenties. All had something to live for. Over half had wives. Many had children. Children who'll never know their fathers."

"So with so few of you left, the war's over for you?"

"Ma'am, until the shooting stops the war is never over if you're a Marine."

"But it's obvious from the bandages on your arm you're wounded. You appear to be bleeding. Are you badly hurt?"

Erickson glanced at the line of blood. "It's really not much more than a scratch. My corpsman fished around in there for a while trying to get the shrapnel out. But he didn't have any luck. Once this is over and the doctors have time, I'm certain they'll take care of it. For now, I'll just have to live with the pain and keep doing my job the best I can."

"So you're going back into combat with a piece of metal in your arm?"

"It looks that way."

"Do you know when you're leaving?"

Erickson rubbed his raw eyes. "We're going to take a couple hours to get our heads on straight. After that we'll head inland. I've heard my battalion got hit hard in a couple of the counterattacks. So as soon as we can, we've got to get to the front lines."

"Then what?"

"What do you mean, then what? What else is there? We're going to fight and keep on fighting until someone orders us to stop. But right now, if you don't mind, I'm going to curl up on this beach and get a little sleep. In two hours it'll be daylight. When the sun comes up, I'll gather what remains of my unit and we'll head out once more."

"Head out for where?"

"Cairo. We're on our way to Cairo to kill the Chosen One and put an end to this thing."

"Cairo. Do you think you'll get there?"

"We'll get there. You can count on it. Those crazy Green Berets are waiting for our help. And by God, the 2nd Marine Division's going to give it to them. Now, if you don't mind, ma'am, I really do need some sleep."

"Oh yes, of course, Lieutenant. Thanks for talking with us." She motioned for her cameraman to shut down his camera.

As the pair walked away, she kept looking back at Erickson.

When they were out of earshot, she turned to her cameraman. "Chuck, let's go find some of those dead Arab girls. It'll make a nice addition to our piece. As soon as it's daylight and things clear a bit, locate a spot on the beach to set up the satellite. Tomorrow all of America's going to wake to see Lieutenant Samuel Erickson's handsome face in their living rooms."

"Handsome face? How could you tell he had a handsome face? He was so filthy I couldn't tell anything about what he looked like."

"Don't worry, Chuck, I could tell. There's one hell of a face under all that dirt and camouflage paint. And, Chuck . . . ?"

"Yes, Ms. Wells."

"I'll tell you something else."

"What's that?"

"When Erickson gets to Cairo and shakes hands with the first Green Beret, you and I are going to be there to film it."

"Sounds like a great idea, but you're forgetting one thing."

"What's that?" she asked.

"If we're going to do that, there have still got to be some Green Berets alive when we get there."

14

I n the murky no-man's-land between the combatants' lines, Army Sergeant Charlie Sanders dangled over the side of the aging bridge. To the west, the landscape teemed with Mourad's zealots. To the east, across the wide span, the safety of the tenuous American defenses was more than a quarter mile away. Fifty feet below, the Nile's historic waters meandered past on their four-thousand-mile journey to the sea.

The autumn night had been unusually cool. A heavy fall mist, gray and clammy, rose from the dark currents. A thick blanket of fog reached out from the passing waters to cover the lengthy expanse. Throughout the beset city scores of great fires burned. The moist river haze mixed with the thick smoke to devour the predawn landscape.

The African American sergeant adjusted the nylon lifeline, bringing himself closer to a massive pylon. Sanders fished around in his rucksack, withdrawing the plastic explosives. The Green Beret engineering specialist, an expert at building or demolishing nearly any structure, pulled a roll of heavy tape from the canvas bag. He started attaching the powerful explosives to the substantial bridge support. Above him, Sergeant First Class Matthew Abernathy and Staff

Sergeant Aaron Porter stood on the damp pavement with their rifles at the ready.

"Sanders, hurry it up," Abernathy said in hushed tones. "It's nearly sunrise. If Mourad's forces catch us out in the open like this, we're dead men."

"Take it easy, Sarge, this is the last one. I'll be finished in five minutes."

"Make it three," Abernathy said.

"My mother always told me when a job's worth doing, it's worth doing right. So do you want it fast, or do you want it right?"

"I want it right and fast. What I really want is to be back on the other side of this stupid bridge before it gets any lighter. And I also want to tell Captain Morrow this thing will be blown to kingdom come when you hit that detonator."

"What the hell's the name of this bridge anyway?" Sanders asked while securing the deadly explosives.

"Who friggin' cares," Porter said. "Just finish up. I'll feel a whole lot better when we're back inside our own lines. I'm not exactly thrilled to be standing here waiting for a bullet to arrive."

"Relax," Sanders said. "I'm almost done."

"Finish it already and let's get out of here," the anxious Porter said. "The enemy's near. I can sense it. And you know I'm never wrong when it comes to stuff like that. What's left of the buildings on this side of the river are crawling with the Chosen One's creepy little friends."

But Sanders wasn't concerned in the slightest. "You've got nothing to worry about. No one's going to bother either of you. With all this gray swirling around, anyone who sees you will think you're nothing more than a couple of ghosts rising up from the Nile."

"We're going to be real ones soon if you don't hurry up," Abernathy said.

Sanders fastened the long strand of detonator cord to the explosives. The final connection had been made. Each of the tired passageway's huge pillars was wired to blow.

Throughout the length of Cairo, on every span across the great river, other Green Beret units were doing the same. Their orders were clear, the consequences obvious—leave a single bridge standing and the city could fall before sunset.

Sanders checked his handiwork. "Okay, all done. Going to be a hell of a show when this thing goes up. Sure glad I'm going to have a front-row seat for the festivities. Pull me up and let's head home."

Four strong arms reached out and lifted the Special Forces A Team's engineering expert onto the wide stretch of steel and concrete. Porter handed Sanders his M-4 rifle.

"All right, let's go," Abernathy said.

"Hold up a minute," Sanders responded.

From his earliest days Charlie Sanders had been bold. Not once had he turned away from a challenge or dare. And he had the ample scars to prove it. He'd always been confident and a bit cocky. But he'd also been quite good at anything he'd ever tried. It hadn't taken long after his entry into the Army for him to recognize that Special Forces was the ideal place for someone with his intellect, talent, and temperament. His assessment had been correct. This was the perfect world for the young sergeant. He'd survived the relentless horrors of Green Beret training with relative ease and quickly learned his new job duties. Through long hours of practice, he'd become exceptionally skilled at destroying things.

The presumptuous Special Forces soldier reached into his fatigue jacket and pulled out his green beret. He fastidiously went about the process of placing it at just the right angle on his head. Then he primped and preened a moment longer. When he was satisfied the headgear was properly positioned, he turned to the others.

"How do I look?" he asked.

"Jesus, Charlie, you've got to be kidding," Porter replied. "Who gives a damn how you look? Let's get the hell out of here while we still can."

Abernathy and Porter turned and started running through the

enveloping gray toward the eastern end of the bridge. Sanders was right behind. Five hundred yards away members of their remote detachment waited behind a makeshift fortification of demolished cars and the crumbling remains of bombed-out buildings. Behind the precarious team's position was nothing but the disintegrating skeletons of Rhoda Island's assailed apartment houses and hotels. The once majestic island near the contested river's eastern bank was scarcely more than smoldering rubble. Mourad's artillery barrages had flattened all but a handful of the historic isle's structures.

"Come on, guys," Sanders called out as they neared their own lines. "I'm serious. This is really important. How's it look? 'Cuz it's critical it be positioned just right. I don't want to take any chances here. I need to be at my best. You never know when you're going to turn a corner and find yourself face-to-face with a pretty girl with love on her mind."

"Sanders," Abernathy said, "I'm afraid the only women you're going to find out here at this time of the morning are carrying rifles. And love's not what they're looking for. The sole thing they're thinking about is putting a bullet into that precious beret of yours."

"That'll never happen. Not to me. Not a bullet's been made with my name on it."

"God," Porter said, "I'd almost forgotten what it's like to be twenty-three and believe you're invincible. So tell me, Charlie, how does it feel to still think you're immortal?"

"Pretty damn good, that's for sure."

"Sanders," Abernathy said, "why in the world are you worried about meeting women? What's the matter, your three fiancées back in North Carolina not good enough for you?"

"Don't forget the pretty German girl who thinks he's on his way back to marry her," Porter added.

"Look," Sanders said, "a guy can never have enough women in his life."

"Take it from someone who's on his third wife and speaks from experience," Abernathy said. "You *can* have too many women. Just ask my second wife. She'll be glad to explain it to you. Just like she never stops explaining it to me when I pick up the kids for the weekend."

The trio was in magnificent physical shape. They swiftly covered the substantial distance across the broad causeway. The instant they reached the eastern bank, all three disappeared behind the makeshift barricades. The overwhelming tension of the previous hour's exceptionally onerous task and Sanders's self-assured attitude were too much for them to bear. The results were quite strange, but utterly predictable. The second they were safe they burst into laughter.

Captain Morrow, the A Team leader, was waiting. A puzzled expression came over his face at the sight of the laughing soldiers.

"What the hell's so damn funny?"

"Nothing, sir," Abernathy said between suppressed giggles.

They glanced at their disapproving commander. Each soon realized they looked like giddy schoolgirls. The laughter stopped.

"How'd it go?" Morrow asked.

"Piece of cake, sir," Sanders answered. "Only thing I need is to hook the leads to the detonator, and we'll be all set. After that, you give the word and boom, no more bridge."

"Go ahead and wire it up. But don't blow it until I give the order. I want to wait until the last possible moment to ensure anyone trying to escape Mourad's army still has a way to cross the Nile."

"There haven't been any civilians on it in nearly two hours, sir. Not since that last big Pan-Arab attack. Obviously, the enemy's cut off the escape routes across the river."

"You're probably right, Sanders. Even so, wait for my signal before you hit that switch. If there's a chance in a thousand of saving one more person, we'll hold out until the last possible second."

"I can't believe when they're captured," Porter said, "the lunatics are giving the Egyptians one opportunity to accept Mourad's brand of Islam and join their side. Men, women, children, it doesn't make any difference to that sorry old fool's followers. From what I heard, even the slightest hesitation and a nasty-looking sword the company political officer carries separates their head from their shoulders."

"At least the Egyptians are getting an opportunity to say yes," the captain said. "If the Mahdi's ghouls get their hands on any of us, they won't ask a single question before the ax falls."

"I tell you what, sir," Porter added. "I'm already so sick of all this I'm about to puke. If I see another innocent person's severed head, I'm personally going on a one-man scouting expedition to locate the Mahdi's headquarters. If I find him, he won't get a chance to say anything either before I slit his throat from ear to ear. I'm sure we'd all love to see how his perverted little head looks once it's dangling from a pole."

Each of those present, however, realized with millions of the Chosen One's henchmen closing in, they weren't likely to get such an opportunity anytime soon. From the looks on their faces, they all understood the grim reality of their situation.

Sanders didn't care to think about it further. He suspected if he stayed busy, the desperateness of the assignment would temporarily fade. The detachment's junior sergeant took the wire cutters from his rucksack and stripped the tips from the primer cord. In the dull half-light, he attached the leads to the detonator. It wasn't until he finished that he realized three of the team's members weren't present.

"Where's Staff Sergeant Donovan's team?"

"They haven't come back from wiring the bridge behind us to blow," Master Sergeant Terry, the team's senior operations sergeant, said.

"I hope nothing's happened to them," Morrow said. "If Mourad's forces have gotten around behind us and captured the second bridge, we'll be trapped on this island with no way of escape."

"I'd be more worried, sir, about being stuck here because Donovan screwed it up and blew the passage behind us by mistake," Sanders responded.

"Okay, Charlie, that's enough," Terry said. "We all know how you feel about Donovan's demolition skills. Why don't you cut the guy some slack? We're short an engineer, so even though it's Donovan's secondary specialty, he's having to fill in."

The Special Forces detachment was supposed to have twelve men: two officers, two operation sergeants, two medics, two weapons specialists, two communication specialists, and two engineers. Each member was proficient in one of the other skills as a secondary specialty. With such an arrangement there'd be redundancy for every activity. Like most A Teams, however, this one was short a few people. Detachment Alpha 6333 had arrived in Cairo thirty-six hours earlier with only ten men. They were minus one officer and an engineer. Thus far they'd been extremely lucky. In their hours on the front lines they hadn't lost a single member. Even so, each understood such good fortune wouldn't last forever.

Minus an engineering specialist, the team's newest member, Staff Sergeant Donovan, had been forced into performing his secondary skill.

"But Donovan hasn't done a single practice demolition right since he joined our team last month," Sanders said. "Captain, why don't I go back and check on them?"

"That's just what I need," Morrow responded. "Send my sole engineer out to search for a missing team. What a brilliant idea. We're going to need someone to handle all kinds of demolition projects in the coming days. What do you suggest I do if you don't come back, Sergeant Sanders?"

"If I don't come back it'll probably be because I'm dead. So to be honest with you, sir, at that point I'd probably not care much one way or another what you do." A silly grin came over his face.

"Very funny, smartass. The answer's no. You're staying right here to blow this bridge."

"Even so, sir," Terry said, "Sanders has a point. They're overdue. It's only six blocks to the other side of the island. Maybe we'd better send someone back to check on them."

"Okay, Abernathy and Porter, if you think you can stop laughing long enough to help us out here, why don't you head over to find them."

"Sir," Abernathy said, "if you'll promise to keep Sanders here, we assure you there'll be no more laughter on our part."

"Count on it. I'll tie him to the hood of this car and let the Pan-Arabs use him for target practice if it'll help this team accomplish its mission."

Fifteen minutes later, the first light of the arriving day pierced the gloomy morning. With the coming of the warming sun, the smothering fog began to dissipate. It wouldn't be long before the dreary mist disappeared and the swirling smoke was all that remained to mask the battered landscape. As the tentative dawn appeared, Abernathy and Porter returned with the missing members of the team.

"Where the hell have you been?" Morrow asked.

"Took longer than I'd anticipated, sir," Donovan said. "But I finally got it wired. The detonator's hidden under a palm tree on the left end of the bridge. All we've got to do is hook up the leads and it'll be ready to blow."

"Run into any of the Chosen One's followers?"

"No, sir," Donovan said. "No sign of them anywhere."

"What about the Egyptian infantry company that's supposed to help defend this sector? They were due two hours ago."

"No sign of them either, sir."

Each member of the team understood the significance of the supporting force's failure to show. If the last thirty-six hours were any indication, there was bound to be a fierce struggle for Rhoda Island, and quite soon. Without the infantry support, the ten men of Detachment Alpha 6333 would be on their own against Mourad's hordes. Nevertheless, the vastly outnumbered Green Berets were too well trained and certain of their abilities to panic.

"Obviously, they're not coming," Morrow said. "With each passing hour, the Egyptians are getting less and less reliable. I guess after three weeks of this shit they've about had enough. Looks like we'll have to handle this ourselves. Everyone get into position. With the sun starting to rise, it won't be much longer before the fireworks begin again. Find a good spot and get ready for another enemy advance. If the past hours are any indication, the Pan-Arab attack will commence soon."

15

Morrow was right. Seven minutes was all it took for a first furtive figure to appear in the dissolving mist on the far side of the Nile. The Pan-Arab scout approached the broad entrance to the bridge. A second stealthy form crept from the fragmented remains of the building directly in front of the wide, eight-lane span. He joined his comrade. The Americans understood thousands would soon follow. Before springing into action, the Green Berets waited to ensure the duo across the river weren't Egyptian civilians.

"Okay," Morrow said, "they're hostiles. Porter, Abernathy, they're all yours."

The A Team's weapons experts put down their M-4 assault rifles and picked up their single-shot sniper rifles. Both raised the thin black barrels and pointed them toward the elusive forms masked in the settling gray.

"I'll take the one on the left," Abernathy said.

"Five bucks says my kill's cleaner than yours," Porter answered.

"You're on."

Porter squeezed the trigger. A shot rang out. The exacting bullet sliced through the dreary dawn. A fraction later, Abernathy fired. The Pan-Arab soldier on the right silently slumped to the ground. The one on the left also dropped. But the second kill wasn't nearly as precise as the first had been. The Pan-Arab screamed as he fell to the rough pavement. He struggled to escape his lethal wounds, painfully dragging himself a few feet before stirring no more.

Abernathy reached into his pocket and took out a five-dollar bill. He handed it to his smiling partner. The money exchanged, both accomplished assassins inserted another round. As they did, a dozen new individuals appeared on the far approaches. The arriving squad inched toward the sedate structure.

"Double or nothing," Abernathy said.

"That's a bet I'll gladly take," Porter answered.

The nebulous images crept forward. They displayed a wariness that hadn't been often seen in the past three weeks. It was apparent none was eager to be the first to reach the avowed paradise this morose morning. The deadly rifles were back on the Green Berets' shoulders. Two more shots rang out.

A second pair fell onto the glum street. Neither moved further. Two clean kills. This time both Americans agreed the grisly competition had ended in a tie. The rest of the startled enemy dove for cover. But there was little protection to be found on the treeless avenue. The entire Special Forces detachment opened fire. The team's machine gun pounded their outgunned foe.

The Green Berets' individual weapons had a far greater effective range than that of the enemy rifles. In their adept hands, the Americans ripped the survivors apart. Their opponents tried to respond with their Czech-made AK-47s. They fired wild bursts toward the distant shore. Still they were no match for their multitalented antagonists. The one-sided encounter was soon over. Each Libyan lay dead on the bloodstained asphalt. Not a single American had suffered the slightest harm. The immensely gifted team stopped firing and waited. To a man, they knew things would get more difficult from here.

Silence gripped the grievous scene. The waiting defenders held their collective breath and watched the decaying buildings on the western edge of the magnificent Nile. Not the slightest sound or movement was detected on the distant side. The anguished day grew strangely calm. Second by second, an interminable minute passed. It felt like an hour to the determined men. Another torturously dragged by. Still nothing. The embattled detachment's ten soldiers were keenly alert. They knew their remorseless foe was out there and probably quite near. They understood the time for great conflict would soon be at hand. Beads of sweat appeared on their upper lips. Rows of sticky moisture formed on Sanders's forehead. It trickled into the corner of his eye. He brushed it away with a swipe of a soiled sleeve. And the detachment waited even longer.

But the tense interval was almost over. For their obsessed rival was, in fact, close by.

The frightening sounds, reaching out to assail them, came first. The thunderous dissonance of uncounted tanks drawing near. The lumbering machines' growling engines sliced through the listless gray to assault the defenders' senses. An eerie chorus, surreal and terrifying, soon joined the rancorous tanks. The indecipherable refrain grew louder. It filled every corner of the dejected dawn, drowning out the scores of armored vehicles. It overwhelmed the Americans' understanding. The Green Berets were at a loss to explain the strange mixture of forbidding noises tearing at their ears.

One by one, the perplexed soldiers recognized the source of the riotous discord. The horrific resonance devouring their world was man-made. The fearful strain belonged to thousands upon thousands of expansive human voices. The Pan-Arabs were gathering their courage. Their acknowledged journey to the astonishing next world was upon them, and Mourad's followers wanted to ensure their God recognized the worthiness of their sacrifice. The frenzied voices, rejoicing while they ran toward their inevitable deaths, were chanting at the top of their lungs.

The reveling drone swelled. The attackers were drawing close.

"Sergeants Terry and Donovan," Morrow said, "grab your Javelins and cover the bridge. Unless you're certain a tank's about to unleash its main gun, hold your fire. We'll permit them to get sucked in so deeply there'll be no chance of escape. If the situation allows, don't release your missiles until the enemy's at least halfway across the river. That'll jam them up with nowhere to go. Let's entice as many onto the bridge as we possibly can. Once they're trapped, we'll blow the sons-a-bitches to kingdom come."

Terry and Donovan picked up their powerful shoulder-mounted missiles. Each crept to the abutments at the eastern end of the broad causeway.

"Sanders," Morrow said, "slide over to that detonator and get ready. But don't set off the explosives until you receive my command."

The anxious soldier crawled over to take his position. He reached for the detonator and waited. The queuing tanks and beseeching voices continued to expand. The enemy was upon them. It wouldn't be much longer before the desperate struggle between ten fearless men and thousands of crazed cultists would be joined.

The Chosen One's followers arrived at the Nile.

A pair of M-60s smashed through the faltering walls of the shattered building in front of the bridge. Side by side, they roared toward its wide entranceway. The instant they reached the river crossing, the rumbling tanks' machine guns blazed.

Their vastly outmanned opponents ducked their heads and waited. Behind the M-60s, hundreds of screaming fanatics scurried through the opening the rushing tanks had created. More armored vehicles appeared. In an endless stream, sprinting men and maniacal machines poured onto the southernmost structure into Cairo. The torrent of agitated humanity and rampaging steel appeared to go on without end. The proficient Green Berets readied their weapons.

A raucous day of reckoning burst upon the great city. The exploding sounds of pitched battles erupted up and down the Nile. The men of Alpha 6333 weren't the only ones facing incredible odds on this grievous morning.

Morrow signaled and the death-dealing Special Forces' rifles opened up upon the surging masses. In large clumps, Mourad's followers fell upon the battered pavement. Many of the mortally wounded stumbled to the lethargic bridge's low railing and dropped the fifty feet into the shimmering waters. The languishing currents were soon a flowing crimson. The Pan-Arabs returned the Green Berets' fire. Shooting in every direction while racing across the broad expanse, they continued their suicidal charge.

Terry and Donovan brought the firing tubes up to their shoulders. The first pair of charging tanks was in their crosshairs. To the right of the assailed bridge, Sanders looked at the A Team commander, desperately searching for the sign to flip the switch. Morrow watched as their endless adversaries continued their frenetic procession toward Rhoda Island.

The lead tanks raced toward them. Behind them, the chaotic mob on the roadway grew. A dozen tanks and thousands of Mourad's adherents were on the expansive bridge and pressing forward. Still more were on the way.

Their numbers were so great, their desire for conquest or martyrdom so powerful, that untold multitudes were crammed shoulder to shoulder onto the entrance to the extended span. The fevered throng was so unyielding that those who lost their footing were being trampled to death by their persistent comrades. Scores more, unfortunate enough to find themselves in an M-60's path, were being crushed beneath a fifty-ton tank's steel treads.

The incited enemy came on.

"Shit," Sanders said as he watched the perverse scene, "I'm not going to have to blow this bridge. Those idiots are going to cause it to collapse on its own."

Yet the overburdened structure somehow held. And the determined frenzy was relentless. The steadily progressing leaders soon reached Terry's apocalyptic firing line. It was now or never for the Americans. Wait any longer and the M-60s would be too close to kill with a Javelin. If their antitank missiles were going to activate in time, they had to unleash them now.

Terry fired his unmerciful ordnance. Donovan's leaped from its tube. The nimble killers were a blur as they ripped across the brief distance. Rather than hitting the monsters head-on, the missiles were set for a top-down attack. Each would penetrate and destroy by striking the M-60's thinner upper armor.

The roaring Javelins ran true. A pair of thunderous explosions rocked the besieged city. An immense fireball, stretching the width of the bridge, swept out from the burning wreckage.

The ravenous blaze swiftly consumed huge numbers of the Chosen One's followers. Fiery figures could be seen staggering to the tormented structure's edges and tumbling into the gathering waters.

Those behind the defeated tanks were trapped. A solid wall of fatal flames blocked any movement forward. And the resolute thousands behind eliminated any chance of going back.

Terry and Donovan raced for the protection of their own lines.

"Now!" Morrow screamed.

Sanders hit the detonator switch.

A surge of electricity rushed down the primer cord. The results of the all-powerful blast that followed were appallingly certain. Five hundred yards of defeated mortar and concrete, steel and flesh, were ripped apart. Huge pieces of defiled bridge and massive weapons of war sailed into the heavens. Limitless bodies, whole, dismembered, or in butchered pieces, flew in every direction. Many of the crucified forms soared so high it appeared they were literally reaching for the promised paradise they so desperately craved.

In less than a heartbeat, thousands died. Debris and dust, stone and metal, rained down in unforgiving torrents upon the American positions. The Green Berets frantically dove for cover in a hopeless attempt to protect themselves from the lethal fallout. A red-hot piece of searing metal, razor-sharp and malicious, found Donovan as he futilely searched for somewhere to hide. From his wrist to his elbow, the metal sliced open his forearm. Blood gushed from the gaping wound. The injured soldier screamed in agony.

The sensation of a great earthquake, the result of Sanders's handiwork, shook the beleaguered capital. Behind the Green Berets, the fragile shells of dying buildings collapsed. They crashed to the ground in a mighty gale.

The imposing river crossing disappeared. Its pulverized remains tumbled into the mighty Nile. The innumerable carcasses of once-breathing souls joined the demolished edifice. The suddenly swirling waters eagerly accepted the lifeless human forms, allowing them to accompany it on its steadfast pilgrimage. Despite being extinct in the wide delta for at least a few centuries, the unspeakable carnage and rotting flesh brought the Nile's crocodiles north once more. They'd soon grow fat and lazy on the immense banquet Sanders had provided. Yet even the voracious crocs couldn't consume so great a bounty. For months afterward, bloated bodies would appear at regular intervals at the marshy entrances to the Mediterranean. Always on the lookout for an easy meal, great schools of circling sharks would form at the edges of the salt water to await the next feast.

Before the dust of the cataclysmic collapse had settled, another thunderous explosion, in the far north, rocked the struggling city. A second passageway over the Nile disappeared. And a few minutes later, a third bridge was torn apart. Throughout the morning, the Green Berets would hold, and then destroy, the stretching links separating Cairo from the vast suburbs of Giza, home of the Sphinx and Great Pyramid complex.

The obscene death and destruction Alpha 6333 wrought upon the world was beyond even their callused comprehension. Each reeling American stared in disbelieving silence at the sordid violence. On the other side of the broad river, Mourad's wounded and dying struggled to their feet and wandered back toward the protection of the western suburbs. The Pan-Arabs' unsated taste for blood and desire for a rapturous eternity had been tempered, at least momentarily, by Sanders's mighty blow. Still it had in no way been destroyed. It would take most of the day for the Chosen One's forces to reorganize and gather their courage for another attack. But they would be back.

The desolate detachment would have seven sorrowful hours to prepare for the next challenge. Few words were spoken for the length of the tense morning. At this point, dazed and disoriented, they took the time to gather their thoughts and prepare for whatever horrifying images lay ahead. With the first seriously wounded among them, each began to comprehend that from this moment on the continuation of their lives would be counted in precious seconds.

The team's medics were some of the best on the planet at performing field surgery. Each Green Beret, anticipating wounded within their numbers, carried plasma in his rucksack. It wasn't long before Donovan was stitched up and back on the line. He'd lost the use of his right arm, but at this point, half a Green Beret was still better than anyone the Mahdi could throw against them.

16

___

There was nothing the detachment could do but wait to see what the Mahdi's next move would be. Once the overwhelming enemy's motives were clear, the small band would attempt to counter them. Throughout the long day, the most outgoing member of the team uttered not a single sound. Until well into the afternoon Sanders sat with his back to the withering slaughter, refusing to look in the direction of the demolished bridge.

From the first moment of planning for the war, Mourad had predicted the Egyptian army would destroy every boat in Cairo in an attempt to keep his troops from fording the Nile. The Chosen One had been right. The hundreds of water taxis, so popular with the tourists, and the thousands of small boats buzzing around the commanding river had been set ablaze days ago. Not one still navigated its historic waters.

With every bridge across the river demolished, and Cairo's boats eliminated, it appeared the Allies had bought a hard-fought reprieve from the ferocious attacks. Their foe's artillery would undoubtedly continue its fierce shelling of the city. His ground forces, however, seemed to be stuck on the western banks without an easy way to cross.

The Americans were certain they'd purchased at least twenty-four hours of precious time in their defense of the sprawling metropolis. They'd soon, however, be proven wrong.

Days earlier, the Chosen One had put his plan into motion to counter the Egyptian army's anticipated actions. From deep within the Sudan and the farthest reaches of southern Egypt, his followers set sail in their feluccas. Traveling only at night to avoid detection, and hiding in the Nile's lush grasses during the day, huge numbers had eased their way up the endless waterway. For quite some time, they'd lain in wait a few miles south of the city.

The insignificant sailing ships had made their homes on the Nile since before the days of Christ. Their simple design hadn't changed since the times of the pharaohs. They'd carried supplies and people upon the river from time immemorial. Throughout the millennia, they'd been used to support a thousand desperate battles. On this day, they'd be called upon to assist in one more.

Detachment Alpha 6333, unsure of what would follow, sweated through the oppressive heat of midday. There was little to do but bide their time while hopelessly attempting to brush away the merciless attacks of biting flies. While the ten soldiers of the southernmost Special Forces unit scanned the western bank for signs of movement, Mourad's edict went out. With every inch of their decks crammed with human cargo, the feluccas were launched.

They'd catch the Americans by surprise, or overwhelm them with sheer numbers. Either way, the result would be the same. By day's end, his forces would control both sides of the wide flow. And they'd begin the final push to capture the sparkling city.

As always, Porter was the first to sense something was wrong. In the distance, the tips of billowing sails appeared on the shimmering waters. The small boats were too far away to determine what they were or who they carried. Porter watched the endless masts approaching. Their numbers were increasing by the minute.

"Captain, I think you'd better get over here. There's something kind of strange going on."

Morrow and Terry rushed to his position. Both stood watching the odd activity as it drew nearer.

"What do you think?" Morrow, his concern obvious, asked.

"I think we're about to be flanked, sir," Terry answered. "Looks like our plan to keep the enemy out of Cairo has failed."

"Epstein," Morrow said to the team's senior communication sergeant, "get on the radio and tell group headquarters significant Pan-Arab forces are landing along the eastern bank. Thousands more are on boats sailing up the river toward the center of the city."

The communication specialist was soon relaying the message. In less than a minute, the 6th Special Forces Group commander would receive the shocking news.

"What'll we do now, sir?" Terry asked. "It won't be long before they enter the little inlet on the other side of the island and get around behind us."

"What we do is get the hell out of here. If not, we'll be dead long before sundown. Pass the word, we're leaving. And we're doing it now. Gather up the weapons and gear."

"Yes, sir!"

There was nothing they could do. If they stayed where they were, the detachment would be cut off in less than an hour. Their demise would soon follow.

The time had come to abandon Rhoda Island. In minutes, loaded down by their equipment, the Green Berets were making their way across the isle's battered landscape. They were heading toward the southern part of the infinite city. Six blocks away waited the small bridge that would take them into the most ancient section of Cairo. From this point on, Old Cairo, with its dark streets and veiled bazaars, would be their home for as long as they survived.

Porter and Abernathy led the way. Both had years of experience at traversing myriad terrains. For the moment, the route appeared open. Yet each understood that looks are often deceiving. In the next doorway, or around the coming corner, death might be lurking. Neither could let his guard down for the briefest of moments. If a trap was waiting, the highly proficient soldiers wouldn't miss it. If an ambush was out there, the odds were great the pair would circle it and slice the enemies' throats before they knew what hit them.

By necessity, their halting actions were precise and caution-filled. Even so, they beat Mourad's forces to the inlet with time to spare. In ones and twos, the Green Berets made their way across the narrow waters.

When the team was safely on the far side, Morrow turned to Sanders. "Might as well not make it any easier than we have to. Once we're clear, blow this thing."

"Yes, sir."

"Sergeant Porter will wait for you in the row of buildings across the street."

Morrow motioned for the detachment to blend into the shadows and move deeper into the sinister surroundings. While the Green Berets disappeared into the restrictive half-light, Sanders located the palm tree where Donovan had hidden the detonator. He knew that even though he appeared to be alone, Porter would be somewhere nearby, alert and ready. Sanders stripped the ends off the primer cord. The wires were soon attached. Everything was ready. There wasn't a moment to waste if he wished to hold a beautiful woman in his arms again. He pushed back the panic rising deep within him. They were in a tough spot. Now, however, wasn't the time for a mistake. He hit the detonator, obliterating the shorter bridge. The last route off the vanquished island disappeared.

After a quick check to ensure unfriendly eyes weren't watching, Sanders turned and ran toward the ever-deepening twilight. He disappeared into Old Cairo's dark world. Porter stepped out from nowhere to join him. The watchful duo inched their way through the maze of fearful streets and menacing alleyways. Every few steps, they stopped to listen for anyone foolhardy enough to follow. The going was slow, their movements calculated.

It would take the A Team an hour to cover the twelve blocks to the rendezvous point. But the careful group of ten all arrived. While the Green Berets scrambled to prepare defensive positions, Sanders said the words each was thinking.

"Someone better get us some help here real soon."

17

The secretary of defense, secretary of Homeland Security, director of the CIA, and the chairman of the Joint Chiefs of Staff settled into their seats for the early morning meeting. The president got down to business. There'd be no pleasantries or small talk on this morning.

"Let's start with Saudi Arabia and Kuwait," the president said while looking at the secretary of defense. "Mr. Secretary, what's the latest from the battlefront?"

"Our forces in Kuwait are holding their own. The Kuwaiti capital is safe for the moment. Wish I felt as comfortable about Saudi Arabia. A battalion from the 1st Cavalry stopped the enemy once again near the city of Sakakah late last night. Iranian infantry made another suicide attack this morning. When that was repelled, Iraqi tanks raced in to duel our Bradley Fighting Vehicles. We suffered heavy losses. But our forces didn't surrender an inch. I've been told there are Iraqi and Iranian dead everywhere."

"Sounds encouraging," the president said.

"Thank God the 1st Cavalry won," the secretary of defense said. "For the moment there's no one behind them. We're trying to rectify that. But should the enemy break through, there's little to stop them from racing across the desert to destroy the Saudi oil fields."

"I still can't believe the Iraqis and Iranians are fighting side by side." The president turned to the director of the CIA. "You're certain, Chet, this was their plan the entire time? When they massed all those troops on their border and threatened war with each other, they sure had me fooled."

"They fooled everyone, Mr. President. But at this point, there's no doubt it was all an elaborate ruse. When you put the pieces together it's obvious Mourad set the whole thing up. The Iraqis and Iranians never intended to do anything but turn and attack Saudi Arabia and Kuwait."

"So you're telling me two countries who've been enemies for thousands of years are fighting together like the best of friends?"

"I don't know if they're the best of friends, Mr. President," General Greer, chairman of the Joint Chiefs, said. "But they're definitely fighting as one on the battlefield. So far, we've found no chink in their armor in that regard. Whatever distrust they have for each other hasn't affected their ability to coordinate their actions."

"You've got to remember," the director of the CIA added, "that while they loathe each other, they despise the West a thousand times more. Their hatred for the Great Satan and for Israel consumes them. Don't forget the old Middle East proverb—an enemy of my enemy is my friend."

"All right," the president said. "Not much we can do about it now other than hold them off long enough to get reinforcements in and save the oil fields. I want all of you to continue working on coming up with an angle to get the Iraqis and Iranians to turn on each other."

"I still think the answer's right in front of us, Mr. President," the secretary of defense replied. "Ask my former wife. Nothing rips a shaky marriage apart like a setback. If we can lay a big defeat on them, I wouldn't be surprised to see their alliance crumble. I've got the best minds at the Pentagon working on a plan to hurt them and hurt them bad. Then we'll see how solid their friendship is."

"You may be right," the president said. "It may take nothing more than a good, old-fashioned butt kicking to get the job done. That's why I've gone along with your recommendation that we concentrate our efforts on Saudi Arabia. Which brings us to our second item of business. General, how are our mobilization efforts proceeding? Are we getting any closer to creating a level playing field? Give me the specifics first, and we'll move to the bigger picture from there."

"The update on the unit movements we previously discussed is a good one. A brigade from the 3rd Infantry arrived in Saudi Arabia yesterday. It took almost every cargo plane the Air Force has, but with them, they brought a full complement of armored vehicles. That's over one hundred Abrams tanks and one hundred Bradley Fighting Vehicles. They're presently headed toward the front lines. Another 3rd Infantry brigade's loading onto those same transports as we speak. Five thousand French troops have arrived along with half as many British. More are on the way. The last of the 1st Cavalry have loaded onto ships in Galveston. The first elements of the 10th Mountain and 101st Airborne Divisions are scheduled to sail from Bayonne and Norfolk tonight."

"How long before they'll reach the Middle East?"

"With the extensive damage to the Suez Canal we'll have to go around the Cape of Good Hope to reach Saudi Arabia. Even at top speed, it could take ten days."

"Ten days? No sooner?"

"No, sir, not if you want them in Saudi Arabia. By ship it'll take at least that long. We could place them in Egypt in seven, maybe less."

"Are the British firm on their commitment to land two armored divisions in North Africa by this time next week?"

"Yes, sir," General Greer said.

"Then let's leave it up to the British to support our forces in Egypt. I'm still worried about Saudi Arabia. We've got to get significant help there as quickly as we can."

"We're trying, Mr. President."

The president turned to the director of Homeland Security. "Jim, what about terrorist attacks?"

"There've been six suicide bombings in Europe in the past twenty-four hours, and three in this country. Boston, Atlanta, and Los Angeles were all targeted. The FBI foiled the Atlanta attack. But the other two succeeded, I'm afraid. We're doing everything humanly possible. Even so, there's no way we can get them all."

The president shook his head. His frustration was obvious. He looked at the chairman of the Joint Chiefs. "All right, General, go on with your report on our troop movements."

"The last pair of fighter wings on the East Coast left early this morning. They'll arrive in the Middle East in another four hours."

"Are our aircraft losses as high today as they were yesterday?"

"I'm afraid so, Mr. President. Eight more in the past twenty-four hours. But you shouldn't overly concern yourself with the air portion of the war. The Chosen One's forces have shown an uncanny ability to use their huge supply of Stinger missiles and Russian-made air defense systems to destroy our aircraft. Still, our operations folks believe we've got more than enough airpower to maintain control of the skies over the entire war zone."

"If that's the case, should I cancel the activation of the Air National Guard!"

"Not at all, Mr. President. If the war runs beyond what we've projected, or our losses increase, we might need them all. The same goes for the Army National Guard."

"Okay, continue the mobilization process. Anything else?"

"One more note, Mr. President. The final battalion of Patriot air defense missiles left El Paso yesterday morning and arrived in Saudi Arabia late last night. The battalion's four firing batteries are in place and fully operational. In fact, one already knocked down three Scud missiles headed for Riyadh. We're convinced the reason the Iraqi and Iranian air forces haven't attempted to enter Saudi or Kuwaiti air space is because of their fear of the Patriots."

"That's something I'll definitely mention during today's press briefing."

"Do that, Mr. President. And tell them one more thing. Not a Saudi city's been touched. The same goes for Israel. We've put a steel curtain in front of every critical Middle Eastern country. If it weren't for the Patriots, Tel Aviv and Jerusalem would've been reduced to rubble early in the war. If that had happened the Israelis would've had no choice but to attack the Iraqis and Iranians."

"What a mess that would be. We'll never extricate ourselves from this situation if the Israelis become any more involved than they already are."

"No doubt, Mr. President."

"Except for our snail's pace in getting ground forces in place, it sounds like things are going as well as we could hope. General, can't we do anything to get our men and equipment over there quicker?"

"No chance, Mr. President," Greer said. "We just don't have the capabilities to get combat units from Europe or America to where we need them. We're doing everything we can. Still our options are limited."

"We've no other solutions?"

"There's a partial one, Mr. President," the secretary of defense said. "But you're not going to like it."

"What's that?"

"Implement the War Powers Act. Take control of our merchant shipping fleet and our commercial airliners. It also wouldn't hurt if you got your hands on every cruise ship you can find. You've the power to do so, and quite honestly, sir, if you don't, we might lose this war."

"But if I seize our commercial aircraft, I'll basically shut this country down. Think of the consequences to our economy. It could take months to recover from such a decision."

"It's still better than the other outcome," the secretary of defense said. "What are the consequences if we lose and the Pan-Arabs control the entire Middle East? Without those oil fields, the world's economy will never recover. Mourad won't have to raise a finger to fulfill his promise of dragging us back to the seventh century. With all that oil gone, it wouldn't be long before the world finds itself back there on its own."

"Anyone heard the cost of gas this morning?" the president asked.

"Seven dollars a gallon in some places," the director of the CIA replied. "Projected to double in the next two weeks."

"Fourteen dollars," the president said. "Hell, that alone will shut us down. Are the rest of you in agreement with the secretary of defense's analysis? Should I seize control of our commercial airline industry?"

"Yes, Mr. President," the secretary of Homeland Security said. "I hate to admit it, but we need to do so. Invoke the War Powers Act and take control over this country's aircraft."

"Will we need them all?" the president asked.

"No, Mr. President," the secretary of defense said. "All of the merchant and cruise ships. Probably half to two-thirds of the aircraft. The shorter-range stuff like the 737s won't be of much use to us. We'll need some of them, but can allow most to remain in the hands of the airlines. Still I'd like to see us get our hands on all the longer-range planes."

The president paused. His answer was a reluctant one. "All right, I'll announce the implementation of the War Powers Act at my noon press conference. That'll give me time to notify the heads of the major airlines before they hear it from the media. At two o'clock, all normal aircraft traffic in this country will be suspended."

"That's fine, Mr. President," the secretary of defense said. "I'll make sure Military Airlift Command is ready."

"Okay, General Greer, the shipping and aircraft fleets are yours. What're you going to do with them?"

"With the airliners at our disposal, I'd recommend we take a serious look at Egypt."

"I'm almost afraid to ask," the president said. "What's the latest word from Cairo?"

"Green Berets blew up every bridge over the Nile this morning. It slowed the Chosen One's advance. But it didn't stop him. The western part of the city's under a fierce artillery bombardment. His followers are crossing the river in countless small boats. The Green Berets are engaged in vicious fighting to stem the tide. They're making Mourad's lunatics earn every inch. Nevertheless, Pan-Arab forces are moving farther into the city as we speak."

"How much longer before everything collapses and Cairo surrenders?"

"We've got no more than forty-eight hours," General Greer said. "The Egyptians are at their end. There's not a single unit that hasn't suffered significant casualties and desertions to the Mahdi's side. Some, even as large as regimental size, have switched en masse."

"Is there anything we can do? Anything that will keep Egypt from being destroyed?"

"With the airliners we can have fifteen thousand of our best men in the Egyptian capital by this time tomorrow."

"How?"

"I've been holding the 82nd Airborne in reserve. They've been specially trained for house-to-house fighting. We can get the entire division there with enough smaller weapons to hold the bastards for a few extra days. By then, if we're lucky, we'll come up with a way to keep Cairo in our hands."

"Are you certain, General? Will the 82nd be enough to keep the city from falling?"

"Yes, sir. We believe they'll turn the trick. Should give us a couple more days minimum."

"Except for the Marine landing, that's the best news I've heard all week. Get the 82nd ready. I'll make sure the CEOs of the major airlines understand the urgency of making their long-haul planes available as quickly as possible."

"That'll help, Mr. President."

"What's the latest word on the Marines?"

"They made definite progress after their landing. Covered about twenty miles before the enemy got organized and launched a series of counterattacks. Late last night, lead elements of the 2nd Marine Division captured a section of the Alexandria-to-Cairo highway and severed Mourad's forces in the northern part of Egypt. With the Marines' help, Alexandria appears to be solidly in the Egyptian army's hands. In the past hours, however, the attacks against our positions have been relentless. One armored division after another has smashed into our lines. The Marines' advance has come to a standstill. Our forces are settling into defensive positions in an attempt to hold off the Chosen One's tanks. At the moment, things are pretty rough. But as long as our air superiority remains, we've got a decent chance of staying right where we are until the 1st Marine Division comes ashore in three or four days."

"No possibility of the Marines reaching Cairo?" the president asked.

"None whatsoever, Mr. President," General Greer said. "At least, not until the British arrive next week. Until then, we'll be lucky to hold on to the territory we've gained. But you've got to realize that even though the Marines aren't directly relieving Cairo, they've accomplished what we sent them there to do. Mourad's had to turn thousands of his tanks away from the city to battle our forces. Without the Marines' help, the Egyptian capital would've fallen last night. His tanks would've reached Israel today. So our plan's working. We just need more time. If we can figure that part out, with seven hundred British Challenger tanks on the way, we might have a chance of winning this thing."

"Sounds like you could describe our situation as desperation with a tinge of optimism."

"Exactly, sir."

"At the moment, I can live with that. What's next?" the president asked.

"We've still no word on Mourad's location," the director of the CIA said. "Based on Pan-Arab radio traffic, we know he's somewhere near Cairo, but so far we've struck out in locating him."

"Keep looking, Chet," the president said. "If we eliminate the Mahdi this thing will collapse. Without his leadership, Islam's dreams of world conquest will be lost. So our top priority continues to be finding and killing the Chosen One. This is one war we can win by eliminating a single man."

"We'll stay on it, sir."

"Do that, Chet. Find the sorry son of a bitch and take him out."

"Yes, sir. He's definitely near the battlefield. So we'll spot him sooner or later."

"Make it sooner." The president paused. "Is there anything else?"

No one said a word.

"Okay, I won't keep you any longer."

The four stood to leave. The president looked at General Greer. "General, I'm curious. Will you give me an honest answer to an honest question?"

"I'll try, Mr. President."

"If you had to guess . . . What would you estimate our chances are of winning this thing?"

The chairman of the Joint Chiefs paused. His answer was a truthful one. "At the moment, somewhere around fifty-fifty, Mr. President."

18

With the Humvee in the lead, the modest formation of bone-weary Marines trudged the final miles toward the American defenses. So far they'd been lucky, surviving the arduous journey without any additional killed or wounded. Each prayed their good fortune would hold. This early in the North African campaign the front lines were ill-defined and porous. The rampaging enemy was taking full advantage of the situation. Roving bands of Pan-Arabs were making the Egyptian Sahara a fiercely inhospitable place.

Sergeant Joyce's hands were wrapped around the .50-caliber's grips. He was ready to squeeze the machine gun's trigger at a moment's notice. The Humvee's fire team was anxious and wary. Should another assault come, it would be on them to repel the insurgents long enough for the depleted platoon to find cover and get organized.

During the twenty-mile trek, they'd successfully survived two marauding attacks. The first, from a battered pickup truck carrying four hooded men holding rifles and rocket-propelled grenades, had happened in the early hours of the march. At the initial sign of trouble, Joyce's team rushed forward to engage the insurgents. The small skirmish was swift and decisive. The sergeant's skillful men hurriedly dispatched their overmatched foe.

The second encounter had been far more serious. Halfway through their desert crossing, they'd stumbled toward three dozen jihadists waiting in ambush in a concealing ravine. The result could have been disastrous for the struggling remnants of Erickson's men. Fortunately, two passing Cobra attack helicopters had spotted the trap moments before the enemy opened fire. With a life-stealing barrage from their Gatling cannons, the fearsome pair swooped in and destroyed the threat.

Behind the Humvee, the remaining ten Marines dragged through the shifting sands. Gunny brought up the rear, encouraging the floundering force to take another step. For seven difficult hours, the fourteen survivors of yesterday morning's battle had made their way across the infinite desert toward the battalion's defenses. Misery was painted on their grizzled features. The relentless winds tore at their stoic faces. The endless sojourn's unmerciful heat pressed in upon them. It threatened to devour the haggard Americans.

There wasn't a cloud in the sky. Yet the dismal heavens were as dark as the bleakest New England January. A blanket of suffocating smoke, so thick it consumed every labored breath, covered the tedious landscape and overwhelmed the sun's light. The smoldering corpses of destroyed enemy vehicles stretched to the horizon. Pan-Arab remains, twisted and rotting, cluttered the landscape. Some of the decomposing bodies had been in the sweltering Sahara for nearly three weeks. With so great a bounty, the vultures and carrion eaters had grown indifferent.

Death's reviling stench clung to the exhausted platoon. Decay oozed into their sand-clogged pores and assailed their senses. The putrid smell of suffering and disease tore at their nostrils. Although the men on the ground couldn't see them, the sounds of soaring aircraft filled the spiteful afternoon. Throughout the long hours, Super Hornets from the aircraft carriers *Lincoln* and *Eisenhower* flew sortie after sortie over the Nile Delta. Attack and reconnaissance drones crisscrossed the dingy heavens. At regular intervals, groups of lethal Cobras screamed overhead. The low-flying merchants of death skimmed the dunes, tearing through the narrow valleys and treacherous landscape as they rushed toward the burgeoning battles. Artillery duels rumbled incessantly. With each painful stride Erickson took, the sounds of the fearsome struggles reached out for him. With every passing minute, the platoon grew closer to the menacing clashes.

The depleted lieutenant adjusted the fifty pounds he carried on his back. The pack's straps dug into his slumping shoulders. It tore at his battered flesh. His left arm throbbed. Mind-numbing pain, sharp and unpredictable, flashed down his wounded biceps and surged toward his tingling fingers. The acidic air overwhelmed him. Dirt crept into every crevice of his distress-filled face. He raised his hand to tighten the filthy scarf covering his mouth and nose. The small cloth secure once more, the platoon leader removed his sunglasses and wiped the sweat from his brow.

It had been an extremely long day for the men of 3rd Platoon. And it was far from over.

A few hundred yards ahead, the glistening blacktop of the Alexandria-to-Cairo highway called to them. The beckoning conclusion to their extended effort was nearing

"Sergeant Joyce," Erickson said. "There's a checkpoint up ahead. Drive up and see if they know where the battalion's located."

"Okay, Pitzer," Joyce told his driver. "You heard the lieutenant. Get this thing in gear and let's check it out."

Kicking up clouds of sand, the Humvee raced ahead of the platoon. A quarter mile away, four Marines waited behind a sturdy sandbagged barrier on the edge of the multilane highway. The vehicle roared up and stopped.

"You guys in 2nd Recon?" Joyce asked.

"Yeah," the corporal in charge of the checkpoint said. "Alpha Company."

"Any idea where we'll find battalion headquarters?"

"Straight up the road about three-quarters of a mile. You can't miss them, they're the ones with all the burning tanks in front of them."

"Thanks. Pitzer, let's go tell the lieutenant there's less than a mile to go."

The team whirled about and headed back toward the laboring platoon.

19

Okay, Platoon Sergeant, fall the men out and have them fill their canteens."

Erickson lifted the flap and entered the battalion command tent. Captain Richards, Bravo Company commander, was standing inside the entrance. He stuck out his hand.

"Been expecting you, Sam. Enjoy the trip?"

"Let's put it this way, sir. Next time I book a tour of the Middle East, I'm going to pick a better travel agent." Erickson attempted to smile, but all he could bring to his tired features was a halfhearted grin.

"Sorry to say your visit to ancient Egypt gets no better from here."

"What've you got for us, sir?" Erickson asked.

"With the division digging in and our forces spread thin, the need for reconnaissance is on the back burner. For the moment, we're assuming a more traditional role. As our recon battalion only has a couple hundred men, each regiment has provided a few units so that we can build our numbers to near a normal battalion's size. I've been given command of three additional platoons. A few hours ago, a rocket attack took out one of the platoon leaders and his senior sergeant. You and Gunny Fife are going to have to take command of their men."

"How many left in the platoon, sir?"

"Thirty last time I was up there. But they've still got three vehicles and ample ammunition. The platoon's TOW-mounted Humvee just received six new missiles an hour ago."

"Thirty. With my men that'll give this new platoon a full complement. Where are they?"

"It's real simple. Go south along the highway for another half mile. You'll pass through three lines of defenders. When you get to the fourth line, your platoon will be waiting."

"How many Marines in front of us, sir?"

"Sam, I'm sorry to say the only thing in front of you is a hundred thousand maniacs intent on killing every last one of us," Richards answered. "You'll have responsibility for holding the eight-lane highway and the desert for two hundred yards on either side. A platoon from Alpha Company's on your left. One of my new platoons is on your right. If things play out like they have been, you can expect an armored attack of at least brigade size soon. At this point, we're trying to keep our losses to a minimum. Should it look like you're going to be overrun, fall back and link up with the next line. Keep falling back until we stop them. Right now we're trying to buy time. Men are the precious commodity. They're far more important than ground. So when in doubt, retreat and save as much of your platoon as you can. Still got one of your vehicles?"

"Yes, sir. Sergeant Joyce's Humvee is right outside."

"Good. A King Stallion landed with Javelins, TOWs, and a number of crates of LAWs a few minutes ago. Brought some claymores too. I'll have your Humvee loaded with as many as it'll carry. From what I've seen today you're going to need every last one. Don't tell anybody, but I also got my hands on some Stinger missiles. I'll make sure you get a few of those too. Last Pan-Arab attack included a helicopter assault by Russian-made Hind-Ds."

Richards stood next to the idling vehicle. Every inch was crammed with missiles and claymore mines.

"Okay, Sam," Richards said, "there are four Stingers in there. Promise you won't let on where you got them. Battalion commander allocated your platoon ten Javelins, eight TOWs plus two tripod launchers, twenty-four of the LAW light antitank missiles, and a dozen claymores. Use the Javelins and TOWs sparingly. Fire the LAWs when you have a choice. They've worked fine against the older BMPs and French armored personnel carriers the Pan-Arabs are using in this sector. But I want to warn you. They've been hitting us most of the day with Russian T-72 tanks. The frontal armor on the T-72s is quite stout. The LAWs can't handle them. Every time we've tried to kill one with a LAW, the missile's exploded against the hull without penetrating its defenses. So make sure you keep the Javelins and TOWs in reserve if you can. Otherwise, you're going to find yourself defenseless against the enemy's heavy armor."

"Count on it, sir. My platoon already knows what that feels like. It's something none of us ever again want to experience."

"With the repeated counterattacks, some of our most critical supplies are running low. Got plenty of ammunition. And we're hoping to have more missiles by sundown. Try to make what you've got last."

"Yes, sir. We'll do what we can."

"Air support's been real good. Call for it at the first sign of trouble. Cobras can be over your position in two minutes. Fighters off the *Lincoln* and *Eisenhower* are sitting with their pilots in the cockpits. They'll be here in less than five if we need them."

"Understood, sir. Anything else?"

"Just one thing, Sam—don't be a hero. With the losses we're sustaining, I'm going to need you with me for the rest of this war. And at this point it's a hell of a long way from over."

"Sir, I've every intention of sticking around to see how this ends. I'll do my best to keep my head down. All right, Gunny, move the men out."

The hard-pressed platoon wasn't difficult to find. Neither were the Pan-Arabs. The boiling desert was littered with recently slaughtered ones. Many of the lifeless figures were still warm. The sated sands ran red with freshly flowing blood. The desolate landscape in front of the Marines also was filled with thousands upon thousands who were quite alive.

Behind each distant dune, in every cleft and gully, the Chosen One's anxious soldiers prepared. They prayed for the sainted word to come. Mourad's followers knew it wouldn't be long before the next impassioned attack. His devotees' hearts soared with the conviction that a place in the glorious beyond would soon be theirs.

It didn't take Erickson long to size up the situation. Captain Richards was right. This was the end of the line. Behind them, the thin layers of immersed Marines waited. In front, the Sahara teemed with the agitated enemy. To the southeast, a short distance away, the barren desert made a remarkable turnabout as its shifting sands met the lush fields and swaying palms of the rich Nile Delta. Hidden within its fertile grasses, Mourad's tanks waited for the order to attack. The time was drawing near. The fifth foray of the day was getting organized.

The instant they arrived, the platoon leader sprang into action.

"Sergeant Joyce, drop the claymores, Stingers, and two of the Javelins here. Leave the TOWs and tripods also. Then go along the line passing out the remaining Javelins and LAWs. Each squad leader gets two Javelins. Each fire team gets two LAWs."

"Yes, sir."

"Tell them there probably won't be any more until sundown, so make every shot count."

"Will do, sir."

After they unloaded the weapons the lieutenant had identified as remaining there, the Humvee sped off toward the far left of the platoon. Joyce's fire team was soon doling out the remaining missiles.

Satisfied with Joyce's efforts, Erickson turned to his recon platoon's remaining team leader. "Sergeant Merker, your team will handle the TOWs. Set a tripod up on each side of the highway. Four TOWs for each one. Once they're in place, take the claymores and string them fifty yards in front of the platoon. Try not to blow yourselves up while doing so. And keep your heads down. Don't get careless and let a sniper pick you off."

"Yes, sir. Trip wires or detonators?"

"Detonators for now. When the attack comes, each team leader will fire his claymore as he sees fit. If we haven't expended them by the time it gets dark, we'll switch to trip wires. After you've finished positioning the claymores, get behind those tripods, ready to release your TOWs."

While Erickson laid things out with Sergeant Merker, Gunny took a quick look around. He wasn't at all satisfied. "Pass the word. The rest of you need to hurry up and fortify your positions. I want to see twice as many sandbags in front of you and your foxholes two feet deeper by nightfall."

Erickson looked in Fife's direction. "Gunnery Sergeant, didn't you once tell me you had experience with Stingers?"

"Yes, sir. Haven't fired one in a few years. But at one time I was pretty damn good with them. I can drop a few enemy helicopters for you if it comes to that."

"That's good enough for me. You've been elected platoon air defense gunner. Mount the firing assemblies onto the first missile and get ready to repulse an attack."

In their foxholes, the sparse Marines crouched behind the sandbagged walls. The merciless sun beat down upon them as it continued its unwavering passage across the afternoon sky. To a man, the scattered Americans knew the killing fields would soon be upon them once again.

First came the unmistakable rumble of three hundred tank engines springing to life. The motors of an equal number of armored personnel carriers howled in unison. Moments later, the high-pitched screech of steel treads was added to the devilish refrain as the rebellious T-72 and

BMPs slithered from the abundant grasses near the river's edge. This was no brigade-size attack. An entire division of armored beasts was on the move. Twenty-four whirling Hind helicopters rose from their hiding places. The Chosen One's artillery screamed into action, intent on softening up their vastly outnumbered opponent. A fierce barrage tore through the disagreeable desert in search of the sheltering infidels.

The determined Marines answered with their howitzers.

Across the unforgiving landscape the vulgar tanks roared. The earth shuddered beneath their immense power. With every yard the T-72s covered, shadowy men carrying assault rifles sprang from their burrows to run alongside the massive hulls.

The fateful directive had arrived. It would be an all-out assault by one of the most loyal of the Chosen One's divisions. Brought to a frenzied state by the political officers, fifteen thousand enraged fanatics would attack the six hundred survivors of the reinforced Marine battalion. The Mahdi's army would concentrate everything it had on smashing the center of the Americans' lines with a swift and crushing blow so awe-inspiring nothing could withstand its mighty force. Their target was the sticky ribbon of wide asphalt leading to Alexandria and the glistening sea beyond.

Eternity was upon them. This time they'd fight to the last man. In the coming battle, the lovers of Islam would stop for nothing until they'd hurled the heretics back into the Mediterranean, or having failed, found their way to a martyr's dream.

Erickson didn't hesitate. He knew they were severely overmatched.

"Get on the radio and call in air strikes," he directed Fife. "Cobras, drones, and fighters."

The platoon's sergeant grabbed the radio handset. As he did, the first of the plundering tanks crested a rippling mountain of sand no more than a mile away. Behind it, Mourad's malignant throngs appeared.

20

With its engines now running, Lieutenant Commander Bradley "Blackjack" Mitchell sat in his F/A-18E Super Hornet's cockpit reading a letter from his wife. The mail had arrived minutes before Mitchell went on deck. It had taken the naval pilot significant time to gather the courage to open the sweet-smelling envelope. The lengthy text was yet another of his pampered spouse's endless harangues. From the look on his face it was obvious he was troubled by its stinging words. There was no way around it. The shrill letter, along with the four equally disquieting e-mails she'd sent since yesterday morning, was a distraction. And in his line of work, distractions could get you killed.

Along with his wingman, Lieutenant Norman "Worm" Sweeney, Mitchell had been sitting in his fighter aircraft on the deck of the *Lincoln* for more than an hour.

To Mitchell's right, another pair of fierce Super Hornets brought their deafening jet engines to life. The frantic preparations on the aircraft carrier's flight deck increased tenfold. All around him, flight personnel raced to their fighters. Deck crews scrambled to prepare the Hornets scheduled to support the embattled Marines.

Erickson's desperate plea had reached the carrier task force. Pan-Arab forces were gathering for another offensive against the beleaguered Americans. In less than a minute, the first of the ground attack fighters would be launched to support the outnumbered defenders. That F/A-18E would be piloted by Mitchell. Twelve of the *Lincoln*'s Super Hornets would be committed to battle the Chosen One's tanks. A few miles north, another dozen waited on the aircraft carrier *Eisenhower.* Should the first dozen fail to stem the tide, the second group would spring into action.

The furious activity on the *Lincoln*'s deck continued to balloon. Every forty-five seconds, an F/A-18F two-seater or F/A-18E single-seater Super Hornet landed. Every minute or two, another pair catapulted down the runway. Each screamed across the rippling waters. All were capable of attacking both air and ground targets. While the F/A-18Es were presently handling the ground attack role, the F/A-18Fs were protecting the carrier battle groups from the threat of hostile aircraft or cruise missiles. Since their recent arrival off the coast of Egypt, such patrols had become routine, and for the most part downright boring. None of the Chosen One's ample air forces had attempted to test their abilities against the fleet's daunting defenses. Not one of Mourad's MiGs had challenged their impressive adversary.

Intelligence sources confirmed the majority of the Mahdi's aircraft had survived the three weeks of air-to-air combat with the Egyptian air force. Even so, no sign of them had been seen in the past two days. They remained on the ground, hiding within the relative safety of their bases in Libya and Algeria. There was nothing astonishing in the Pan-Arabs' unwillingness to tangle in the stained skies with the world's best pilots. That surprised no one. Why the Mahdi had failed to use his generous supply of cruise missiles at any point in the war was far more puzzling. The Americans were beginning to believe they were facing a seventh-century warrior in a twenty-first-century war.

That was exactly what the little Algerian wanted them to think.

Mitchell's radio crackled to life. "Blackjack, this is launch control. Massive attack has commenced against Marines holding the Cairo–Alexandria Highway. Your aircraft will move into position on catapult one."

"Roger, Control."

Mitchell shoved his wife's letter into his flight suit and started preparing for the launch. His life would soon be on the line. For now, he'd push his family problems into the deepest recesses of his mind. It was something he'd long ago trained himself to do. His overindulged wife and her incessant demands forgotten, he sat watching as his staunch aircraft was towed onto the catapult.

Lieutenant Sweeney's settled onto the one next to Mitchell's.

Tow bars were being placed on another pair of Super Hornets. It wouldn't be long before all four of the aircraft carrier's steam-operated catapults were occupied.

The time had arrived for Mitchell's third mission of the day. The veteran pilot turned to watch the catapult control officer standing on the deck to his left. The launching system gained power. Mitchell revved his jet engines in preparation for takeoff. His F/A-18E's engines were so powerful he wouldn't need to go to afterburners to slingshot off the deck. Without the tremendous waste of fuel involved in firing his afterburners, he'd be able to spend far greater time over the battle-field.

The catapult control officer held up his chalkboard, indicating everything was ready.

Mitchell checked his instruments. Satisfied, the Hornet pilot gave a thumbs-up. The green light lit on the controller's panel. The blast deflector rose behind the aircraft. Mitchell put his hands on his helmet so the deck crew could verify there was no possibility he could accidentally hit the wrong switch and release his weapons while sitting on the deck. The armament specialists raced in and removed the safety pins from the Hornets' loads of bombs and Sidewinder air-to-air missiles. The show was getting under way. The control officer signaled. Mitchell increased his F/A-18E's power even further. The controller held up a green flag. Everything was ready. The accomplished pilot saluted. With a crisp chop of the controller's right arm the flag fell.

In an instant, the catapult fired. With incredible force it threw the lethal plane down the abbreviated runway toward the open sea. The aircraft leaped from the giant ship. It soared into the steaming afternoon. Sweeney soon joined him. The pair raced into the heavens at tremendous speed.

The control officer headed over to the Super Hornets on catapults three and four. Another pair of F/A-18Es moved up to catapults one and two. It wouldn't be long before twelve angry Super Hornets were swarming over the unbounding desert to annihilate the Pan-Arabs.

"Echo Control," Mitchell said into his radio, "this is Blackjack Section. We're armed and ready. Request flight instructions."

From high above the southern Mediterranean the EC-2 command and control aircraft answered. "Roger, Blackjack. Enemy has launched a division-size ground attack. Tanks and armored personnel carriers are attempting to break through our lines. Cobras have arrived and are dueling Mourad's attack helicopters. They'll join you in protecting the Marines as soon as they chase the bad guys away. Attack drones have been launched. We need you to blunt the lead elements of the tank column and slow them down. Once you've used up your munitions, return to the *Lincoln* to rearm and refuel. Looks like you can plan on a few return trips to the desert before this day ends. With the persistence of those lunatics, we anticipate you'll spend most of the coming hours greeting the Chosen One's followers."

"Roger, Echo Control. Battle zone still masked by smoke?"

"Affirmative. No significant change in conditions from this morning. Your systems will handle it just fine. Should be able to put your ordnance right on target."

"Any bandits in the area?"

"Negative, Blackjack. Just like it's been since the carriers arrived. No sign of enemy aircraft. Even so, we've got Super Hornets at thirty-five thousand feet to cover your heads."

"What about Pan-Arab air defenses?"

"Still plenty of Stinger missiles and antiaircraft systems around. Growler aircraft will hit the strike zone with chaff and electronic countermeasures moments before you arrive. That should jam their radar and disrupt their air defenses. It'll help with the advanced Russian stuff the Pan-Arabs are using, but once you drop your bombs and head down to attack with your Vulcan cannons, you're on your own against the Stingers. So don't be a hero. Use the smoke to hide your position. Drop flares and take evasive measures at the first sign of a Stinger firing."

"Roger, Echo Control. We're on our way."

At fifteen miles a minute, the Hornet pilot and his wingman sprinted toward the evolving battle. The remainder of the attack squadron would be right behind. The first of the help the Marines needed was three minutes away.

The soaring duo had been flying as a section for two years. In their significant hours in the sky together, they'd learned to read each other's thoughts and anticipate each other's actions. Each had absolute confidence in his partner's abilities. In a tight spot, Mitchell knew he could count on his wingman. And Sweeney knew he could depend on his section leader to make the right decision.

The swift pair passed over the North African coastline. Just over a minute before the attack would begin.

Even with a thick blanket of gray obscuring the trackless ground below, with the F/A-18E's sophisticated instrumentation it wasn't hard to find the unending targets.

"Worm, this is Blackjack, oncoming armor confirmed on highway and surrounding desert," Mitchell said to his wingman. "Pan-Arab lead elements are just south of our lines and closing fast."

"Roger, Blackjack, I've got them spotted."

"There are five Hornet pairs scheduled to follow us in on the attack. They should be showing up in one-minute intervals. Let's hit the lead elements of the enemy armored column first. That should blunt the Pan-Arab attack and give the Marines a little breathing room while they wait for further Hornets to arrive. Be real careful, though, the last thing I want is to hit our people by mistake. Bombing run first, then we'll circle around and strafe the hell out of them with our cannons. Hopefully, the Growlers jammed things real good. But just in case, keep your eyes open for air defense radar locks or Stinger firings."

"Roger, Blackjack, I'm wide-awake back here. Make your pass, I'll be right behind you."

Mitchell raced toward the surging T-72s. Sweeney hugged his tail. The F/A-18Es lined up the release point on their cockpit displays. At precisely the right instant, Mitchell dropped tons of high explosives from the ruinous stores beneath his fighter's shimmering belly and wings. A line of thousand-pound killers tumbled from the ashen skies. They headed straight for the inviting prey striving to cross the potent desert two miles below. A brief moment later, Sweeney also hit his release. A second set of death-laden armaments fell toward the mournful earth. For the Super Hornet pilots it was a routine task. Their exceptional aircrafts' computer systems had performed the majority of the work. When the systems told them to fire, they dropped their toxic payloads onto the targeted area. As the lethal pair circled to the rear to set up their strafing run, they didn't give their actions a second thought.

Even so, for the followers of Islam the compelling acts of the American pilots held far greater importance. Without warning, a demonic swath of contested desert a quarter mile long erupted in a blazing corridor of death and destruction. The wide highway disappeared. Directly in front of Erickson's position, two dozen tanks and half as many armored personnel carriers were ripped apart in a blinding flash. A ghastly inferno filled with suffering and damnation fell upon the Mahdi's attackers in a thunderous series of explosions. The inescapable flames of an unspeakable maelstrom reached out to consume three hundred once-breathing souls. Most never knew what hit them. In another sixty seconds, a second pair of F/A-18Es was scheduled to do the same. And behind them would come another, and another, and another, almost without end, until the dreary sands in front of the Marine positions would become an inhospitable no-man's-land filled with the charred remains of vanquished flesh and ravaged machines.

"Echo Control," Mitchell said, "this is Blackjack Section. Have completed our bomb run. Beginning cannon attack."

"Roger, Blackjack Section. Second section is thirty seconds out. They'll commence their assault the instant you clear the area."

Mitchell and Sweeney lined up their position behind the endless enemy. Now would come the most exhilarating, and most dangerous, part of the pilots' mission. Screaming in so low over the blighted sands that they could see the anguished faces of those they were destroying, Mitchell and Sweeney would assail the enormous armored column with their Vulcan cannons. From above and behind, their 20mm armor-piercing shells would penetrate the upper and rear armor of a T-72 to mutilate and kill those sheltering within. Suffering and death would follow in the Hornets' wake.

The avenging F/A-18Es roared in side by side with their shining wing tips nearly touching the rolling dunes. They streaked across the ill-prepared column at thirteen hundred feet per second. The attacking armor was right in front of them. Mitchell made a first brief squeeze of his trigger, allowing the weapon's burst controller to determine the number of shells expelled. The shattering shells spewed from beneath the Hornet's nose. At four thousand rounds per minute, without the burst controller he would've emptied his Vulcan's chamber in six seconds. He fired another lightning burst. Sweeney unleashed a quick blast of his own. Their armor-piercing cannons tore into the stretching lines of faltering tanks and personnel carriers. At such incredible speed, the T-72 commanders had no time to react with their antiaircraft machine gun. The perishing hulks were defenseless against the shrieking raptors' infinite power.

But the Chosen One's air defenses were not. Thirty Stingers were lifted onto the shoulders of Allah's warriors. The Stinger gunners fought to track the wailing bandits. If they could lock on to one of the despicable aircraft and destroy it, when their own death arrived their honored place in a blissful eternity would be assured. The air defenders begged to hear the firing tone go off telling them their heat-seeking Stinger had found the lusting target. Even so, none of the unsophisticated little missiles was capable of distinguishing the intense heat of the ground-hugging F/A-18E engines from the burning tanks and scorching sands all around them.

In seconds, the pernicious Hornets completed their run. Two hundred additional beings departed the world of mortal man. The solemn journeys across the River Styx would be many on this day. Both aircraft rocketed over the American defenses and raced back into the morose heavens. As they passed, each pilot saw the situation on the ground below. The swirling clouds of ever-darkening fires soon covered their escape.

"Christ, Blackjack," Sweeney said. "Our efforts barely slowed them down. Did you see those sons-of-bitches? They're right on top of our guys."

"I saw them. Looks like the Marines are about to catch hell. We've still got half our 20mm shells. Let's circle around. After the next pair of Hornets makes their bomb run, we'll complete another quick pass before heading back to rearm."

"Roger, Blackjack. I'm with you."

"Echo Control, this is Blackjack Section. Our guys are in big trouble. Get the other sections in here as fast as you can. We're about to turn and make another run to buy some time."

"Blackjack, this is Echo Control. Negative on that. Cease your engagement immediately. All Hornet sections are to break off their attack at once."

"What?" Mitchell said. "Did you hear me, Echo Control? The Marines are going to be slaughtered if we don't give them a hand."

"Roger, Blackjack, we heard you loud and clear. But there's something very odd going on. All of a sudden we've got bandits all over the place on our radar. More and more are popping up every second. And they're headed this way. Hornet sections are to switch from ground attack to dogfight modes. Find a clear piece of ocean to jettison your bombs before heading west to meet the enemy."

21

M uhammad Mourad was no military genius, but he wasn't nearly the fool the Americans believed him to be. His air forces were quite powerful. Yet the Mahdi understood no winged force in the world was a match for those he faced. His MiGs and Mirages performed well during the initial advance into Egypt. In days, they'd gained a modicum of control in the skies over North Africa. He realized, however, that they couldn't hold on to their delicate domination against the accomplished Americans. So the moment the Allied planes arrived, he withdrew his five hundred fighters to wait for precisely the right moment.

His overly confident opponent had been lulled by the Pan-Arabs' failure to provide any heaven-based opposition. There'd been significant losses of American aircraft to ground-based missiles, but the threat to the pilots and ships from an airborne enemy was presumed to be nearly nonexistent. This was exactly what Mourad wanted them to believe. The moment he'd been searching for had arrived. To return to his primary task of throwing everything he had into seizing Cairo, he had to destroy the impudent American Marines who'd brazenly landed behind his lines. To do so, he needed to eliminate his adversary's air superiority.

Without air support, his dogged opponent would stand no chance against his massive army. He'd wipe them from the face of the earth as easily as one would dispatch an irritating insect. And with the Marines no longer biting at his backside, Cairo would be his by sundown tomorrow.

The time had come to spring the trap. In a surprise assault, he'd launch every fighter he had against the carrier-borne aircraft. Once the Super Hornets were engaged and pulled away from their ships, he'd fire scores of cruise missiles, each with a thousand-pound warhead, at the naval fleet. Sink an aircraft carrier and the American military might struggle to recover. Sink both carriers, and he would gain air superiority over North Africa for at least a week. And with eleven thousand infidel bodies floating in the Mediterranean, he might gain far more than control of the skies. With such casualties, a stunned America could lose the taste for war.

The Iraqis and Iranians would undertake a similar air assault against Saudi Arabia. There was no way either country's air forces could penetrate the Patriot missile defenses or buzzing fighter aircraft. But that was never their goal. Their attack would be a well-timed ploy to tie down the land-based aircraft in Saudi Arabia and carrier-based aircraft in the Arabian Sea. With those forces engaged, the two carriers hovering off the Egyptian coast would be isolated.

It was a gamble. Mourad was rolling the dice. He was risking his air armada in a bold strike designed to destroy the Americans' ability to stop him in Egypt. He knew his skyward forces would suffer heavy losses against his opponent's planes and pilots. Yet it was a risk worth taking. From Algeria and Libya, hundreds of French-made Mirages and Russian-made MiG-25s and SU-24s rose from their runways on a sweltering fall afternoon. The American surveillance satellites spotted them the instant they left the ground.

At the moment of Mourad's surprise attack, there were twenty-four Super Hornets in the far-flung heavens over northern Egypt. Those twenty-four would have to defend the fleet until help appeared in the skies behind them.

"All aircraft, say again, all aircraft. This is Echo Control. Pan-Arabs have launched a massive fighter attack. Approximately five hundred bandits are headed east at a high rate of speed. *Eisenhower* and *Lincoln* will launch all fighters immediately. First groups are to hold the enemy until reinforcements arrive."

The carrier battle group had nearly one hundred and eighty planes that had so far survived the intense combat. Of those, eighty-eight were top-of-the-line F/A-18Es and F/A-18Fs. Those eighty-eight would bear the brunt of the Chosen One's invasion.

Blackjack Section would limp into the air battle with half its cannon shells expended and a single heat-seeking Sidewinder on each of its pilots' wing tips. Mitchell would've felt much better about engaging the enemy with two AIM-132 and four AIM-120 missiles also nestled under his wings. But there was nothing he could do to change that reality. For the moment, there was no time to return to the *Lincoln* to reload. The Americans didn't have a minute to spare, and the thirty minutes Blackjack Section needed to land and rearm couldn't be considered.

From his field headquarters beneath the lengthening shadow of the Great Pyramid, the Mahdi waited. The moment his hemmed-in foe took the bait and sent their aircraft to battle his MiGs, he'd initiate the second part of his plan.

One hundred Tomahawk cruise missiles were sitting on the coast of Libya waiting to be fired. Their targets would be the *Lincoln* and *Eisenhower.*

A smile came to the Chosen One's weathered face. The unbelievers were about to feel the full power of Allah's wrath.

The Marines were all but forgotten as the fighters rushed west.

With only the Cobras and drones to aid them, on the shifting sands of Egypt the confounded defenders were on their own.

22

A Cobra fired another of its air-to-air missiles at an overmatched Hind-D. The streaking shadow ripped through the low heavens at incredible speed. The Sidewinder rushed headlong toward the intense heat being produced by the Hind's engine. There'd be no chance of escaping the fiery death soaring through the macabre skies to seize the Pan-Arab crew. The older-model Russian helicopter exploded. It fell in flaming pieces upon the grappling lines of the Chosen One's foot soldiers running across the weighty sands.

The harrowing helicopter clash had started minutes earlier, with twenty-four Hinds facing nine Cobras. With the American helicopter's latest kill, the numbers had dropped to sixteen against seven. At the present rate, it wouldn't take but another quarter hour for the Marine pilots to sweep their overmatched opponent from the battle zone. The surviving Cobras would then turn their attention toward cleaning up what remained of Mourad's forces after the Hornets were through annihilating their ground-based foe.

In a completely unanticipated move, in the center of the swirling battle, a Hind boldly rushed past the fierce Cobras. The instant it breached the darting defenders, the Pan-Arab helicopter dove for the protection of the desert floor. The Hind bobbed and weaved at over one hundred and eighty miles per hour. With its engine running full out, it sped toward the Marine battalion.

A smile came to the roaring pilot's face. He was almost there. Over the next rise their abhorred opponent awaited his vengeful wrath. His machine guns and rockets would soon be ripping the first line of out-classed defenders apart. As he raced past his own lines, the Hind cleared the last of the barren dunes separating him from his saintly purpose. The Americans were right in front of him. His glorious moment had arrived. Uncontrollable joy swept over him.

His surging elation would, however, be short-lived. The firing tone went off, ringing in James Fife's ears. He squeezed the trigger. The Stinger rocketed off his shoulder. Straight as an arrow, the scant missile roared toward the hurrying Hind.

The helicopter's radar screamed for its pilot to take evasive action. But the determined Stinger was so near he'd almost no time to react. The mindless killer was closing at ten times the Hind's speed. In an instant, the pilot's euphoria was replaced by the stark terror of his impending defeat. His only chance was to turn skyward while dropping strings of white-hot flares in a desperate attempt to fool the unsophisticated little heat-seeker streaking across the skies to destroy him. Maybe, just maybe, a scalding flare would confuse the Stinger and cause it to chase a false target. It was a long shot at best. And with so short a distance between attacker and prey, there was scarcely any possibility of success. Still, a slim chance was better than none at all.

The hell-bent assassin was nearly there. The panicked pilot raced into the hazy firmament while clawing at his flare release. But his frantic efforts would do little good. Before the first shielding flare could free itself, the relentless executioner was upon him. The Stinger's death-tipped nose flew into the Hind's engine. Another numbing blast shattered the horrific world above the battlefield.

On the ground, the gunnery sergeant paid scant attention to his victory. There'd be no revelry on Fife's part. With the first of the rampaging Pan-Arab armor and infantry cresting the final rise, there was no time for that. The enemy was scarcely two hundred yards away. Both sides opened fire. From every corner, the horrendous battle exploded with relishing fury.

While a solid curtain of rifle fire stung the intemperate desert, the platoon's senior sergeant placed the empty missile tube on the ground and started disassembling the firing mechanism. With the spent tube discarded, he reached for a replacement missile. In less than a minute another Stinger would be attached, ready to leap from the wily Marine's shoulder once more.

Defense of the platoon from an aerial assault was in capable hands.

Yet at the moment, it wasn't the airborne threat that worried Erickson. It was the overwhelming actions of their land-based adversary that consumed him. In combat this intense a few seconds were going to be a lifetime. And this pitched battle was going to last much, much longer. An entire division was surging toward the paper-thin American lines. In an endless stream, their unflinching opponent continued to appear in front of the bedraggled platoon. In steady succession the Marine rifles cut them down. Nonetheless, their menacing numbers, both in armored vehicles and infantry, swelled

For the initial five minutes, things went exactly as the accomplished platoon leader had anticipated. Their foe's ground attack was fierce and unrelenting. Straight down the inviting asphalt roared the bulk of the division's power. The unending Pan-Arab tanks, along with the supporting foot soldiers and armored personnel carriers, hit the Americans hard. The Marines reeled beneath the immense blow. Missiles and small arms ripped through the melancholy afternoon. Both sides' death tolls mounted. The depraved scene's distorted images continued to expand. The hideous screams of the dying and wounded went on without pause.

The imperiled defenders staggered but held on, blunting the savage attack long enough to keep Mourad's forces from smashing through the initial line. They clung by their fingernails and prayed for air support to arrive.

Mitchell's Hornets appeared right on schedule. The F/A-18Es' precision bombing and murderous cannon fire soon laid waste to the leading edge of the massive armored column. The Mahdi's losses were great. With Blackjack Section's assistance, the Chosen One's promise beckoned for untold numbers to undertake their brief life's final passage. The brutal onslaught raining down upon Mourad's army stunned the obsessed attackers. It slowed their unending furor, giving the Marines the briefest glimmer of hope. Still it failed to stop them. When the aircraft completed their runs, the columns of fearsome tanks and determined men regrouped and pressed their advantage once more. For a second time, the Mahdi's followers charged down what remained of the wasting highway.

Again the Americans bent but didn't break beneath the withering advance. They scratched and clawed at their overriding enemy, forcing the fanatical attackers to consume precious time.

Their strafing mission at an end, Blackjack Section's F/A-18Es roared low over the platoon's lines. The fighters raced away. As the Hornets finished their destruction, Erickson expected others to take up the attack. From now until Mourad's last fevered disciple died or retreated, there'd be no letup in the indiscriminate death screaming from above. The plan was for havoc from heaven to continue falling upon the Chosen One's followers until none still stood. The F/A-18Es were coming to escort them to their avidly awaited resting place.

But for some unexplained reason, it didn't happen. Inexplicably, rather than increasing as the tenacious battle went on, air support for the embattled Marines suddenly vanished.

On came an overriding force of T-72s. Guns blazing, they churned down the hot pavement toward the Americans' makeshift positions. The ferocious fray's agonizing texture turned one-sided.

There was little the belabored defenders could do. Without air support, the lightly armed American ground forces were severely overmatched. For five additional minutes, a thousand eternities in a clash of such magnitude, the forestalling Marines held their own. They wouldn't, however, be able to do so for much longer. Erickson frantically scanned the swirling skies for signs of additional assistance. Yet none appeared.

With no fighter attack to slow their advance, Mourad's tanks and armored personnel carriers rushed forward. Behind them, the desert filled with thousands of wrathful men intent on wiping out the destitute battalion. The Pan-Arabs sprang toward their besieged opposition. The Marine rifles and machine guns cut down the exposed figures. Still, for each jihadist the Americans killed, dozens more arrived to take his place.

Despite their mounting losses, the agitated aggressors were un-yielding. They were going to slaughter the Americans. They were going to prevail in the reverent battle. Or die in the attempt. Their dreams of a wondrous forever spurred them toward their insatiable goal.

The intensifying conflict dragged on through incalculable life-times. While he watched his men fight and die around him, Erickson's angst changed from quiet concern to mounting desperation.

They'd been told to conserve their armor-slaying missiles. Never-theless, they had no choice.

Six hundred armored vehicles were rushing across the trackless sands to destroy them. Thousands of armed men were on the way. Faced with such adversity, the first row of Americans fired all of their Javelins and TOWs. With quelling effect, half the platoon's smaller LAW missiles were sent out to greet the armored personnel carriers. One dreadful explosion after another rocked the girding scene. As the gathering flames found the dying armored vehicles' stores of ammuni-tion, secondary blasts splintered the afternoon. Thick plumes of nox-ious smoke further masked the ghastly battlefield.

The Marines' hopeless efforts slowed the ruinous force just a little longer. Yet once more, it didn't stop them. The determined enemy pressed his advantage. The obsessed zealots weren't going to be de-nied. With each passing second, they closed with their outgunned adversary. Menacing tanks and ireful men were everywhere.

Erickson fought to control his platoon's actions. Even so, like every battle, this one was chaotic and disjointed. It was happening in slow motion. It was happening at the speed of light.

He grabbed the radio handset. "Two-Six, this is Bravo-Three-Six."

"Roger, Bravo-Three-Six," the battalion radio operator answered.

"Two-Six, what the hell happened to our air support? The bastards are crawling all over us up here. Without immediate help, we're going to be overrun. And the Chosen One's army isn't going to stop until they're standing on the beach staring at the Mediterranean."

"Bravo-Three-Six, be advised the Hornets have been pulled for a higher-priority mission."

"Higher-priority mission? What higher-priority mission? How the hell could there be a higher-priority mission than this one? My men are getting slaughtered."

"Understood. We're as confused as you are. All I can tell you is we've already taken steps to remedy the situation. Attack drones will be here shortly. And the division commander's freed up eighteen additional Cobras. They're itching for a fight and on the way. They'll be here in ten minutes. He's also released twelve M-1s to support our position. They should arrive a few minutes after that."

"Roger, Two-Six. But with the intensity of this attack, ten minutes is going to be forever. There's no way we can hold that long. What do you suggest we do until the drones and Cobras reach us?"

"Initial orders are still in effect. Don't worry about hanging on to real estate. Ground's cheap. It's live bodies we're short on. Save your men any way you can. It'll be your call. If you can't defend your position, fall back on your own initiative. Don't forget, there are three lines of Marines behind yours."

"Roger. Will do what I can. Even so, with what's headed this way, don't be surprised if when we next talk we're standing side by side with a T-72 bearing down on us."

Erickson slammed the headset down. The uneven battle was worsening. To his left and right, Marine foxholes were eliminated in a single blow from a pair of tanks' thundering main guns. Huge holes appeared in the American lines. The lieutenant realized without question that his small force would soon be overrun. He had to act. In the middle of the horrifying onslaught he had to find a way to retreat to the protection of the next line. And he had to do so while limiting his losses.

Two churning T-72s burst through the platoon's defenses to the right of the highway.

Ignoring the gunfire all around him, Erickson leaped up, hurtled the median, and raced across the road. The platoon leader snatched a LAW from the gnarled hands of a dead Marine. He turned toward the speeding tanks with the small, bazooka-like launch tube perched on his shoulder. The little rocket couldn't penetrate the frontal armor of the T-72s. But if placed right, it could damn sure puncture the thinner armor on a ravaging tank's rear. The trailing tank was in Erickson's sights. He was a shallow breath away from pulling the trigger. But before he could loosen his scant rocket, both tanks erupted. Each disappeared in a mighty blow from the hellish power contained in a pair of TOWs. The second row of Marines had beaten the frantic lieutenant to the punch.

A continuous stream of Mourad's infantry rushed across the depleted landscape. Erickson searched his meager defenses, looking for a glimmer of hope. There was none.

The platoons on each side of him were having no better luck than his. He was out of time. And options.

There was nothing he could do. If they stayed where they were, their devastating adversary would destroy them with ease. In seconds, they'd be wiped out by the rampant attackers. Despite the extreme danger of his exposed position, he furiously signaled his men.

"Pass the word! We've gotta fall back!" he screamed into his headset over the deafening noise of the blood-soaked butchery. "Humvee machine guns are to cover our withdrawal. Team leaders, fire your claymores then extricate yourselves. Each man's on his own. Get out of here any way you can. Link up with those behind us!"

He'd be risking his Humvees, but to cover the platoon's retreat, he had no other choice.

A dozen claymores were fired at nearly the same instant. A solid wall of voracious steel reached out to slaughter the first line of Mourad's infantry. Many of the oncoming assailants were cut in half. Their disemboweled corpses, severed at the waist, spilled onto the crimson sands. The scorched earth eagerly soaked up their dying essence.

"Gunny, grab the Stingers and get the hell out of here! I'll cover you."

There'd be no chance for an orderly withdrawal. The Marines staggered from their foxholes. A volley of grenades leaped from their hands and arched toward the enemy. The Americans didn't pause to watch their final efforts. The instant the plummeting killers were released, the platoon's survivors turned and ran toward the second line.

As the platoon retreated, a trio of Reaper drones appeared. Each carried four tank-killing Hellfire missiles. From their monitors in Nevada, the drone operators unleashed one after another of the armor-slaying ordnance. Once again, the attackers' leading edge was ripped to shreds. Explosion after explosion rocked the contested sands.

Moments later, the first of the buzzing drones went down. With no defenses against Stingers, it was easy prey. A second soon followed. The third, at least for the moment, continued its assault.

The retreating Marines had one hundred yards of open ground to traverse to reach the protection of the next row. For many it would be forever. Even with the Humvees and surviving drone covering their retreat, many would never make it.

Dragging their equipment with them, the fleeing men ran, dove, hobbled, and crawled toward the waiting row of sandbags.

With their compatriots in the way, the stalwart Marines of the second line could do little to help. There was far too great a chance of hitting one of the retreating Americans. From the safety of their defenses, they encouraged their countrymen's progress. They fired at the rabid enemy wherever the situation allowed for a clear shot. And they steadied themselves for the depraved tidal wave reaching out to engulf them.

The worn platoon ran as fast as they could toward the illusory protection of the next row of rifles. The incensed rabble was right behind.

On foot, or in armored vehicles, they nipped at the withdrawing lines' heels. Steel and flesh chased Erickson's men.

On the left of the lurching Marines, an American fell beneath the persistent rifle fire. He stumbled to his feet, dragging himself on a shattered leg across the heavy sands. His pitiful journey was slow and tortured. A trail of bright red marked his labored movements. Three eager attackers pounced. The wounded figure used every hand-to-hand skill he knew. But it was no use. The Pan-Arabs overwhelmed him. A glistening sword, long and terrifying, rose into the air. The wicked result was ruthless and certain.

With the defeated Marine no longer in the way, his obsessed killers were out in the open. An M-16 muzzle flashed from behind the second row of sand. From fifty yards away, the skilled marksman wouldn't miss. The exposed executioners fell to earth and stirred no more.

On the right, another Marine dropped in a hail of gunfire.

In the center, a Humvee exploded. The withdrawing Americans' losses continued to soar. Erickson turned and fired a full burst at the solid wall of marauding warriors. A handful fell. Thousands came on.

The spent platoon leader ran down the sticky pavement as fast as his weary legs would carry him. The instant he reached the second line, he dove into the foxhole of a pair of encouraging Marines.

Joyce's Humvee roared past. The moment he reached his own defenses, he turned to meet the attackers. The desert in front of this level of sandbags was finally clear. Once more, armor-destroying Javelins and TOWs ripped through the frightful afternoon. Once again, rifle fire and LAW missiles struck down the enemy. And still the Chosen One's masses came on.

Erickson had scarcely controlled his breathing before the second layer was overcome. This time there'd be no need to tell the hopelessly outnumbered force to withdraw.

The Marines turned and ran toward the third array.

23

Mourad's faithful could sense the noose tightening around the exposed Americans' necks. It spurred his rapturous followers. Their lust for blood knew no bounds. They would annihilate the invaders. Not one of the nonbelievers would still be breathing when sundown came.

There was no longer any doubt. This would be the moment for which all had waited. This would be the time of conquest over the hated infidels. Satan's unholy servants would be destroyed. Theirs would be the victory that would turn the tide of battle back toward Allah's chosen. They'd drive their contemptible adversary into the sea and reclaim northern Egypt before night fell.

Once they wiped the heretics from the face of the earth, the Mahdi's followers would return to capturing Cairo. With the destruction of the great city complete, they'd make a headlong dash across the Sinai to face the one true curse upon the Arab world. The sainted battle with Israel would begin. Revenge for decades of indignities, real and imagined, would be theirs for the taking. After today's unqualified mastery, nothing would stand in their way. The Chosen One's tanks would be rolling into Jerusalem within the week. Islam's triumph over the world of the faithless was taking shape.

With unbound fury, the Pan-Arabs chased the struggling Marines. Victory was within their grasp. Another one hundred yards of fallow ground was lost as the stumbling Americans ran before the pillaging armored division. Another round of agony and death reached out to claim the defiling Americans. The narrow third line held their positions and waited for their comrades to clear the field. Their weapons were locked on the unending targets.

The last of the faltering figures was soon out of the way. The instant they were clear, the anxious defenders unleashed everything they had. Missiles and machine-gun fire stung the immense attackers. And as before, scores of fierce eruptions rocked the desert air.

But Mourad's army wasn't going to be denied. The assured aggressors barely slowed. The third line rapidly consumed their insignificant reserves. Yet their unbending antagonists were still coming. What remained of the first three orders was soon struggling toward the final defensive positions.

For a fourth time, the maligned scene would be repeated. Death, turmoil, and destruction ruled the day. There was nothing the halting Americans could do except use the limited supply of weapons in the remaining row's arsenal. To slow the Pan-Arabs, the Marines fired everything they had. The last of the battalion's antitank missiles were unleashed. More burning intruders were added to the perverse display.

Still the suicidal attackers didn't stop.

The resigned Marines were out of options. There was nowhere left to run. And nothing remaining to slow the lusting tanks. Even so, the Americans would stand their ground.

Thousands of Pan-Arab soldiers and hundreds of weapons of war surged forward, determined to claim a share of the hallowed conquest. Mourad's armor crowded together in a mad dash to vanquish their debased opponent. The Chosen One's victorious infantry rushed shoulder to shoulder toward what remained of the disappearing defenses. The onerous battle was at its end.

The lethal blow would be swift and certain.

Side by side, eighteen Cobras roared over the shifting landscape. The instant the overpowering executioners reached the scene, they released a barrage of Hellfire and TOW missiles so mighty nothing could withstand its concussive force. It was a supremely powerful blow. Four hundred yards of desert erupted in a frightful no-man's-land of blistering fires and searing infernos. A sizable portion of the Pan-Arab armored division disappeared in one swift strike. The earth shuddered and collapsed beneath the Mahdi's fanatics.

On the ground, the startled Marines watched as fiery figures emerged from the unspeakable holocaust. Fully ablaze, the sightless forms staggered a short distance into the desert before their suffering mercifully ended.

Even the most hardened of the Americans turned away in abject revulsion at the lurid sight. The anguished wails of those who'd been caught in the furious attack would never be forgotten by the horrified men of the Marine battalion. The endless streams of tormented cries would shatter their fitful dreams for the rest of their days.

Within the targeted area, nothing survived. Men and machines perished in a swirling witch's caldron of death and destruction.

The consuming Cobras, however, weren't finished. Always on the alert for Stinger launches, they swooped in low with flares falling. Their bulging rocket pods were filled with further agony for those intent on a beckoning paradise. The frenetic helicopters' armor-piercing guns also soon roared.

In an instant, the combatants' roles had been reversed. Now it was Mourad's dazed forces facing defeat on the Alexandria highway. Yet the Pan-Arabs didn't yield, unwilling to admit that in a handful of fleeting heartbeats certain mastery had been taken from them. They responded with everything they had. T-72 antiaircraft machine guns fired in every direction. Stinger gunners futilely attempted to break through the staunch Cobras' defenses and lock on to the daunting attackers.

The Mahdi's devotees were outmatched. Still they were by no means defenseless. The first of the Cobras soon discovered how much fight remained in the stunned enemy. A Stinger suddenly reached through the confusing clutter to snatch an American crew. A second Cobra went down moments later in a hail of antiaircraft fire. The crippled helicopters smashed into the desert near their own lines. An earth-shattering blast accompanied each life-ending explosion.

For the Chosen One's disciples such victories served no tactical purpose. They were far too few, and much too late. Yet it no longer mattered.

When the Marine division's Abrams arrived, the Pan-Arab defeat was forever sealed. The twelve tanks waded deep into the scattered survivors to obliterate and plunder. The T-72s were excellent tanks. Nevertheless, they were no match for the top-of-line American armor. The M-1s were far too advanced, and the Marine crews much too polished, to suffer even a single defeat.

What the Cobras didn't eliminate, the M-1's methodically dispatched. The precision of the Abrams' kills was a thing of distorted beauty to behold. The four-man crews loaded their huge rounds, located their targets with their fully computerized systems, and fired in such quick succession it was impossible for those on the battlements to keep up. What few rounds the T-72s got off against their superior adversary failed to penetrate the foot of frontal plating protecting the technologically superior armored vehicles. The massive shells harmlessly exploded against the M-1s' thick hulls.

The fleeting hopes of the Chosen One's armored division forever disappeared when the five surviving Cobras from the earlier air battle arrived at the rear of the Pan-Arab lines. The flailing division was caught in an ever-constricting death grip. The lethal Americans closed in from all sides to squeeze the final, fading embers from the defeated force. Even when their loss was there for all to see, not a single one retreated. Mourad's obsessed adherents had arrived on the blood-stained vista intent on triumph or martyrdom. They'd come within an eyelash of the first. In the end, however, they'd have no choice but to settle for the second.

The spirit-seizing slaughter went on without letup. It wouldn't be until early evening that the final gunfire would cease. But end it eventually did.

The remnants of the platoon settled into the defensive positions they'd held at the beginning of the grotesque battle. At the conclusion of the day, the Chosen One's forces hadn't gained an inch of ground. As the unforgiving sun disappeared, fifteen thousand fresh bodies lay on the piteous landscape. The smoldering shells of their crushed armored vehicles littered the sorrowful ground. Two hundred of the Marine battalion's men had been killed or seriously wounded during the afternoon assault. Barely half those Erickson had taken command of a few hours prior were still in the fight.

The battalion's final four hundred would harden themselves for the next attack. With every fiber of courage they could muster, they'd attempt to hang on until help arrived.

In three days, the 1st Marine Division would reach the North African shore. Until then, all the scarred Marines could do was lick their gaping wounds and wait for Mourad to make his next move.

Second Battalion had suffered greatly. So had many of their brethren along the defensive front. It had been an extremely difficult day for the entire division.

The same could be said for the carrier battle groups sent to protect the skies above.

24

A dozen F/A-18Fs led the way. Armed with AIM-120, AIM-132, and Sidewinder missiles, they were a formidable adversary. It wouldn't be long before the Pan-Arab pilots tasted the immense power of the American aircraft. The Navy interceptors would attempt to stun the leading edge of the attack, buying the Americans valuable time. With a dagger's thrust to the heart, they'd fearlessly dive into the center of the fray to disrupt Mourad's huge air assault. Chaos would follow in their wake.

A similar number of F/A-18Es, their ground attack missions aborted, were right behind. The second wave was taking a more passive posture. They'd wait to see how the battle unfolded and try to hold the line against the numerically superior enemy until help arrived. Hopefully, they could screen most of the MiGs away from the carrier fleet. They had no other choice. This first group of F/A-18Es was limping into battle with a severe handicap. Sent skyward to destroy tanks, none was loaded with a full complement of munitions for air-to-air combat. Not one of the F/A-18Es was carrying its most powerful weapons. Without their radar-guided AIM-120s and AIM-132s, the Hornets would have to work their way relatively close to make a kill. The range of their Sidewinders was limited to about twenty miles, less than one-fifth of what an AIM-120 missile would provide.

Blackjack Section, with only a single heat-seeking Sidewinder hanging from each of its pilots' wing tips and much of its cannon shells expended, trailed the leading groups.

All were headed west at speeds of over a thousand miles per hour.

Five hundred enemy fighters smothered the skies over the southern Mediterranean. Twenty-four of America's finest aircraft were rushing to meet them. The opposing groups were on a collision course seven miles above the ocean's breezes.

The initial advantage belonged to the Chosen One. Still, the Americans' chances were improving with each passing minute. They'd been caught off guard. Yet their response to the attack was measured and proficient. Every thirty seconds, another combat aircraft leaped from one of the carriers' decks and raced to join its countrymen. Within the hour, the entire strike force would be airborne. Even with the five-to-one odds against them, they'd be more than a match for Mourad's inferior pilots and planes.

But the Mahdi had no intention of giving the Americans an hour to prepare. His orders were to attack with all the malice his MiGs could muster before their opponent got organized. The Pan-Arab pilots didn't hesitate. They made a headlong rush toward the oncoming Navy fighters.

The battle was joined.

The initial dogfights were scarcely under way when the first of the Chosen One's MiGs burst into flames. The defeated fighter, the lifeless body of its vanquished pilot strapped in his seat, began a long, slow spiral toward the waiting seas. Moments later, a second crippled Pan-Arab aircraft, a French-made Mirage, followed.

Things were heating up. One by one, pairs of freshly launched Super Hornets arrived on the scene. More were on the way. By well before the dinner hour, all eighty-eight of the carrier fleet's combat fighters would be engaging the enemy.

The expanding battle continued to evolve.

While the hot afternoon sun made its journey toward the western horizon, the match of calculating men and streaking machines wore on throughout the length and breadth of the heavens. Like a giant game of tic-tac-toe, crisscrossing vapor trails covered the distant skies.

The "shoot" symbol appeared on Mitchell's cockpit display. A MiG-25 was dead center in his kill envelope. He fired the last of his missiles. The Sidewinder dropped from the tip of his Hornet's left wing. It raced across the sky. Six miles separated the F/A-18E from the fleeing aircraft. The Sidewinder would cover it in seconds.

There was nothing more for Mitchell to do than watch as the fire-and-forget heat-seeker closed with its target. The MiG's radar screamed for its pilot to take evasive action. The panicked Libyan dove for the beckoning seas with the Sidewinder in pursuit. Flares poured from the diving plane. But it was no use. The Sidewinder couldn't be fooled. At the last possible instant, the pilot hit the eject lever and parachuted from his craft. The MiG exploded. Pieces of the defeated plane, Mitchell's second kill of the afternoon, fell into the watery world below.

Throughout the spanning blue, scores of Pan Arab aircraft were meeting the same fate.

Mourad's struggling fliers had one-tenth the training of their American counterparts. And it showed. Even with the initial twenty-to-one odds against them, the assured Navy pilots dominated the unanticipated air battle. As the extending heavens behind the first groups filled with Super Hornets, the contest turned one-sided. In the early stages, some of the Mahdi's fighters broke through the twenty-four defenders. Those that did ran headlong into the rising formations of F/A-18s. Only a scattering of Mirages reached the fringes of the naval battle groups. Each of those was effortlessly dispatched by the swarming cruiser and destroyer air defenses. Not a single invading pilot got within thirty miles of the aircraft carriers.

The first desperate hour passed. With the Pan-Arabs' superior forces, the Americans lost a few of their number in the solemn conflict spreading for hundreds of miles in every direction. A handful of defeated Navy planes plunged into the Mediterranean or crashed into the trackless Sahara. Sixty of the enemy were gone. All eighty-three remaining American fighters from the *Lincoln* and *Eisenhower* were engaged in the life-and-death drama. Not a single combat aircraft had been left in reserve. With so immense a strike, holding back even one was a luxury the defenders couldn't afford.

The battle drifted west toward Libya. It looked quite reasonable to the F/A-18 pilots that their inexperienced rival was being pushed back by the Americans' remarkable skills. Everything seemed perfectly natural. A slow retreat by their overmatched opponent was exactly what the Navy fliers anticipated would occur. A steady elimination of Mourad's aircraft was under way. It wouldn't be much longer before the Pan-Arab flight commanders would have to decide between withdrawing to their bunkered bases or facing certain annihilation over North Africa.

Things were proceeding exactly as the Americans had hoped. At least, that's how it looked. In reality, the conflict was developing precisely as Mourad had laid it out. The Mahdi's orders were for his planes to draw their opponent toward the sunset, away from the carrier task force. They were accomplishing just that. The closest American aircraft was one hundred miles from the fleet.

The Chosen One's aim was to lure the swarming Super Hornets from their guardian positions surrounding the carriers. And by the end of the first hour he'd succeeded. The towering skies above the fleet were clear of friend and enemy alike.

Mourad had achieved his initial goal. He'd temporarily eliminated a crucial layer of the naval strike group's defenses. The AIM-120 and AIM-132 missiles of the F/A-18s wouldn't be waiting on the perimeter of the American fleet to shoot down his cruise missiles. He knew, however, that even with the soaring aircraft out of the mix, there were still no guarantees of success. The highly accurate shipborne Aegis air defense system would have to be overcome. This would be an impressive task. Most of his lethal missiles were bound to fail.

The great majority would never reach their destination. Of that, he had no illusion. Yet with one hundred launches within moments of each other, there remained a decent chance of overwhelming the two carrier battle groups and killing one or both of the giant ships.

The Chosen One's plan was evolving right on schedule. With the shielding fighters pulled away, the carriers were at their most vulnerable. The time had come to unleash his concise executioners to seek out and destroy. At the launch sites in Libya, the crews readied their ground-hugging missiles. One hundred nearly simultaneous firings were about to take place. With a top speed of five hundred and fifty miles per hour, the unwavering American-made Tomahawk cruise missiles would need just under sixty minutes to reach the inviting aircraft carriers.

As he'd accomplish many times in this war, Mourad was going to slaughter the Americans with weapons of their own design.

The countdown began. A first missile rose from its launchpad. Following its on-board computer's preprogrammed data, it headed straight for the open sea. Another soon followed. Still more spewed forth. It didn't take long for the deadly pack to form. Somewhere out there, the enormous quarry awaited. The guiltless killers picked up the scent. A monumental game of hounds and foxes was taking shape. And the hounds' sharp teeth were bared and lusting for blood. A fast and furious contest of hunter against hunted would soon be waged off the coast of Egypt. To the victor would go the spoils.

The Chosen One's prize was the two carriers' eleven thousand lives and the destruction of a pair of the world's greatest warships. His ultimate goal, control of the skies over North Africa and defeat of all Allied forces in Egypt, would be at hand.

In the next hour, the Pan-Arabs' chances for conquest and Mourad's eventual world domination would become much clearer. Win this afternoon, and triumph over the infidels was all but assured. Lose and face the stark reality of a forever-steepening struggle to defeat those who stood in Allah's way.

Unaware the second act in the Mahdi's life-and-death drama was playing out, Bradley Mitchell contacted the EC-2 command and control aircraft.

"Echo Control, this is Blackjack Section. Have expended our missiles. And our Vulcan cannons are almost empty. Request permission to return to the boat to rearm and refuel."

"Okay, Blackjack Section. We've got a few other Super Hornets that are low on fuel and will reach the *Lincoln* ahead of you. But by the time you arrive, you should be able to land immediately. Bring it on in."

"Roger, Echo Control, we're on our way."

After searching the widely scattered clouds to ensure the enemy wasn't hiding nearby, the pair of Hornets swung around and rushed back toward the east. In seven minutes, they'd reach their destination. Alert for lurking Pan-Arab aircraft, Blackjack Section closed with the fleet.

It wasn't long before the fearsome aircrafts' screeching wheels reached the deck and each Hornet's hook grabbed one of the stout runway's arrester wires, slamming them to an abrupt stop.

The tired pilots crawled from their cockpits. The maintenance and armament crews were there to meet them. Mitchell searched out his crew chief.

"How much time until we're back in the air, Chief?" he asked.

"Normally I'd tell you an hour, sir. But with the present tactical situation, our orders are to have you strapped in your cockpits and headed to the catapults in thirty minutes."

"Looks like there'll be no rest for the wicked today."

"No, sir. Word is this probably won't be the last time in the coming hours we prepare you to launch. Fuel and weapons teams are ready and waiting. They'll start getting your Hornets into dogfight mode before you've cleared the deck."

"Thirty minutes," Mitchell said. "Worm, we're going to earn our paychecks today. Let's go below, grab some coffee, and shove down a sandwich or two while we can."

"Sounds good to me," Sweeney said. "While we're at it, maybe we should stop by and talk to Naval Pilot Union Local 114's shop steward about putting us in for some overtime. That time-and-a-half money will sure come in handy with all the pretty girls in Naples who're waiting for my handsome face to return. Ya know many of them believe I'm some sort of deity whose every command mortal women must obey."

"You wish. It's not those homely features of yours that makes you so attractive to the women around the Naples piers. None of them care a lick about what you look like. It's that fat wallet of yours they're really interested in. But you're right about the money. After what we've gone through this week, I know why on my first day in the Navy they made it clear we were being paid twenty-four hours a day, three hundred sixty-five days a year. If they ever gave me overtime for all the hours I've put in during the past twelve years, I could retire tomorrow."

Side by side, the pilots of Blackjack Section swaggered across the deck and disappeared down the stairs.

The Chosen One's cruise missiles had been in the air for fifteen minutes. If not stopped, a fiery end would reach the floating cities in three-quarters of an hour.

Just a few feet from the water, the missiles skimmed the whitecapped sea. As they crossed the twenty-minute mark, each reached the outer edges of the EC-2's three-hundred-mile radar limit. A large cluster of unexplained symbols, their outlines vague and distorted, appeared at the fringes of the controllers' screens. The command and control aircraft was nearing the end of its five-hour shift. All three battle controllers were consumed with the enormity of guiding the intensive air combat. None picked up the images hugging the ocean's waves.

Another ten minutes passed. Mitchell finished a first sandwich. He glanced at his watch and reached for another.

The air battle was reaching its peak. The EC-2 controllers had their hands full. Straight and steady the cruise missiles came on. They were ninety miles closer to their goal.

Finally, the lead controller spotted the immense threat to the fleet's survival.

"What the hell?" he said. "Am I seeing what I think I'm seeing?"

"What have you got, Commander?"

"Take a real close look, Lieutenant Boyles. Chief, give me your opinion too. Two hundred and ten miles west, right above the waves."

The controllers focused their attention on the strange radar images. The trio stared intently at the scores of hazy reflections huddled together near the outer reaches of their screens. The objects, their speed and course constant, were moving east toward the ships.

"Oh God, as much as I don't want to admit it, sir," the lieutenant said, "there's only one thing that flies so low at those speeds and could be launched in such great numbers."

"Cruise missiles," the chief added.

"Everyone's been wondering why the Mahdi hasn't used any of them. Well, now we know. He's been saving them all for one big attack."

"How many do you think there are, sir?"

"Impossible to tell for sure, Chief. The ground clutter's distorting everything. My guess, from what I see, would be no less than fifty and possibly three times that. One thing's certain: with so many on the way, we've got our hands full. No doubt they're headed for the carriers. Lieutenant, notify the task force to prepare to repel a massive cruise missile attack. Get the cruisers and destroyers into position for an airborne assault coming out of Libya. Have the carriers get under way and initiate full evasive maneuvers. If all the cruise missiles have is their preprogrammed data to go by in tracking down the ships, they're going to have a heck of a time hitting a carrier moving over thirty miles an hour. Without a GPS system to help adjust their flight paths, when they arrive the carriers will be fifteen miles away from where the missiles are headed."

What the Americans didn't know was that months earlier Mourad's technicians had figured out how to hack into the American military GPS satellite system. Not only were they using American-made cruise missiles in their heinous task, but also the enemy's GPS to hunt down their mammoth prey. No matter what the carriers did in the coming minutes, the cruise missiles would know right where to find them.

"Yes, sir."

"How much time do you estimate before the missiles arrive, Commander?"

"With their present course and speed, I'd say no more than twenty-five minutes."

"We've got to stop them, sir. Can the task force's ships handle the attack, or should we call the fighters back to knock the missiles from the sky? If they return at top speed, many of the Super Hornets should be well within range before the threat reaches the carriers."

"We don't have a choice here, I'm afraid. The ships' defenses will have to battle the missiles. We can't expect help from our Hornets. At this point, that's not even an option. If I call for fighter support and most of our F/A-18s withdraw from the air battle, the skies will be wide open. I'm afraid it wouldn't take long for the Chosen One's MiGs to find openings and pour through to attack both carriers. Better our ships tackle Mourad's cruise missiles than face four hundred heavily armed fighters. I'd rather have the fleet fighting mindless machines coming in at a five hundred miles an hour than bandits with humans in control flying twice that fast. I don't know if the escort ships can stop that many cruise missiles coming in so close together. We've never faced more than one or two in an actual combat situation. Even in the computer simulations the numbers have never been so great. Maybe we can handle them, maybe not. But one thing's for certain. In the next half hour, we're going to find out."

"Isn't there anything we can do to help the ships?" the chief asked.

"How many fighters have returned to the carriers to rearm?"

"Four F/A-18Fs and a pair of F/A-18Es are on the deck of the *Lincoln*, sir. Another handful are on the way back to the boats."

"How long before they're ready to launch?"

"Ten minutes, maybe a little less for the 'Fs. Fifteen for the two 'Es. None of those headed to the carriers can possibly rearm in time."

"First priority is getting the ships ready. I'll coordinate that part. Chief, once the Super Hornets launch, have them attack the oncoming missiles. You'll handle the six fighters. We've got to get maximum use of their AIM-120s and 132s."

"Yes, sir."

"Lieutenant Boyles, you'll continue to coordinate our efforts against Mourad's aircraft. Lest we forget, we've still got that little problem on our hands."

"Will do, Commander."

"All right, gentlemen, let's see how good at this we really are."

The approach to security for the great ships was to layer the defenses. The Super Hornets normally comprised the first line of protection. Flying twice as fast as a cruise missile, they could easily close with an invader. Once the cruise missiles were in range, AIM-120s would be launched from over one hundred miles. After the AIM-120s were expended, the shorter-range AIM-132s would be sent to search and destroy. With plenty of luck, and much skill, a Super Hornet could eliminate six cruise missiles.

Under normal conditions the carriers' fighters would have handled the oncoming threat with relative ease. Unfortunately, the initial element of the American defenses was tossed throughout the far-flung heavens. Nearly all were tied down by the air-to-air conflict. Fifteen minutes before the first cruise missile's arrival, four Super Hornets would rise from the *Lincoln*. With ten minutes to spare, Blackjack Section would careen off the same deck loaded with four radar-guided AIM-120s, a pair of AIM-132s, and two heat-seeking Sidewinders.

Even if the six aircraft destroyed an incoming assailant with each of its radar-guided missiles, sixty-four undeterred thugs would be left unharmed. And with the targets small, close to the waves, and little time remaining to find and eliminate, the fighters might not come close to so great a number of successful engagements. At this early stage, it was evident the majority of the battle groups' defenses would have to come from the support ships.

Each carrier was being escorted by two cruisers and four destroyers. Of the eight destroyers, three were equipped with Aegis air defenses. Among the potential threats it had been built to address, the Aegis system had been designed to defend against cruise missiles. The three Aegis ships had a Sea Sparrow quadpack ready to fire on a moment's notice. Each also carried a five-inch air defense gun, one Phalanx gun capable of firing forty-five hundred rounds per minute for close-in defense, and two chaff launchers to fool the approaching missiles. The entire process was computerized and fully integrated to obtain the maximum from the system's components.

The remaining ships of the task force, and the aircraft carriers themselves, also were equipped with ample weapons. The first to spring into action would be the eight Harpoon missiles on each of the cruisers. Seventy nautical miles was their range.

The ships bristled with air defenses. There were more than enough missiles and guns to destroy the intruders many times over. With each passing minute, another protective measure would become available to the fleet. The only question was whether there'd be sufficient time to use them before so impressive an arrangement of lethal armaments arrived. It was time, not missiles that was the Americans' true enemy.

The task force sprang into action. The cruisers and destroyers aligned to confront the threat.

One hundred trudging missiles were headed their way. Death's sadistic shadow skirted over the rolling seas. In twenty-five minutes, unless stopped, Muhammad Mourad would reach across the shimmering waters to claim his prize.

For the Americans, the seconds were slipping away. With each sweep of the clock, the Mahdi's grand ambitions were nine miles closer to ending the game.

25

As Mitchell and Sweeney appeared on deck, four F/A-18Fs filled the catapults. In rapid succession, they ripped down the runway and tore into the sky. There was scarcely a quarter hour remaining before the first searching killer would arrive.

Mitchell's Super Hornets rocketed off the *Lincoln*. Beneath both aircrafts' wings, four AIM-120s and two AIM-132s glistened in the late afternoon sun. A Sidewinder hung from the end of each wing.

"Echo Control, this is Blackjack Section. Where do you want us?"

"Blackjack Section, cruise missiles are seventy-five miles out. Unless stopped, they'll arrive in eight or nine minutes. The bulk of the attack's coming from the southwest. Estimate approximately seventy missiles in that grouping. They appear to be heading for the *Lincoln*. First four Super Hornets are closing in to cut them down to size. All four cruisers are concentrating on that formation. If they have time after the Super Hornets are finished, the cruisers will fire thirty-two

Harpoons at the survivors. Two Aegis systems are also going to be sent against this primary grouping, along with one of the five remaining destroyers. There's another group of thirty that's broken off from the rest. They're trying to sneak in from the west. At the moment, with nearly everything we've got focused on the main body, we're as concerned about the second formation as the bigger one. From their latest course change, we believe they're aiming for the *Eisenhower*. All we've got left to stop them is one Aegis and three regular destroyers. And you. We want your Hornets to go after the smaller formation. You've got to handle as many cruise missiles as you can."

"Roger, Echo Control. We'll do everything possible to knock 'em down. We're picking up both formations on our radars. We'll drop this instant to hug the waves and hit them head-on. Intercept of thirty cruise missiles is estimated at three minutes."

"Roger, Blackjack Section. Good luck."

Mitchell dove for the ocean's swells with Sweeney on his tail. Flying directly into the sun, a dozen feet above the blinding waters, they raced west.

Both of their radars tracked the approaching targets. The pilot's job was to get his aircraft to the attack point, and once there, unleash his AIM-120s and 132s. While they flew toward the cruise missiles, the F/A-18Es' computers would select and prioritize their victims.

To the southwest, a Super Hornet fired its first AIM-120. The initial clash of the desperate defense had begun. This opening match, the precursor of many to come, would be no contest. At six times the cruise missile's speed, the streaking bird of prey roared across the relentless waves with sharpened talons raised. The AIM-120 soon plucked the helpless pigeon from the low skies. The impacting projectiles exploded. One cruise missile would never reach the fleet.

Ninety-nine to go. And seven minutes left.

A second AIM-120 leaped from its perch beneath a Super Hornet's wing. A third and fourth went in search of conquest moments later. Three more cruise missiles would never reach their monumental goal. Another took up the chase. And another. Few would miss the mark.

Even with the extreme pressure, most of the aircrafts' air-to-air missiles would find the speeding sharks. The game would go on until the last of the F/A-18Fs' munitions reached its implacable adversary, or failed in its quest and, its fuel expended, spun into the sea.

Behind the sea-hugging Super Hornets, the cruisers' Harpoon missiles waited. The first of the cruise missiles already was well within range of the ships' air defenses. As soon as the Super Hornets finished their task and cleared the area, the Harpoons would fire. And behind them, the Aegis, missiles, and guns of the destroyers sat at the ready. It was all a matter of time.

Yet with so few ticks of the clock remaining, time was not an ally of the Americans.

The unrelenting moments continued to run. Another minute passed. The fatalistic enemy reached the fifty-mile mark. In fewer than six minutes the Mahdi's minions would find the fleet.

Blackjack Section neared the release point for its AIM-120s.

"All right, Worm, looks like we're all set. Computer's got them prioritized. I know we're in a hurry here, but let's attempt to eliminate as many as we can. Six kills in six shots from each of us would make me quite happy."

"There's not much time left, Blackjack. And the cruise missiles are awfully small targets."

"I know. But we'll do our best and hope the ships can handle the rest. Okay, my first shot's all set. Here we go."

Mitchell fired an initial missile. The fast-flying armament leaped from the Hornet. The tables had been turned on one of the oncoming killers.

Another frantic chase had begun a few feet above the cool Mediterranean. And the result would be predictable. The selected cruise missile was overmatched. The smaller pack of Mourad's assassins would soon be down to twenty-nine.

Sweeney had a parrying shot lined up. Away went a second slayer. Mitchell fired another a moment later. The F/A-18E pilots were methodically knocking one after another of the Chosen One's dreams from the low skies.

There were less than five minutes left.

A final Super Hornet's AIM-132 went forth to seek and destroy. One last kill from the F/A-18Fs. Of sixteen missiles fired, fourteen had found the mark. Still, in the main group, fifty-six of Mourad's avenging angels remained in the air. With single-minded determination the survivors came on. The quartet of Super Hornets had done what they could. They raced skyward. It was now the cruisers' turn. The ships fired. An initial volley of Harpoon missiles filled the air in search of prey. Others would soon follow.

More cruise missiles were about to be destroyed.

Four minutes before death's arrival. Thirty six miles out and coming on fast. But the first of the Harpoons would soon be upon them.

At three minutes, the destroyers entered the fray. A barrage of Sea Sparrows soared forth. An immense curtain of readying destruction rushed west to meet the invaders. The cruisers raced to prepare their Harpoons once again. Scores of defensive missiles were on the way. The covering ships gave it everything they had.

A hastening Tomahawk fell. It was followed seconds later by another, and another, and another . . . The action was so fast and remarkably furious it was impossible for Echo Control to follow. The steady elimination of the Mahdi's missiles was relentless. It seemed to go on forever. Explosion after explosion flashed on the western horizon.

No one had a handle on what was occurring. One thing was certain:

Mourad's brutal clans were being destroyed in huge numbers. One by
one, and in dying handfuls, their shattering fragments tumbled into the
deep waters. In the space of sixty frenetic seconds, nearly thirty were
pulled from the sky. Twenty-seven remained in the main group.

The survivors came on.

The second hand reached twelve once more. The sands remaining
in the hourglass were few. Two minutes before the interminable enemy
would reach their objective.

Sweeney brought down another target. In the distance, his impacting
AIM-120 tore apart a crusading missile. So far, Blackjack Section had
knocked down seven ducks with eight shots. The smaller gathering of
steadfast huntsmen was reduced to twenty-three.

Their radios crackled to life. "Blackjack Section, how many missiles do you have left?" Echo Control asked.

"A pair of AIM-132s each and our Sidewinders," was Mitchell's
reply. "But with the nominal heat source emanating from the cruise
missiles and so little time left, I don't think the Sidewinders will be of
any use."

"Hold your AIM-132s for now until we see how many the ships can
handle. We'll send you back in to eliminate any surviving cruise missiles once the ships complete their volleys."

"Roger, Echo Control."

The pair roared skyward, intent on circling behind the onrushing
formation. Blackjack Section would position itself and wait to see
where the last of their missiles was needed.

The swarming destroyers took over from the Hornet pair. Twelve
ships were firing everything they had at the two groups of oncoming
assailants. Explosion after explosion filled the western horizon. The
feverish invaders were dwindling. Seventy would fly no more. Mourad's grand plans were resting on thirty sets of stubby wings. The fixated survivors wouldn't relent in their determined quest.

The Americans had a scant minute to go. Death was nine miles out and drawing near.

Panic was setting in. The carriers instituted severe evasive actions. The fleet's immense array of guns prepared to enter the contest.

Blackjack Section's Hornets chased the cruise missiles across the buffeting waves, hoping to do what they could. The fleet's incessant firing never faltered. And cruise missiles steadily fell. But the Americans' time was nearly up. And the lurid clock refused to stop.

The destroyers never gave in. They fired missile after missile at the incoming threat. A steady destruction of the little Algerian's twisted plan could be traced across the ocean's crests. Another Tomahawk exploded. The others maintained their unwavering course. Twenty missiles left . . . seventeen . . .

Forty-five seconds to go. Fifteen missiles remained. Thirteen . . .

"Blackjack Section, we're almost out of time and there are far too many on the way to the *Eisenhower*. Select your targets on your own initiative and knock them down!"

Mitchell instantly responded to Echo Command's directive. A first AIM-132 sprang into action. Sweeney was brief seconds behind. Neither would have the luxury of watching his lethal missile hunt down its perishing prey. They had to act without delay.

"Worm, we've no more time! Fire your last 132."

"My system's not ready."

"Neither is mine, but it no longer matters. Fire now!"

Both released their final radar-guided missile.

Both hurried shots missed . . .

Each aircraft pulled well away, out of the line of fire. They would have front-row seats for the final breaths of the life-and-death struggle.

The antiaircraft guns erupted in a continuous spray. Computers, radar, guns, and missiles, working as one, the anxious ships fought on. Four miles to go. Eight unrelenting murderers skimmed across the blinding waters. At three miles, chaff and decoys sailed skyward to fool the Chosen One's cold-blooded butchers. Two missiles heading for the *Lincoln* swerved off course, chasing the false images north toward the open sea. Somewhere far out in the Mediterranean, they'd sputter into a watery grave.

Six cruise missiles . . . Just six out of one hundred had escaped the Americans' grasp. Yet if placed just right, six might be enough to sink both carriers.

The last half dozen came on. Two were headed for the *Lincoln*. Four for the *Eisenhower*. One short mile before the end arrived. A handful of ticks was all that remained. It was too late for any of the ships' missiles to activate in time to stop them.

The fleet was down to its final level of defense. Spewing thousands of rounds per minute, all eight destroyers' and both carriers' Phalanx and Vulcan gun systems sprang into action. Broad streams of tracers spewed toward the setting sun, searching for the elusive enemy.

A cruise missile headed for the *Lincoln* was destroyed in a hail of gunfire. The final five came on. Their steadfast journey was near its end. Six hundred yards remained before the target would be reached. They had to be stopped. The guns went on without letup.

Four hundred yards and closing much too fast. The watchful crews could see the unearthly silhouettes skimming across the shimmering ocean to claim them.

Three hundred yards . . . Another, the final missile aimed at the *Lincoln*, exploded and dropped into the ocean's depths. Mourad was down to a final quartet. The last four were headed for the *Eisenhower*. Two hundred yards . . . The guns raged. One hundred yards . . .

Every weapon the Americans had was focused on the rolling waves. Given enough time, they'd get them all. But time was a gift the defenders no longer had. The fleeting seconds of a merciless clock ran out.

It was the *Eisenhower* that would suffer the effects of their failure. The initial one-thousand-pound warhead struck near the rear of the floating city. Twenty feet below the flight deck a massive explosion staggered the carrier. It found one of the multitudes of self-contained ammunition storage areas. A fraction of a second later, the three remaining hangmen hit a handful of feet from the first. Four nearly simultaneous explosions rocked the early evening. They obliterated that portion of the floating giant. The ammunition stores erupted, ravishing the last third of the aging carrier. Goring flames roared high into the air, singeing the clouds a mile above the crippled vessel.

Hundreds perished in the immense explosions. The death toll mounted. Despite the ship's sophisticated suppression systems and the crew's actions, the raging blaze was soon out of control. Fierce fires tore through the crippled aircraft carrier, consuming everything in its path. Within hours it would become apparent the *Eisenhower* was finished.

Circling high above the blackening heavens, Blackjack Section watched the horror unfolding. Silence filled both cockpits. A sickening feeling overcame the astounded pilots. Both understood that if they'd locked on to a single additional cruise missile the ship might have withstood the smaller assault. It was possible that even though the mighty ship would have been significantly damaged, a major part of the tragedy might have been averted and the *Eisenhower* saved. Innumerable lives had been lost because of the failure of each pilot to kill one more Tomahawk.

Many distant families would soon face a hideous reality.

Deep down, the somber pilots realized they'd done their best. Yet at this moment, as they witnessed the beginnings of the anguished drama to follow, such was of little solace.

To make room for the dying carrier's F/A-18s the *Lincoln* would send away most of its nonfighter aircraft. Each flew to air bases in eastern Egypt, Israel, or Saudi Arabia. With its less critical planes and helicopters gone, the surviving Super Hornets would find a home on the final carrier's crammed decks. For days, the *Eisenhower*'s fires would burn. Despite everything its dejected crew attempted, the howling flames couldn't be contained. In the end the fiery metropolis, home to over five thousand, would have to be abandoned. At the conclusion of a tortured week, the listing ship would sink. The *Eisenhower* would settle into a watery grave two thousand feet below the ocean's crest. Eleven hundred bodies would be carried into the depths with it. Millions of disbelieving Americans would sit watching their televisions as the once-invincible ship disappeared.

The Mahdi's goals had been temporarily met. He'd destroyed one of the carriers. He'd shaken an American populace that had to this point viewed the war as little more than detached entertainment to be brought into their homes each evening.

In the end, however, Mourad's grand plan didn't succeed. He wanted a day's control of the skies to eliminate the Marines. He wanted a week to crush Cairo and lead his tanks onto Jerusalem's timeless streets. But he wouldn't receive more than a few confusing hours of tentative mastery of the heavens. During the short window available, there was nothing he could do to capitalize on his advantage. His battered planes and demoralized fliers had suffered severe losses in the afternoon clash and were in no condition to press on toward victory. And after what had happened, the American pilots were out for blood. They were ever more determined to command the skies. If necessary, they'd fly missions around the clock to avenge the loss.

Within hours of the shocking attack, the great country took bold steps to remedy the situation. The planet's most powerful nation dispatched its newest aircraft carriers from Virginia. By the *Eisenhower's* final gasp, the *Gerald Ford* and the *John F. Kennedy* would arrive to take the defeated ship's place. Ninety-six new American fighters would join the *Lincoln's* air armada. From this point on, the Super Hornets would dominate North Africa. For as long as the war continued, the Marines would have the air cover needed to maintain their tenacious foothold.

The die had been forever cast. The Chosen One had given it his best. Yet his victory was incomplete. If he was going to conquer Egypt, he'd have to do so without mastery of the skies. If he was planning on crossing the Sinai to smite the Israelites, he'd have to contend with the swarming Americans overhead. In the days and weeks that followed, his forces were bound to suffer countless casualties as they chased their dream of world domination.

Yet none of that mattered for Muhammad Mourad. With the help of the Iraqis and Iranians, his prophetic struggle to subjugate the planet would go on.

26

S tanding in the open commander's hatch of his Bradley Fighting Vehicle, Army Staff Sergeant Darren Walton pointed his flare gun toward the heavens. He pulled the stubby gun's trigger. A phosphorus flare arched into a star-strewn sky. Directly over the killing field, the soaring flare exploded.

In the expansive desert in front of the cavalry battalion's positions, the shimmering image shined down upon the unseeing eyes of thousands of disjointed Iraqi and Iranian bodies. In places on the gruesome battleground, mutilated corpses were stacked three high. In the distance, the ravaged remains of countless Iraqi tanks littered the sands.

The Iraqis and Iranians made no effort to remove their dead. Even the injured, no matter how extensive their wounds, had been left to fend for themselves.

Those who could, crawled back to their own lines. Those who couldn't, remained where they fell. With razor-sharp pieces of shattered limbs piercing their pliant skin, or holes in their anguished bellies so large their ruptured intestines spilled onto the blowing sands, the wounded beseeched Allah for mercy. In wails and whimpers, in plaintive pleas and pious prayers, the grievously injured begged for the end to come. The horrifying cries of the dying carried across the distant field upon the strong winds. They came to rest upon the Americans' ears. For days without end, the living nightmare of the abandoned beings had gone on without letup. Even after a week, the pitiful sounds of unbridled suffering were something none of the men of the cavalry battalion had learned to tolerate.

They never would.

Whenever the Americans spotted the source of one of these unearthly appeals, a burst of gunfire reached out to extinguish the agony and escort another ill-disposed soul to the next world.

The flittering flare slowly descended toward the valley of death. Walton looked away, shielding his eyes. A wretched smile came over his face. For a week, their maniacal opponents had kept Walton's platoon from finding all but the briefest moments of sleep.

In his battle-weary mind, turnabout was fair play. Interrupting their rivals' fitful dreams was one of the few pleasures he'd enjoyed in the countless hours since his unit's arrival outside Sakakah.

Other than the falling flare's unsettling effect, there'd been no strategic reason for firing it. The Bradleys had state-of-the-art thermal night vision. In combination with the smoldering fires from the last Iraqi armor attack, these systems ensured nothing could move an inch on the piteous ground without the battalion's men spotting it.

Even so, the Americans continued firing the flares at irregular intervals to keep their adversaries on their toes. If nothing else, they served to remind the Iranians and Iraqis that the vestiges of the proud battalion were still here, ready and willing to take their lives.

Of the thirty-four fighting vehicles with which the cavalry unit had arrived, only twenty-two had survived. There'd been four Bradleys in Walton's platoon when they took up defensive positions six miles in front of the Saudi city and its critical crossroads. Now there were only three. Seven days earlier all four had been placed in sloped holes so only their turrets were exposed to the disdaining enemy. Even so, Lieutenant Field's fighting vehicle had been destroyed in the fierce combat two nights prior. A lucky shot from a T-72's massive cannon ripped the twenty-five-ton Bradley apart.

Walton glanced at the burned-out shell on his right. The skeletal remains of Field's Bradley sat in its hole. Its scorched hull was a continual reminder of how tenuous were the lives of the cavalry soldiers. The defeated tracked vehicle's turret was smashed beyond recognition. When Walton dragged them from the blazing Bradley, the charred bodies of its crew of three also had been unrecognizable.

Laid out in shiny coffins, the vanquished fighting team was on an Air Force cargo plane high over the Atlantic. The C-17's hold was filled with identical silver coffins. Each contained the remains of a soldier who would, at least in this lifetime, fight no more. America's dead were coming home. The long journey of the defeated armored vehicle's men was nearing its end.

There were moments in the past days when Walton envied them.

The platoon's Bradleys had carried thirty-six soldiers into battle. After a week of intense struggles, most of the six infantrymen each armored personnel carrier had transported in its rear compartment were gone. Dead or wounded, one by one, 4th Platoon's members had been carried away.

Only fifteen of their original number endured. The three surviving Bradleys' drivers, gunners, and commanders were still in the fight along with six of the cavalry platoon's foot soldiers.

With the death of the platoon's lieutenant, Walton was now in charge. The previously undistinguished thirty-two-year-old sergeant wasn't the typical military leader. His approach had never been the stern autocratic one of the Army's textbooks. He commanded the platoon more through his ample abilities than through his rank. Such a leadership style worked well for the brown-haired, hazel-eyed sergeant. The piles of bodies in front of their position were all the proof needed to show the success of the soft-spoken Walton's methods.

While the settling flare sputtered and died, Walton glanced over at his Bradley's gunner. Specialist Four Miguel Sanchez's eyes were nearly shut.

"Miguel, you sure look like you could use a nap. Wally's been asleep in the driver's compartment for a couple of hours. Why don't you get him to relieve you? If the Iraqi tanks attack again, we'll wake you up."

"Naw, Sarge, I'm okay. Got twenty minutes of sleep yesterday. And a half hour the day before. Let Dimmit sleep. When the time comes to leave, I want our darling private first class wide-awake to drive us out of here as fast as he can."

"Leave? I hate to say it, Miguel, but what makes you think we'll ever leave this place? We've been in this godforsaken hellhole forever. And with each passing hour, I become more and more convinced here's where we're going to stay until the end of time."

"Man, you couldn't be more wrong. Haven't you heard, Sarge? This is our last night in this filthy little corner of nowhere. We're leaving in ten hours. By midday we'll be on our way out of here. Two brigades from the 3rd Infantry arrived yesterday. A friend at battalion called on the radio while you were out checking on the platoon. At this moment, one of those brigades is headed this way to relieve us."

"An entire brigade to take our place? Miguel, your stories get wilder by the minute. I'm afraid this sounds like nothing but wishful thinking. Wasn't it two days ago someone told you the 82nd Airborne was making a parachute drop behind our lines? And yesterday your best source had it from the battalion commander himself that a Marine division was going to land in Kuwait and fight their way across the desert to reinforce our position."

"I know I said those things, Sarge. But you've got to understand, those were just crazy rumors created by guys with too much time on their hands. You really can't pay much attention to that sort of stuff. I'm telling you, though, this one's no rumor. It's really true. There are one hundred and twelve M-1s, one hundred and twelve Bradleys, all kinds of artillery, and more Apache attack helicopters than you can shake a stick at on the way. They'll be here by noon at the latest."

"Is that a fact? And what happens to us when they get here?"

"My friend didn't know for certain. Word is we're headed back across Saudi Arabia to the Persian Gulf. We're to wait for the rest of the division to arrive from Texas. They won't be here for at least another week. Until then, unless these lunatics break through, we kick back and relax. When the division gets here we're supposed to lead some kind of top secret mission to crush the Iranians and Iraqis."

"Oh my God, now we're going on a top secret mission? Miguel, you know I like you and everything. You're the best damn gunner I've ever served with. You don't miss with those TOW missiles of yours. But where do you come up with some of these insane ideas? I swear, the lack of sleep is causing you to hallucinate."

"Sarge, I've spoken nothing but the truth. We're getting out of here. Twelve o'clock, you'll see. This is our last night in these lousy holes. By this time tomorrow, this will be nothing more than a distant memory. We'll be lying on the beach dipping our toes in the bright blue waters while Red Cross donut dollies feed us grapes and caress our tired brows."

"Miguel, you're losing it, man."

"Okay, I made up the donut dolly part. But the rest is true. Come midday we're leaving."

"Then I guess it's official. Specialist Miguel Sanchez has announced for the world to hear that by noon the desert behind us is going to fill with M-1s. Looks like I'd better start packing. Sure wouldn't want to be in the way when all those Abrams show up."

"Sarge, they're on the way . . . You're going to be sorry you ever doubted me when the 3rd Infantry gets here."

"All right, Miguel, whatever you say. Let's hope for the next ten hours those idiots on the far side of the dunes leave us alone. Who knows, maybe they'll decide to sleep in tomorrow. If we're lucky, their commanders might elect to catch up on their beauty rest. Because it sure would be a shame to get killed at this point when you've stated so much help's coming."

An exhausted smile spread across Walton's face.

"I can't believe you're even questioning me," Sanchez said. "You know darn well I'm one of the best sources of information in the entire battalion. Remember back at Fort Hood when I told you they were calling a surprise inspection to check the barracks for drugs with one of those dogs? I was right then, wasn't I? Then there was the time Dimmit got caught doing the colonel's daughter on the parade field. I was right about that too. And I'm right now. With my track record I can't understand why you're doubting what I'm telling you. This is starting to tick me off. I mean really tick me off. Just for that, for not believing me, when this war's over remind me to never speak to you again."

"Whatever you say, Miguel. Now why don't you try to get some sleep? Everything's quiet. Sure looks like the enemy's sleeping right now. So should you."

"Naw, Sarge. I'm staying right here to wait for the 3rd Infantry to come over those ugly hills behind us. Don't want to miss the look on your face when the M-1s arrive."

"I hope you're right about those tanks. Nothing would please me more than being wrong about this one. Unfortunately, I'm afraid I'm not. And I'm sure going to hate seeing the expression on your face when they don't show up tomorrow."

Walton couldn't know it, but Sanchez's rumor was, in fact, true. A brigade from the 3rd Infantry was rolling across the monumental sands at that moment. They were ten hours from relieving the battered battalion.

All the 1st Cavalry soldiers needed to do was live that long.

Because despite appearances the enemy wasn't sleeping.

Deep inside the hastily constructed command bunker, the argument had been raging for hours among the Iraqi leadership.

"Omar, sit down, you're making a fool of yourself," Lieutenant Colonel Yousef Haddad said. "The men are weary of all this killing. They need to rest. Why don't we let them get some sleep? Paradise can wait for a few hours more."

But his best friend and fellow battalion commander, Omar Sura-dein wasn't about to be silenced. "We're nearly there. I can sense it. Victory's within our grasp. The Americans have suffered many losses. They're as exhausted as we are. And they grow weaker with each at-tack. If we concentrate everything we have at one key position, we can break through. Once we do, we'll dash across the desert before anyone figures out what's happened. By this time tomorrow, we'll be setting fire to the Saudi oil fields. Won't that be a pretty sight? Come on, where's your courage? The Iranian infantry's ready. They've even got one of their martyr battalions prepared to show the way. All they're waiting for is our tanks to back them up."

"Omar, the men are tired. And like our previous assaults, this one calls for bravery. Tired men are not courageous men. Many have lost their taste for the fight. They need to sleep if they're going to rebuild their strength. Let's go to bed. We can die as easily in the sunlight as we can now."

"Cowards! Every one of you is nothing more than a coward. I'm ashamed to call myself an Iraqi soldier. Our friends the Iranians are willing to find a blissful beyond this night if that's what Allah wishes. Their martyrs are eager to lead. The political officers have brought them to a fever pitch. There'll be plenty of time to sleep in the honored place we go, my friends. And beautiful virgins to share our beds for eternity. Hear this, each of you, my battalion's going to start its en-gines this instant. I've got thirty-six T-72s ready to support our coura-geous allies in their holy venture."

"Omar, if you insist on this foolish thing, let me call for artillery. We'll soften the Americans before you attack. Maybe we can find a few helicopters to support your operation."

"Allah's true believers need nothing to aid their efforts. Save the artillery shells and helicopters for your soldiers. Maybe after they're given such help and a few days to relax, they'll be brave enough to at-tack the heretics whose presence forever stains the Prophet Muham-mad's sacred homeland."

Suradein stormed out. It wouldn't be long before his tanks would be supporting a five-thousand-man Iranian infantry brigade's attack on the American lines.

The Iranian plan was to first send one of their martyr battalions to cause the enemy to expend the majority of his munitions. With their opponent weakened, they'd concentrate everything they had against a single position in the defenders' lines.

That position was being held by Walton's platoon.

There would be no rest for the fatigued platoon sergeant on this night.

27

Walton's eyes momentarily closed.

"Sarge!" Sanchez called out. "Sarge, we've got company."

"What? Where?"

"Where? There's movement everywhere I look. Got to be at least a battalion of infantry out there, maybe more. Looks like they're preparing to attack."

Just then, three dozen T-72 engines roared to life. The first of the hideous tanks crept toward the front lines.

"Aw, shit. They're bringing their Iraqi friends again." Walton spoke into the radio. "Two-Six, this is Alpha-Four-Five. Two-Six, this is Alpha-Four-Five."

Three miles south, the call was answered. "Roger, Alpha-Four-Five," the familiar voice of the battalion radio operator said.

"Two-Six, be advised we've got a strong infantry force directly in front of us. They're getting ready to attack. Sounds like lots of armored vehicles headed this way too. Request immediate air support."

"Okay, Alpha-Four-Five. I'll call for fighters. Then I'll wake the battalion commander and see if he'll release our last three Apaches to hold them until the jet jockeys arrive."

"While you're at it, Two-Six, can you scrounge up some ammunition for our Bushmaster cannons, machine guns, and rifles? We're running low. And some additional TOWs wouldn't hurt. My three Bradleys only have about a dozen missiles between them."

"That I can do, Alpha-Four-Five. We received a complete resupply an hour ago. Got more stuff than anyone knows what to do with. You'd think with all the support helicopters left, they were servicing a brigade rather than a battalion. I'll get one of the reserve platoons headed your direction. We'll put a few crates of TOWs and all the ammunition they can hold into their Bradleys and bring it to you."

"Make it fast. It looks like the infantry could charge at any second."

"They'll be there in fifteen minutes."

Walton put down the handset.

"Sarge," Sanchez said, "I've been watching the Iranian preparations. This one looks different somehow."

Walton peered across the far field. "Different? What's different?"

"The pieces don't fit. Something's not quite right about their actions. There's some strange goings-on over there."

"What's so strange? The Iranian infantry's about to charge and the Iraqi tanks are backing them up. There's nothing unusual about that. It's like they've been doing every few hours for the past week."

"Maybe so. But I swear there's something odd about their activity. I haven't put my finger on it yet, but those bastards are up to no good."

"Wake Wally and get him out there with his M-4. We're going to need every rifle we've got for this one. As soon as he's outside, button up good and tight."

Sanchez spoke into the intercom. "Dimmit, you awake?" The corporal banged on the driver's compartment. "Can you hear me, Dimmit? Get your ass up and get outside. The Iranians are getting ready to attack."

The sleepy PFC emerged from the driver's area in the front of the Bradley. He wandered over to a sandbagged foxhole twenty yards to the left. The armored vehicle's driver rubbed his tired eyes, let out a wide yawn, and took the safety off his rifle. In the distance, the first group of Iranians marched single file onto the humble field. They continued forward until they passed the last of the burning tanks. Once there, they began spreading out side by side to create a lengthy line three hundred yards long in front of the demolished Iraqi armor. The moment the stretching formation was in place, a shrill whistle sounded. The Iranians started running across the chaotic ground. The lovers of Islam were screaming at the top of their lungs. The martyr battalion's initial wave of three hundred had entered the coming contest. A thousand yards of open ground separated them from the Americans. An identical arrangement of anxious participants appeared behind the first on the crest. As the preceding array had done, they marched forward until they reached the front of the armor and started to disperse. They were ready to race forward upon command. Behind the small hill, out of sight of the Americans, two more queues waited.

"Here they come!" Sanchez said. He dropped into the compartment, grabbed his hatch, and pulled it shut.

Walton took one last look at the charging enemy and slipped inside the Bradley. He reached up and secured his hatch cover. "Get ready to line up your TOWs, Miguel. If they do this one like the others, the tanks will appear as soon as the last of the infantry comes over the top of the hill." The platoon sergeant spoke into the radio again. "Fourth Platoon, reinforcements and ammunition are on the way. Nobody panic. Hang tight and get those machine guns and Bushmasters ready. Make every shot count. Hold your fire until they're within range, then let them have it with everything you've got. We'll attack the infantry at three hundred yards. Open fire on my cue. When the tanks appear, select your targets and release your TOWs as you see fit."

Walton and Sanchez watched the approaching formation through their night-vision system. The Iranians didn't hesitate. Stretching one hundred and fifty yards in both directions, they rushed toward the American positions. Each Iranian was exactly three feet from the ones on his left and right. Hurdling the piles of ever-increasing bodies, they were running at top speed. The sprinting file was perfectly straight. Not one of the advancing souls surged ahead or fell back. Fifty yards behind the opening wave, political officers, swords in one hand, pistols in the other, trailed the procession.

"That's weird," Walton said. "Usually the Iranian attacks are really sloppy. But this one's coming toward us with absolute precision. How are they staying together like that when they're running as fast as they can?"

"I'm telling you, Sarge, something's wrong here."

At that moment, in the center of the column, one of the Iranians tripped over the putrid remains of a long-dead countryman. Instead of staying where he'd fallen, the faltering soldier was dragged across thirty yards of rock and sand. The far-off figure clawed his way to his feet. None the worse for wear, he returned to running.

Both Americans witnessed what had transpired.

"What the hell?" Walton said.

"Rope! That's what it is. They're tied together with a thick rope. If you look real hard, you can just make it out. They've got it wrapped around their waists. It's connected to those on either side of them."

"But that's crazy. Nobody in their right mind sends foot soldiers into battle with those kinds of restrictions on their movement. Infantry needs flexibility if it's going to succeed. Tied together these guys don't have a chance. They're begging to be slaughtered. Why in the world would they do something so stupid?"

The Iranians had covered two hundred yards. The fierce whistle, long and eerie, sounded again. A second screaming formation, identical to the first in every respect, started running toward the bewildered soldiers. Behind them, more political officers raced forward. A new group of devotees appeared on the crest and moved forward to take their places in front of the crushed tanks. They watched the events unfolding in front of them with rapt attention.

Each knew his turn would soon come.

The lead elements were eight hundred yards away. There were five hundred to go before the platoon would open fire. In the command Bradley they watched the oncoming file, waiting for the Iranians to reach the attack point Walton had drawn in the sand.

Another two hundred yards were painfully crossed. The nearly immeasurable bodies littering their path was growing. The initial order's piercing cries of death for America weren't as loud or as determined as they'd been two minutes earlier. The formation had completed four hundred yards of running at full speed. It was impossible to maintain such a torrid pace any longer. The extreme exertion involved in the self-destructive effort made every breath a painful one. The tethered line slowed. Yet, propelled by its own weight, it struggled forward. The political officers, berating and cajoling, spurred their floundering charges. The second group followed, an eighth of a mile behind. Another piercing whistle blast could be heard over the screaming martyrs. In front of the burning armor, the third three hundred started toward the paradise promised by the American guns.

"Fire a flare," Sanchez said.

"What?"

"Open up and fire a flare. I want to check something."

Both soldiers popped their hatches. Walton pointed the flare gun into the heavens and pulled the trigger. Another flare sailed into the ominous night. It burst over the center of the angst-covered ground. Its offensive glow had no effect on the shrieking Persians. Conventional infantry tactics called for the exposed order to drop to their chests and lie perfectly still until the betraying light went out. Yet even under the harsh glow, the maniacal charge didn't pause in the slightest. The cavalry soldiers shielded their eyes and peered at the persistent enemy.

"That's what I thought I'd seen," Sanchez said. "I can't imagine why but take a good look, those in the first formation don't have rifles."

"What? How can that be?"

Walton searched the faraway sands. Miguel was right. With the exception of the political officers, there wasn't a weapon to be found. He scanned the more distant second and third arrangements. The results were the same. None of the agitated figures was carrying a rifle. An inquisitive expression, filled with confusion, came to the platoon sergeant's face. What was occurring was completely illogical. He'd no explanation for any of this. And not the slightest clue what the Iranians were doing.

It wouldn't be much longer, however, before an answer to the madness would appear. It was a result Walton never would've imagined, even in his wildest dreams.

For some inexplicable reason, one of the stumbling figures attracted his attention. The muddled form looked like all the others, but something about the striving Iranian caught his eye. He raised his binoculars. From across the cluttered landscape, he stared at his ardent adversary. With the blinding flare's sheer light raining down, the oncoming individual was as clear as if he were standing a few feet from the Bradley.

Walton could see every crease in his ragged uniform. The fatigue-clad Islamic was racing as fast as his despairing legs would carry him toward a certain death. The platoon leader raised the binoculars to look at his fateful foe's face. Unbelievably, the doomed figure was actually smiling.

Through the field glasses, Walton watched the soldier's painful progress, trying to comprehend what was so powerful it could cause a person to ignore the instinct for survival. For a moment, his thoughts wandered.

Suddenly the startled cavalry soldier realized there was something else hidden in the features of his dirt-streaked opponent. Something so horrible his mind denied its existence. For a split second, he refused to accept what his eyes were seeing. Yet it couldn't be rejected for long. Like a bolt of lightning, the truth of Walton's discovery struck deep within him. The startled Bradley commander froze. He did a double take, hoping against hope his sleep-starved brain had erred in its observations.

He lowered the glasses to his chest, unwilling to accept the sinister secret he'd uncovered. He shoved the binoculars back to his face and took a second look. He had to ensure he wasn't mistaken.

But the results were the same. There could be no doubt what he beheld.

The running Iranian was a child.

28

Walton quickly focused on the screaming image to the boy's left. He held the binoculars steady, searching a second set of features. Once again, the outcome was the same. It was another child. He frantically scanned the procession, hoping for an answer. When he was through, he let the binoculars drop.

He instantly understood the monstrous result the enemy was going to force upon him. Sadness overwhelmed the stunned American. Pain welled deep within his disbelieving psyche. His sorrow burst forth, racing through him with electrifying speed. Consuming agony came to rest in the platoon sergeant's eyes.

"Miguel, they're children. Boys of nine or ten. Got a few little girls mixed in."

"What? Are you sure, Sarge?"

Walton passed the binoculars to his gunner. Sanchez looked upon the grievous ground. It didn't take long for the normally animated specialist to confirm his platoon sergeant's findings.

"My daughters are that age," Walton said.

"I don't understand. This doesn't make any sense. What are children doing in the middle of this nightmare?"

"I wish I knew."

"Wake me up and tell me this isn't happening. They should be home playing Little League or dressing their Barbies. Instead they're running to their deaths in this godforsaken place. Jesus, they don't even have a way to defend themselves. Give me one good reason why they're sending children out to be butchered."

The answer came to Walton. "The bastards are using them as cannon fodder, Miguel. I'd heard they did similar things when they fought the Iraqis back in the 1980s. Gave mothers extra food if they handed over their children to be used as human minesweepers. Until this moment, I hadn't believed those stories. But there's no doubt what they're doing. They're sacrificing the children to force us to expend our ammunition. Once we've run out, they'll send their regular units and the Iraqi armor to finish us off. What they don't realize is with the battalion's last resupply, their plan will fail. As of an hour ago, we've got enough ammunition to kill all the children the Iranians send against us until time itself runs out."

"What're we going to do? I sure didn't enlist to murder helpless babies."

Walton paused. He turned to his gunner and spoke in a voice devoid of emotion. "What choice do we have? It'll be like gunning down my own daughters. But we're left with no options. We're going to kill those children. If we don't, with or without weapons, they'll sweep across this disgusting desert and overwhelm us. Once they have, those sweet children you're worried about will take your knife and slit your throat from ear to ear. When they're through they'll rip out your entrails and joyously dance upon them. So there's nothing we can do. Whether we want it or not, this has been forced upon us. We're going to aim our machine guns and rifles onto that field and we're going to pull the triggers. We're going to kill them. And we're going to continue doing so until none are left. Now button up your hatch and get ready."

The martyrs' march came on. The first wave was five hundred

yards away. The American guns were ready. And the condemned children were relentless. The Iranians struggled toward the platoon's positions. Four hundred yards. The death whistle blew a final time. The fourth sequence began running across the clamoring desert. The last group's venomous wails joined with those of the earlier conscripts. Their voices filled the night with bloodcurdling hatred for the contemptible servants of Satan. Twelve hundred children were headed toward a certain end. Behind the final group, regular Iranian infantry, armed to the teeth, appeared. Their attack would commence once the lambs finished their esteemed purpose. Throughout the length of the strife-filled no-man's-land, running, yelling children hastened toward their end.

The stilled cavalry platoon waited. The harbingers of death would soon be upon them.

Three hundred yards. The boundary was crossed. Walton blocked all conscious thought.

He pulled the trigger on his machine gun. In unison, the remainder of the platoon opened fire.

As the relentless slaughter continued, from the area behind his platoon, four fighting vehicle machine guns joined in on the unmerciful serenade. The reserve platoon had arrived. Soldiers, M-4s at the ready, poured from the rear of each Bradley.

"Miguel, before the Iranian infantry charges, take Wally and get the ammunition and TOWs from the relief platoon. Make sure all three Bradleys and each of our men have enough of everything to withstand a determined attack."

"Okay, Sarge. I'm on my way." Sanchez opened the hatch and disappeared into the night.

Alone in the compartment, Walton continued firing at the unrelenting lines of screaming children. They'd seen the holocaust reaching out to devour the initial order. Yet their visions of the remarkable place the mullahs professed propelled them toward that same vilified end.

From the Bradleys' machine guns and soldiers' rifles, death spilled forth upon the fiendish field.

Walton's stomach was churning. Yet with each pull of the trigger, his mind felt less and less. The platoon sergeant's trance was only interrupted when Sanchez and Dimmit arrived beneath the weight of machine-gun cartridges and cases of TOW missiles. The resupply was soon accomplished.

"Got a few more deliveries to make, Sarge," Sanchez said. "Then I'll be back to lend you a hand."

It wasn't long before he returned to his position next to the Bradley's commander. "Took a look around when I was out there. Using the children to screen their advance, Iranian infantry's sneaking forward."

"All right, Miguel, get those TOWs ready. Iraqi armor will be close on their heels."

As if on cue, the first of the T-72s appeared in the distance. The Iraqi tank fired a hurried round from its main cannon. The shot went high, harmlessly smashing into the trackless lands behind the platoon's position.

Sanchez lined up his TOW through the Bradley's periscope. "In about ten seconds you can scratch one Iraqi tank."

"He's all yours, Miguel. After what they've done to these children, hell's hottest fires are too damn good for any of them. But I'm afraid that's the best we can do as retribution for the suffering they've caused. Send the sorry son of a bitch on his way."

Sanchez fired the first of his pair of online TOWs. The deadly missile ripped across a thousand yards of disorderly battlefield. It smashed head-on into the malignant tank. A thunderous explosion followed by a billowing ball of flames rose skyward. It was a sight the sands of the Middle East had witnessed innumerable times in the past three weeks.

"There's one less tank to worry about," Sanchez said. "As soon as another shows its ugly head, I'll make the score good guys two, Iraqis zero."

"That's fine, Miguel, I know you'll do your best. But tell me, where's the air support we were promised? This is going to be a whole lot harder if we've got to do it by ourselves."

Walton was back on the radio. "Two-Six, this is Alpha-Four-Five."

"Roger, Alpha-Four-Five."

"Where's the air support? The T-72s are about to attack."

"Hang tight. Apaches are on the way. ETA's four minutes. Six Air Force F-16s are airborne. They're eight minutes out and itching for a fight."

"Roger, Two-Six, thanks for the encouraging news."

The handset was returned to its receiver, and Walton's fingers firmly wrapped around his machine gun's grips before he even realized. On this night, the killing wasn't nearly complete.

What followed wasn't so much a battle as a bloodbath. The Iranians' tactics had failed. Each Bradley was fully stocked and more than ready to dispatch a perverse enemy willing to hide behind the deaths of its children. The Iranians had the numbers. But the Americans had the skill, solid defensive positions, and superior weapons. The Bradley gunners were lethal in their ability to unleash their missiles, destroy two tanks, and quickly reload to initiate another round of devastation. And the attack helicopters turned up right on schedule. The Army's top-of-the-line Apaches were as strong and lethal as the Marine Cobras. With their appearance, the T-72s were forever overmatched.

When the F-16s arrived, there was little to do but clean up the scattered remains of the doomed Iraqi armor. With smart bombs and deadly cannons, the fighters eliminated the last of the overwhelmed tanks and infantry.

At shortly after four on a hideous black morning, the firing finally stopped. When it did, Walton and Sanchez opened their hatches to survey the incomprehensible display. The defeat was total. Thirty-six Iraqi tanks had been destroyed. Five thousand Iranian infantry and twelve hundred children were dead or severely injured.

American losses were a single Bradley, nine dead, and sixteen wounded.

In the hours following the ill-conceived struggle, the frightful screams of the mortally wounded, many of them children, pierced the poisonous battlefield. Once again, the enemy turned his back and left the dying to the Americans.

Walton's machine gun spit out a distorted world's final judgment in short, injurious bursts. Each child's cringing death stabbed ever deeper into the platoon sergeant's heart until he sensed nothing from the top of his head to the tips of his toes. Yet despite his determined efforts, the cries of those in unbearable agony went on until he believed they'd never stop.

To the relief of all, there'd be no more attacks prior to the 3rd Infantry's arrival.

With the coming of the long-awaited dawn, the Bradley commanders continued the distasteful task of locating and eliminating the Iranian casualties upon the banishing ground.

Shortly before ten on a smoke-filled morning, a final burst of gunfire brought an unearthly calm to the crimson-choked sands. Walton's hands, frozen in place, had to be pried loose. While he surveyed the anguish he'd wrought, tears poured down the platoon sergeant's face. His tears would eventually stop. For the remainder of his days, however, the overwhelming damage to his anguished existence would never be fully repaired. In the long years that followed, not once did he talk to anyone outside his platoon about what had happened in the bleak desert outside Sakakah.

After loathsome days and sleepless nights, the stillness of the ruinous scene was deafening.

They heard them before they saw them. For over an hour, the growing sounds of the relief column reached across the far-flung Arabian dunes to fall upon the embattled battalion's ears. The 2nd Brigade of the 3rd Mechanized Infantry was drawing near.

With each passing minute Sanchez's smile grew. As the first of the Abrams peaked over the ocher hills behind them, the specialist's satisfaction reached from ear to ear. He glanced over at Walton. The astonished sergeant sat in a disbelieving hush.

"What'd I tell ya!" Sanchez exclaimed. "You and I are minutes away from leaving this place."

"I guess you were right, Miguel. Who knows, maybe the rest of your prediction will come true. After last night, I'd believe almost anything. We might really be headed back to rest and prepare for some top secret mission."

As the sun reached its highest point, the scorching sands behind the embittered battalion filled with M-1s and Bradleys.

At least for the moment, Darren Walton's ordeal was over.

But for another soldier caught in this suffocating war, the anguish was about to increase tenfold.

29

For half a century the burgundy-bereted soldiers of the 82nd Airborne Division had shared Fort Bragg, North Carolina, with the green-bereted members of American Special Forces. Throughout their history, there'd never been any love lost between the two organizations. In the tough bars of Fayetteville they'd battled for as long as anyone cared to remember.

A bleak October day may have been the sole time in the two units' histories when Special Forces soldiers were glad to see the appearance of a burgundy beret.

It hadn't been long after Alpha 6333's retreat into Old Cairo that the welcome word had come—help was on the way. The 82nd Airborne's soldiers would soon be loading onto commercial airliners for the ten-hour flight to the Middle East. And as the news spread, even the despondent Egyptian army rallied. The Egyptian infantry company scheduled to support Alpha 6333 was twelve hours late in arriving. Yet arrive they finally did. Without them, the Green Beret detachment would've had no chance of surviving the night.

Late in the morning, the first of the airliners appeared. Carrying two hundred men and as much equipment as their jammed cargo holds could contain, the planes landed one behind another throughout the afternoon and well into the evening.

Close to sundown, nearly thirty hours after the A Team's abandonment of Rhoda Island, a company of burgundy berets showed up in the section of Old Cairo being held by what remained of the detachment. After an infinite black night and torturous gray day of house-to-house fighting, the Special Forces team and their Egyptian support had fallen back even farther into the heart of the city. And the Americans' numbers had dropped from ten to eight. They'd left the bodies of two of their countrymen, victims of a direct hit from a Pan-Arab mortar shell, in the bombed-out skeleton of an ancient marketplace.

Not one of the team's survivors had escaped the long hours unharmed. Each had suffered the indignities of fierce combat. Their wounds ran the gamut from light to severe. In time, if they survived to the war's conclusion, their physical injuries would heal. The damage to their struggling psyches, however, probably never would. Yet each fought with every ounce of courage and strength he could muster. And finally the burgundy berets appeared. Battered and staggering, but still unbeaten, the Green Berets prepared to temporarily turn their sector of the city over to the airborne company.

There was one task remaining before leaving for a welcome respite and their first sleep in three days. Captain Morrow agreed with the 82nd Airborne company commander's assessment. Further demolition needed to be performed to secure the area from enemy tanks.

Morrow found Sanders sitting in the shadows of a crumbling building with his rucksack and equipment packed to leave. Beneath his tattered beret a trail of blood, thick and coagulating, peeked through the soiled bandages on the right side of his skull. A solid red line reached down the brash sergeant's neck, staining his uniform's collar.

Sanders looked up at his commander and smiled. "So when are we leaving, sir?"

"Shortly. Just a few loose ends to tie up and we'll be on our way. How's your injury?"

"I'll live, sir," Sanders replied. "I'm still a little groggy from the blow I received from that falling beam. And this headache won't stop."

"Even so, you were extremely lucky. If Donovan hadn't screamed a warning, you'd have been a goner for sure."

"Yes, sir."

"I wouldn't sweat the headache too much. I've been assured by the team medics it's nothing more than the lingering effects of the slight concussion you received."

"The Chosen One's 'gift' isn't going to stop me, sir. All I need are a few days of sleep and a pretty woman or two to whisper words of love and adoration and I'll be fine."

"I'm afraid," Morrow said, "that before we find those soft beds and adoring women, I need you to do something for me."

"What's that, sir?"

"Pan-Arabs have succeeded in building some makeshift bridges over the Nile. Despite our air support knocking them out as quickly as they erect them, a handful of tanks have crossed the river and joined Mourad's infantry. More are sure to follow. Something has to be done to counter the enemy's actions. We've got to blow a few of the buildings in front of us to block the tanks' paths. That will force them to enter the city through some traps the 82nd's setting up. That's where you come in. Still got plenty of explosives in your rucksack?"

"Sir, you've got to be kidding. We're all exhausted, and that certainly includes me. My head's pounding so hard it's coming apart. I can barely keep my eyes open. Like everybody else, I'm more than ready to get out of here. And you want another demolition job?"

"That's exactly what I want, Sergeant Sanders."

"Why doesn't the 82nd blow the buildings themselves?"

"We're being relieved by an infantry company. You know there aren't any demolition people with them. Most of their ordnance folks have yet to arrive. They're spread real thin right now. There's demolitions work all over the city. Who knows when they'll wander out here to handle this one? The 82nd company commander doesn't want to sit around and hope they show. That could take hours. Maybe even days. If they wait, it might be too late to stop Mourad's tanks from smashing through our lines. And you know what'll happen next. All hell will break loose. Everything this team's suffered, every horrible attack we've beaten back, will've been for nothing. Once the armor's in the clear, there'll be nothing to stop them. The Chosen One's forces will reach the center of the city by midnight. If that occurs, you can forget about getting any rest. Tired or not, we'll be thrown back into the front lines."

"But, sir, I—"

"Look, Sanders, there's nothing to it. One simple mission and we'll be relieved. All I want you to do is blow a handful of buildings at three intersections a few blocks west of here. For someone with your skills it'll be a piece of cake. You'll be back in an hour. Abernathy and Porter will go along to provide support."

"But, sir, everything west of here's in enemy hands. What if when we get there, the whole place is crawling with Mourad's troops?"

"Then I'm afraid you'll just have to deal with the situation. Come on, Sanders, it's not going to be that difficult. Blow a few buildings and I'll personally find you the prettiest woman your eyes have ever seen."

"Sir, what good are women if I don't make it back? Another mission, even if it's as simple as you claim, really wasn't what I had in mind. Isn't there another way to handle this? Maybe the 82nd could call in a few well-placed artillery rounds to blow those buildings. That might work as well as sending me smack into the middle of thousands of lunatics who'd enjoy nothing more than lopping off my head."

"Enough already. I know we're tired and ready to go, so I've tried to be more tolerant than usual. But I'm still in command here. I'm the one who gets paid to make the tough decisions. And this one's been made. I don't know why I've wasted time trying to reason with you. When I give an order I expect it to be obeyed. Is that clear, Sergeant?"

"Yes, sir. Perfectly clear."

"Then the subject's no longer open for debate. This is something that's got to be done. So you're wasting your breath trying to get out of it. It'll be dark soon. The faster you accomplish your assignment, the faster we find those soft beds. Now stop stalling and get up off your rear. Let's go over what I want you to do."

30

With Abernathy and Porter to watch over him, the fresh-faced sergeant headed into the half-light. The sunset was drawing near. It would be upon them well before they returned to their own lines. Down narrow, twisting streets the silent trio moved. The initial target was three blocks west and two south. The going was cautious and calculated. Slipping in and out of the lengthening shadows, the phantomlike figures made their way toward the first intersection. To all but the most highly trained eyes, their presence couldn't be detected.

In ten minutes, they arrived. They'd reached one of the main crossroads in Old Cairo. The trio took a careful look around. Their enduring rival was nowhere to be found.

"Okay, this is one the captain wants blocked," Abernathy whispered. "And there's no sign of any of the Chosen One's followers. But that could change at any moment."

"It's about time for prayers," Porter said. "Hopefully, they're busy fulfilling their duty to Allah, and we've got a few minutes to get the job done without interference."

"Maybe," Abernathy said, "but I wouldn't count on it. We need to stay alert. Sanders, figure out what you're going to do, do it, and let's get out of here."

The demolition expert appraised the situation. He examined the damaged buildings to determine what it would take to create a pile of rubble so high and deep it would ensure a forty-seven-ton T-72 couldn't breach it. It wasn't long before he had his answer.

"I'll need to demolish the apartment building on the far corner and the storefront on this one. Might have to take down a third building if those two don't finish the job."

"How long's it going to take?"

"Ten . . . fifteen minutes maybe. No longer than that. I'll start with the apartment. Once I've blown it, we'll have a better idea what more we need to do."

"Okay. Wait for us to find a place to cover you and then get to it."

Porter and Abernathy started withdrawing from the crossroads, each hugging the frail edges of the fading afternoon.

"Hey, where are you two going?" Sanders asked. "Don't leave me in the open by myself. I want you out front, not hiding somewhere behind me."

The pair stopped and looked at each other. Grins spread from the corners of their mouths.

"Charlie," Porter answered, "think about what you just said. We've got to be behind you. If we're in front when you destroy the first building and you succeed in blocking things, how do you propose we get back on this side?"

A sheepish smile came over Sanders's filthy face. "Oh yeah. What the hell am I saying? Man, I'm tired. Three days without sleep has scrambled my brain. And this headache I've been walking around with for the better part of the afternoon isn't helping."

"Look," Abernathy said, "after what we've gone through, no one's thinking clearly. And neither of us wants to be on this assignment any more than you. But we've got a job to do. So let's focus the best we can. As soon as we find safe vantage points, you can get started."

With their rifles at the ready, the duo turned and edged down the roadway. Thirty yards behind, they took up covering positions in heavily shaded doorways. Sanders turned toward them. Even to his skilled eyes, neither was visible. He nervously glanced at the deserted streets around him.

The Sahara winds suddenly stilled. In the distance an abandoned dog, its belly empty, eerily howled. Sanders glanced toward the east once more, searching for his cohorts' hiding places. He knew they were there, watchful and vigilant. Yet for the life of him, he could find no trace of either. The apprehensive engineer had never felt more alone, or more vulnerable, in his life. He could sense death's whisper lingering in the twilight, waiting for him to make a mistake.

"You two better stay alert for the bad guys," he mumbled. "It's my ass hanging out here."

With the deepest hues of a developing dusk taking hold of what remained of the day, Sanders edged across the broad street. He stopped in front of the four-story apartment and took another hurried look around. Everything was strangely quiet. Not a single sound or hint of movement reached his well-defined senses. There were no signs of friend or enemy alike. He reached into his rucksack and withdrew the explosives.

It wasn't long before the job was completed and the lethal team on the move again. The destruction of two buildings was all it took to ensure Mourad's tanks would find the critical intersection impassable. Four blocks north and one farther west waited their next objective.

Other than a brief pause for Porter and Abernathy to slit the throats of a couple of careless sentries, everything was on schedule.

The second crossing, smaller and already partially blocked by the haphazard remains of several decrepit dwellings, wasn't as challenging as the first had been. The task was effortlessly accomplished, and in minutes they were on their way. Night was falling full upon them.

Two blocks north and one east, toward their own lines, waited their final responsibility. Hiding behind the ongoing prayers, the deadly assembly arrived without incident.

Yet as they reached their last objective evening prayers came to an end.

"Okay," Abernathy said, "here's the third one. Sanders, how many buildings do you need to take down to do the job?"

He surveyed the scene. Every timeless structure in the area had suffered severe damage from the Chosen One's artillery attacks.

"Just this one right here," he said. He pointed to an old six-story hotel on the southwest corner. He glanced at the nearly indistinguishable sign on the front of the run-down building. In the half-light he could make out the words *Hotel Louraine*.

"Reminds me of an old fleabag hotel I stayed in while passing through Memphis a few years back. The place was a dump. But the girl across the hall soon made me forget all about it. You know, I think her name might have been Louraine. Or something like that. Sure made for one hell of a weekend. Man, that woman was wild, and more than eager for some Sanders action."

"Here we are in the middle of nowhere. The Mahdi's soldiers are probably crawling all around us," Porter said, "and Charlie's thinking of a woman."

"Yep. We could be dead before we knew what hit us," Abernathy added. "Leave it up to Sanders to see a dumpy hotel and find a girl to reminisce about."

"If you'd have seen her, you'd be reminiscing too," Sanders answered. "But enough of that Louraine. Once I'm through, this one will leave a pile of rubble twenty feet high right in the middle of the road. Nothing will be able to get through here."

"Do you have enough explosives to finish the job?" Abernathy asked.

"Hell, it won't take much. This place is so rickety if you breathe on it hard it's likely to fall. In ten minutes, it'll be nothing but a pile of sticks and mortar. And we'll be on our way to rest, relaxation, and pursuit of the opposite sex. I can't wait for those women the captain promised."

"You should be so lucky," Porter said. "I suspect as soon as we get back, Captain Morrow won't remember one word of what he's told us. So before you get carried away with your erotic visions, wait for us to find a good spot to cover you."

The stealthy pair crept into the darkness. Eighty feet east, Abernathy and Porter dropped into the gloom on opposite sides of the foreboding street. Sanders glanced in their direction. He'd seen exactly where they'd entered the frail wisps of light, yet neither was visible. He knew they were there. Yet for the life of him, he couldn't tell where. He shook his head in amazement at their remarkable abilities.

"I swear those two aren't human," he muttered, his words barely audible. "The way they appear and disappear. The devil himself must have trained them to do what they do."

He started attaching the explosives to the final building. A smile came to his haggard face. It was nearly over. The weight of this last mission had been lifted from his shoulders.

Sanders, however, had relaxed too soon.

Porter sensed their presence well before he saw them. In the distance, a strong infantry force was moving down the narrow street. Leapfrogging from building to building, the careful Pan-Arabs edged forward. There appeared to be close to one hundred in their number. For now, there was no need for the Green Berets to panic. The point element of Mourad's soldiers was two blocks away. Porter signaled to Abernathy. The senior sergeant indicated his awareness of the approaching formation. Both crouched in the black void of the filthy gutters, watching their adversaries' movements. So far, none of the Americans had been spotted by the advancing enemy.

Busy with his preparations to destroy the aging building, and forever lost in his burgeoning fantasies of soft beds and beautiful women, Sanders didn't notice the threat drawing near.

"How many do you count?" Porter whispered.

"Can't tell. But it's way more than we can handle," was Abernathy's response.

"Want me to slip up there and get Charlie?"

"Negative. There are too many watchful eyes coming this way. Even as good as you are, there's not much chance of getting to him without being spotted. If that happens, he'll have no chance. And they'll likely get you too."

"What're we going to do?"

"We're going to wait. Maybe they'll turn onto one of the side streets, or Sanders will spot them and figure a way out."

Unfortunately, the young Green Beret was too distracted by his idyllic dreams to worry about the growing danger.

"Charlie, look up," Porter pleaded.

But Sanders continued to absentmindedly prepare his explosives. The Pan-Arabs closed to within a block and a half. They'd yet to locate the figure kneeling deep within the darkness of the downtrodden structure.

"Dammit, Sanders," Abernathy said, "what the hell's wrong with you? Where's your head? Look up, you crazy bastard."

Yet Sanders's mind was anywhere but there.

"What're we going to do?" Porter asked.

"What else can we do? Give them another fifty yards. If they don't turn when they reach the final side street, we'll open fire. That's sure to get Sanders's attention. Hopefully, he's still in good enough shape to run like hell. Because if he doesn't they're bound to nail him. If he catches a break and makes it to our position, we'll disappear down one of the streets behind us and hightail it for home. Our lines are only three blocks away. I know we can get to safety no matter how many of Mourad's followers are prowling around."

They waited and watched, praying for Sanders to notice the overwhelming band headed for him. Straight and steady, the Chosen One's soldiers came on. Doorway by doorway, house by house, they moved up the roadway. They'd nearly reached the point where Abernathy and Porter planned to open fire. The ambush team stared intently at the approaching enemy. There appeared to be no doubt. The potent force was headed for where Sanders was working. In the heavy half-light, two M-4s were raised and pointed in their direction.

Without warning, a Pan-Arab soldier stepped out of a constricted alleyway not more than twenty feet in front of the waiting pair.

"What the hell?" Abernathy screamed.

He opened fire. The Libyan fell to the sidewalk, bullet holes painted across his chest.

A second poked his head out. Porter blew it off with one quick burst. The slender passage was full of movement. A significant element had surprised the Americans.

"Where'd they come from?" Porter excitedly asked.

"Who knows? We were so busy watching Sanders that we did what he did. We got distracted. Wherever they're from, there are way too many of them. Let's get out of here while we still can."

"What about Sanders?"

"There's nothing we can do for him. He's on his own. Let's go."

Both sprayed a final volley toward the sheltered opening. By the time the echoing sounds of gunfire stopped, they were gone.

A dozen of the Mahdi's followers edged toward the front of the alley. The minute they were certain it was safe, they took up positions on both sides of the street.

A startled Sanders's soaring daydreams were forever shattered. A hundred of the enemy were headed toward him. Still more blocked his retreat. He looked south down the side street only to find rifle-carrying figures in the distance. He was cut off. He frantically searched for a way out. None, however, presented itself.

The detachment's junior member edged deeper into the murky protection of the old hotel. The developing night continued to mask his presence. The peeling door to the Hotel Louraine was ajar. The entrance was a few feet away. He peered inside the shrouded doorway.

He could see nothing but darkness beyond the slender opening. He waited and listened. The decaying hotel was frightfully silent. Sanders took a frenzied look around, hoping to find another solution. Yet once again, no answer appeared.

With as little movement as possible he scooped up his rucksack and rifle. He eased inside the smothering building, and without the slightest sound, closed the tired door behind him.

31

The dingy lobby was dank and musty. The air in the room lay heavy and stale upon the encroaching night. It pressed down upon the grimy hotel's reluctant visitor. The pungent odors of rotting carpet and the thousands of unwashed bodies who'd passed through this place in the past century filled every corner of the cramped entryway. The fading furniture was strewn about. It was obvious, even in the scant threads of light penetrating the old structure, that the location had been abandoned in a great hurry.

To his right, Sanders could make out a timeworn stairway leading to the upper floors. A small dining area nestled behind it. Next to the stairs sat a primitive elevator of long-forgotten design. Feeling his way, his rifle poised, Sanders moved farther into the room. Step by wary step, he crept through the small foyer. His senses were keenly alive.

Smothering himself in the sheltering darkness, he eased into the hotel. He needed time to adjust to the sparse light. But he was unsure if the enemy had spotted his hasty actions. For all he knew, one hundred angry souls were closing for the kill. He stumbled over the pieces of a cheap lamp lying on the threadbare rug. He reached for his flashlight but thought better of it. With nothing but his instincts to guide him, he pressed into the nearly sightless world. Well within the room, he stopped for the briefest moment to listen for the sound of footsteps either inside or out. A haunting quiet greeted him. Nothing but calm reached his ears. The humble hotel appeared to be empty. And the Mahdi's soldiers were moving slowly, unsure what their compatriots had stumbled upon moments earlier. They'd yet to reach the modest crossing.

Sanders knew a formidable presence was drawing near. The trap was tightening. He had to find a way to escape—a side street or alleyway still clear of sword-wielding zealots. If nothing else, he had to uncover a sheltering rock to crawl beneath to plan his next move.

He spotted what appeared to be a doorway at the far end of the lobby. Always on the alert, he eased past the antiquated check-in counter. Patiently, Sanders opened the creaking door and peered inside. A small, windowless kitchen waited in the blackness. He could just make out the far wall. The modest enclosure couldn't be wider than fifteen feet in either direction.

"I'll bet if there's a way out of here," he whispered, "it'll be on the other side of this room."

He moved forward, hoping against hope that the dim kitchen would hold the priceless treasure of freedom at its end. To his disappointment, the only thing he found on the far side was an impenetrable wall of mortar and brick. It had to be at least a foot thick. He felt his way along it, searching for a glimmer of salvation. But none appeared.

Like so many of the structures in Cairo's oldest section, this one had been built wall-to-wall with its neighbors. Still he needed to ensure he hadn't missed an escape route within the meager space. The apprehensive sergeant reached for his flashlight. Its light soon shined, piercing the stifling void that closed in around him to feed upon his fears. A cursory check with the penetrating beam did little good. The results of his investigation were the same. The stout wall was a dead end. There appeared to be no way out except through the front of the hotel. And with death waiting in a hundred rifles, that was no way at all.

Sanders was surrounded. If his presence was discovered, he'd be no match for the overreaching attackers. He'd go down fighting to the last. Even so, his end would soon come.

He couldn't chance the light any further. His flashlight was quickly extinguished.

Maybe the answer for which he was searching could be found in another part of the broken-down building. He turned to retrace his steps. That's when he heard them—excited voices drawing near. Whether they were inside the squalid edifice or gathering in front of its framework, he couldn't determine. It didn't much matter. Either way, he couldn't chance a return to the lobby. He was trapped in the kitchen. And sooner or later, they'd stumble upon his hiding place. The sounds grew louder. He froze. Not a muscle moved. That's when he saw it out of the corner of his eye. Waiting in an obscure niche sat another door, small and narrow.

Tucked in the wall separating the kitchen from the lobby, the indistinct area had been ignored in his initial search. The door was partially open. Sanders didn't have the slightest clue where it went. Nevertheless, it seemed his best chance, possibly his only chance, of avoiding detection.

He moved across the room toward it, measuring each step to avoid making the slightest of sounds. He soon found himself facing the gaping doorway. He peered inside. He was greeted by absolute darkness. He had to know where it led. He had to risk the flashlight, to gamble on it not being seen once more. It was back in his hands.

With its bright glow, the riddle was partially solved. On the other side of the entryway, wooden steps led underground. To where, Sanders couldn't determine. Yet with the enemy so near, anywhere was better than where he was. The door was ajar enough to allow him to squeeze past. He moved around it, edging inside. The first of the deteriorating steps sagged beneath his weight. He glanced back toward the kitchen, taking a final look.

He pulled the sheltering door closed and reached to bolt it. But there was no latch. He'd no way of securing it from the inside. For now, however, such problems would have to be ignored.

Ever vigilant, with the beam to guide him, he headed down into this new world. On the creaking stairs and rotting banister were the unmistakable signs of blood. Its age was impossible to determine, although it gave every indication of being reasonably fresh. From where it had come, and who'd left it, he hadn't a clue. The solitary Green Beret's senses heightened.

It didn't take more than a handful of steps to realize what he'd discovered. A tiny, windowless basement. A dank environment filled with rows of wine racks. The sunken opening was the hotel's humble cellar. In its day, each of the cobwebbed racks had held the finest wines. The British colonists had demanded no less. Now the majority of the racks stood empty. Even so, enough grit-crusted bottles were scattered about the small room to satisfy the thirst of an entire A Team for many a week.

A fleeting smile came to Sanders's face. Upon reaching the bottom of the short staircase he picked up one of the reclining bottles, examining its label with his flashlight.

"What do ya know, after all I've put up with this afternoon, things are finally looking up. Thank goodness this is a moderate Islamic country where such gifts can still be found. At least I know one thing. Dying of thirst's not going to be a problem."

He carefully placed the bottle back on the rack. He knew it was far too soon to feel at ease. His lethal antagonists were out there, swarming over every foot of pavement between here and the American lines. And for the moment, the Special Forces sergeant had no idea what he'd find in the remainder of the tight cavern. He had to secure his hiding place. With the piercing light illuminating his path, he started checking between the wooden rows. As he made his way down the slender aisle his search was uneventful. At least that's what he thought.

It was at the end of his brief sojourn that the biggest surprise of the day awaited. In the corner, hidden behind the final rack, a body lay with its face in the dirt. The instant his gleaming beam fell upon it he recognized the Pan-Arab uniform. The left shoulder had turned black beneath a thick pool of blood.

"Now, where the hell did you come from?" Sanders reached out and cautiously turned the Pan-Arab over. He stared at the lifeless image, the unhappiness with his discovery evident upon his face. "Look, I hope you're not offended, but it really is kind of cramped down here. And I sure wasn't planning on sharing this hole with a roommate. Especially a dead one." He glanced at his surroundings. "I've got to tell you the selection of this dump as your final resting place definitely has me confused. If I were going to die, this is the last place I'd choose to do it." He looked toward the doorway at the top of the stairs, his concern undeniable. "Although considering my situation, with so many of your sword-wielding friends swarming around this place, I wouldn't be surprised if this sorry crypt's where I'll also take my last breath."

It was obvious Mourad's disciple had stumbled into the hotel after being struck by a bullet and had found the sheltering basement during the fierce fighting on the previous evening. Without medical aid, the wounded soldier had bled to death inside the solemn room. Sanders shined the light onto the enemy face. He reached down and lightly brushed away the dirt covering the Pan-Arab's features. He was stunned by what he found. Much to his chagrin, beneath the layer of grime was the most incredible girl he'd ever seen. Even in death her beauty radiated.

"Oh, man, what a waste. You were so damn pretty. And you can't be over twenty. What a way to complete my day. Send me a beautiful woman like the captain promised, but with one small caveat. She's a corpse. I've waited for someone like you all my life and what happens?

God hands me a dead one. What a sick joke. And I wouldn't be shocked to discover I was the one who killed you. Seems to me we fought somewhere around here last night. Or maybe it was early this morning. If it was me who shot you, I want you to know you have my sincerest apologies. I'd never intentionally harm someone as attractive as you."

Sanders bent down to examine the decimated figure. Her body was still warm to the touch. He pulled back his hand in astonishment. She couldn't have died more than a few minutes earlier. He stared at her, wondering who she was and from where she'd come. It was then he spotted what appeared to be the slightest movement in the girl's chest. At first he dismissed his surprising discovery as wishful thinking. But then he saw her chest rise a second time. He brought his ear next to the sweet face and listened.

She was alive. Though barely.

"Jesus Christ!"

Sanders grabbed his rucksack, digging for the plasma and medical supplies within its protective canvas. "Hang on, sweetheart. I may not be the best field medic there ever was. But I've been told I'm pretty damn good at this. And you're one patient I've no intention of losing."

He knew his situation was filled with desperation. The desolate American was trapped behind a ruthless enemy's lines. An opponent who, should they stumble upon his hiding place, would show no mercy.

He'd no idea how and when his life would meet its end. Nonetheless, if he lived long enough, Charlie Sanders had every intention of saving the beautiful Arab girl.

His, however, would not be the only life that would find itself on the line.

32

Norm Sweeney walked into the sparse quarters he shared with his section leader and four other pilots. Bradley Mitchell was alone in the room. He lay on his bunk aimlessly staring at the low ceiling.

"Mail's in," Sweeney said. "You got another letter from your wife." He tossed it onto Mitchell's chest.

Mitchell glanced at the expensive pink envelope, sent express mail, and frowned.

"They want us in the ready room in fifteen minutes," Sweeney said.

"Another raid on the Libyan air bases?"

"Looks that way."

"Have you noticed since the *Eisenhower* was hit we've done nothing but fly routine missions against stationary targets?"

"I've noticed," Sweeney answered.

"Every time they need someone for a high-priority mission another section's been chosen. I doubt it's coincidence, Worm. We used to be this wing's fair-haired boys. Now we're drawing assignments normally going to the least-experienced crews. Appears they've lost some faith in us."

"Kind of looks that way. To be honest, for the past couple of days I suspect we've acted like we've lost faith in ourselves."

Mitchell held his wife's letter. "Might as well read this before we go. My afternoon's shot anyway."

He sat up, ripped open the envelope, and unfolded the pages. His wife's handwriting was precise and flowing. There could be no misreading what the letter said. Her stinging words spewed forth.

Dearest Bradley,

Every day for over a week I've written asking you to call me. And yet, as I stare at the phone, it refuses to ring. Each of my e-mails has also gone unanswered. I cannot understand your continued refusal to do what I've asked. Such a simple request and still you choose to ignore it. The only conclusion I can reach is your failure to respect my wishes is a direct reflection of your lack of concern for my problems.

Mitchell shook his head.

"What now?" Sweeney asked.

"Still bitching about the fact I haven't called her."

"Look, it's obvious she isn't going to stop. I know it won't be fun, but why don't you go up to the satellite telephone area, call her, and get this over with? Maybe that'll shut her up."

"I wish it were that easy. But knowing Brooke, it will have the opposite effect. It'll just give her another way to continue haranguing me. Once my calls begin, she'll be demanding I spend every minute on the phone listening to her incessant demands. If she finds out how easy it is for me to call, she'll make my life even more of a living hell than it already is. I'm still upset she found out we had e-mail."

Mitchell returned to his reading.

*How could you leave me in this dreadful situation? I hate this
horrid backwater town. I'm sick of Norfolk. I wish I'd never
seen this sorry excuse for a naval base and its awful base
housing. And I'm sick of being the proper officer's wife, expected
to act in a certain way in order to further her husband's career.
There was nothing to do here as it was. Now all anyone talks
about is that stupid war you've gotten yourself involved in.
With each passing day I'm getting more disgusted with the
whole thing.*

*The children have become unbearable. I don't know how I
make it through the long hours. If it wasn't for the time they
spend at school and the young girl down the street who's willing
to babysit on a moment's notice, I believe I'd lose my mind. All
they talk about is what Daddy's doing and when Daddy's
coming home. Because of your refusal to call, I don't know
what to tell them. They can't comprehend what's going on. To
tell you the truth, neither can I.*

*My parents have invited me to the Hamptons for a few
months. Of course, the invitation doesn't include the children.
After Joshua hit Mitsy with that stick during our last visit,
Mother refuses to allow him and Jennifer within five hundred
feet of the house.*

*Who can blame her? She's had Mitsy for nearly ten years.
That dog means everything to her.*

*Your parents said they'll take the kids, but with your
mother's health, they've refused to come get them.*

*They made it clear it's up to me to get Joshua and Jennifer
to California. The good news is the airlines said since the
children are now five and seven they're old enough to travel
without an adult. The bad news is because of the president*

taking away most of the planes for the war, the waiting list for
travel is presently two weeks and growing by the day.

They're starting some kind of priority system, so I may not
be able to send them at all. My father's trying to call in some
favors to get them on a flight, but so far nothing's worked. I
don't know what to do. With gas nearly ten dollars a gallon
and rationing beginning, even if I was capable of driving across
the country to California, it's simply out of the question. You've
got to tell me what to do about these children.

If you care even the slightest, you'll call the instant you get this.

Your loving wife, Brooke

Mitchell dropped the letter, letting it fall to the floor.

"What's the matter this time?" Sweeney asked.

"Same old stuff. Wants to dump the kids on my parents so she can hobnob in the Hamptons. But because of the nasty old war she's having trouble getting them there."

"Sounds familiar."

"One thing about Brooke, she never changes," Mitchell said.

"What are you going to do about it?"

"What can I do? I still think answering her e-mails and letters would be a mistake. That'll only encourage her to continue her tirades. And there's really nothing I can do until the war ends and the *Lincoln* makes its way back to Norfolk."

"You're probably right. Until we return to the States, there's not much you can do. Look, it's really none of my business, but if I were you I know the first thing I'd do when we get home."

"What's that?"

"Find a good divorce lawyer."

"Don't you think I've thought of that, Worm? Unfortunately, it's not an option. If I even appear to be thinking about doing anything he perceives as halfway threatening to his precious little girl, Brooke's father's going to have me hung out to dry. File for divorce and he'll make sure my military career's over. Shortage of pilots or not, I'd never see a Hornet cockpit again. Or the cockpit of any plane, for that matter. He's got friends on the board of every major airline. Not only will I be kicked out of the Navy and unable to fly fighters, I'll be blackballed from any chance of a commercial pilot's job."

"Isn't there anything you can do about your situation?"

"Nope. I'm stuck. I'm the fool who had to have his trophy wife. Nobody held a gun to my head and made me marry her. And one thing's clear. Divorce is out of the question."

"You know, sometimes I wish we'd run off with those showgirls we met in Las Vegas last year. The dark-haired one really took a liking to you. She was dead serious about her interest in dashing Navy pilot Bradley Mitchell. After that weekend, we should've turned in our resignations. We could've taken off for Mexico like they wanted."

"Geez, I hadn't thought about them for quite some time, Worm. To tell you the truth, I barely remember that dancer's name. Gwen . . . I think. But I definitely remember that face of hers. Those two were absolutely gorgeous. Gwen was every bit as pretty as Brooke when I first met her. I've got to admit I was tempted to take her up on the offer to accompany me to my room that night. But bad marriage or not, I'm still a married man with two small children to consider and a vengeful wife at home ready to pounce on even the slightest transgression. So there really was no other answer I could give. Sadly, I had to tell her no."

"Thank God I've no such issues. Lisa turned out to be as good in bed as she was as the lead dancer in the Riviera's topless review. Wow, that woman was something. Too bad we only had the weekend. Those two were dead serious about providing us with some long-term lovin'. We made a big mistake, Blackjack."

"But throwing away our careers in the middle of advanced fighter training to run away with a couple of showgirls? You know we couldn't do that."

"I don't know," Worm said. "I'm beginning to wish we had. Right now we'd be romping naked in the surf on some isolated beach in Baja, each clutching an incredible woman with one hand and a stiff drink with the other. We wouldn't have a care in the world."

"Worm, you're probably right. Even so, I can't believe you're bringing up Mexico and drinking in the same breath. After what happened when we went to Tijuana a few weeks later to celebrate our graduation, I'd think you'd never want to talk about Mexico again."

"Now that you mention it, I believe I'm still a little hungover from our sordid adventure south of the border," Sweeney said.

"That really was one lost weekend. But at least something positive came out of it. We might've never come up with a good handle for you if it weren't for that trip. After a two-day stint of evil deeds and drunken debauchery 'Worm' was the only thing anyone could call you. The way you bravely downed the last drink and the worm that went with it."

"What's so brave? I was so drunk I couldn't stand up. You think I'd have considered doing anything that stupid if I'd have been even halfway sober? But at least the worm didn't stay in my stomach for long."

"Yeah, I couldn't believe it when we reached the border and you leaned out the window and threw up the contents of your stomach, worm and all, on that custom agent's shoes. Let me tell you, that guy was pissed. For a while I didn't think they'd ever let us back across."

"And the legend of Worm was born," Sweeney proudly said. "But legend or no, I'm telling you, Blackjack, as soon as we're stateside I'm heading straight for Vegas. Got to see if sweet Lisa's still interested in sharing the Worm's bed. Hopefully nothing's changed, and between our unending bouts of lovemaking she'll be eager to hang on every word of the daring exploits of a Navy pilot fresh from the wars. If Lisa's serious, I'm going to have to think long and hard. After the past few days, I'm tempted to give up the Navy and look for greener pastures. And if I were you, I'd consider coming with me."

"You know I can't. I love my kids too much to ever do anything like that. And besides, aren't you forgetting the vow I took to never again set foot in Las Vegas? Don't you remember what happened? While you were in your room romping in the sheets with Lisa, I was in the casino losing my shirt at the tables."

"And that's how the legend of 'Blackjack' Mitchell was born," Sweeney said.

"That's right. Remember what the dealer told me as he took the last of my chips? I was one of the best blackjack players he'd dealt to in some time. And possibly the most unlucky person he'd ever met. Considering the money I'd lost, I didn't think it was funny. But you and Lisa got quite a laugh out of it."

"Well, you know what they say, Blackjack . . . lucky at love, unlucky at cards."

"If that were true, I shouldn't have lost once."

"Next time, take Brooke with you so the gambling gods can get a good look at your luck at love. Once they take a gander at what you're up against, you'll probably win every hand."

"No chance," Mitchell said. "I'd never get Brooke within a thousand miles of Las Vegas. It's far too crass for her tastes. Having to rub elbows with the common people they let into those places would never do. You know how she hates having to subject herself to the masses. She needs to surround herself with her equals."

"There's no doubt rubbing elbows with us ordinary folk is something Brooke would find disgusting. Remember how she acted when you brought me home for dinner?"

"How could I forget?" Mitchell said. "I was so embarrassed."

"She made no effort to hide her displeasure. How dare you bring some simple farm boy from Kansas to share your table?"

"Unfortunately, you're right, Worm. After meeting you, she spent the week in bed recovering from the ordeal."

"Don't feel bad, Blackjack. She's not the only one that's happened to. Lots of women have needed a week in bed to recover from their adventures with the old Wormman. Most take at least that long to get the smile off their face."

"You wish," Mitchell said. "And Brooke sure wasn't smiling."

"Well, Brooke or no Brooke, it's time to hit the ready room."

Mitchell got up and headed for the door. Sweeney was right behind. As they did, the computer sounded, indicating the section leader had received a new e-mail. Both pilots heard the machine's announcement.

"Let me guess," Mitchell said.

Sweeney glanced at the screen. "It's from Brooke."

Mitchell shook his head. Both turned and left the room.

The catapult fired. Lieutenant Commander Bradley Mitchell's Super Hornet roared down the runway and leaped from the *Lincoln*'s deck. Lieutenant Norm Sweeney was half a minute behind. They took to the heavens and headed west across a sparkling fall sea.

To the northwest, twenty miles distant, the *Eisenhower*'s raging fires burned. If anything, the uncontrollable flames appeared worse than they'd been when the pair undertook their last mission a few hours earlier. Each tried to ignore the horrific sight, but neither could do so. They couldn't deny the anguish they felt each time they viewed the burning aircraft carrier. The fierce blazes tore at the pilots' wounded spirits.

The F/A-18Es ripped across the afternoon sky. The target was thirty minutes away.

Mitchell considered this an easy mission, well below his immeasurable skills. Most of the fleet's pilots, however, wouldn't have agreed. Despite the determined efforts to eliminate them, the Pan-Arab air base Blackjack Section was scheduled to attack bristled with air defense weapon systems. A careless American could easily forfeit his life on a mission such as this. Nevertheless, to so adept a pilot, even with the air base's deadly defenses, the assignment was a routine one.

For the first time, he couldn't put his family problems behind him.

The relentless distractions were starting to get the better of him. Brooke was there in the cockpit, her complaints weighing heavily on his mind.

They reached the Libyan coast. The target would soon appear. The mission could no longer wait. He did his best to push Brooke aside.

Mitchell spoke into his radio, "Echo Command, this is Blackjack Section . . ."

But Brooke was never far from his thoughts.

33

O n the ground, figures raced toward the relative safety of their bunkers and gun emplacements. Blackjack lined up the target. The aircraft hangar was within his sights. Hidden within the buttressed shelter were a half-dozen MiGs. One right after the other, Mitchell released a quartet of thousand-pound bombs. Sweeney did the same.

This wasn't the first attempt to take out the fortified structure. The hangar's roof showed the scars of the daily raids against it. So far, the stout enclosure had withstood the pounding. Still, the framework was clearly weakened by the continual assaults. And it couldn't resist the bombings forever. With any luck, Blackjack Section's plummeting armaments would penetrate the building and destroy the aircraft inside.

The lethal ordnance sailed toward its purpose. A series of mighty explosions hit the hangar.

The F/A-18E pilots had performed their task perfectly. The only thing remaining was for the intelligence experts to determine the extent of the damage. They'd do so using the Super Hornets' video of the attack and the spy satellites' next pictures of the air base. If the Americans were fortunate, the images would confirm the objective had been destroyed. If not, another bombing run would be undertaken tomorrow and on each day following until elimination of the shelter and its aircraft was complete.

"All right, Worm," Mitchell said, "looks like we nailed it. Let's move on to the secondary targets." There was no enthusiasm in the section leader's voice.

"Confirm your assessment, Blackjack. Moving on to targets two and three."

"Even though there've been no sign of them, keep your eyes open for enemy radar locks."

"Roger, Blackjack," Worm said. "With the vivacious Lisa awaiting my return, the only desert I want to find myself standing on has a big 'Welcome to Fabulous Las Vegas' sign stuck in the middle of it. I've no intention of letting an air defense missile sneak up on us anytime soon."

"Roger, Worm. Let's begin our next run."

A trio of bombs would soon be unleashed to assault a smaller aircraft hangar. And once that task was completed, the pair would move on to attacking the air base's runways with their Vulcan cannons. The second hangar was soon within their sights. The bombs were released. And once more, the target was struck dead center.

The pilots moved on to the third, and by far the most dangerous portion of the mission.

Screaming in wing tip to wing tip a few hundred feet above the ground, they'd fire untold 20mm shells into the glistening black pavement of the air base's primary runway in an attempt to put it out of commission.

"Let's get set to nail that runway. Once we're done, we'll head for home."

"I don't even know why we're bothering, Blackjack. We tear them up and they come out five seconds after we're gone to fix them. No matter how much damage we do, an hour from now they'll have repaired this thing good as new."

"I know. But orders are orders. And we've been directed to unload our Vulcans on that runway. So let's get to it and head back to the boat."

The speeding pair raced across the featureless desert. As they reached the runway Mitchell released a quick burst from his Vulcan cannon. Armor-piercing shells poured forth from the aircraft's lethal nose. The striking armaments tore huge gashes in the three-mile ribbon of patch-marked asphalt. Sweeney squeezed his Vulcan's trigger, spewing further angst upon the hot tar.

As they neared the attack's midway point, the Mahdi's air defenders let loose with their antiaircraft guns upon the low-flying Americans. Both rocketed through the fierce streams of gunfire. When they reached the western edge of the base, the duo turned to make a final approach. With a few hundred rounds remaining in each of their cannons, their assignment was close to its end.

Blackjack Section soared into the solemn skies, turned, and plummeted toward the ground. Entering a teeth-rattling dive, they headed for the black ribbon once more. It was then Worm spotted the first serious threat to their survival.

"Blackjack! I'm picking up a radar attempting to lock on to us."

"Roger, Worm. My system confirms."

"I'm picking up a second one."

The Hornets continued plunging toward the sultry air base. Mitchell watched his screen.

Mourad's air defenses were doing their best to grab hold of the immense prize.

"Did you copy, Blackjack?" Worm said. "These guys are getting close. Maybe we should abort and get the hell out of here."

Suddenly Mitchell's system screamed the warning. A searching radar had achieved a lock on the leading Super Hornet. An enemy missile would soon rocket skyward to destroy the first of the invaders. No longer was this a routine mission.

For a split second, he didn't react. If anything, the knowledge his death was imminent seemed an odd relief. An ironic smile came over his masked face. He'd never thought of his life's end being a solution to the problems he faced in his difficult marriage. Yet there it was, unexpectedly. He'd found an answer to his nagging concerns. Succumb to the Chosen One's missile and there'd be no more Brooke and her petty annoyances.

Mitchell was stunned by his response. He fought against the startling impulse. His innate need for survival seized control, shaking him from the momentary lapse and forcing him to respond.

"Worm, I've got a missile lock! Break off the mission! Break off the mission!"

Mitchell's F/A-18E raced skyward. A Russian-made, radar-guided SA-6 ground-to-air missile fired. Both pilots hit their afterburners and roared into the heavens. Each instituted evasive actions. The devastating missile closed with the lead Hornet. The nimble F/A-18E twisted and turned, dodged and wove. On the ground, the missile system's operator matched his every move. The killer drew near. One of the Navy's best pilots was locked in a life-and-death struggle in the bright skies over Libya. Mitchell's thoughts were racing at incredible speed, yet he remained perfectly calm. Now wasn't the time to panic. The tracking executioner was right on his tail. Blackjack released chaff and a long string of flares. If that didn't fool the unmerciful assassin, there'd be no choice but to blow his canopy and bail out. If the ejection didn't kill him, he'd soon be dangling at the end of a billowing parachute floating toward the Sahara. He'd find himself on the scorching desert, alone and vulnerable, deep within enemy country.

Whether he could elude his pursuers would require both luck and skill. With only a Beretta pistol, he'd be no match for any armed unit in search of him. If he could evade capture after his fearful descent, he'd try to find a deep hole in which to crawl. There he'd turn on his rescue beacon and wait for help.

He scanned the staid terrain with one eye while watching his screen with the other. The ground beneath him looked barren and sparsely populated. Maybe, just maybe, if no one spotted his parachute he'd stand a chance. A search-and-rescue helicopter would be launched immediately. With so great a distance to travel, however, they'd need at least three hours to arrive, pinpoint his location, and pick him up. And with so bleak a landscape for him to hide in, three hours would be a lifetime. He realized his odds weren't good. There was an excellent chance his head would be severed and stuck on a pole long before the rescuers drew near.

He was out of time. He could die a certain death in the heavens or take his chances on the inhospitable ground. He reached for the canopy release. But luck was with him. The falling curtain of chaff and long line of flares fooled the system's inexperienced operator. The SA-6 swerved off course, pursuing a falling flare. The misguided killer raced after the descending decoy. It exploded a few hundred yards behind the fleeing fighter.

Mitchell was safe. He brought his aircraft under control, cut back his afterburners, and headed northeast toward the Mediterranean. Worm soon returned to his place on his section leader's wing. They hurried home.

Blackjack Section neared the fleet. The *Lincoln*'s arrester cables waited to catch the arriving Super Hornets. Mitchell aligned his aircraft for landing.

He'd never before had the briefest thought of ending his life. Yet in the crushing skies over Libya, with his death imminent, such a desire had sprung to the forefront without the slightest warning. He was clearly shaken by the close call. As he neared the welcoming deck, his response to the all-too-real dangers astonished him. His haunting questions and mounting self-doubts would be there for him to examine once he was safely on board the *Lincoln*.

34

Quite unexpectedly, the second fierce storm in a week blew in from the ebbing Mediterranean. There could be no denying the sparse rains were arriving early this year. And with more intensity than anyone could recall.

Ominous black clouds thundered across the broad seascape to hammer the North African coast with a fury rarely seen by mortal man. Huge waves pounded the beaches, tearing at the fragile sands and carrying them out to settle in the ocean's depths. Over the coming millennia, new sands would form on the battered shoreline to replace those lost to heaven's rage. With the passing of time, the mighty storm's scars would be forever healed. By then, if man still existed on this insignificant planet, the promises of a twenty-first-century oracle would be long forgotten by the descendants of those who'd fought and died here.

For now, however, nature's impressive power was there for all to witness.

Incessant lightning strikes stung the shadowy vistas with a frightful fireworks display that tore at its all-consuming veil for hours without end. One after another, unpredictable currents leaped from the flittering heavens to perform their dance of alarming inspiration. With each startling image, the night's mantle was momentarily shattered. The eerie desert world became disjointed and surreal. Terrifying claps of rumbling thunder provided the orchestration for the electrifying performance. With every new chorus of the fearsome overture, it was as if the gods themselves were voicing their displeasure with mankind's evil follies.

The winds howled and a sticky gray, smoke-tinged rain fell in stinging sheets upon the exposed Americans. In their foxholes, hidden beneath their sheltering ponchos, they futilely attempted to find protection from the raging storm's power. Their efforts failed miserably. Yet there was a silver lining to their suffering. For the abominable conditions accomplished one wonderful thing. They halted the ruthless battles, and gave the Marines an opportunity to catch their breath for the first time in three days. Even Mourad's followers had lost the will to fight in the deplorable conditions. Except for occasional sniper fire, there'd been no sign of them since early in the afternoon.

For twelve hours, to the relief of all, the killing was halted by the biting desert rains.

Within the American defenses, a nearby bolt illuminated a pair of hunched figures moving near the front lines.

"He's over here, sir," James Fife said, "in the foxhole next to the highway."

"How bad is he?" Captain Richards asked.

"I think you'd better see for yourself."

Richards gingerly stepped into Erickson's hole. He lifted the thin poncho covering the platoon's leader and stared at the distorted form lying in three inches of muddled rainwater. He placed his hand on the platoon leader's chest. Much to his relief, Richards could feel the lieutenant's labored breath rising and falling. He put his palm to Erickson's forehead. It was impossible to miss the fever raging through the motionless Marine.

The company commander looked up at the platoon's sergeant. "At least he's breathing. How long's he been like this?"

"Don't know for sure, sir. I checked on him about an hour ago. He wasn't doing very well then. I tried to get him to go back for medical attention. But he refused. Said after all that's happened he wouldn't leave what remained of the platoon until the 1st Division arrives. Claimed the men, those alive, and those who weren't, deserved no less. To tell you the truth, he was pretty much out of his head. A lot of what he said didn't make sense. A while later I heard him talking real crazy like. I swear, it sounded like he was having a conversation with those who died while taking the beach. Then I heard nothing from the lieutenant. So I thought I'd better come back and check. Found him like this a few minutes ago. That's when I sent for you."

"You did the right thing, Gunny. Let's get him out of here. I'll take him to the battalion aid station so one of the corpsmen can have a look."

They pulled the inert figure from the murky hole and carried him to the company commander's Humvee. As they did, a particularly impressive lightning strike flashed in the distance. A nasty refrain of threatening thunder soon followed.

Richards turned to File. "Doesn't look like Lieutenant Erickson will be back anytime soon. For the time being, you've got command of 3rd Platoon."

"Yes, sir. I'll do my best to hold things together until the reinforcements get here. Has there been further word on the 1st Division?"

"The rumors were true. They're on the way from Naples. Last I heard, the lead elements are scheduled to land before sunrise. But the storm's slowed them a bit. If the seas calm, we can expect them here early in the afternoon."

"Let's hope so, sir. Two days ago we had a pair of Marines in each of these foxholes. Now about a third of them don't have anyone in them at all. We've got gaps in our lines so wide you could sail the

Queen Mary through here without anyone noticing. We can probably stop a few modest attacks as long as the air support remains strong. But any major offensives and there won't be anyone alive to hold off anything."

"I know, Gunny. Hang tight. Help really will be here soon."

"Yes, sir. Any idea what the higher-ups have planned for us?"

"Nothing definite. A couple of days lying on the beach licking our wounds is the most likely scenario. Let the 1st Division slug it out with the Chosen One while we get reorganized."

"Sounds good to me, sir."

"All right, Gunnery Sergeant, 3rd Platoon's yours."

The corpsman laid Erickson on an examining table in the battalion aid station's tent. With the lull in the fighting, for the first time in days the grave table wasn't surrounded by a river of red.

Richards stood nearby, anxiously waiting for him to finish his examination. The medic spotted the discolored rip in the lieutenant's sleeve and the faint signs of dried blood. He poked around long enough to be convinced he might have discovered the source of his latest patient's perplexing problems.

"Captain, can you give me a hand? I need to get his shirt off to take a better look at his arm."

Richards lifted the unconscious lieutenant and held him in a sitting position while the corpsman carefully removed Erickson's rain-soaked fatigue shirt.

"Go ahead and lay him back down, sir."

On his swollen left arm, a filthy bandage covered much of his biceps. From his elbow to his shoulder the arm was bright red and swollen twice its normal size. Discolored crimson streaks flashed across his chest. Others ran down the length of his arm. A few reached his blackened fingertips.

The corpsman carefully removed the old dressings. When the last fold of deteriorating cloth was gone, the source of Erickson's condition was there for all to see. In the area where the shrapnel had penetrated the skin, thick puss oozed from an angry wound.

"How long's he had this injury, sir?"

"Four days. Got hit while taking the beach. His corpsman tried to get the shrapnel out, but he failed."

"Why didn't you make him take care of it before now?"

"Because I didn't realize it was even a problem. He hasn't said anything about it to anyone."

"From the looks of this, he must've been in a hell of a lot of pain for the past few days."

"The crazy bastard hasn't complained once. With the constant attacks, he probably felt he needed to stay with his men no matter what. Can you get the shrapnel out?"

"In his condition, I'm not even going to try. I'll let the doctors handle that. He's already unconscious. If I do something wrong, he could slip into a coma. All I'm going to do is get a drip started and pump him full of antibiotics. Once he's stabilized, we'll load him in an ambulance. If we're going to save that arm, we've got to get him back to the hospital they've set up near the landing zone."

"What are his chances for recovery?"

"Who knows, sir? With all the swelling his injury may look far worse than it actually is. If things go well, in a few days it's possible the lieutenant might be good as new and ready to rejoin the battalion. You'd be surprised what clean sheets and good living can do to a person. Especially when there's a pretty face, filled with smiles, bringing you your medicine."

35

The storm rushed south, its immense display surging unchecked down the Nile Delta. As morning neared, the ominous clouds' downpours continued their assault upon the beleaguered city. The sorrowful heavens gave no indication the tumult would soon end. Silt-clogged eddies of swirling rainwater raced down the timeless streets of Old Cairo. But there existed few outlets for the deluge's bounty. The confounding rains were finding a home wherever they could.

The hotel's fading lobby was immersed in an ankle-deep pool of filthy rainwater. The damaged remains of the tattered building creaked and groaned with each blustery gust. So far, the surprisingly resilient structure had stood fast against the appalling conditions. Yet with each of the gale's fierce blasts, its brittle walls threatened to surrender their tenuous hold and end their defiant stand against nature's overwhelming power.

Water seeped into the windowless cellar from a dozen widening cracks in its worn walls and ceiling. In much of the dank enclosure, the dirt floor had turned into a soupy mud. Humid morning air, stale and oppressive, hung upon the soiled room like a suffocating blanket.

Kneeling over her, Sanders brought the candle's flickering light nearer the wounded girl's face. She was awake again. Despite her attempts to mask her discomfort from the revolting American, pain was etched upon her delicate features. It settled deep within the corners of her eyes. Her vivid eyes held something else. Something she made no attempt to hide. Her eyes were filled with an all-consuming contempt for the man who'd saved her life.

"Good morning, Reena," he said.

The girl looked up at him in astonishment.

"That's right, I know your name. Found your ID card when I removed your shirt to doctor your shoulder. Couldn't make out what most of that scribbling was in Arabic, but your name, age, and address were there in English. You're Reena Sharma. You're nineteen years old. And you come from some place in Tunisia I couldn't possibly pronounce."

She attempted to move, trying to put a little distance between herself and the black soldier hovering over her makeshift bed. It was no use, however. Even the slightest action sent daggers deep into what remained of her mangled shoulder. The pain was too much to bear. The agony of her efforts soared through her. Reena fought to keep from losing consciousness. She lay perfectly still, praying for the anguish to pass. Her vile captor continued to talk, his foreign words meaningless.

"There's something else about you. And I didn't need any ID card to discover it. I knew it the moment I laid eyes on you. Reena, you're the most beautiful woman I've ever seen. And let me tell you, I've seen lots of women. I mean lots of women. But don't you worry, none of them mean a thing to me now."

She stared at him, the unbearable discomfort slowly receding from her face.

"I wonder if you believe in love at first sight. I never did. At least I didn't until I found you. I know you're probably thinking this is kind of impulsive. But I've had lots of time sitting in the dark to reflect on it. So I don't think I'm being the least bit impetuous. As I stare at that sweet face of yours, there's no longer any doubt. I'm certain I'm falling in love with you. I've no doubt you'll soon learn to love me back. I really am a nice guy when you get to know me. And we could be great together. So my mind's made up. Don't even think about trying to talk me out of it. When this is over, if I'm still alive, I'm going to take you with me to America. I realize you're in no condition to discuss it right now, so I'm not expecting an answer right away."

He looked at their squalid surroundings. "Let's face it, there's no hurry. Neither of us has anywhere to go. I'll give you all the time you need to make your decision. I know it would be quite a change in lifestyle. But it's truly a great country. And a wonderful place to raise our children. I bet you'd like it there. It'll take some work to get all of Mourad's crap out of that brain of yours, but eventually we'll turn you into the loving wife every man would envy."

The wave of misery subsided. The disgust returned to the girl's face. Lost in his fantasy of what life with her would be like, Sanders didn't notice.

"Reena, I'm afraid I don't speak Arabic. Is there any chance you understand English?"

The expression on her face never changed. It was obvious she didn't comprehend a word he was saying.

"Well, no matter. It would've been nice to be able to talk. But I guess that wasn't meant to be. There'll be plenty of time to teach you later. For now, it looks like your shoulder's really hurting. Let me see what I can do to put you at ease."

Sanders adjusted her pillows, trying his best to make his patient as comfortable as possible. As he did, he accidentally brushed against her wound. She writhed in agony once more.

"I'm sorry," he said, "I didn't mean to do that." He grabbed his rucksack. "Look what I found during my last foraging trip." Sanders held up a half-full bottle of aspirin. "Wish I had a more powerful painkiller. But you've got to understand. It's not like I can wander out to the drugstore to pick something up. Your friends have seen to that.

They're crawling over every inch of ground outside. I've already pressed my luck as far as it'll go. Three trips into the hotel during the night was more than any sane person would've chanced. And when I'm upstairs I'm sure you understand I can't spend a lot of time looking around. As it was, I was lucky to find the aspirin. It'll have to do."

He got up and headed for the nearest wine rack. "Let's find something to wash the pills down. After that, if you're up to it, maybe you could try eating a bit of the food I discovered in the kitchen."

Sanders returned with a soot-covered bottle of the finest French wine. He inserted the corkscrew he'd discovered in the little restaurant on one of his precarious ventures outside the basement. As he did, a severe blast of wind rocked the hotel's structure. Even in the cellar, there could be no mistaking the impact of the powerful storm. The lovestruck sergeant stared at the low ceiling. A momentary fear flashed across his face.

"This old dump probably can't take much more. I sure hope the ceiling holds if the rest of the building collapses. To tell you the truth, being buried alive wasn't the way I wanted to go. Lying here trapped beneath thirty feet of rubble with no chance of escaping wasn't what I had in mind. No slow, agonizing death for me. No, sir. That's not what I want. When it happens, make my end swift and certain."

He took out two aspirin. She reluctantly opened her lips to receive the painkiller. He put the wine up to her mouth and started to pour. The instant she realized what he was giving her to drink, she spit the dark liquid in his face. Her outraged form was defiant.

"Look, I know it's against your religion to drink alcohol. But despite the fact it's raining like crazy outside and there's water everywhere, none of it is fit to drink." He held the bottle to her lips once more. "You need to swallow those aspirin."

She looked at him with an all-encompassing hatred in her dark eyes. Her jaw was clenched tight. Sanders realized he wouldn't be able to force open her mouth without risking the loss of the tips of his fingers. There was no way she'd drink the wine.

He shrugged his shoulders. "What do I care? Have it your way. Down the damn pills any way you can." He stared at her ireful face. His tone softened. "Look, I know they've got you brainwashed to hate me. But I've thought about that too. To tell you the truth, I don't get it. Someone as pretty as you shouldn't hold so much anger inside. So how about cutting me some slack. I saved your life, for Christ's sake. That should count for something. I could've left you to die and tried to sneak back to my own lines that first night. That's what most people would've done. It was only a few blocks. I bet I would've made it. Right this minute I'd be curled up on a soft bed with a lovely little wench who wanted nothing more than to give old Charlie pleasure. Instead, I've been stuck here with you for the past thirty-six hours. It's now five days since I've slept. And there's no longer any chance of my escaping. That ship has sailed. So now I'm trapped until your sick friends discover this place and put an end to me. And the sad part is, there's nothing I can do about it. After a day and a half of hiding in this hole, I'm probably five miles behind the Mahdi's lines. For all I know, all of Cairo's fallen into his perverted hands."

Her rebellious expression didn't change. Sanders stood. He turned and headed over to the far wall. He found himself a reasonably dry spot and dropped to a sitting position with his back against the aging mortar. The girl never took her eyes from him. The cruel death she wished with every measure of her being couldn't be ignored.

"Have it your way, Reena," Sanders said with a shrug.

He blew out the candle.

36

As the late morning rains withered and the first wisps of sunlight peeked through the clouds, twenty-four exacting Super Hornets rocketed down the Nile.

The city was drawing near.

Blackjack Section, with the farthest to travel, was in the lead. Beneath his mask a smile spread across Bradley Mitchell's face. This was an exceptionally dangerous, highly arduous task. One demanding the most skilled of the American fliers. And Mitchell's had been the first name the wing commander called at the early morning briefing. The struggling pilot had done nothing to hide the pride he'd felt in being designated to lead the furious assault.

It was exactly the type of action-laced mission he enjoyed. The coming hour would be filled with tension and significant uncertainty for the members of the advancing force. Mitchell's every thought would be consumed by the enormity of the swiftly unfolding events. The assignment would require lightning-quick reflexes and split-second decisions. Just the thing to allow him to break free from his essence-consuming funk.

With the storm-induced lull in the attacks upon the Marines, the Americans had been able to focus, at least for a few hours, on another critical component in their defense of Egypt. Before that window closed they needed to strike.

Over the past days, they'd been able to use their carrier-based aircraft to destroy every temporary span the Pan-Arabs built across the Nile. Only a few of the hastily constructed pontoon bridges had survived long enough to be of any use to the Chosen One's armored forces as they attempted to ford the wide waters. The Hornet pilots' determined efforts had ensured no more than meager numbers of the Mahdi's tanks reached the streets of Cairo.

They'd been far less successful, however, in stopping Mourad's infantry from arriving on the eastern shore. Most of the ardent enemy had traversed the broad currents unopposed. There hadn't been the time, or the resources, to halt the streams of resolved warriors from setting foot upon the eastern banks. From the northern edge of Cairo to its far southern reaches the agile feluccas had continued to cross the Nile filled with soldiers ready to join in on the visceral attack. If the Americans didn't soon stop them, their growing numbers would permanently tip the scale in favor of the fanatics.

The outmanned defenders had no choice. They had to eliminate the legion of sailing ships to have any chance of holding on to the city. And they had to do it now.

With Mitchell in the lead, the F-18Es had sprung from the *Lincoln* intent on doing just that. None would return to the carrier until they had destroyed all the little boats, effectively limiting Mourad's ability to place additional numbers on the other side. The daunting fighter aircraft would swarm over every inch of the dark waters until not a single sail remained.

Each of the deadly Hornets was configured for an air-to-ground attack. All were armed with pods filled with Hydra and Zuni rockets. Their 20mm Vulcan cannons were loaded to the brim for the close-in offensive.

Death was on the way to stalk the ancient river.

As they reached their sections of the time-honored flow, Hornet pairs began peeling away until only the final two aircraft remained. Blackjack Section had drawn Cairo's southernmost area. They were tasked with razing every Pan-Arab sailing on the troubled currents from the northern tip of Rhoda Island to the final expanses of the great city. To do so, they would be conducting the merciless onslaught from scarcely two hundred feet above the immense currents.

"Rhoda Island coming up on our left, Worm. Get set to undertake the attack. Growler aircraft should have jammed things up real good before we arrived. Even so, there are going to be lots of Stingers in the area, so be ready to drop flares and chaff the moment your system identifies even the smallest of threats."

"Roger, Blackjack."

"I'll handle the left half of the river and the eastern bank. You've got the right."

The duo split, each taking a position in the middle of the targeted area. Three hundred yards apart they began hunting their prey.

Everywhere they looked there were billowing white sails on the storm-surged river. In seconds, Mitchell spotted the first that would find its way into his gunsights. The modest craft was nearing the ravaged island. Every inch of its deck was crammed with well-armed men. The struggling felucca had been built to hold no more than ten. But thirty or more fixated souls clung to its bobbing wooden deck.

The Super Hornet roared toward them. At the last possible instant, those on the ill-fortuned launch spotted the low-flying assassin. Even so, there was little Mitchell's startled foe could do to save their lives. Their fate had been sealed by the screaming assailant's sudden appearance. The Chosen One's promise was coming for them all.

Many of those on the targeted sailboat began firing their assault rifles at the onrushing executioner. Hundreds of hurried rounds rushed skyward. It was nothing more than a useless gesture, filled with noisy symbolism, but little else. The fierce American aircraft was impervious to small-arms fire, no matter how accurate or intense. As he lined up his shot for this initial encounter, its pilot ignored the hapless efforts of those trapped on the accursed vessel.

Mitchell made a passing pull of his six-barreled cannon's trigger. It was followed by a second. And then a third. Scores of 20mm shells poured from the overpowering killer. The venomous rounds raced toward the august waters. They would be more than sufficient to finish the task. The unmerciful munitions ripped into those firing from the felucca. Huge, fatal wounds appeared. Like a well-rehearsed demon's medley, those on the boat tumbled from its crowded deck. Each fell into the reddening waters. Not a soul was spared.

The crippled craft began taking on water. Within seconds it sank.

Fifty yards beyond his first victim, the Hornet pilot spotted a further offering. Having deposited its weapons-carrying cargo on Rhoda Island, this one was headed toward Giza to gather a fresh load. Mitchell was so close he could see the terrified expressions on its flailing sailors' faces. A single burst tore from his Vulcan cannon to devastate yet another of the floundering skiffs. The vessel disappeared beneath the waters, heading for the river's bottom.

Nearing the island's southern tip, he found three fiercely blowing sails. Each was just reaching the decimated isle's jumbled shoreline. The crush of soldiers on the small decks was readying to leap onto solid ground. In all, their numbers approached one hundred. The feluccas and their human cargo were tightly bunched as they touched upon the riverbank.

A wide grin appeared on Mitchell's face. A huntsman's feast awaited the voracious predator. The targets were far too tantalizing to resist. The American pilot moved in for the kill. He fired the first of his Hydra rockets from a pod beneath the Hornet's right wing. The rocket leaped from the eradicating aircraft. It was a whirling blur as it rushed toward the ground.

It took no more than a heart-stopping moment to arrive. An existence-devouring blast, filled with thousands of high-velocity steel fragments, struck in the center of the arriving enemy. An immense explosion tore into the docking boats. Each was ripped apart in the all-consuming assault. Little would remain of the devastated feluccas.

The furious detonation's crushing power reached out to cut down the luckless Pan-Arabs. Not one would survive the encounter. When the fierce rocket was through, what remained of the battered boats' ravaged travelers scarcely looked human. Both in the crimson waters and on the blood-splattered shore, the dead and dying were everywhere.

Further targets awaited.

The F/A-18 roared south.

Norm Sweeney was experiencing even greater luck than his section leader.

He had destroyed a pair of fully loaded feluccas near the center of the wide river when he spotted an immense prize. He couldn't believe the treasure he beheld. Just ahead, on Giza's shores, more than a dozen sails sat motionless as their troop-carrying decks were being filled with anxious soldiers. In all, nearly four hundred of Mourad's followers were assembled on the embankment as the loading process continued.

The naval aircraft roared forward. Its pilot released the first of his large Zuni laser-guided rockets at the widespread throng. It flashed across the low skies. The stalwart Zuni pounced upon the stationary targets, devastating the northernmost elements of the impressive gathering. The crushed pieces of four feluccas were soon ablaze. In a twinkling, well more than a hundred of the enemy were gone.

On the ground, the survivors turned to run from the horrific scene. They'd, however, be far too late to save their fading lives. Another rocket, and seconds later, a third, went in search of the Chosen One's followers. In a handful of passing moments, the toll on the western shoreline reached uncountable proportions. For hundreds, their final journey had begun.

Sweeney followed upon his murderous siege with intense bursts from his Vulcan cannon to ensure none survived. Upon the venerated river's western shore, the slaughter was beyond description. Yet the lieutenant had neither the time, nor the desire, to consider the result of his actions. For there was a great deal of work remaining.

Like his section leader, he moved on.

Both reached the southern end of Rhoda Island at the same instant. Beyond the disappearing landfall, there were white sails without end upon the sweeping river.

Yet with Blackjack Section rampaging up and down this portion of the Nile, there wouldn't be for much longer. The surging Hornets raced forward, making attack after attack as they dispatched those trapped on the waters below.

As they reached the southern end of the city, the destructive aircraft turned to make another run. Further victims called to them. And they were determined to dispatch them all.

For sixty relentless minutes, the hounding twosome made pass after pass. With each run, the gruesome result grew. Minute by minute, the sails dwindled until there were no more.

All along the Nile, the American fighters tore after the Pan-Arabs with a vengeance. The attacks went on without pause. As the hour reached its end, not a single felucca would remain on the wine-colored waters.

The Americans turned and headed home. They'd lost three of their number, downed by Stinger missiles during the furious assault. But considering the intensity of the mission and the tactics they'd been forced to employ, the result was well below the naval strike force's expectations.

Because of the Hornets' resounding victory, few more, if any, of the Chosen One's disciples would find their way onto Cairo's streets.

Blackjack Section's day was far from over. There would be three additional assignments to undertake in widespread corners of the battle zone before the exhausted pilots would find their beds at shortly before midnight. The oozing scars on Bradley Mitchell's soul were far from healed. And the unending concerns involved in dealing with Brooke remained. Still, the day's successes had helped his battered psyche. And for the first time since his perceived failure to protect the *Eisenhower*, he was able to settle in for a decent night's rest.

The same, however, couldn't be said for another in this horrid conflict. For his sleep was far from comforting.

37

S am Erickson was having the strangest dreams. For hours on end incoherent images, vivid and distorted, raced through his subconscious at breakneck speed. Scenes of long-ago days of childhood brought momentary peace to his pummeled spirit. Wondrous pictures of the women he'd loved, and those he'd lost, teased and taunted him. Revelries filled with passion and joy were his for the taking. Fantasies littered with life's fleeting victories, or tinged with the bitter memories of everlasting defeat, fought for center stage. Terrifying emotions crammed with fear and loathing tore at him. Surging impressions clouded with the recent remembrances of flowing blood and horrific suffering found a place to display their appalling visions.

As the lieutenant reached the twentieth hour of drug-shrouded sleep, his mind's roller coaster neared its end. The searing nightmares of desperate battles crowded out all other thoughts and seized his tortured intellect. The angst-filled images grew grim and violent. The faces of the dead locked on to his core, refusing to release their accusatory grip upon his anguished existence.

He fought against his mind's frightening illusions, sinking deeper into a morass of despair and pain. He had to find a way out of the agonizing dream world. If he didn't, it wouldn't be long before the gruesome visions would destroy him.

He awoke with a start. His crusted eyelids fluttered. His eyes struggled to open. He stared at the tent's low canvas ceiling, unable to comprehend the unfamiliar surroundings. The aftereffects of his mind's conflicts were evident on his disconcerted face.

Next to his bed, an attractive woman sat on an uncomfortable folding chair. In her lap lay a novel filled with mystery and romance. She looked at him and smiled, her relief evident.

"What do you know, our wayward patient's finally awake. Glad to see you've decided to rejoin the living. Remember me?" Lauren Wells said. She spoke quietly in deference to the wounded around them.

"I remember. Where am I?" Erickson asked. His voice was strange, his throat hoarse.

"You're in the mobile hospital on the beach."

"How'd I get here?"

"They dragged you in yesterday morning. The shrapnel caused your arm to become infected. The doctors removed it, sedated you, and stuck you in with the walking wounded."

He painfully raised his arm to examine the heavy bandages and dangling tubes.

"The good news is in a few days you'll be just fine," she said. "The bad news is in a few days you'll be just fine. So it looks like your time in this insane war isn't close to over."

"I expected no less. Where's my platoon?"

"They're camped about a quarter mile from here. First Marine Division relieved your battalion early this afternoon. Your guys are catching up on their sleep and getting ready to enjoy a few precious days of R and R."

"That's good," Erickson said.

"Your company commander and some of your platoon have been

by twice tonight. They seemed genuinely concerned. I got the impression they weren't real excited about heading back into this mess without you. They spent quite some time regaling me with glowing descriptions of their valiant lieutenant's daring deeds in the deserts of northern Egypt."

"It's nice to know I'm appreciated. But don't let their tales fool you, Miss Wells. Stories of wartime exploits are like children's rumors. They have a tendency to grow with each telling. Despite what they might have said, I didn't do any more than anyone else out there. It was simply a matter of trying to stay alive. One of the things I've discovered in this line of work is oftentimes people mistake necessity for bravery."

"That may be. Or it might be I've stumbled across a rarity in today's world, a truly modest man."

"I doubt I'm rare or modest. I'm just a guy doing a difficult job the best he can."

"Believe what you want. But I know your men will be relieved to hear you're awake. I think I'll wait until morning, however, to let them know you've returned to the world of the living. They looked totally exhausted."

"You would too if you'd been through what they have."

"I can only imagine. But that's behind your guys for the moment. My guess is your battalion will stay out of the front lines for at least three or four days. Two British armored divisions sailed from England a few hours ago. They're headed straight for this beach. Figure you'll wait for them and then take off across the desert to support their attack on Mourad's forces. Seven hundred Challenger tanks are on the way. Once they land, you won't be fending off any more Pan-Arab assaults. It'll be the Mahdi's turn to hold on against a superior opponent."

"That's a sight I know I'll enjoy. Helping dig Mourad's grave is something I want to be a part of."

"I wouldn't worry about that too much," she replied. "Unless the doctor's misdiagnosed your injury, it looks like you're going to get your wish. There's no doubt this thing's going to wait for you to return before reaching its conclusion."

"That's good. I wouldn't want the end to come without my being right in the middle of it. So tell me, since I've missed what's gone on today, how are we doing at fending off the fanatics?"

"Not much has changed. Pan-Arab divisions continue to attack our lines. We continue to beat them back. In the past few hours, the 1st Marines have gotten a strong taste of the Chosen One's fury. They're knee-deep in blood, Arab and American, but their defenses are holding."

"Glad to hear it. I'd hate to think our efforts had been for naught. What about Cairo? Has it fallen to the sorry bastards?"

"There's been nothing but good news from there. The *Lincoln*'s Hornets are making the Nile run red. Every bridge the enemy's built has been blown up. And they were able to launch a successful air assault to destroy all the feluccas the Chosen One had. So none of his armor or infantry has reached the other side in quite a few hours. Between the storm slowing the Pan-Arabs and the arrival of the 82nd Airborne, Mourad's operations have ground to a halt. With the way things are going, a decision was made to save Cairo at all cost. So the British diverted two battalions of mechanized infantry headed for Kuwait and the French did the same with one of their best armored brigades. Both have arrived, been unloaded from their transport aircraft, and set up defensive positions throughout the city. The lines have stabilized. Word is the Mahdi's forces haven't gained a foot of ground. Each side's where it was yesterday."

"That'll play right into our hands. The longer we hold, the stronger we become." He paused for a moment, puzzlement on his face. "Look, I know my brain's a bit addled, but there's something I've been wondering since the moment I woke up . . . What're you doing here?"

"Just after you arrived, a friend alerted me they'd brought you in. Since they've got us confined to the area on the beach surrounding what's been not so affectionately dubbed 'Press City,' I'd nothing better to do. So I headed over. Figured there might be a good follow-up story."

"Follow-up to what?"

"Oh, that's right, you don't know, do you? From the reports I've heard, you've probably been a little too busy to pay attention to what's going on in the outside world. I suspect you've had no chance to watch television since we last met."

"Television? No. Mourad's seen to that. Since we talked on the beach, I haven't had time for anything except keeping a zealot's sword from my neck."

"That's what I figured. Anyway, the interview I conducted with you was a big hit. For the better part of a day it played on all the major news networks."

"To tell you the truth, I barely remember talking to you. I was so exhausted when we met on the beach. Still am. What time is it, anyway?"

"A little after one in the morning."

"How long have you been sitting here?" he asked.

"Off and on for about twenty hours."

"You've sat for nearly a day hoping for another story? Lady, I thought I was serious about what I do, but you've got me beat by a mile."

"Well, if we're being honest, it wasn't just the story keeping me glued to this chair."

"Oh?"

Her words were a bit reluctant. "How do I put this without it coming off the wrong way? Let's just say there's more than professional curiosity here. I know we only talked for a few minutes the other day, but your interview really stood out. There was something about you. I don't know how to describe it exactly. There was a quality to you. There was a spark in your eyes telling me you were someone I wanted to know more about."

"As a journalist?"

"Yes, as a journalist. And after I confirmed there was no wife and children cluttering up your life, also as a woman."

There was an uneasy lull in the quiet conversation. Her discomfort with the direction of the discussion couldn't be missed. She was accustomed to being in control. Yet this time she'd let down her guard. And her embarrassment showed.

"Look," she said, "why don't we talk about this later. You look like someone who needs a lot more sleep before being ready to rejoin the living."

"You're probably right. I don't know what the doctors gave me. But I'm feeling no pain."

"Then it's settled." She got up to leave. "I'm going back where I belong and let you get that sleep. To tell you the truth, I could use a little myself."

"What about the story you wanted to get?"

"It can wait. And so can any other vague reasons I've got for being here. Why don't we leave it like that for now? When you're up to it, if you want, we'll take a stroll and talk."

She gave him a broad smile and gently touched his hand. Without waiting for a response, she headed out of the stuffy tent.

Erickson watched her go. He lay wondering whether what had occurred was real or nothing more than another in an endless line of fantasies. It wasn't long, however, before his eyes shut and he drifted back into the world within his dreams.

This time, with Lauren Wells's beautiful image to hold on to while crossing through the darkest recesses of his mind, his sleep would be a pleasant one.

38

Lauren walked up to the wounded lieutenant's bed carrying a hospital-issue robe. Even in an olive-drab military T-shirt and camouflage fatigue pants, she was strikingly appealing. Erickson smiled as he saw her approaching.

"You look a hundred times better than the last time I saw you," she said. "Obviously the doctors were right about your rapid recovery. Ready to take that walk we talked about?"

"More than ready," he replied. "Any excuse to get out of here. I've been staring at these walls for hours. And they're really starting to get to me. I'm not used to being cooped up like this."

"I know exactly what you mean. I swear I'm going to lose my mind if I don't find a way to get off this beach. I feel like some sort of criminal. They've had the entire press corps confined to Press City for the past five days. We're not allowed to leave the area without the military's permission. They've spoon-fed us reports every few hours. But so far, we've not been able to go to where the fighting is."

"With what things are like up there, that's probably a good idea," he said. "You're far too likely to get your head blown off. Or because of your presence, cause someone else to lose theirs."

"Maybe so, but don't you think the American people have a right to know what's going on? You know, freedom of the press and that sort of stuff. And I sure can't tell the public what's happening if all I've got are the vague reports we've been receiving here on the beach."

"Have you talked to anyone about it?"

"I've talked to everyone. From the commanding general down to the pimply-faced private dishing out food in the mess tent. I've pleaded, I've threatened, I've even shed a few tears, trying to find a way out. But so far, nothing's worked. All my requests, both official and otherwise, have been denied. I've been told the same thing over and again. Until things are more secure, the press must remain at the landing zone. When the military's gained control of the situation, they've promised to let us go out under armed escort to take a look around. I figure that'll be about two weeks after the war's over."

"I'm sorry, but you've got to understand," he answered. "After seeing what those on the front lines are going through, I don't know how much sympathy I can muster. At least you've got the freedom to move around the beach when you want. Being allowed to wander the shore sounds like a pretty nice thing to me."

"Then if you're up to it, let's go find a nice piece of sand to walk on with a gleaming chunk of sky overhead. The winds have blown the smoke away and there's a big, bright slice of moon out there tonight."

"I'm up to it. They removed all the tubes a couple of hours ago. And the swelling in my arm's way down. I'm a bit weak, but starting to feel like myself again. The doctor said as long as I don't overdo it, it's okay to take a walk with you."

"Then let's take a stroll along the beach."

He struggled out of bed. After nearly two days off his feet he fought against the dizziness that suddenly appeared. The light-headedness quickly passed. She handed him the robe. He strained to put it on over his injured left arm. With her assistance, and a momentary flash of lingering pain, the robe found its way onto the wounded lieutenant. He looked around. There was no sign of anyone waiting outside to accompany them.

"Not bringing your cameraman?" he said.

"You won't have to worry about that. Chuck's busy trying to get the dirt from this afternoon's sandstorm out of his precious equipment."

"That's good. I wasn't looking forward to you shoving that camera in my face again. But even without it, what about questions, Miss Top-Notch Reporter? Are we taking this walk because I'm too weak to resist and you're hoping to ply me for information?"

"You can relax. There'll be no interviews tonight. This time it's strictly personal. I've only got one reason for being here. I'm doing this because I'm a woman who in the short time we've spent together finds you fascinating. So it's really quite simple. I want to get to know you better, Samuel Erickson. And that's all there is to it. I went off duty the instant I left Press City."

Kicking up the sands as they went, the couple walked arm in arm along the crashing waves. Lauren had described the evening perfectly. Other than the distant rumble of artillery and the perverse smell of battle pervading every inch of the North African landscape, the night was heavenly. The winds had chased away the blanketing layer of smoke. A shimmering moon and multitudes of flickering stars filled the evening sky.

The only blemish in the sparkling heavens was the distant red glow from the fiercely burning *Eisenhower*. Even thirty miles distant, its great conflagration was there for all to see.

For the first few minutes, he was oddly silent. He seemed quite distracted. She didn't know if this was his usual manner or if something was on his mind.

"Is something wrong?" she eventually asked. "Are you feeling all right?"

He stopped and looked at her. Her wondrous eyes sparkled in the Egyptian moonlight. "Why do you ask?"

"Because you haven't said a word since we left the hospital."

He looked upon the swirling waters. The tides were high and more than a bit furious.

"I'm okay. It's nothing really. It's just I've seen this beach before under far different circumstances and those memories aren't exactly the best."

"I'm sorry, Sam, that didn't enter my mind when I planned this evening," she said.

"Everywhere I look, I see things reminding me of the misery and suffering that happened here a few days ago. It's all around us. As we wander along, I can identify the critical elements of the battle as if they were happening this moment. All the cries for help from the wounded. All the places where the dead took their final breaths. I'll bet if you examine things closely you can still see the bloodstains on the sands. And if you look to the right about two hundred yards, you can see the spot where Sergeant Fife and I lay trying to figure out how to stop that final Pan-Arab tank."

"Yes, I know. I've seen that spot, Sam. I've seen what remains of that tank. After I interviewed you, my cameraman and I toured the beach. I've seen it all. The dead Arab girls, the bloody sands, everything you must've gone through. But it's over now, it's in the past."

"You don't understand. No one ever will who hasn't experienced it. For as long as I live, it will never be over. I can hear their screams, Lauren. I can see their faces. It's as if they're right here walking along with us. And that may never change. Those gruesome images might be with me the rest of my life." He paused. A frown appeared. "I'm sorry. Why did I bring this up? I . . . I didn't intend to ruin your evening. It's just so damn hard to overcome the horror of that morning when it's staring right at me."

"You've nothing to feel sorry for. I'm glad you brought it up. It's obviously something you needed to do. No one expects you to ever get over it completely. I certainly don't. All I'm asking is with my help you try to move forward. One of the best ways to do that is by talking about what's bothering you. And until you put all this as far into the past as you can, you and I have no chance of ever seeing if we can build a relationship."

He looked at her with an inquisitive expression. "Is that what we're trying to do here?"

"I don't know. I hope so. But I also understand by being so bold and announcing my intentions, I'm probably scaring you to death. It's much too soon for such talk, and I'm rushing things. And that's not like me at all. I'm always Miss Cool, Calm, and Collected. Miss Always in Control. At least until I met you. Maybe it's this damn war that's making me want to hurry things to see where they might lead. Maybe it's something else entirely. At this point, what's going to happen is something neither of us can know. To tell you the truth, I've no idea if you're the slightest bit interested in me. I've never asked, and you've never said. And you may not be. I've found in the past some men find me more than a bit intimidating and want nothing to do with a strong, independent woman like me. You might be one of those men, Sam Erickson. But I'm here tonight, willing to take that chance."

"You certainly don't have to worry about me being intimidated," he said. "You're obviously extremely smart. And unbelievably attractive. Just the kind of woman I've always enjoyed being around. I can't imagine how any man wouldn't find you fascinating."

"There've been a few. Even so, even if you're as interested in pursuing this as I am, there are no guarantees things will work out. There never is. We'll just have to play it by ear and see what happens. Maybe there's something between us, maybe not. Does that sound fair? Because if you look inside and find you've no real interest in me, that won't change a thing this evening. We can take this walk as friends and let it go at that."

"That's more than fair, Lauren."

"As friends, Sam?"

"As whatever, I guess. Friends, more than friends, whatever. I mean you certainly are an engaging woman. And I can't think of a reason in the world not to pursue this further."

"Then I'll tell you what. Let's turn around and walk down the beach in the other direction. Maybe when we're far away from here, we can figure out what it is we're really trying to do tonight."

"Sounds good to me," he said.

They turned and headed back toward the west.

"And besides, it'll give you a chance to tour the beautiful tent-lined streets of Press City, my wonderful home away from home," she added.

They trekked along the breakwaters. Sam's horrifying visions faded as they moved away from the scene of the earlier battle. Nevertheless, he didn't say much until they were a significant distance from where the initial landing had occurred. This time she let his silence go unanswered. The ground rules had been established and she was willing to do nothing more than hold on to him on this engaging night. So she walked on in silence, content to let him set the evening's terms.

They were two miles down the beach before he decided to restart the conversation. "I know you're off duty, but I've no idea what's happened since we spoke early this morning. Got any updates on today's events you can provide a curious Marine?"

They were now in her element and she immediately perked up. "Absolutely. My sources, both great and small, tell me other than the Iraqis and Iranians continuing to give us hell, things are going pretty well. In Egypt, most everyone I've talked to couldn't be happier. The regiments sent west have fought their way to the Libyan border. At the moment, things are quiet there. They're digging in and fortifying their positions. Still no sign of those seven million reinforcements Mourad told me he had. But so far, so good. On the front lines, the 1st Marines are under constant attack, but the fighting's not as intense as it was when you guys were there. In Cairo, not only have things stabilized, but with the assistance of the French tank brigade and British mechanized units, the 82nd Airborne's actually gained back some ground in parts of the city. With our help, the Egyptian army inside the capital's continuing to rally. We're definitely keeping the pressure on the Mahdi's followers. And I wouldn't be surprised if we counterattacked soon with the top-of-the-line French LeClercs to push them back across the Nile. I think we'll make our big push inside Cairo in the next few days. I've not been able to confirm it, but rumors are we've seen the first signs of the Pan-Arabs retreating."

"You're kidding. That's a sight I'd love to see."

"Intelligence folks believe it might be an indicator of things to come. There's a school of thought gaining acceptance with our military analysts. Even though Mourad's got millions of soldiers on the battlefield, many of the best, the most fervent of his followers, have been wiped out in the relentless attacks of the past few weeks. The majority of his elite units are gone. What's left believes in him and his message. But not to the point where they're eager to forfeit their lives without a damn good reason."

"Sounds like the tide's slowly turning."

"Hopefully it'll turn even faster, and this will be over before anybody knows it. Because now that I've found you, I'm not anxious to give you back to the Marines. And the sad part is because of my connections, I've already been told the exact hour that'll happen."

"I know too. I just hadn't said anything. Guys from my platoon stopped by the hospital this afternoon."

"When I met them they seemed like a real nice bunch. How are they doing?"

"They're okay considering. Their spirits seem real good. Getting lots of sleep and eating their first actual meals in quite a long time. My platoon sergeant told me the British tank divisions are due to arrive in a couple of days. To cram all seven hundred onto the ships they had to leave their infantry support behind. So we're going to be tasked with that mission. We'll be heading out the moment the British are ready to roll."

"I know. Unless something slows them, this beach will see its initial Challenger tank at first light on the twenty-fifth. That's just over two days from now. One of my best sources confirmed that a few hours ago on my promise not to release it until you guys leave. Any chance my prayers will be answered and you'll not be discharged from the hospital in time to join your platoon?"

He stopped and looked at her once more. "Not going to happen. Even if the doctors told me I couldn't go, I'd go. They're my men and it's my job to lead them."

"You didn't have to tell me. I knew what your answer would be. But a woman can dream, can't she?"

"It's what I do. I'm a Marine and I plan to stay one. I wouldn't have it any other way."

"Not even if leaving the Marine Corps would allow you to spend the rest of your years in the arms of the woman you loved?"

"Lauren, I learned long ago to never say never about anything. But I need to be honest. I'm doing something with my life that I love. Something I've dreamed of for a long time. I've wanted this since before my father was killed. That doesn't mean something new couldn't find its way into my heart. Or this new love couldn't be so strong it forces my love for my job to lose all meaning. Anything's possible. Still, even after the horror I've lived through the past few days, I don't see myself ever doing anything but what I'm doing right now."

"Well, I asked," Lauren said. "And you were truthful. I can't expect more than that. After all, you did say never say never. So there's still hope."

"What about you? You're already famous. And have quite a reputation as a hard-charging, career-driven newswoman. Would you consider giving that up for the man you loved?"

"My answer might surprise you, Sam."

"How so?"

"There's definitely a part of me that would like a family life. If possible, I'd want to balance that with my career. Still, if the right man came along, who knows what I might decide to do?"

"So if the right man appeared you'd give your plans up just like that?"

"Just like that? You know better. You and I are so much alike it scares me. So you already know my answer. I also love what I'm doing. I don't want to quit anytime soon. But I too say never say never. Because you can't know what curves life's going to throw you. It's not likely I'd trade my career for a cozy house and some bright-eyed children, but you never know. If the right man came along, it's something I'd have to think about long and hard before making my decision."

"Fair enough. Two honest people with two honest answers. Hopefully, we can live with that for now."

They turned, heading back along the beach toward Press City and the hospital and landing zone beyond. While they walked, Sam grew quiet once again.

They soon entered the long rows of tents composing the area that had been dubbed Press City. They strolled between the drab canvas with Lauren beaming as she showed off her dashing date to the envious women in the press corps. The smile on her face left no doubt of her satisfaction with the stately Marine clinging to her arm. Without letting a hint of it appear in his movements, Sam was beaming also. He too was quite satisfied with how events were progressing. They stopped in front of a nondescript tent. Lauren threw back the flap.

"Well, this is it," she said. "My home away from home. I know it doesn't look like much, but don't let that fool you. I'm planning on adding a few rooms later on. Thinking of putting in a nice deck and an Olympic-size swimming pool."

"Looks pretty good compared to the filthy foxhole I spent most of the week in. Got the place to yourself, I see."

"You know what they say, rank has its privileges. And besides, rumor has it the other women reporters are terrified of having to live with me. So I've got a tent intended to sleep four to myself. Looks like it's going to stay that way for the time being. If we're stuck here much longer I'm going to plant a garden."

For the first time she heard him laugh. He looked out at the barren desert. "Don't think much would grow."

"I know, but it might be the insane thing that convinces the brass they have to let me out of here." The night's pleasant breezes tugged at their silhouettes. She turned to face him, moving in close and wrapping her arms around his waist. She looked into his eyes. Her voice was soft and sweet. "I know I'm being far too forward, but after tonight there's no longer any doubt. I want to get close to you, Sam."

"But you don't even know me. Counting this evening, we might have said all of a few hundred words to each other. How can you decide from so little information I'm someone worth getting to know better?"

"I know a whole lot more than you suspect. I've got to admit, I was fascinated by the battle-scarred lieutenant I interviewed on the beach that morning. So I did a bit of checking. Okay, more than a bit. I've spent a lot of the past five days finding out everything I could about that brave Marine. What I learned was astounding. Solid upbringing. First-rate athlete and class valedictorian. Adored by his men. And at least according to his mother by every eligible girl in his hometown in Indiana."

Lauren couldn't see it, but Sam's face was turning a bright shade of red.

"My God, you talked to my mother?" He tried to hide his embarrassment but his words gave him away.

"Sure did. Extremely nice lady. Quite proud of you. But at the moment also extremely concerned. Claimed when I called that I needed the information for a follow-up story I was doing. After watching my interview with her brave son about a hundred times, she was happy to oblige. I felt bad lying to her like that. In reality, it was the only way I knew to find out about my competition. Fortunately, there doesn't appear to be any. Because I've had a long-standing policy about involvements with involved men. But you passed the test with flying colors. No wife. No kids. No fiancée. No lasting relationships whatsoever. According to your mother, and much to the consternation of scores of pretty Midwest girls, the only serious relationship you've ever had was with the United States Marine Corps. Well, have I adequately described First Lieutenant Samuel Erickson to your satisfaction, sir?"

"To the point of nearly scaring me to death."

"Well, don't be too scared, my motives were truly honorable. It's just when I set out to do a job I always do it right. In that respect we're also a lot alike, you and I."

They looked into each other's eyes. The moonlight shined down upon them. The pounding waves crashed upon the shore. Lauren reached up and kissed him. It was a long, slow kiss filled with passion. For Sam there was no doubt this was a woman who'd been kissed before. And one he'd want to kiss again.

"Want to come inside?" Her voice was as alluring as any he'd ever heard.

He looked into her inviting tent. And for some strange reason hesitated.

"What's the matter?" she said. Disappointment replaced sensuality in her words.

"I don't know. No man in his right mind would turn down such an offer. So I must be crazy, but I'm going to decline, if you don't mind. I want this too, but more than anything I want things to be just right before we move on to the next level. To be honest, after our walk I'm exhausted. Anything further we attempt tonight wouldn't be when I'm at my best. And I suspect if we want this to last beyond tonight, it's almost too important, and too soon, for us to carry things beyond where they are. I also want you to understand if my superiors find out I turned down such an incredibly attractive woman's offer, I could be drummed out of the Marines for gross stupidity."

Lauren let out a little laugh.

"Still," he said, "why don't we take a few hours before we go any further? Would you mind if I took a rain check until the moment's right for both of us?"

A smile came to her face. Her gallant lieutenant had confirmed everything she'd suspected about him. "I don't mind at all. Even if the British arrive on time, we've got two great days and two incredible nights before we have to face reality. So let's see where those hours lead. Because I'm planning on spending nearly every one of them at your side. For now, my precious Marine, since you've graciously turned down my offer, I think we need to get you back to that hospital bed of yours."

39

C harlie Sanders awoke with a start.

There could be no denying, even in his addled state, that he'd been dozing. His catnap had lasted an hour this time. His faltering mind was confused and disoriented. He struggled to clear away the cobwebs. This wasn't the first time he'd fallen asleep in the past three days. Despite his efforts, after a week without the briefest moments of relief, his body had succumbed to its need for slumber. He understood letting his guard down could prove fatal. If he were sleeping when the enemy discovered his hiding place, he'd stand little chance. So he fought hour after hour against the overpowering craving for unconsciousness.

He took the lighter from his pocket and felt for the candle at his side. Its flame soon burned, illuminating his cramped surroundings. Deep within his taut belly the stranded American was feeling the morning's hunger pangs. With the flickering light to guide him, Sanders searched the contents of his rucksack. His investigation confirmed what he already knew. The meager amount of food he'd found in the hotel's kitchen had been consumed. The only provisions remaining were enough packets of MREs, meals ready to eat, to feed a single person for three days. He shook his canteen. There wasn't sufficient water to prepare the final packets. Even so, he wasn't concerned. The next time he ventured into the kitchen he'd drain enough from the rusting water heater to fill the canteen.

He was still kicking himself for failing to notice the ample water supply until a couple of days ago. If only he'd thought of the obvious source earlier, the failed attempt to force Reena to drink the wine wouldn't have happened. And her hostility toward him might not be so great.

Water wasn't the immediate problem. They had enough of it to get through the coming days. He was certain at least twenty gallons remained within the old water heater. More than adequate, if rationed properly, to last for a long time to come.

Still, they needed far greater amounts of food to sustain them than what they had. Sanders would have to figure out a way to rectify the situation as soon as possible. He glanced at his watch.

He'd no idea how far behind the lines the hotel was situated. From the way things looked on the day he was surrounded, Cairo could have capitulated days ago. Even if such had happened and the war in Egypt was over, he understood he couldn't surrender. To do so would be to sign his death warrant. If he gave up, his life would be over in no more than a few tortured minutes.

A sharp sword would sever his head.

He'd had endless hours to search the farthest reaches of his mind to discover a way out of his predicament. Yet so far, he'd drawn a blank. With no idea what the tactical situation was, there was no chance of finding a means of escape. His best option, his only option, was to stay where he was and wait. For what exactly, he'd no idea. Nevertheless, the Special Forces sergeant had little choice. Unless discovered by the Chosen One's soldiers, he suspected his stay in the musty basement would go on indefinitely. He anticipated being trapped in this dark world for far longer than the couple of days his remaining rations would last. It wasn't beyond the realm of possibility they'd be here for countless weeks. He might have to hole up for months in the suffocating cellar before his chance for freedom appeared. As he stared into his rucksack and its scant supply, he faced the awful truth. Death by starvation was becoming a reality.

Sanders understood what he needed to do.

He got up and headed across the narrow aisle to the girl's resting place. He held the candle near her face and verified Reena was asleep. With her severe wounds, she'd slept for the majority of the past three days. He'd performed well in addressing her injuries. Her wounds were healing nicely. His stitches were a bit crude, and there'd always be a nasty scar. Yet given the circumstances, he'd excelled in his secondary specialty. There was no doubt she'd survive the bullet that had mangled her beautiful shoulder.

The young soldier smiled as he viewed her face. His peculiar love for her was stronger than ever. Although he'd seen no signs she'd changed her attitude toward him, he believed she'd eventually come around. Despite the bleakness of his situation, he was convinced things would turn out exactly as he desired. Someday, somehow, Reena Sharma would become his adoring wife.

"We're going to be out of food soon," Sanders quietly said to the silent figure. "And I'm certain we've cleaned out what there was to eat in the kitchen. But there might be a bounty capable of sustaining us for many days waiting in some unexplored corner of this old dump. The hotel was evacuated in one hell of a hurry, and they left a little food in the kitchen. So maybe, just maybe, there hadn't been time to gather any remaining elsewhere. It's a long shot, I admit. Still I thought I'd check as many of the rooms as I can to see if there's some elsewhere. I know I'm risking being discovered, but it's a chance I need to take. So I've decided to go upstairs and stay as long as I dare while searching for something to fill our bellies. The sunrise won't be here for over an hour. That should give me enough time to look around on the upper floors. You lie real still while I'm gone and dream a sweet dream of mountains of tasty morsels just waiting to be discovered."

Sanders grabbed his rucksack and rifle. He headed for the wine cellar's creaking stairs. The cautious sergeant blew out the candle. He couldn't risk any light once outside his protective den. Even a faint glow might be detected from the corner in front of the hotel. And the result would be inevitable. Within minutes, Mourad's soldiers would be swarming over every inch of the place.

It was a chance he couldn't take. He'd have to work in near darkness.

To avoid making more noise than absolutely necessary, he cautiously placed his boot upon the first step. The aging wood groaned. His senses heightened.

He had to be careful. Until he'd returned to the dank cellar, every movement would be adroit and calculated. He understood any ill-positioned action could be his last. Placing his weight to minimize the noise, he eased up the rotting staircase until he reached the narrow door into the kitchen. Sanders took the safety off his M-4. He held his breath and pushed the door open a fraction of an inch. He stood on the top step for nearly a minute, listening for any sound of impending danger. The morning was hauntingly quiet. Outside only a light desert breeze disturbed the early hours. Neither footsteps nor voices reached his ears. He waited, searching in the blackness for anything out of place. Nothing, however, appeared.

Sanders carefully opened the door. He hesitated, adjusting to the dark void within the windowless room and waiting for his mind to confirm it appeared safe to move on. The air in the kitchen hung heavy and stale, but it felt like heaven when compared with the stifling cavern he'd left. He took a tentative step into the kitchen. Without warning, the room came alive. It was filled with furious movement and unwelcome noise.

Something brushed against his boot and rushed past his leg.

Something else raced by a fraction later. Sanders froze. He knew in an instant what he'd uncovered. The space was filled with scurrying, squeaking rats. He could feel their sordid presence around him. He waited, never moving a muscle as the vile scavengers hurried to find a hiding place. It didn't take long for the bloated Nile vermin to locate a safe hole. Their frantic movements subsided as swiftly as they'd begun.

He waited to ensure the rats were gone. Hopefully, no one outside the kitchen had heard the rodents' actions. If they had, they might come to investigate the cause of the din. He listened for the telltale signs of man-made sounds. Yet nothing out of the ordinary emerged. Slowly, measuring each step meticulously, he felt his way across the small enclosure. He pressed his ear against the lobby door and waited. Once again, nothing but the rustling noises of the morning's gentle winds greeted him.

He pushed the door open and peered into the lobby. On the other side of the lightless passage, near the foyer, the enticing stairway waited. Now would come the most harrowing moments of his plan. To reach the stairwell he'd have to cross the room, coming perilously close to the hotel's front door and the street beyond. As he did, he'd be at his most vulnerable. If his adversary entered at an inopportune moment, or a passing Pan-Arab soldier spotted movement inside the hotel through the dirt-crusted windows, the game would be over. After a brief but furious struggle, his life would end. Nevertheless, traversing the decrepit space was a chance he'd have to take. He needed to discover if more to eat could be found within the Hotel Louraine's crumbling walls. He knew he was risking it all in hopes of finding something to nourish them. He understood the chance he was taking. He'd few choices left, nevertheless. It was a gamble he had to take.

The anxious Green Beret moved across the dingy chamber. The tattered rug was impregnated with filthy rainwater from the earlier storm. Its surface squished beneath his feet. He did his best to make the minimum amount of noise. Halfway through the cluttered space, he stopped and listened once more. The hotel was deathly silent. The ancient street in front of the timeworn building was the same. He sensed nothing either inside or near the hotel. For the first time, his keen hearing picked up the sounds of distant small-arms fire. There was fighting going on somewhere in the city. Yet he couldn't determine its source or intensity. Sanders moved on, coming nearer to the entrance.

Finally, the tantalizing stairs were within reach. He felt for the deeply shadowed handrail. Once more, he froze, waiting and listening. A less experienced individual would have headed up the steps and away from the obvious dangers the hallway presented. But Sanders wasn't going to make such a mistake. Instead, at the bottom of the stairwell he stood motionless, letting his finely tuned senses examine his surroundings for signs of danger. He had to ensure nothing outside the structure seemed amiss. If his movements had been detected, the odds were good that excited voices would fill the street in front of the building. Even more, he needed to verify that nothing on the upper floors indicated the enemy's presence. In his long hours in the wine cellar he'd heard no indication of anyone inside the hotel. Even so, he didn't know whether voices in the lobby or floors above would've carried to his well-insulated hiding place. And with his luck, Mourad's men could've arrived and headed upstairs while he snoozed. For all he knew, every inch was filled with sleeping Pan-Arabs. So he held his ground in the foyer.

His eyes never left the door leading into the dirty street while he waited and listened. The doorway and the pavement beyond were scarcely an arm's length away. Sanders would've loved to look at what awaited outside the hotel. He was severely tempted to take a quick peek through the tattered curtains. Yet he thought better of it. A glance out the slender windows, even a brief one, might prove fatal if a careful sentry was posted nearby.

Satisfied there appeared to be no one within the building, he turned and headed up at a slow, calculated pace. After pausing on each landing to allay his fears, he intended to go to the sixth floor and work his way down. He'd search as many rooms as he could in the time he had to find the banquet he craved. Long before the sun arrived, he planned on returning with as much food as his strong arms and rucksack could carry.

Shortly before the lobby's tired clock chimed six, the anxious American reached the top floor. He made his way to the end of the hall and mindfully opened the door on the right. Always conscious of the need to avoid the windows, he started his determined search.

There was nothing in the first room he checked. Or the second. And nothing still in the third. In the darkness, it took twenty minutes to examine the contents of the twelve rooms on the sixth floor. His search found nothing in any of them. There was no food on the top floor.

Disappointment showed at the corners of his mouth. Still, he wasn't ready to give up. He'd thirty minutes remaining before being forced to crawl back into his hole. He moved to the fifth floor. A first room awaited his inspection. He hoped what he required would appear. If not, he'd keep checking for as long as the coming morning would allow.

Maybe a king's feast waited in the next room . . .

40

S anders had come up empty. For nearly an hour he'd searched for anything they could eat. He'd covered every room on the top three floors. But no food had been revealed. And he'd stayed much too long. The dawning day was near. The creaking hotel was growing far too light to continue with his quest. Maybe tonight, well after dark, he'd resume his mission by scouring the rooms on the first, second, and third floors. He knew from the previous hour there wasn't much hope of finding anything. Nevertheless, he had to try. Maybe this evening he'd uncover the supplies they desperately needed.

The discouraged sergeant stepped out of the final room on the fourth floor. In the growing twilight he moved like a whisper through the depressing hall. Despite the lack of meaningful sleep and despondency from the futile search, he attentively edged down the old stairs. Every muscle was alert, every sense vigilant. Now wasn't the time to let down his guard.

Sanders reached the third floor. He paused, listening and waiting. He moved on, a single step at a time. The second-floor landing would be his last stop before the lobby. He soon arrived. He held his breath at this final resting place and examined his surroundings. Nothing seemed out of the ordinary.

He started down the final staircase. One exacting movement after another, he made his way for home. He was halfway to the foyer. Five minutes from now, after stopping at the water heater to fill his canteen, he'd be back in his burrow.

Suddenly, the hotel's door flew open wide. Two figures were standing in the half-light. Both were carrying rifles. Each appeared to be wearing a Pan-Arab uniform. The intruders began speaking in a language he didn't understand. The arriving pair weren't particularly vigilant. Neither spotted the murky form on the fragile stairs. They moved into the foul-smelling lobby.

"What the hell are they doing here?" Sanders said in a voice so soft only he could hear it.

They soon answered the bewildered American's question. The first pulled a pack of cigarettes from his pocket. He removed a couple, handing one to his companion. He lit both with the lighter he'd liberated from a dead Egyptian soldier a week earlier. As they smoked, they continued their relaxed conversation with no more than a curt glance around the tussled room.

"You two may be careless," Sanders muttered. "But you're no fools. It's still dark enough outside you'd have been spotted three blocks away lighting those cigarettes. Bet you didn't want to tip off your superiors you were having a smoke, so you snuck in here to make sure you wouldn't get caught."

The leader dropped upon the tattered couch in the middle of the lobby. It was obvious the enemy was in no hurry to return to the street. So far, Sanders had been lucky. They hadn't noticed his presence. Even so, he couldn't expect his good fortune to last much longer. The day was growing lighter. It wouldn't take much for the Pan-Arabs to spot him. He needed to find someplace to hide. And he needed to find it fast.

Anywhere was better than where he was. The hundreds of hours of hard training he'd endured in learning how to avoid detection were going to be tested to their limits in the coming seconds. Without the slightest sound, he slowly turned and headed up the stairs. His foot placement on the faltering staircase was critical. Even the faintest noise would be heard by those below. He was eight steps from the second-floor landing. A mistake on any and the game would be over. He pushed aside his fears and focused. A single stair was conquered, and then another. One at a time, he addressed the final six. Undetected, he returned to the second floor.

He slipped inside the room at the head of the stairs. Sanders dropped behind the shaded door. He held his breath and listened, searching for telling footsteps.

He looked around. It wasn't much of a hiding place. Nevertheless, it was a significant improvement over where he'd been. He pulled his knife from its sheath. Even if it meant all day, he'd stand motionless and wait.

Reena awoke. As she'd done often, she lay perfectly still pretending to be asleep so the infidel wouldn't bother her. She waited in the devouring darkness, her breathing measured, her body unmoving. For reasons she couldn't quite determine, she sensed she was alone. She raised her head and scanned the pitch-black room, searching for noise or movement.

There was none.

She held her breath and listened. The small enclosure was silent. Her tormentor didn't seem to be there. She was becoming more confident her suspicions were true. Her captor had disappeared. When he'd left, and where he'd gone, she hadn't a clue. She instantly understood one thing with resounding clarity. Her chance to escape and alert her countrymen of the American's presence had arrived. Her wounds were extremely serious and she'd barely moved in the past days. She wasn't, however, going to let that stand in her way. Freedom waited at the top of the cellar stairs.

Using the peeling clay wall for support, she started lifting herself to a sitting position. Her efforts were slow and awkward. Her breathing strained. Still, she wasn't going to be denied. Inch by inch, she struggled against the all-encompassing pain until her back was against the ancient mortar. She placed her good arm on the earthen floor and strove to stand. The attempt resulted in an unqualified failure. She slumped against the wall, fighting the surging torment and compelling nausea that threatened to engulf her. Reena tried again, but didn't get far. She rested, resisting the misery and steeling herself for another effort. Against all odds, she had to succeed. A third attempt . . . her body tenuously rose. It took every measure of strength she could muster to complete the undertaking.

Yet she'd done it. She was on her feet. Despite her best efforts, her suffering was so intense she nearly let out a piercing scream. The floundering girl fought her need to cry out. If she did, and her antagonist was near, it would alert him of her attempt to escape. She could tell the resolute movements had reopened her wounds. She could sense warm liquid oozing down her back. She could feel a line of red trickling upon her breast.

She leaned against the wall, fighting to maintain consciousness. She had to hold on. She had to escape. With her good arm, she grabbed the nearest wine rack and took a stumbling step toward freedom.

The lounging Pan-Arab ground his cigarette into the soggy carpet. He said something to his partner and started toward the stairs. His friend was right behind. As the duo climbed toward the second floor, they continued their animated discussion. Neither seemed particularly aware of, or the least bit troubled by, their surroundings. They soon reached the landing.

The first soldier spotted the open doorway at the head of the staircase. While continuing to chatter away, he entered the small room where the deadly sergeant was hiding.

Sanders's body stiffened. He held his breath and waited.

The leader went directly for the unmade bed. He threw himself upon its rumpled sheets. The second stood just inside the dusky entrance. He was inches from the skilled assassin hiding behind the gloomy door.

Sanders raised his knife. He suspected he'd have little difficulty killing them both. He'd reach out a powerful arm and slit the nearest one's throat before the Pan-Arab could react. The other would prove more difficult. With any luck, the startling American's sudden appearance would allow little time for his languishing foe to respond.

Along with his fellow Green Berets, he'd spent endless hours rolling around in mock knife combat in the red dirt of North Carolina. It was his favorite way to pass the time on sultry summer days beneath the swaying pines. He was lethal at his task. He wasn't concerned with his ability to succeed in the coming fray. He knew he'd win. His only worry was whether the one on the bed could unleash a wild shot before he reached him, alerting anyone nearby of the presence of an intruder. If before he died the soldier got off even a single round, Sanders's efforts over the past few days might have reached their end.

The Pan-Arabs continued to chatter, oblivious to the danger within their midst. The confident Sanders calculated his task. Reach out, slice the first throat, then pounce upon the other before he had time to react. He went over the murderous process in his mind, visualizing the details of his furious attack. Ten seconds from now the room would be filled with the flowing blood of the Chosen One's mortally wounded followers. And he'd be headed back to the cellar.

He raised his arm ever so slightly, moving the knife into the precise position for the furious advance. He was a fraction of a second from springing into action. He suddenly recognized the fatal flaw in his plan. It was likely he'd prevail in the one-sided combat. Of that he'd no doubt. Still, he was just as certain of something else. Once he'd slain the enemy soldiers, it wouldn't be long before they were missed. Sanders knew the Mahdi had no tolerance for deserters. A thorough search would be undertaken of the entire area. If anyone had seen them going into the hotel, they'd soon find their battered remains. And their killer's underground hiding place within minutes of that. Even if they hadn't been spotted entering the ramshackle building, eventually the old structure would be searched, with the results for the lone American the same.

Sanders pulled back the knife.

If he wanted to survive another day, he couldn't slay either of them. All he could do was wait to see if they spotted his presence and forced his hand. For their sakes, and his own, he hoped neither would.

The lurid moments crawled by. It was obvious the one on the bed was in no hurry to leave. Finally, his partner glanced at his watch. He looked at it again in the dissolving dawn. He announced something in an anxious tone. The sentence was barely out of his mouth when he rushed from the room. The other leaped from the bed, grabbed his rifle, and headed out the door in a great hurry. Sanders could hear their running feet on the stairs. Moments later, the front door slammed. The hiding Green Beret let out a deep breath and sighed.

Reena also heard the sudden clamor. She'd no idea who or what had made the unexpected noise. Maybe the infidel had left her at last. Maybe it was something else entirely.

She stumbled toward the rickety cellar stairs, supporting herself by grasping the heavy wine racks. Each teetering step was filled with suffering. She stopped after nearly every movement to rest and recover from the extreme exertion. She was far too weak to be attempting anything half so demanding. Nevertheless, it was an opportunity she couldn't let pass.

The grappling form needed five agonizing minutes to cover the ten feet from the corner of the cavern to the bottom of the enticing stairs. Even so, her determination didn't waver. She looked at the deteriorating steps, unable to make out much in the blanketing space. She did, however, recognize that the slender door above was partially open. Even if it took all day to climb to the top of the decaying passageway, she'd make her way out of the underground prison.

Reena gripped the stairs' railing with her good arm. With all her might, she pulled herself up onto the first step. Her knees buckled. She fought to stay on her feet. She knew if she fell, she wouldn't have the ability to stand again. Despite her best efforts, she let out a muffled scream. She battled against her mind's insistent urging that she sit down. Her breathing was sharp and intense. Her heart was racing, pounding in her throat. But she understood she was one step closer to her reward. Her days confined with the vile heretic were nearing their end.

Daylight was upon Cairo. Sanders peeked out the second-floor doorway. He waited and listened. He was certain the Pan-Arabs were gone. Yet now wasn't the time to get careless.

He stepped into the hallway and made his way toward the stairwell. The dank lobby awaited.

Reena's battle continued. She edged onto the second, and shortly thereafter the third step. Her body was gripped by a pain so demanding it nearly caused her to lose control. She could feel the blood rushing from her head. The struggling girl fought the overpowering impulse to rest. She leaned against the brittle railing once more. She was nearly halfway there. Only five stairs remained to conquer and she'd be in the kitchen. The door above swung open. The American was standing there. He looked at her wretched figure. There was a stunned expression on her face. Even in the half-light, he could see the crimson flow beneath the thick bandages he'd applied.

"Reena, what the hell do you think you're doing?"

He hurried toward her. The wavering girl collapsed before he

arrived. She was unconscious before she tumbled to the floor. He carefully lifted her sprawling form and carried her to the makeshift bed.
Sanders began examining the damage she'd inflicted. He gently removed the blood-soaked bandages from her injured shoulder.

"Aw, Reena, why'd you do something so stupid?" His voice was soft
and gentle. But the motionless girl heard none of the love in his ad-
monishing words. "You've ripped your stitches. I'm going to have to
sew you up all over again."

Late in the afternoon, despite his best efforts, he nodded off anew. He
was slumped over, half-sitting, half-lying against the pitiful wall. His
breath became steady and rhythmic. He started to snore. It was the moment for which Reena had been waiting. Her near escape had heightened her desire for freedom. She understood, nonetheless, that as long
as the enemy soldier lived, she'd be trapped in this limiting place, unable
to flee. There was no other way. Despite her fragile state, she'd have to
take matters into her own hands. She'd have to kill her captor.

Reena worked her gashed body into a sitting position. She was even
weaker than before. The swallowing anguish was deep and overwhelming. It wouldn't subside. She bit her lower lip to keep from cry-
ing out. It was a long, difficult effort, but eventually the girl fought her
way to her feet and took a halting step. Sanders lay a short distance
from her. A trembling Reena was soon standing over his sleeping
form. She knew his rifle would be resting against the wine rack to her
right. She felt her way, inching with her hand until her fingers reached
his M-4. Silently she picked up the foreign rifle, cradling it beneath her
good arm. One quick shot in the dark and her troubles would be over.

She pointed it in his direction. The end of the barrel was nearly
touching his chest. Her wretched body was shaking. She didn't have
the strength to hold the weapon still. At so short a distance, however,
it wouldn't matter. The bullet would find its mark. She'd kill the unbe-
liever. And her freedom would come.

The time had arrived to dispatch her oppressor.

She held her breath and squeezed the trigger. There was a clicking sound as she pulled it. But nothing happened. No cartridge fired.

The Special Forces soldier reached out and grabbed the end of the rifle's barrel. He ripped it from her hands.

Charlie Sanders had survived his second close encounter of the day.

"Didn't they teach you anything in your weapons training, sweetheart? You've got to take the safety off if you want the damn thing to fire."

He got to his feet. At well over six feet, the forceful American was a foot taller than his captive. He hovered over her, the anger in his words unmistakable. She was helpless in his presence. He could easily have reached out and strangled her. He could've snapped her neck without giving it a second thought. It would take no effort for the well-trained expert to end her life. That was what she expected. She steeled herself for the end. Instead, he put down the rifle and picked up a candle. Its flame soon filled the room with haunting light. She could see the rage in his eyes. And the disappointment. The anger soon passed. He took her gently by her good arm.

"After all the time I spent patching you up this morning, I can't believe you've reopened your wounds again. I'm going to have to rip up more bedsheets for bandages and start over. Reena, your injuries are serious. You need to get back into bed and lie still if you're ever going to recover." He led her over, settled her in, and reexamined the damage. "When are you going to learn?"

He dressed her shoulder. When he was finished he shook his head and blew out the candle.

41

The loving couple stood on the windswept dunes. Both were staring at the restless waters. Each clung to the other as if their life depended upon it. The thick haze from the unrelenting battles had returned to cover the landscape in a sickly hue. Only a handful of faint stars and hint of a waning moon could be seen through the perverse smoke's cover.

Still, their bliss hadn't been dampened by the bleak surroundings. They'd found a lovers' paradise in a dreary place called Press City. For two days, they'd hardly been out of each other's arms. For forty-eight hours, they'd seldom left the uncomfortable cot in Lauren's tent. Even so, they couldn't get enough of each other. Both wished their time together could go on without end.

Despite the idyllic appearance of their embrace, neither was smiling as they looked upon the choppy seas. The reason for their concern was obvious. Each was staring at the British fleet anchored beyond the breakwaters. The unspoiled hours with few cares about the world beyond her tent were nearing their end.

"How many ships do you count?" she asked. He could hear the tension, with the slightest hint of panic, in her voice.

"Enough to hold two divisions of armor, I'm afraid."

"I guess this means you'll soon be rejoining your platoon and heading into the desert toward who knows where."

"I didn't have the heart to tell you, but I've already gotten my orders. This is our last night together. The tanks start landing at sunrise. By noon, their advance elements will move south. My platoon will be joining the lead unit and heading for Cairo."

She brushed away the hair from her vivid eyes. "Well, we knew this moment would come. We've been living on borrowed time from the beginning. Even so, I've cherished every minute of our brief hours together. I hope you feel the same."

"You know I do."

"Please don't tell me this is the end for us, Sam, and what's happened was nothing more than a wartime fling."

"How could you think that way? I'll be back in your arms the minute the shooting stops. I still don't know where we're going with this relationship. But one thing's certain, if I've anything to say about it, the wonderful days we'll spend together have just begun."

She glanced at her watch. "I guess we'd better make the most of what little time we have left. So what do ya say, mister, want to go back to my tent and show a girl a good time?"

"To be honest, I don't know if I've got the strength. Morning, noon, and night, we've been at it without pause for two straight days. I'm beginning to suspect you're some kind of spy who has been sent to kill me."

"Yeah, but what a way to go, making passionate love to the woman who adores you. And think of what it'll do for my reputation."

"I assure you, Lauren, your reputation doesn't need any assistance."

"So are we going to stand here wasting time, or are we going back to my tent?"

"What do you think?" he said. "We're going back to your tent."

They turned from the flotilla and headed toward Press City. A few bouts of joyous lovemaking remained before the fortunes of war would pull them apart.

Neither slept a wink as they held on tight and relished every passing minute. The intensity of these dwindling moments knew no bounds. In between, they talked a bit about the past, and even more about the future. Admittedly, neither was certain of what the future held. There simply hadn't been time to know what it was they had here. But whatever it was, each recognized it wasn't your run-of-the-mill romance that would fade with the final echoing gunfire. For Lauren, the spark she'd recognized the first time she saw him had burst into a roaring flame. And Sam felt the same. The final night's lovemaking was beyond either of their exceeding expectations. It was far more than primal lust, however. There was something about it, something each recognized, telling them this was a love affair that might last for the remainder of their days.

The night soared on toward the cold reality of morning. The desperateness of their final hours weighed heavy on their minds.

"Sam?" Lauren said softly.

"What?"

"Don't try to talk me out of it because I've made up my mind. Even if I have to call the president to get permission, I'm going with you tomorrow."

"No, you're not, Lauren."

"Why not? It's not just because of you I want to be there. I've got a job to do. And I can't do it while confined to Press City. The American people need to know what it's really like out there. They need to know what you guys are living through."

"You're out of your mind. It's far too dangerous."

"Danger comes with the territory for a good reporter. Do you have any idea how many times I've had bullets flying around me the past few years? I've probably seen more action than you."

"Not like this you haven't. This isn't some crazy palace revolt with a few wild shots fired into the air. This is out-and-out war at its worst. These guys mean business. They'll kill anyone and anything that crosses their path. They won't care who you are. Being a big-shot reporter isn't likely to protect you this time."

"I'm going, Sam. I can't take being locked up on this beach while this all passes me by. I can't take knowing the man I'm falling in love with will be facing the enemy and I won't know what's happening to him. So tomorrow, when your battalion moves out, my cameraman and I will be in the Humvee right behind you."

"Lauren, please don't. For my sake, don't. Think about what my response will be if you're in that Humvee. If you're there, there's a far greater chance of my not surviving. I'll have enough to worry about keeping my guys alive. But with you tagging along I'll have doubled the problems I'll face. Making sure you're safe might cost me, and the men under me, our lives. So if you care about me in the slightest, if you care about the Marines you've met from my platoon, you'll do what I ask and not come with us."

She lay in silence, taking in his words. She knew he was right. Being with him would significantly increase the danger. For once, she couldn't think just about herself. She couldn't focus solely on her own selfish ambition to get the story ahead of everyone else. Her growing love had seen to that. Her voice was almost a whisper. "All right, Sam. When you leave tomorrow, you leave without me."

With the day's first glimmer, they stood on the beach watching the initial landing craft coming ashore. The moment the lead tank headed down the ramp and crashed into the surf, a tear trickled down her cheek.

42

B arely a week earlier, to keep Cairo from falling, the Americans had been forced to attempt a desperate landing behind enemy lines. And for the eight days following, the Marines had held on, waiting for help to arrive. With the appearance of the British tanks, the Allies suddenly were brimming with confidence. It wouldn't be long before they crushed the Mahdi and annihilated his forces. On every Egyptian front, the war had turned. Optimism abounded. Among the Marines there was wild speculation they'd triumph in as little as four days.

The steady process of bringing men and equipment ashore continued without letup. The first arriving division's tanks were on dry land. Over three hundred imposing Challenger 2s had reached the glistening sands of the Egyptian coast. The foul-smelling beasts covered every inch of shoreline and the scowling desert beyond. The few days of rest Erickson's Marines had enjoyed were at their end. It was time to return to the slaughter. The bloody-nosed Americans of the 2nd Marine Division, survivors of endless hours of fierce combat, would provide the infantry support the British division required. The 1st

Marines, presently holding the front against Mourad's forces, would leave their foxholes to give similar support to the second of the British divisions.

By today's sunset, nearly seven hundred of some of the world's best tanks would be upon the open sands of North Africa and the Allied offensive well into its initial stage. Waiting to face them were the Chosen One's eight thousand surviving T-72s and M-60s supported by four thousand armored personnel carriers and more than two million warriors. In their day, the Russian T-72s and American M-60s had been excellent tanks. But only the T-72 could be considered so now. And even it had severe limitations when compared with the Challenger. Each of the Mahdi's tanks was capable of holding its own in most combat situations. Yet neither had the fully integrated shoot-on-the-move capabilities of their adversary. The enemy tanks were capable of firing upon a target from only a stationary position, a severe handicap their opponent didn't face. In a one-on-one confrontation with the technologically advanced British, the Chosen One's armor would stand scant chance of victory.

Fortunately for the Pan-Arabs, their armored vehicles greatly outnumbered the invaders. So tank-against-tank battles would be few. Mourad's forces were depending upon sheer numbers and relentless determination to prevail in their holy crusade to conquer the Middle East, and beyond that the world.

In two hours, the Allies would attack across a one-hundred-mile front. Losses for both sides in so monumental a struggle would be severe. With the Americans' dominance of the skies, such would be especially true for the Chosen One's disciples.

At the moment, it was organized chaos along the beachhead. The steady shifting from the transport ships to the historic sands went on unimpeded. At the landing zone, men and equipment were moving in every direction. With the initial division ashore, the time had come to start the proceedings. The lead battalion's thirty-six Challengers roared to life. Accompanied by the three hundred surviving Marines of Erickson's battalion, they'd spearhead the attack on the eastern edge of the Pan-Arab lines. As they'd done in the beginning, his men would be out front. With a handful of replacements bolstering their numbers, Erickson's twenty-three-man platoon, with two battle-scarred Humvees, would accompany four Challengers in their efforts to locate and destroy those who stood in their way.

The lieutenant, in full battle dress, approached the forward British platoon leader's tank. His Marines were ready to go. Each was either in one of the Humvees or clinging to a Challenger's hull for the ride through the sun-soaked desert. Gunny reached out and gave Erickson a hand up. The lieutenant scrambled onto the broad metal shell and found a spot next to the tank commander's position. He turned toward the beach, searching for Lauren. In the confusion, she was nowhere to be found. For the life of him, he couldn't understand her unexplained disappearance. She'd been called away for something urgent moments before he'd headed for the tanks. He looked toward the fluttering tents of Press City, hoping against hope she'd appear. Still, he couldn't locate her.

The command was given. The time had arrived to drive the maniacal cultists from Egypt. The pair of Humvees headed toward the seemingly unending desert. At a cautious ten miles per hour, they'd point the way. The tanks began churning through the deep sands. Behind them, the remainder of the British battalion and its Marine supporters edged forward.

At the last possible instant, Wells pushed through the crowds watching the initial Allied advance. Erickson spotted her.

She ran toward the slow-moving formation. "Sam!" she yelled. "I'm sorry we didn't get to say good-bye. But this was too important. We just got word. The French armored brigade, supported by the British mechanized infantry and the 82nd Airborne, attacked this morning. We've retaken all of Cairo! Other than a few scattered pockets, our forces have pushed the Pan-Arabs back across the Nile." She couldn't tell whether he'd heard her. "Did you hear me? The French tanks annihilated them. Cairo's back in our hands."

He gave her a thumbs-up. "Lauren, there's no need to say good-bye. We aren't going to be apart that long. With the way things are going, I'll see you in Cairo in a few days."

Wells stopped running. The armored array continued to move onto the vast plain. She gave him a huge smile and a final wave.

The Americans were certain the end was near.

Their fervent opponent, however, wasn't ready to agree with their assessment. For the Mahdi had significant tricks yet to play.

There wasn't a cloud in the Sahara sky and the smoke had momentarily dissipated. A sweltering North African day beat down upon the procession. The Challengers steadily progressed. They were alert for a surprise attack by Pan-Arab helicopters or marauding raiders. Fortunately, neither appeared. Other than the occasional stray camel, and a slithering asp or two, the Allies saw little in the monotonous world.

Death's disordered form, they viewed everywhere. Widely spaced, or in twisted clumps, the festering bodies littering their path stretched to the horizon.

The twenty miles to the front lines were soon crossed. They reached the wide asphalt of the Cairo-to-Alexandria highway. The Americans' forward foxholes were ahead. Erickson and a handful of his foot soldiers dismounted and took up positions supporting the tanks. The advancing elements soon passed through the cheering 1st Marine Division's lines. Between here and Cairo, there was nothing in front of them except two million well-armed zealots intent on taking their lives. From this point on, the bitter battle could burst upon them at any moment.

The lead platoon's Challengers spread out and rumbled forward. The Humvees settled in on the flanks, running twenty yards ahead of the armored monsters. The ever-vigilant Sergeant Joyce and his three men held the right flank. Sergeant Merker, now in command of the Humvee on the far left, was just as wary. Both vehicle commanders had their hands on their .50-caliber machine guns. Erickson was in the center of the formation, a few feet to the left of the British platoon leader's Challenger. While he walked, the tough lieutenant turned and looked behind.

The thirty-six tanks had taken up attacking positions. The British battalion was spread across an area two miles wide and one deep. The sounds of their thundering engines could be heard for miles. There'd be no surprising their adversary this time.

A dozen Humvees were mixed in the tank formations. The majority were armed with machine guns. A third of the Marine vehicles were equipped with TOW missiles. The battalion's men were spread throughout the rumbling armor. Reconnaissance drones passed over the formation, heading out to scout the terrain. A dozen Marine Cobras rushed to join the advance. The low-flying attack helicopters kept a keen eye on the unyielding landscape. Their mission was twofold: protect the advancing tanks from an assault by Pan-Arab Hinds and attack the Chosen One's armor whenever the opportunity arose. A further layer of Allied aggressors was overhead. High in the skies, Super Hornets from the recently arriving *Gerald Ford* and *John F. Kennedy* crisscrossed the heavens. Even higher, still others prowled to protect those below from the sudden appearance of Pan-Arab fighter aircraft.

From those on the ground to those well above, the Allies were anxious and watchful. There'd been no signs of opposition. That, nonetheless, could change in a passing thought.

The Allies continued their persistent movement forward. Each step brought them closer to Cairo and an end to the war. Erickson had expected to encounter severe resistance the minute they left their own lines. Yet much to his amazement, it didn't happen.

Two long hours passed as the dauntless Marines plodded through the taxing environment. The torrid sun continued to hammer the exposed Americans. They were seven miles beyond their forward defenses. And there had been no sign of Mourad's followers.

To a man, they knew the Pan-Arabs were out there, waiting and watching.

Each understood it was all a matter of time.

43

A reconnaissance drone was the first to spot the danger. Their elusive opposition had appeared. Over the next rise, as the highway went through a confining canyon scarcely a half mile wide, a brigade of M-60s, supported by armored personnel carriers and infantry, waited. More than one hundred Pan-Arab tanks were positioned in the rocky gorge. The stationary M-60s would attempt to hold off the aggressors within the enclosed space to limit the superior maneuverability of the Challengers. Three thousand infantry, many armed with antitank missiles, were hidden within the steep crags or scattered among the tanks and armored personnel carriers.

Until the last instant, Mourad had insisted on fighting in attack mode rather than defending the ground they held. He finally had relented. Even so, none in the canyon had been given time to dig in or fortify their defenses. It was a result that would severely hamper the M-60s' chances.

The Cobras raced toward the canyon. The Hornets plunged from on high to strike the armored brigade. The British tanks, having stopped to allow the remainder of the Marines to dismount, picked up speed. Those on foot started running across the flowing sands.

Mourad's brigade of aging M-60s was going to be hit by three groups of overriding assailants, one right after another. The tank-destroying helicopters crested the final ridge. The bristling canyon unfolded in front of them. There were targets everywhere the pilots looked. A Cobra's weapons acquisition officer unleashed an initial TOW. He guided it toward an exposed Pan-Arab tank near the gorge's northern end. As the missile reached its impact point the M-60's hull was ripped apart by the ordnance's irrepressible power. Burning pieces of the demolished giant surged skyward. Ear-shattering sound and soul-stealing fires rushed into the heavens. The stark violence stunned defenders and attackers alike. The deafening explosion echoed throughout the limiting space. The defeated tank's consuming flames rose, singeing the gorge's time-weathered walls.

A second attack helicopter followed with a Hellfire missile. The result was lethally startling and brutally predictable. Another wrecked tank exploded, its objecting roar crushing the contrite afternoon. Two Pan-Arab crews had found the promised paradise. Many would soon join them. Always on the alert for Stinger firings, the voracious Cobras sprinted through the canyon to seek and destroy. The stalwart avengers gave it everything they had. Death and destruction followed in their wake. A solid wall of cannon fire, missiles, and rockets tore into Mourad's exposed force. A dozen hapless giants were soon ablaze upon the canyon floor. Ten crushed personnel carriers joined the mounting fires. Scores of infantry went down beneath the darting Cobras' profound attack. Explosion after explosion ripped through the struggling garrison. The dazed defenders tried to answer back. But they were overmatched.

The M-60s' air defenses were ordinary at best. They posed little threat to the spitting Cobras. A hundred tank-mounted air defense machine guns opened fire at the same instant. As they raced through the modest strait, the insatiable helicopters continued their unerring mission to maim and devastate. As quickly as they had begun, the swirling attackers finished their run. They soared over the jagged outcroppings and disappeared. Behind them the devastated canyon was burning. They formed for another assault.

A Hornet duo appeared in the blackening sky above the exposed brigade. Each dropped a string of five-hundred-pound bombs upon the center of the striving defenders. The deadly warheads screamed toward the earth. As the high explosives reached their impact point, a grimacing refrain of life-taking detonations shook the anguished world. The results of the run were swift and certain. The calamitous desert shuddered and yawed beneath the impaling ordnance. The men and equipment caught in the awe-inspiring assault were torn apart. The fearsome aircraft swooped in to follow up on the onslaught. Their armor-piercing cannons blazed as they raced forward. Two additional pairs of F/A-18Es were right on their tails. They screamed in for the kill. More were on the way. In the choked terrain, striking bombs and spewing cannons went on without pause. Mourad's armor withered beneath the dismaying attack. The flailing opposition was being hacked to pieces. Thirty tanks were on fire. As the swarming Hornets left the canyon, a third of the Mahdi's force was gone.

And the uneven struggle was scarcely two minutes old.

The Pan-Arabs staggered beneath the airborne offensive. The British crested the final rise and reached the soiled ground. The Marines were with them. Out of breath, Erickson looked upon the hideous scene. Everywhere he surveyed, a grinning Mephistopheles was making his rounds. The Challengers surged forward, intent on finishing their crippled foe. The lead platoon's tanks spewed smoke from the five-barrel dischargers on the fronts of the lumbering beasts. The swirling gray clouds would mask the attackers' positions from the M-60s and the soldiers waiting with antitank missiles. Even with the self-induced haze, using their sophisticated thermal systems the Challengers could see their targets as clearly as if it were the brightest of days.

The British would concentrate their fire on the remaining M-60s and wait for the Cobras and Hornets to return. Erickson ordered his men forward. The foremost platoon's tanks locked on to their quarry. The Challengers' computers verified their targets were ready for the kill. All four tanks fired within seconds of each other, each destroying his floundering adversary. The one-sided battle's deaths grew.

The Humvee machine guns fired upon the force hidden along the condemned canyon's edges. Another Challenger platoon unleashed its 120mm main guns. Erickson's men opened up with their M-16s. Additional Marines rushed to join them. The British tank commanders fired their machine guns. Those in the canyon answered back.

The venomous Cobras returned. The horror began once more. The Pan-Arab commander attempted to rally his scalded force. But there was nothing he could do. The stark chaos and consuming terror were beyond anyone's control.

An arriving pair of Hornets released long streams of bombs. Hell's merciless images had nothing on the spectacle below. The overwhelmed Pan-Arabs broke and ran. On foot, or in armored vehicles, the survivors turned and scurried toward the safety of the south. Erickson watched as the turbaned political officers attempted to keep Mourad's defeated followers from retreating. Yet it was no use. What remained of the ravaged brigade couldn't be stopped. The desperate mullaho fired upon the fleeing soldiers, killing more than a few. Even so, they couldn't slow the panic-stricken elements from running for their lives. In a matter of minutes, what remained of the devastated force was gone.

As the fleeing enemy disappeared, the Hornets and Cobras gave brief chase before returning to their guardian positions. Their primary responsibility was to protect the British, and no matter how tempting the prize, they could not leave the tank battalion vulnerable to a Hind counterattack.

The Challengers would've loved to press their advantage. What remained of the defiled Pan-Arabs could easily have been annihilated. Still, it couldn't be done. For the moment, the flaming canyon was impassable. And the Allies were trapped on its northern side. Their advance was halted by the raging fires and constant secondary blasts on the horrid gorge's floor. There was nothing they could do until the persevering blazes subsided. They'd have to wait for things to die down before crossing the simmering inferno.

Erickson organized his men into a defensive perimeter as far into the canyon as he dared.

44

Eventually, it was safe to move on. The Allies passed through the smoldering wreckage, continuing their relentless advance. Nothing in the past hours had shaken their confidence. Each was certain in a few sunsets they'd reach Cairo and end the war.

The victorious attackers had survived the unequal battle with a dozen wounded and six dead. Erickson's Marines hadn't suffered a single casualty. Even so, the platoon leader understood such good fortune wouldn't last forever.

They left the essence-stained canyon and the wide highway behind. They were back on the open Sahara. The lead elements pushed south, heading toward the Egyptian capital. The sunset would soon be upon them. The Marines and the British armor trudged forward.

Since their earlier dominance, there'd been little sign of their rival. A few hit-and-run skirmishes and a halfhearted defense by a battalion of T-72s were all the dogmatists could provide.

Erickson had anticipated significantly stiffer resistance than what they'd encountered so far.

It had been a long day, but with their successes, and their superior night-fighting abilities, they'd no intention of stopping for even the briefest of moments. They were going to press their advantage and continue attacking throughout the infinite night.

As he walked, Erickson watched the progress of his Marines, judging their ability to carry the fight to the elusive enemy. Over the Challengers' bellowing engines he talked with the men, testing their resolve. Even those taking a turn riding on the tanks or in the Humvees looked as he felt—thoroughly exhausted and ready for relief.

Always observant, they continued to shuffle along. The encroaching sunset was on their right as they moved across the unrelenting landscape in search of prey. From the distant sounds upon the featureless hills, there was meaningful fighting occurring elsewhere. But their corner of the conflict had become strangely still.

The platoon leader sensed it was almost too quiet. They'd soundly defeated their battered adversary, pushing him back. Nevertheless, something didn't quite fit. The Mahdi had limitless divisions waiting in the Allies' path. Where they were, and why they weren't putting up more of a fight, he couldn't comprehend.

It wouldn't be long, however, before the answer would come.

Without warning, the late afternoon's malaise was shattered. On the left, thirty yards from Erickson's position, a violent blast hurled a plodding Marine into the air, dumping him upon the rock-strewn ground. Erickson turned toward the unexpected sound. The severely wounded private lay screaming at the top of his lungs. He flailed about, the all-consuming pain tearing at his anguished brain. His right leg, from the knee down, was gone. His left was shredded and bleeding. Erickson took an additional step and froze.

The injured American was one of those he'd taken command of earlier in the week. He wasn't one hundred percent certain, but he believed the private's name was Ruiz. On the far right, near James Fife, an earthshaking explosion pierced the growing evening less than a heartbeat later. Like a discarded rag doll, the British platoon's westernmost tank was tossed upon its side. Smoke poured from the ruptured Challenger's belly. Its left track was gone.

Erickson knew it could only be one thing. The advancing battalion had walked into a minefield. The area around them had been saturated with both antitank and antipersonnel mines.

Erickson searched the listless ground, looking for clues to where the mines had been placed. Yet he couldn't spot anything out of the ordinary. Despite the short time they had, their opponent had done a masterful job of planting the mines and disguising their locations.

The surviving British tanks and the Humvees ground to a halt. The critically injured private continued screaming.

"Nobody move!" Erickson yelled. He signaled the platoon to freeze. "We've hit a minefield. Platoon Sergeant!"

"Yes, sir!"

"Take a couple of men and head over to that crippled Challenger. Before it blows, get the crew out and check on our guys who were riding on it. Once I've got everybody organized, I'll try to reach Ruiz and see what I can do until we get a corpsman up here."

"Will do, sir." Gunny turned to the nearest Marines. "Williamson, Ayers, nice and slow move over to that tank and give me a hand. We've got to get them away from there before the fires reach its ammunition."

"Private First Class Gardner," Erickson said to the platoon's new radio operator, "tell battalion we've stumbled upon a minefield. Inform them of the need for a couple of corpsmen up here on the double." With Petty Officer Bright's death earlier in the war, the platoon no longer had its own medic and would have to wait for outside help.

"I'm on it, sir."

"The rest of you retrace your footsteps. Should you step on a mine, try not to panic. Leave your foot where it is, notify those around you of your situation, and wait for help to arrive."

Erickson looked around. His men were doing exactly as he'd directed. A step at a time, each was easing away from the baneful field. The three remaining tanks and the Humvees began slowly backing, using their earlier tracks to guide them to safety. Satisfied with the platoon's actions, Erickson edged across the leering desert toward the screaming Ruiz. With each movement, the platoon leader waited to hear the telltale *click* from an antipersonnel mine. The anguished teenager continued to writhe upon the bitter ground, out of his mind in pain.

Fife and his men headed toward the disabled tank. Each moved warily across the open ground. The tank's commander and gunner, riding with their hatches open, had been blown clear by the massive explosion. They lay a dozen feet from the smoldering Challenger. The loader and driver were trapped inside its immense walls.

Williamson reached the tank commander. The British sergeant lay in a heap. His right arm was shattered. A jagged piece of bone had pierced the skin inches below his elbow. Blood ran down his face from a nasty scalp wound above his right eye. His left leg was twisted in such a manner there was no doubt it was broken. Williamson pulled out his meager first-aid pouch. He applied a compress to the gaping head wound. Hopefully, a corpsman would arrive soon. If not, he'd attempt to carry the British soldier across the minefield before the ravishing flames blew the Challenger apart.

The tank's gunner had survived unharmed, but a bit disoriented. Lance Corporal Ayers helped him up and after looking him over took him to stand in the tank's tracks. He then went after the two Americans who'd been riding on the Challenger. There was nothing he could do for the first. He moved over to the second, who had already gotten to his feet. His injuries were little more than a twisted ankle along with some deep cuts and bruises.

With his eyes scanning every inch of ground, Ayers walked him over and placed him next to the tank's gunner. "Don't either of you move until we tell you to," he directed the pair. "Gunny, Nolan and the tank's gunner are ready to be evacuated. But Corporal Reeves is dead. Looks like he broke his neck in the fall. What do you want me to do?"

Fife had reached the burning leviathan. He glanced at the fires growing within its punctured frame. He knew even with the Challenger's excellent fire suppression system there was little time remaining before the disabled tank would explode.

"Step over here real careful like. We've got to get the other two crewmen out before it's too late. I'll crawl in after the loader. You free the driver from the front compartment."

"I'm on it," Ayers responded while taking a first careful step toward the crippled tank.

The pair commenced the highly dangerous task. Each knew the clock was ticking. But luck was with them. Both trapped crewmen were alive and neither was seriously injured. The crewmen were soon out of the distressing mass. Ayers took his four charges and with the tank tracks as his guide headed toward safety. Fife went over and did what he could to assist Williamson with the badly injured tank commander. As quickly as they dared, they picked him up and left the field.

Moments later, the tank exploded.

Erickson neared Ruiz's position. It felt like forever, but eventually he was at the private's side. The lieutenant examined the obscene results. There was no denying the injuries were life threatening. He put tourniquets on both legs using his belt and Ruiz's. The wounded private continued yelling. An ashen-faced corpsman appeared with a stretcher. A shot of morphine and they placed the disabled private upon it. They were soon on their way out of the deadly field, carrying the stretcher toward safety. Erickson led, searching for the most likely location to place his feet. He was certain each footfall would be his last. Yet somehow they made their way out of the danger.

Within minutes, a medevac helicopter arrived and whisked the wounded away. The crisis was over as rapidly as it had begun.

The platoon would get the rest they craved. In the approaching darkness, it would take the British minesweeping tanks three hours to reach their location. And with no idea of the width or depth of the minefield, the Allies weren't going to risk a nighttime clearance. The Marines would dig deep foxholes to support the Challengers.

Well after sunset, Erickson settled into his sandbagged world. From the beach, they'd traveled thirty-five miles on the opening day of the advance. For the next twelve hours, however, they'd be going nowhere. The platoon's euphoria from the afternoon's mastery was gradually ebbing.

To a man, the worn Americans suspected their dreams of reaching Cairo in four days had been wildly optimistic. All understood their triumph was going to take much longer, and involve far more suffering, than any of them cared to admit.

45

The brightly colored nomad tent sat in the middle of the pyramid complex. A blustery wind tore at its sides. The silken structure flapped with each strong breeze, pulling at its moorings and making significant noise. Those inside its sheltering form paid no attention to its distracting efforts.

For the past week, Muhammad Mourad had called the once-sacred hilltop home. From here he commanded his massive army. Upon the mesa, the Mahdi was surrounded by Egypt's most recognizable landmarks.

To the north sat the magnificent Great Pyramid of Khufu. East and west of the Great Pyramid were large fields of rectangular, aboveground tombs containing the remains of the pharaohs' families and the royal courts.

To the east, reaching to the broad plateau's edges, rested the jumbled peasant houses of the encroaching Giza suburbs. The modest homes stretched unending to the Nile.

To the southeast, a quarter-mile walk from the billowing tent, the enigmatic Sphinx reclined.

To the west were the pyramid of Khafre and the smaller pyramid of Menkaure. Beyond the western edge of the plateau, after a mile or so of additional homes, waited nothing but the inhospitable desert.

The historic elevation buzzed with activity. Soldiers assigned to the command element moved in every direction. Near the huge tent, the landscape bristled with the antennas, trucks, and vans of the Pan-Arabs' primary communication complex. On the perimeter, air defense weapons protected the sanctified ground. In every direction the eye surveyed, Mourad's mujahideen, his two hundred fiercely loyal bodyguards, stood at the ready. Each had vowed to give his life to defend the Chosen One. Farther out, around the hilltop's edges, Mourad's handpicked armored division waited with their tanks and personnel carriers. They were prepared to repel an attack of any sort. The fifteen thousand soldiers of the division were the best trained and most dedicated of the Mahdi's combat troops.

Inside the tent, he sat cross-legged on a stretching rug of indeterminate origin. The vivid hues and intricate designs of the woven fabric had lost none of their vitality throughout the long years of use. The spreading carpet reached from corner to corner in the spacious shelter. Two dozen of Mourad's religious, political, and military advisers sat with their leader in the center of the space. Each understood that in this setting they could speak their minds without fear of recrimination. While the decisions were ultimately his, Muhammad Mourad had learned long ago to carefully consider the advice of those who served him.

"Chosen One, if you don't act soon, all will be lost," General Khalil el-Saeed, commander of the army, said. "This morning the last of our units was expelled from Cairo by the French tanks and the British and American soldiers. Our warriors were ill-prepared for the enemy's assault. They didn't fare well when faced with the French armor. In the city's northern section, small pockets of Allah's warriors were cut off by the forcible advance. Those in this desperate predicament are battling the intruders with every ounce of courage they can muster.

They've sworn to fight to the death. Much of our force is gathering in Giza, waiting for your order to launch a counterattack. They're eager to renew the battle to cast out the unbelievers and continue with Allah's conquest."

"General, as we discovered this morning, it'll do no good to cross the river if we can't hold the territory we gain." Mourad turned to General Jehan Akhtar, el-Saeed's second-in-command. "Like General el-Saeed, I am anxious to renew the attack. Have you devised a plan that will place enough of our tanks on the eastern banks to expel our adversary from this land?"

"No, Chosen One, we have not," General Akhtar said. "We're continuing to look at all options. At best it will take two or three days to develop a viable approach and an equal amount of time to prepare our soldiers."

"Such is probably acceptable, General Akhtar," Mourad said. "It'll allow our warriors time to rest and gather their strength for the final assault. But we can afford no further delays. With the infidels mounting their forces in the north, time is of the essence. We must take the city before they end our chances of prevailing. Do our commanders understand the urgency of their efforts?"

"They understand full well," General Akhtar said. "They're quite aware of the enemy's progress. They recognize the situation's growing more difficult by the day."

"What's the latest word from the north, General el-Saeed?"

"This afternoon our forces in northern Egypt were attacked by two divisions of British Challenger tanks. The American Marines are with them. At the moment, we're putting our efforts into placing strings of great minefields in their path. We're building tank traps and fortifying our positions as rapidly as possible. Even so, we've lost significant ground. And the minefields will eventually be breached, even if they delay our foe's actions for a few additional days. We've had to divert more divisions from the battle for Cairo and send them north to face this new threat. Our forces are numerous and powerful. We greatly outnumber those we face. But the Challengers are far superior to our armored vehicles. And the British crews are extremely proficient. With the American domination of the skies, we cannot expect to succeed without severe losses of men and equipment. We've lost many brave souls this day. Even so, our defenses stretch from the front lines to just a few miles north of here. So there's little chance of the British breaking through and routing our army. We'll make this a time-consuming battle of attrition for our adversary. We'll force him to pay in blood for each meter of ground gained."

"I expect no less, General el-Saeed."

"Chosen One, it's my duty to give you an honest assessment of our military capabilities. As things stand, I don't believe we can defeat our opponent. He's growing stronger by the day and we're growing progressively weaker. After a month of fighting, many of our soldiers have lost their enthusiasm for battle. I'm ashamed to report that there have been incidences of retreating, deserting, and surrendering on the battlefront in the north and in our struggle for Cairo."

Mourad turned to Kadar Jethwa, the high cleric of Algiers, and his handful of religious advisers. There was indignation in the Mahdi's voice. "Such cowardice won't be tolerated! This is your responsibility. You're the ones charged with watching over our political officers. You must ensure they've properly instructed our legions. They must instill the desire to emerge victorious or die a martyr's death. It's you who must answer to Allah for such blasphemy. It's your immortal souls that are at risk if our soldiers aren't prepared. Is that understood?"

"Yes, Chosen One," the bearded mullahs muttered.

"Contact those within your charge. Have them relight the flame in the heart of every soldier. They're to ensure no one draws away from their rapturous duty. Their swords are to bring swift retribution to anyone attempting such acts. We may not emerge triumphant from this, the first chapter of our holy struggle, but in defeat our every action will be to honor Allah. I promise you in my lifetime Islam will rule the world. Yet, as I've always professed, so great a victory, so momentous a venture, will involve extreme sacrifice from all true believers."

"Yes, Chosen One," Jethwa answered. "It will be done."

The Mahdi turned to General el-Saeed. "Even if our political officers do everything possible to bolster our warriors' resolve, how long before our army's overwhelmed?"

"If things stay as they are, two weeks at the very most."

"We've two million soldiers still involved in the battle," Mourad said. "There must be something we can do."

"Of that, you're correct, Chosen One. All's not lost. Satan's disciples have left a fatal opening that will lead to their demise. If we move quickly, success is within our grasp. If you'll change our plan of battle, Islam will prevail."

"What do you propose, General?"

"Bypass Cairo and attack Israel. There's never been a better time. While we're struggling within the great city and the far north, such is not the case everywhere. The enemy's wide open to a flanking movement. Right now the only things north and south of Cairo are demoralized Egyptian units whose lines are perilously thin. Behind them there's nothing. If we move immediately, we can begin an overwhelming assault under the cover of tonight's darkness. When we undertake this operation, we will stretch the American air forces beyond their breaking point. They won't be numerous enough to stop the bridge building taking place in countless locations. In a few hours, much of our armored force will cross the Nile and smash the insignificant defenses we'll face. Once we do, our tanks will race across the Sinai and reach Israel in less than a day. When the Israelites respond, Syria and Lebanon will seize the opportunity and strike from the north while the Palestinians do battle from within."

"Do you believe the plan you propose will achieve such results?"

"Our emissaries assure me all of Islam is awaiting a sign to begin the final battle to conquer the heretics. And this time, when we attack Israel, things will be quite different than in the past. It won't be like the fruitless battles in previous wars. We're too strong, and too determined. We'll place a death grip upon the interlopers. From every direction, we'll squeeze the life out of those who for more than seventy years have shamed us and denied the Arab world's rightful place in Palestine. In three days, you'll ride triumphantly into Jerusalem. It will be a grand sight, forever uniting two billion believers under your banner. We won't be denied by the Jews this time. Victory will be ours. With your own hands, you'll tear the first stone from the Wailing Wall and forever remove the Hebrew scar from the sacred mosque at the Dome of the Rock."

"Chosen One," General Akhtar added, "General el-Saeed's assessment is correct. The enemy's flanks are exposed. There's nothing but a token force opposing us. We can change everything with a bold strike against Israel."

"But what about Cairo?" Mourad asked. "Surely you're not suggesting we abandon our effort to purge Egypt of those who stand in Allah's way?"

"With the forces opposing us inside the Egyptian capital, it will take days, possibly weeks, to liberate the city. We don't have time for the prolonged effort the house-to-house fighting will entail. The only way to assure our success is to turn from this place and head across the Sinai."

There was much to be considered. Mourad got up. He signaled for his advisers to remain where they were. He walked east across the plateau until he neared its end. From this vantage point he could see great distances. Beyond Giza, on the eastern side of the sainted river of antiquity, Cairo began. In every direction its millions of citizens had built their structures for as far as the eye could survey. Great minarets rose above the skyline. Non-Islamic holy places also dotted the landscape. In the south, ancient handiwork and narrow alleyways were the way of life. In the northern and central parts, modern streets ran through the heart of the city. Towering hotels and sparkling office buildings accompanied the urban blight. Among them were hundreds of nightclubs and cafés where alcohol was sold to foreigner and Egyptian alike. A dozen glittering casinos, their decadence there for all to behold, were scattered about the metropolis. There could be no denying the Egyptian capital was filled with corruption and sin. Surely Sodom and Gomorrah, mentioned in the Christian Bible as having drawn Allah's wrath, couldn't have been more perverse than the debauchery Mourad saw before him. This hedonistic lifestyle in the middle of the Islamic world couldn't be allowed.

He looked upon the Middle East's greatest city. Anguish gripped him as he viewed the scene. The overpowering fear of such places, so much a part of his psyche, rose up to seize him. He couldn't let stand this immoral blight, an affront to the pious throughout the globe. To do so, to ignore the need to crush those whose shallow beliefs made a mockery of everything for which the Mahdi stood, was beyond comprehension.

General el-Saeed was right. An attack upon the Hebrews would unify the factions waiting for a sign to join Allah's holy battle. The general's plan was tempting and provided a real opportunity for conquest. Nevertheless, there was no other answer. Cairo had to be vanquished before any other action could be considered.

His mind was made up. He walked back to the tent and took his place with his advisers.

"General el-Saeed, I've considered your suggestion. There's much in what you say that makes a great deal of sense. Nevertheless, until we place all of Islam upon the proper path, we cannot move forward toward any other goal. Destruction of our non-Arab enemies must wait until our brothers are positioned under the one true God's banner. Egypt must fall before we face the outside world."

"I understand your position, Chosen One," General el-Saeed said. "But if you insist upon the destruction of Cairo before moving on, our chances are nearly gone. We won't prevail and many will've died without tasting victory."

"An eternity in paradise will be their victory. They can ask for no greater reward."

"Please, Chosen One, I beg you to reconsider."

Mourad paused, going over things in his mind a final time. But he'd already made his decision. In the end there was nothing anyone could do to change it. "Our conquest will be in the manner I've decreed. First we destroy Cairo, then we cross the Sinai."

The dejected general understood that the Mahdi had let the chance for world mastery slip through his fingers. His disappointment was evident. "It will be as you wish, Chosen One."

"General, don't be unduly alarmed. Our armies aren't finished. Plenty of opportunities remain. At the conclusion of this afternoon's discussions, I'm ordering our reserves to join us in our virtuous struggle. In two days, no more, they're to begin the honored trek. They're to commandeer every truck, bus, and automobile within our federation and cross the Sahara to become a part of our devout conflict. That should be more than enough to sway things toward Allah's chosen. With so many new faces on the battlefield, victory will be assured."

"Thank you, Chosen One," General el-Saeed said. "Seven million additional fighters will certainly give our opponents cause to reflect. I'm not certain, however, how much good such an order will do. This will be an extremely difficult journey. Some will have to travel two thousand kilometers to reach Cairo. Many of their vehicles are old and unreliable. They'll break down on the desert or run out of gasoline along the way. Our reserves from the Sudan, with no one defending the southern entrances into Egypt, should find the most success in reaching us. Nevertheless, we've left few soldiers with combat experience behind. So it's uncertain how effective the reinforcements will be. Most of our efforts will, by necessity, be piecemeal."

"That's understandable, General el-Saeed."

"From the west, our Libyan units will be the first to arrive at the Egyptian border. Many will complete the task in a day. There they'll run into twelve thousand American Marines in well-fortified positions. Whether we can penetrate such defenses is yet to be seen. Our reserves from Tunisia and Algeria will have to travel a minimum of sixteen hundred kilometers to reach us. There are few roads for such a difficult crossing. The Americans will send their aircraft to destroy those highways long before our soldiers reach them."

"Of that, I've little doubt."

"The going will be slow and torturous. Many of our reserves are old men and young boys. Those who survive will be less than battle ready. Only ten percent have been issued military weapons. Another twenty percent will bring weapons of their own. The rest will arrive at the Egyptian border unarmed. We've left no air defenses behind to protect them. The Americans, the minute they've spotted our troop movements, will unleash their fighter jets to annihilate those they find crossing the trackless sands. Many, possibly most, won't endure so hazardous a venture."

"General, are you saying our conscripts will do us no good?"

"No, Chosen One. Should the majority make it to the front, their presence would likely sway the battle in our favor. I just don't believe most will survive the arduous trip. I'll leave it in your hands to decide whether to call them forward on so dangerous an undertaking."

"Jihad's been called. And those we've left behind are anxious to answer its call. As you said, our reserves can turn the tide once they reach us. We must find a way to hold on until they complete their devout journey. To do that, we've got to delay the nonbelievers' advances in the north. We must also find a way for our arriving troops to survive the travail. It may take every aircraft we have, but I'll release our air forces to battle the Americans and protect our reserves as they cross the great desert. That should help. Still, the one thing that will aid us more than anything is getting them headed this way without delay."

"Yes, Chosen One, I will issue such a command."

"Anything else, General el-Saeed?"

"Just one more thing. You're so exposed in this place. Even with the air defense weapons we've assembled around the hilltop, we cannot promise to defeat a determined air attack. I urge you to consider moving your headquarters inside the King's Burial Chamber in the Great Pyramid. The passageway through the structure only takes moderate effort. And there's satisfactory space inside the pharaoh's tomb and antechamber for you and your advisers. It's the one location where you'll be secure from enemy aircraft."

"Nonsense, General. I'm as safe here as I would be anywhere. Allah will protect me."

"But surely Allah doesn't mean for the one he's selected to lead the way to continue tempting the fates. Even with the forces we've gathered on the plateau, my men can't guarantee your safety when you insist on remaining out in the open like this."

"I'll so note your request. But there's no need for concern. No harm will befall me. My tent will stay where it is."

"As you wish, Chosen One."

46

Bradley Mitchell rocketed down the *Lincoln*'s deck. His Hornet roared skyward. Norm Sweeney's catapult fired a half minute later. Blackjack Section formed and headed south. Having drawn another demanding assignment, both were feeling good about themselves.

It wasn't a difficult task. Bombing a huge communication center in the middle of a wide plateau didn't require much skill. It was the location that made the mission one calling for the most trusted of pilots. The facility sat in the middle of the hilltop where some of the most important relics of ancient Egypt rested. Just a quarter mile north and west were the three major pyramids. And a quarter mile southeast sat the eroding remains of the Sphinx. Miss the target and risk destroying some of the world's greatest symbols of man's resolve.

They rushed toward the coastline. As much as they tried to push the tortured image from their minds, they couldn't forget standing in stunned silence watching the final gasps of the *Eisenhower* as it sank on the previous evening. Nor had Mitchell's family concerns lessened in the slightest. Brooke had gone so far as to have her father call one of his friends in the Senate. This one was a powerful member of the military appropriations subcommittee. The senator had willingly complied with her father's wishes. Generous donors always received their due. He made a few calls to the Pentagon. His demands were simple. The Navy was to release Mitchell from combat duty so he could return to Norfolk to take the couple's children to his parents' home in California. Citing the war's pressing priorities, the Pentagon had politely withstood the unmasked pressure. How much longer they could continue to do so was anybody's guess. Needless to say, the air wing commander wasn't thrilled when he called in one of his favorite pilots to give him the news.

In front of Blackjack Section, six aircraft raced toward the critical target. Overhead, additional Super Hornets prowled to ensure no enemy fighters appeared to disrupt the mission. Both Mitchell and Sweeney had visually identified the sections in front of them. And the Super Hornets above.

The mission contained the classic elements of an American air assault. The leading aircraft were Growlers. The pair would arrive at the objective first. Their job would be to temporarily disable the plateau's air defense systems using electronic countermeasures and chaff.

The Pan-Arab radars would be disoriented by the Growlers' actions. In the confusion, the first two teams of F/A-18Es would rush in to eliminate the air defense systems. Blackjack Section would be clinging to the vapor trails of the others. At ten thousand feet they'd each release a single smart bomb to demolish the communication complex. The destruction complete, all eight aircraft would turn and race for home. It was nice and simple. Except for the added pressure of unwittingly destroying four-thousand-year-old monuments to the human race's ingenuity and perseverance, there was nothing to it.

In eight minutes, the Growlers arrived. They instituted the countermeasures necessary to jam the radars. The first section of Hornets was seconds behind. Their objectives were the air defense complexes on the northern and western sides of the plateau. The deft Americans lined up their shots. Smart bombs were released. The pilots guided them dead center onto the targets. Without warning, the radars exploded. Shattered steel and crippled electronics flew in every direction. Razor-edged pieces of defeated equipment mowed down the unlucky. The second Hornet team was right behind. Five seconds later, the radars protecting the southern and eastern approaches were ripped to shreds. More death and destruction befell the crowded hilltop.

The regal plateau trembled beneath the high explosives falling from the towering skies. The sensation of a small earthquake gripped the revered ground. Mourad and his advisers scarcely had time to struggle to their feet, and no time at all to seek shelter, before the final Hornets arrived.

"Okay, Worm, it's our turn," Mitchell said. "Looks like everything's right where it was when the reconnaissance photos were taken this morning. The communication center's dead ahead. The radars are destroyed, so there's little to concern ourselves with other than completing the mission. Take your time, line up your shot, eliminate the target, and let's get the hell out of here while the getting's good."

"Roger, Blackjack, I'm right behind you."

Those on the ground spotted the final pair of Hornets. Hundreds of tanks opened fire with their deafening antiaircraft machine guns. Uncountable lines of twisting tracers roared skyward. Even so, the ceaseless firing of the tanks' weapons was beyond useless. Mitchell and Sweeney ignored the T-72s' distracting actions and focused upon the task.

In the middle of the immense gathering was the unmistakable objective. The F/A-18E pilots aligned the victim in their sights and each released a single smart bomb. They guided their plummeting ordnance toward the objective. The screaming munitions plunged toward the consecrated earth. Mitchell's smashed into the tangled mass. A fraction of a second later, Sweeney's did the same. Two mighty blasts shook the ancient setting fifteen seconds behind the initial attacks. The middle of the hilltop was torn apart. Limitless lives were stolen. Blackjack Section's pilots turned and headed back toward the fleet without giving it more than a passing thought. Not one of the Americans had the slightest notion they'd dropped tons of high explosives upon the Mahdi's head.

Those inside Mourad's tent were knocked from their feet by the precisely timed raid. The powerful blow sent searching shrapnel flying in every direction. It carried with it the shattered remains of the communication complex and the surrounding vehicles. The flowing tent was little more than fifty yards distant. The tenuous structure was far too close to ever hope of surviving unscathed. Chunks of flaming metal reached out for those within its walls. Unending scores of terrifying shards tore through the shredded tent's sides. Those clustered upon the ancient carpet would soon be receiving the brunt of the corrupting assault.

The rushing carnage ripped through the flimsy framework, slicing up the waiting flesh and exiting on its eastern end. Strife and chaos followed in the attackers' wake.

Five of Mourad's most trusted advisers lay dying. Two were already dead. The remaining sixteen had received wounds running from mild to severe. Within seconds, from all around the mesa, the Mahdi's frantic followers were running toward the shredded shelter. Medical help would arrive before the dust had settled.

Of the two dozen within the tattered tent, a single person had escaped the onslaught unharmed. Incredibly, Muhammad Mourad didn't have a scratch on him.

The Americans' attack would be yet another thing added to the prophetic legend of the Chosen One. Word would soon spread on the swirling desert winds of the miracle occurring near sundown beneath the shadow of the Great Pyramid. For his obsessed multitudes, it was an unmistakable sign of Allah's intentions.

The little man stared at the death and destruction. As he observed the grisly scene, there was true sadness in his eyes. Many of those who'd fallen had been with him since the beginning. Yet his God had chosen this moment to take them. Even so, his grief wouldn't linger.

For he knew each who'd succumbed had died a valiant death in a holy struggle. And an exquisite eternal existence would be their reward.

There was blood running down General el-Saeed's face. His right leg was badly injured. He spoke through clenched teeth, fighting the incredible pain. "Chosen One, now will you listen? You're much too exposed here. You must do what we've been urging. Move your headquarters inside the burial tomb of the Great Pyramid. It's the only way to guarantee your safety."

Mourad looked at his bloodied leadership. There was no other response he could give. "All right, General. Following my walk to honor my mother, I'll move inside. Have your injuries tended to. Then have your men move our command element into the pyramid."

"Thank you, Chosen One. It will be done."

The decision had been made. For the remainder of the war, Muhammad Mourad would make his home within the consecrated walls of the pharaoh's burial chamber.

47

For the first time in a month, the president was all smiles. Even the *Eisenhower*'s sinking couldn't put a damper on today's events. "Let's start with the good news," he said. "How do we look in Cairo, General Greer?"

"A hell of a lot better than we did a week ago, sir. The Nile's running red with Pan-Arab blood. Other than scattered fighting with those cut off by our advance, the city's in our hands. The French Leclercs and British mechanized infantry did the trick. And the 82nd Airborne and our Green Berets did a magnificent job of holding on until help arrived. We couldn't have asked for more from them. Because our aircraft kept blowing up every bridge he built over the river, the Mahdi was never able to get more than a handful of tanks across. As soon as we hit them with the French armor they collapsed. Still, we don't think that's the end of it. He's got more than a million men in Giza alone. We expect him to counterattack at some point. Even so, our forces in the city are ready."

"That's excellent news." The president turned to the director of the CIA. "What about Mourad, have we located his headquarters?"

"Not yet, Mr. President. We're certain he's near the front. Beyond that we haven't a clue."

"Okay, Chet, keep looking for the sorry bastard. Original orders remain—find him and kill him."

"Yes, Mr. President."

"Unfortunately, Mr. President," the secretary of defense said, "not finding Mourad isn't the only bad news, I'm afraid."

"How so, Mr. Secretary?"

"We've got a major problem on our hands, sir. One that could spell disaster if the Chosen One identifies it and moves swiftly to press his advantage."

"I'm almost afraid to ask," the president said.

"In order to keep Cairo from falling, we put every unit we could get our hands on inside the city. That left our flanks totally exposed. Both north and south of the capital there are only a handful of Egyptian infantry guarding the Nile. It would take no effort for Mourad to defeat them. We know his ultimate goal's to drag Israel into this war. If he takes advantage of the situation and succeeds in attacking Israel, we're going to have a new set of problems on our hands."

The smile was gone from the president's face.

"I knew General Greer's news was too good to be true. Have there been signs of enemy buildups near the weak points?"

"Not yet. Maybe we'll get lucky and Mourad's intelligence folks won't spot the opening we've left."

"What do you and General Greer propose we do?"

"There's not much we can do for the next day or so. If we pull rifles from Cairo to protect the flank, we're making ourselves vulnerable within the city. Despite the good things that have happened, Egypt may fall if the Chosen One launches a massive assault and we've weakened our forces inside the capital. So that's no option. We've got to leave our units where they are."

"There's no one we can use to reinforce the flanks?"

"Not if he strikes soon. All we'll have is airpower to harass his tanks as they cross the Sinai. That'll slow them. And I'm positive we'll exact a heavy toll. But I'm also certain it won't stop them. Airpower alone never will. You've got to have boots on the ground."

"What do you suggest we do, Mr. Secretary?"

"For the next forty-eight hours pray Mourad doesn't figure out how tenuous our position is. Because if he does, we're in serious trouble. Beyond that, we may be okay. We've been holding the 1st Infantry for such an emergency. They'll have to go without the majority of their heavy equipment, of course. But along with the arrival of the *Gerald Ford* and *John F. Kennedy* off the Egyptian coast, we should be able to hold the line against all but the most determined attacks once they get there."

"All right, Mr. Secretary. Get the 1st Infantry on the move. Let's look at the next topic. Where do we stand in northern Egypt?"

"We're fifteen miles closer to Cairo than we were yesterday, Mr. President," General Greer said. "Both British armored divisions have landed. The first entered the conflict sixteen hours ago. The second moved south a few hours later."

"Fifteen miles in sixteen hours, that's impressive. At that pace we should reach the city in three or four days, right?"

"Mr. President, I wish it were true. Despite the progress our forces made, they've been stopped cold by an endless succession of minefields. They're absolutely everywhere. British tanks armed with mine-sweeping equipment have moved forward to clear them. But some of the minefields are quite extensive. It's going to take hours to create safe passages. And no one's anxious to undertake such delicate operations in the dark. They're going to wait for sunrise to begin establishing paths through them. And Mourad's using that to his advantage. He's finally recognized he's on the defensive. His armor's digging in. So unless I'm mistaken, the northern Egyptian battlefield's going to turn into a time-consuming war of attrition."

"That doesn't sound the least bit encouraging. Even so, you haven't answered my question. What's the best estimate of when the Marines will reach Cairo?"

"Based upon what we've run into today, it'll be anywhere from five days to two weeks before we defeat Mourad."

"Not exactly the answer I wanted. But we will win, won't we, General? No more of that 'fifty-fifty' stuff, right?"

"There are lots of variables, but yes, Mr. President, we should win. That, of course, is contingent upon what happens in the next few days. If the tactical situation stays where it is and the Chosen One doesn't attack Israel, we should be okay."

"All right, I guess I can live with that. Let's move on. How are we doing in Saudi Arabia and Kuwait?"

"Iraqis and Iranians are keeping the pressure on, but with the entire 3rd Infantry and most of the 1st Armor Division in place, we're more than holding our own. The enemy's not made any progress in the past three days."

"That's good to hear. Anything else?"

"Lots of things, Mr. President. The interrogation of the Iraqis and Iranians we've captured has provided some real insight into what's going on with our adversaries."

"How so, General Greer?"

"There's apparently a rift forming. We've always known the Iranians were far more fanatical than the Iraqis. That is causing the two sides to bicker over the proper course of action. The Iranian leadership continues to push for one attack after another. They don't appear to care how suicidal their efforts are. The Iraqis are more concerned with staying alive. They've been advocating for a more cautious approach. They only want to attack when the odds are in their favor. The Iranians are frustrated with the Iraqis' refusal to continue taking the fight to us. And the Iraqis are upset with the Iranian insistence they keep fighting even when there's nothing to be gained."

"Can we use that information to our advantage?"

"We believe so, Mr. President. The Iranians are so upset they've taken matters into their own hands. They're gathering a half-million men with lots and lots of armored vehicles near the front lines in Saudi

Arabia. Their best units, spearheaded by five divisions of Revolution-
ary Guards, are involved. It looks like they're planning a huge attack.
The prisoners told us the Iranians are expecting the Iraqis to hold the
flanks while they unleash their massed army on the center of our defenses. They're certain with so concentrated an attack they can smash
through our lines and race to capture Riyadh and destroy the Saudi
oil fields before we figure out what hit us. The final Iranian units
should be in place and the attack undertaken within the week. Our
satellite photos confirm what the interrogations told us about the Iranian intentions. We've suspected they might try something like this.
So we've been perfecting an approach to counter it."

"The ships carrying the rest of the 1st Cavalry Division, 101st Airborne, and 25th Infantry will arrive in Saudi Arabia in three days," the
secretary of defense said. "Once they do, we're going to put our plan
into motion to destroy the Iranians. We'll launch an attack on the thin
Iraqi flanks five days from now. Our forces will breach the Iraqi lines
and race to encircle the Iranian army. The trap will be sprung before
they know what hit them. With the Iranians surrounded, the 1st Armor and two French armored divisions will hit them head-on. The
destruction of half a million of Iran's best soldiers will be under way."

"And the best part," General Greer added, "is we're going to make
sure what few Iranians survive know the Iraqi failure to hold the
flanks was the cause of their slaughter. That should put an end to their
questionable partnership."

"Are our divisions and the French units enough to handle the task,
General Greer?"

"Along with the airpower we've assembled, it's more than enough.
Our forces will destroy the Iranians with relative ease. And we'll keep
the 3rd Infantry in reserve to protect the Saudis should our efforts
come up short. If the Iranians break through and the 3rd Infantry
somehow fails to stem the tide, we've got another answer. The 4th Infantry's ships are scheduled to arrive the day after the battle begins.
The 10th Mountain Division's a day or two behind them. So the

Iranians will run head-on into two fresh divisions. The M-1 tanks and Bradley Fighting Vehicles of the 4th Infantry and the highly trained soldiers of the 10th Mountain will stop them in their tracks."

The president turned to the secretary of defense. "You're certain this will work, Mr. Secretary? I'd sure hate to have to explain to the public that we've lost the Saudi oil fields."

"It'll work exactly like we said it would. We're going to move fast and hit hard. The enemy's got a snowball's chance in hell of surviving our ambush, Mr. President. And even if they do, we've got two top-notch divisions arriving to finish them off."

"In fact, Mr. President," General Greer said, "we're so certain of success we'd suggest not unloading the 4th Infantry and 10th Mountain until we see how the battle's progressing. If things go as we suspect, we probably won't need them in Saudi Arabia. If that's the case, we'd like to divert their ships to Egypt. Have them rush across the eastern desert to hit the Chosen One south of Cairo. We figure they're just the force necessary to put an end to things."

48

Charlie Sanders relit the candle. He glanced at his watch. The dinner hour had arrived. He looked at Reena. She made no attempt to pretend to be sleeping.

He reached into his rucksack, withdrawing the final packet of MREs. He opened it and got out his canteen. The evening meal was soon ready.

Sanders helped her into a sitting position, with only a modicum of pain involved. As he'd done at every meal for the past four days, he handed her the food. She looked at him and smiled. Reena was certain he hadn't eaten in all that time. She held the food up, indicating she wished for him to share. Yet, as at each previous meal, he declined her offer. She couldn't comprehend his generosity. Even though she'd attempted to kill him, he'd done nothing but treat her with kindness and dignity since. He'd given her all the remaining food, turning down even a single morsel. For ninety-six hours he'd gone without. He held up the canvas bag so she could see it was empty.

"That's the last of it, Reena. I've stretched it as far as I can. There's none in my rucksack and I've searched this place from top to bottom. There's no food in the hotel."

She looked at him while she ate. His strange words meant nothing.

"I wish I knew what's going on. The last time I went into the kitchen for water I didn't hear anything remotely sounding like gunfire. I guess the city's surrendered and is under Mourad's control. All of Egypt's probably fallen. It's possible most of his army moved on days ago and are hundreds of miles from here. I'm thinking about a trip outside the hotel to see if I can find something to eat. It'd be real dangerous, but maybe late tonight I'll sneak out and take a quick look around. To be honest, I know it's not a very good idea. Even if most are gone, Mourad's bound to have a few guys hanging around. And I'd probably be spotted no matter how cautious I was. Besides, I really wouldn't know where to look. I'm willing to bet when they left, his soldiers cleaned out every kitchen and food stall within fifty miles of this place."

She continued to eat the final meal. He watched as she consumed the last of the MREs. She returned his gaze, the hostility in her eyes a distant memory.

"God, Reena, you're even beautiful when you're eating. I don't think I could stand watching while you starve to death. I'd have to do something. But let's face it, we both know a trip outside the hotel would be plain stupid. And my mother didn't raise a stupid child."

Reena continued looking at him. A pleasant look came to her face.

"Look, I didn't want to bring this up, but I know of a plentiful food supply well within reach. I've waited to mention it until I absolutely had to. There's lots and lots to eat right over our heads. The kitchen's only a few feet away. And it's full of big, fat rats there for the taking. It wouldn't take much to kill a few. The only problem is we won't be able to build a fire down here, so we'd have to eat them raw. I know that probably doesn't sound too good when your belly's full. But wait a day or two. After a while you won't care what you're putting into your mouth. I ate worse things while going through Special Forces training. And it isn't so bad when you're as hungry as I am right now. Look . . . I'll tell you what. I can hold out a little longer. Let's wait a bit before I start catching them. That way you'll be good and hungry. How's that sound?"

Her expression never changed.

"All right, it's a deal. I won't go outside the hotel until it's totally necessary. Instead, I'll catch our meal each night at the top of these stairs. That should work for quite some time."

She took the last bite of food and slowly chewed it.

"Looks like you're about done; time to extinguish the candle."

The flickering light was soon perched in front of his lips. As he prepared to blow it out, she motioned for him to stop. For whatever reason, she didn't want him to douse the light. He didn't have the slightest idea why. She struggled to her feet, signaling for him to stay where he was. Reena leaned against the wine racks and stepped toward where he was sitting. It wasn't long before she was standing over him.

"Reena, what in the world are you doing? You need to sit back down."

She smiled at him. Surprisingly, she bent over and gave him a gentle kiss on the cheek. A grin came to his face. It soon turned into a devouring smile. She dropped to the floor and moved around until she was next to her captor. She returned his smile. Scooting up close to him, she took his arm and placed it around her uninjured shoulder. She reached over and blew out the candle.

Sanders's dream of a marvelous life with the beautiful Arab girl was taking form.

49

Walton and Sanchez stood near the busy docks. They were watching the cargo ships unload one armored vehicle after another. The 1st Cavalry Division's remaining brigades were coming ashore. By midafternoon, the entire Texas division would be on dry ground.

The fifteen thousand soldiers of the 25th Infantry Division, with their three hundred Abrams tanks, an equal number of Bradley Fighting Vehicles, and scores of Strikers, already had unloaded. Along with the 25th were stretching lines of artillery pieces, attack and transport helicopters, air defense weapons, and ordnance and support elements of every kind. The first of the arriving divisions was moving to its designated staging area.

By sunset, the 101st Airborne Division would also be ashore.

Sanchez spotted someone he knew from the 1st Cavalry Division's 3rd Brigade. The cavalryman was sitting in the open commander's hatch of an M-1 Abrams easing past their position.

"Hey, Smitty!" he yelled. "Sure took you long enough to get here. Where the hell you guys been? Did you figure 1st Brigade could whip the Iraqis and Iranians all by ourselves so there was no need to hurry?"

"What we heard was you guys were sitting on the beach getting a tan while the 3rd Infantry did all the dirty work. So we took our own sweet time. Didn't want to cut short you 1st Brigade prima donnas' leisure time." The tank commander laughed.

Sanchez raised his middle finger to indicate his displeasure with the snide comment. "You wish. I've killed more tanks than the entire Army did during Desert Storm and the second Iraq war. I'm told the enemy's so afraid of me that when they want their children to behave, they just mention my name."

"Or show them a picture of that ugly face of yours. That would scare the hell out of anyone." The M-1 drove away before Sanchez could respond to this latest good-natured barb.

Walton burst into laughter. "He's got you there, Miguel."

"Forget him, Sarge. He's just some second-rate tanker who couldn't hit a T-72 with a water pistol from three feet away. Besides, I know what you're doing. And it won't work. You're trying to change the subject so you won't have to admit my information was right all along. What'd I tell ya? Our division's unloading. The 25th's already here, and see those ships offshore? The 101st is in those. Three divisions, like I said."

"You were right, Miguel. I don't know why I ever doubted you."

"Two days and we head north for our top secret mission to destroy the Iraqis and Iranians."

"Seems to me you first told me about this so-called plan on our last night outside Sakakah. After more than a week of fighting, I thought you'd lost what little was left of your mind. Some wild idea about a top secret mission. It sounded so crazy. But with your recent batting average, I'll bet you were right even then. Looks like your info's coming to pass. I've been ordered to assemble the platoon in the staging area this afternoon to outfit our Bradleys for combat. There's a battalion briefing for all platoon leaders and platoon sergeants set for three. We should know for sure after that."

"I already know. It'll be just like I told you."

Walton walked into the wide room filled with double-decked bunks and cheap metal lockers. It was nearing the dinner hour. Behind him were eight replacement soldiers. The men of his platoon were waiting. They crowded around their platoon sergeant.

"Did you guys finish prepping the Bradleys after I left for the battalion briefing?"

"All done," Sanchez said. "Fuel's topped off on all three and we've got a combat load of everything. We're ready to move out when the order comes."

"Good, 'cuz if you hadn't, I was going to haul your asses back down there to finish the job, even if it took all night."

"You don't have to worry about that. Even Dimmit pitched in. I swear he broke a sweat at one point."

"Wally did some real work? That's a sight I would've loved to have seen."

"Looks like they sent some replacements."

"Sure did, Miguel. Eight new guys to support our Bradleys."

"Well?" Sanchez said. "What's the word from battalion?"

"We move out first thing in the morning. We're heading north. Attack begins at dawn the day after tomorrow. There's a massive concentration of Iranian forces, over thirty divisions, gathered inside Saudi Arabia. They're planning a surprise attack in a few days to breach our lines and destroy the Saudi oil fields. But it's us who're going to surprise them."

"How so, Sarge?" someone in the group asked.

"Their flanks are exposed. All they've got holding them are a few battalions of Iraqi armor. First Cav's job is to hit the left flank hard and smash through as quickly as we can. We'll race around the Iranians and meet up with the lead elements of the 25th Infantry. They'll be coming in from the right. Once we've encircled the sorry bastards, the 1st Armor and two French armored divisions will hammer them head-on."

"What about the 101st?" Sanchez asked.

"The 101st will use their huge supply of helicopters to transport reinforcements wherever they're needed. There are a half-million Iranians waiting in the trap and the 101st's mobility will definitely help our cause. The slaughter will have begun. And we're not going to stop until the last Iranian's either been killed or has surrendered. Because of our combat experience, this platoon's been chosen to lead the way. So get a good night's sleep. It might be the last time you see a real bed for quite a while."

"Not a problem," Sanchez said. "After what we've been through, we know what to expect."

"From this moment on, you're confined to quarters. Miguel, take the replacements and divide them up between the three teams."

"Will do, Sarge."

The impromptu meeting broke up. It was obvious the platoon's members were less than happy with being restricted to the barracks. And after their previous combat, none was excited about returning to the front.

The cavalry platoon dispersed. Walton returned to his room. Sanchez, his task completed, soon appeared.

"What'd I tell you? Big attack to put an end to this. And our battalion's going to be out front."

"It's like you said, Miguel."

"Yep, when you want the scoop on what's happening in the 1st Cavalry Division, I'm the guy to see. Hey, Sarge, I almost forgot, mail arrived while you were at the battalion briefing. Got a letter from your wife." The specialist dug the envelope out of his shirt pocket.

"Thanks, Miguel."

Walton ripped the envelope open and stood next to his bunk as he started reading.

Dearest Darren,

I know you're busy, but I wanted to drop a short note to let you know the girls and I are fine. We watch television as much as we can, hoping to catch another glimpse of you and your guys. All over Fort Hood, the war's the only thing on everyone's mind. There are lots of nervous people back here. I've got to admit I'm one of them.

Sarah's project went well. She took third place in the school-wide competition. She worked very hard on it, and we're all proud of her efforts. Her teacher heaped lots of praise on her in front of the entire class. Jessica's been acting quite jealous of her big sister. It's fun watching their antics since the awards ceremony. I know you'll get a kick out of it when you get home.

That's the good news. I'm not sure how you'll take the rest of what I'm going to tell you. I think it's absolutely wonderful, but I'll let you make up your own mind. I know we weren't planning on having more kids, but when you got orders to leave for Saudi Arabia in such a hurry, I guess I let things slip. I don't know how to tell you other than to just say it. The doctor confirmed this morning what I've suspected for a couple of weeks—you're going to be a father again. I'm definitely pregnant. Your third child's on the way. Maybe this time you'll get that son you've always wanted. With any luck, it won't be long before you're coaching Pee Wee football with your own child on the team. I hope after not having to change a dirty diaper for so many years, you haven't forgotten how. Because by next summer, you'll be getting lots of practice, whether you want it or not.

*I don't know what more to say. I pray you won't find my
news too disappointing. The girls and I love and miss you very
much. We can't wait for you to get home. Say hi to Miguel for
us. Write if you get the chance. Please take care of yourself and
hurry back as fast as you can.*

My love always, Beth

The surprised sergeant sat down on the edge of the bunk. A sheepish grin appeared on his face. It turned into a huge smile.

"What the hell's going on?" Sanchez asked.

Dumbstruck, Walton stared at his Bradley's gunner. His smile stayed right where it was. "Beth and the girls said hi."

"What? That can't be it. You didn't get that stupid smile on your face because your family said to say hi."

Walton paused, gathering his thoughts. "Miguel, Beth's pregnant. I can't believe it. I'm going to be a father again. Isn't that great!"

The specialist took a moment to let the words sink in. "It sure is." A smile to match his platoon leader's appeared on his face. "I'm really happy for both of you."

"I'll need to write before we move out to tell her how pleased I am. With the two girls, I hope it's a boy this time. Although as long as the baby's healthy, I really don't care what it is."

"After all we've been through, what I hope," Sanchez said, "is if it's a boy, he grows up in a world where people aren't shooting at each other all the time. And in his entire life he never finds himself on either end of a rifle. That's my wish, Sarge."

"That would be fantastic, Miguel. I hope that too."

"You know, it's funny how things work. A little over a week ago you and I had no choice but to end the lives of so many little boys. In a strange way, your wife's news of a new baby . . . it's almost as if God's trying to make a little bit of what he made us do up to you. Kinda like he's paying you back for what he put you through."

"I hadn't thought of it like that. But that's sure a good way of looking at it. One new life entering the world after the loss of so many others. It won't replace them all, but it's a nice start."

"A real nice start. Ready to head to chow?"

"Nah, Miguel, you go ahead. I'm going to sit here for a while and take this in."

50

C atapult three fired. Propelled by its powerful blast, an F/A-18E hurtled down the runway. It leaped from the *Lincoln*'s deck and took to the rippling skies. A second Hornet soon followed. The lethal fighters headed southwest toward the Libyan-Egyptian border.

Bradley Mitchell was feeling better than he had in some time. And his confidence was growing.

Even so, his family problems continued to spread. Brooke had been unrelenting. But his missions had been both frequent and challenging. They'd been more than sufficient to keep his quick mind occupied for ample segments of the day. As he soared into the heavens, he was determined to keep his wife from reentering his cockpit.

The present assignment was both demanding and critical. They'd be providing close-in support to a handful of embattled Marines. The besieged Americans were holding a crucial oasis from the onslaught of Mourad's burgeoning reinforcements. More and more, all three carriers' Hornets were being called upon to support those holding Egypt's western border. This was going to be Blackjack Section's first mission to assist their countrymen in fending off the Mahdi's swelling ranks. With every mile of harsh sands, from deep within Algeria to the Egyptian border, covered with the Chosen One's reserves, it wouldn't be their last. In the days to come, they'd return on incalculable occasions to dissuade and destroy.

The Allies understood the implications of Mourad's orders. Seven million fresh faces on the battlefield would forever change the conduct of the war. If his multitudes reached the Nile, events would turn decisively in the Pan-Arabs' favor.

Five million reinforcements were traveling east from Algeria, Tunisia, and Libya. More were headed north from the Sudan. At the moment, the Americans could do little to stop the two million journeying along the Nile. Egypt's southern border was wide open. There were no Allied forces between the Sudanese border and Cairo. The area was firmly within Mourad's grasp. And with the existing situation, no combat units were available to place in their path. With the relatively short range of the American naval aircraft, there was no way to defeat the northerly-flowing masses.

How the Americans would respond to the Sudanese would depend upon events in Saudi Arabia. If tomorrow's attack went as planned, the 4th Infantry and 10th Mountain would be freed for combat in Egypt. The ships carrying both would rush from the Persian Gulf to ports on the Red Sea. There they'd unload their armored vehicles and men. They'd make a hurried trip across the Sinai. Five days from now they'd reach the Nile one hundred miles south of Cairo. Their appearance would trap the majority before they could reach the battlefield. From that moment on, not one would prevail in his quest to reach Giza. The 10th Mountain would push south toward the Sudan, intent on securing southern Egypt.

The 4th Infantry would help stabilize the defensive lines against the Sudanese. After that they'd rush up the western bank of the Nile toward Giza. When their M-1s and Bradleys were in place, they'd unleash a furious attack upon the Pan-Arabs. Their compelling action would create an additional front against Mourad's partisans.

That was the American plan. If, however, the 4th Infantry and 10th Mountain had to be committed to the battle in Saudi Arabia, significant changes would be undertaken. The carriers would be forced to handle both the western and southern advances. When the Sudanese were within range, the fleet would send its Hornets to slaughter the approaching reserves.

For now, the Americans would concentrate on the five million coming from the west. After two days on the Sahara, many of the Chosen One's followers were drawing near.

The Allies were confident they'd prevail even if a million additional Pan-Arabs reached Giza. Any more would likely tip the scales. They had to stop the human tsunami before it overwhelmed them. Their objective was to allow no more than insignificant handfuls to arrive at the front lines. With such an ambitious goal, the twelve thousand Marines dug in at the Libyan border were spread perilously thin.

So far, the attacks of the oncoming multitudes had been ineffectual. With little effort, most had been defeated. How much longer things would remain this way was anybody's guess. By the hour, the situation was becoming more arduous for the sparse fire teams. The assaults were growing far more frequent and much more intense. Mourad's incessant supporters were appearing at an alarming rate. Scattered groups of defenders were beginning to feel the impact of the Mahdi's fiercely determined disciples.

In the past day, thousands of those the Chosen One had called forward had reached paradise at the ends of the smoking American guns. The body counts were rising in front of the Marines' bunkers—men and women, the young and the not so young, their shattered remains were there for all to see. Immense numbers also were perishing without coming near the border. The cruel wastelands were consuming them by the tens of thousands. Grotesque deaths at the end of chattering rifles, or at the unflinching desert's hand, would continue to soar with each coming sunset. Yet such results didn't deter the Mahdi's dutiful servants. No matter what had befallen those who'd arrived before them, seven million were fixated upon a single aim. They'd reach Cairo and seal the heathens' fates. Islam's world rule was poised to begin, and Allah had decreed they'd play a crucial role in that wondrous event. Their desire to be part of the great religion's triumph knew no bounds. Those on the monumental pilgrimage weren't going to be denied.

As General el-Saeed had predicted, at the first sign of mobilization, carrier-bound aircraft destroyed North Africa's scattered roads. With no other choice, the struggling reinforcements were crossing the endless plains any way they could.

Thousands were struggling across the unrelenting sands in long caravans of sputtering automobiles. Multitudes were crammed into the rear of dilapidated trucks. Some had appeared alone. Many had come in ancient buses. A few had reached the border on the backs of protesting camels. Still more had shown up on foot. No matter how they'd gotten there, the Chosen One's devotees had been staunchly determined. Seven million tortured journeys wouldn't end until they reached the pyramids and joined in the momentous fight, or died in the attempt.

Seventy percent were without weapons. Of these, the small numbers successful in breaching the Marines' lines had done exactly what Mourad had told Lauren Wells they would do. They'd scavenged the bloody fields, taking rifles and ammunition from the stilled hands of their vanquished countrymen. With those lethal arms, they were heading for Giza to join the assault upon the great city.

The fevered dreams of long-awaited conquest drove them all.

51

The North African coastline appeared. Blackjack Section left the dazzling waters of the Mediterranean behind. Six miles below, a colorless world settled beneath their wings.

Mitchell spoke into his headset. "Echo Control, this is Blackjack Section, we're crossing into Egypt thirty miles from the Libyan border. Where do you want us?"

"Blackjack, we've got an outpost that's catching hell. It's at a tiny oasis eighty miles southwest of you. You can't miss it; it's the only place with palm trees for as far as anyone can see. There are two fire teams along with their squad leader trying to hold off a huge assault. It's critical we keep its waters away from Mourad's hordes, so withdrawing our guys isn't an option. Many of the attackers have weapons. We've one dead and a couple of badly wounded. They're about to be overrun. Cobras have been dispatched, but they're twenty-five minutes out. M-1s are also on the way. Even so, the Abrams won't reach the spot until well after dark. We need you to go in and eliminate as many of the fanatics as you can. You've got to take the pressure off the Marines until further help arrives."

"Roger, Echo Control."

"Be aware. Although it's quiet at the moment, MiGs have been extremely active this afternoon. F/A-18Fs have shot down over a dozen in the past two hours. They'll do their best to keep them as far from you as possible. But stay alert for enemy fighters."

"Understood."

"Things are really tight at the oasis. You're going to have to be exceptionally precise. There's almost no separation between our fire teams and the attackers. The minute you appear, the defenders will pop smoke and head for cover. You handle it from there."

"Roger. We're on the way. We've every intention of taking the enemy out so near our guys none of the Marines will need to shave for at least a couple of days. Tell them to keep their heads down until we arrive. ETA's less than five."

"Roger, Blackjack. We'll pass the word."

The Hornets raced south. From their position both pilots could see for incredible distances. And what they glimpsed was truly astonishing. Upon the featureless ground, millions were moving in a single direction. Toward the descending sun, the scene unfolding on the desert floor was beyond description. Pan-Arab reinforcements stretched to the horizon, and for hundreds of miles beyond. From one end to the other, the somber wastelands were covered with vehicles of every sort, size, and description. Some were traveling swiftly, some at moderate speed. Others were moving not at all. Scattered among the endless vehicles were countless forms who'd experienced a breakdown or run out of gas. Those who'd suffered such a fate were undeterred. By the thousands, they were abandoning their transports and walking across the scorched landscape toward the Egyptian border.

There was little rhyme or rhythm to the muddled migration. Mourad's fragmented forces were making their way across the trackless world any way they could.

"Jesus, Blackjack," Worm said, "get a load of the stuff to our right.

I couldn't add up all the people down there if you gave me five years. I've never seen anything like it."

"Nobody has, Worm. Just shows the Chosen One's power. He snaps his fingers and they blindly follow. They're here to do his bidding, no matter how hopeless the attempt becomes."

With no time to lose, Blackjack Section roared toward the faltering Marines.

The Hornets were four miles out. They'd passed through five thousand feet and were continuing their steep descent toward the teeming Sahara. Ahead, the blowing palms were unmistakable.

"Target's coming up, Worm. Four or five scrawny trees at two o'clock. Doesn't look like much. But that pitiful oasis must be heaven to those on the ground."

The F/A-18Es continued to reach out for the swaying trees. The frenetic desert clash was coming into view. The fierce skirmish's ruthless intensity couldn't be denied. Muzzle flashes and running figures were everywhere.

"Man, that looks rough. Are you picking up the situation on the ground, Blackjack?"

"Roger, Worm, I see it. I'm waiting for the Marines to pop smoke. Once they do, we'll hit the sorry bastards with everything we've got."

"I count a couple dozen cars, trucks, and buses near the oasis, with more on the way. Must be at least three hundred Pan-Arabs within a few hundred yards of our guys. And it could easily be twice that. Want to take them out with a bomb run and then attack with our guns?"

"Let's play it by ear. If they're about to overrun the place, we'll use our cannons first. Otherwise, if we've got time, we'll drop our bomb loads on the vehicles and then use the Vulcans for close-in support."

They roared toward the watering hole. The desperate aggressors continued their furious assault. The Americans spotted the onrushing aircraft. The sergeant in charge of the nine-man outpost popped a smoke canister. He tossed it in front of their bunkers.

"There's the smoke, Worm." Mitchell viewed the incomprehensible scene, trying to determine the correct approach. "Things are just too tight. Let's slide down to the deck and hit 'em with our Vulcans."

"Roger, Blackjack. I concur. Strafing run first then finish them with cluster bombs."

The Hornets dove for the beseeching flats. At the last possible instant they leveled off. Fifty feet above the sands, they raced forward. The pair was wing tip to wing tip as they screamed toward the perverse display.

The onrushing Pan-Arabs spotted the surging birds of prey. The threat to their existence was unmistakable. There was perilous quarry everywhere Mitchell looked. In stark panic, fleeing figures, most carrying rifles, raced in all directions. Yet there were few places to hide upon the featureless ground. Hundreds of the Mahdi's followers raised their rifles. They squeezed the triggers, firing long, noisy bursts. Still, as those on the dying feluccas had discovered days earlier, it was hopeless. Their efforts would have no impact upon the thundering Super Hornets. The pilots ignored the futile actions and prepared to bring a life-seizing whirlwind to the world of mortal man.

"Worm, I'll take the big group in front of the Marine positions. You hit the ones on the far side that are trying to work their way behind our guys."

"Roger, Blackjack."

Both pilots were so near they could see the terrified peasants' faces. This time the killing would be up close and personal. The moment had come to lay waste to their ill-fated prey.

The Marines dove behind their protective walls of sand. They plunged into their foxholes and smothered themselves within the earth's protective cover. The last thing they wanted was to be killed by friendly fire.

Mitchell aimed at a plentiful collection of armed figures thirty yards from the American defenses. He squeezed his cannon's trigger. A murderous salvo spewed forth from the voracious gun.

Sweeney did the same, spewing death and destruction toward those caught in his sights.

The huge 20mm shells were designed for far more challenging targets. As the silenced victims of Blackjack Section's earlier assaults had found, crushing pliant flesh with the powerful munitions would be a simple task.

Blackjack Section's firing was exacting and accurate. At incredible speed, far-flung numbers of striking shells screamed across the remorseless sands. They chewed immense holes in everything within their path. In front of the shielding bunkers, well more than four score went down beneath the fearsome assembly. Hit by cannon fire, most of the tumbling figures were blown apart. Even a partial blow was enough to seize a life. With their positions exposed, none of the intruders had a chance. The omnipotent rounds hammered home. In front of the sturdy sandbags, not one was spared from Mitchell's offensive.

Sweeney's overriding Hornet had a similar effect on the forty or so attempting to work their way behind the Marine positions. His Vulcan chewed them to pieces. Death's image fell upon them in scalding waves. In an instant, all but a struggling handful had perished. The threat from those attempting to encircle the embattled defenses was no more.

A fraction of a second later, Worm fired another startling burst. The destructive shells ripped into the mass of stationary vehicles on the distant side of the palms. A doomed truck soon smoldered. A shattered car burst into flames. Still more followed. Those cowering behind the blighted victims were ripped to shreds by the powerful offensive.

The Hornets roared skyward.

"Nice job, Worm. Looks like we nailed the lunatics nearest the bunkers. Let's make another pass at the ones closest to reaching the trees. We'll then eliminate those farther out with our cluster bombs. Once we finish the next run, I'll move on to the groups to the south. You hit that tangle of cars and buses heading in from the northwest."

The F/A-18Es plummeted. They skimmed the sweating sands in pursuit of the wavering aggressors. After the initial fury, the panicked survivors had turned and fled, hoping against hope to uncover a hint of concealment.

Only a smattering of vehicles near the rustling palms had survived Sweeney's assault. Their drivers turned and sped away. Those on foot began racing after them. Farther out, others joined in the terrified flight. Yet upon the passive lands it was folly. Mitchell took aim at the running forms, speeding cars, buses, and trucks. He squeezed the trigger again and again. Hundreds of shells spewed forth from the avenger's nose. A few seconds was all it took for a dozen vehicles to be torn apart. As the deadly fighter passed, figures dropped in twisted clumps and moved no more. Those upon the accursed Sahara were overwhelmed. Beneath the screeching American wings, splintered bodies fell to earth like fading fall leaves. Blackjack continued the grievous raid until his six-barrel Vulcan had emptied its ammunition storage drum. He headed back into the limitless blue.

Sweeney tore after the generous groupings closing in from the northwest. A flashing squeeze of the trigger and a truck filled with two dozen of the Mahdi's fervent burst into flames. Another quick pull and a pair of automobiles were torn to pieces. One after another, he eliminated those closest to the summoning waters. A trail of existence-denying devastation followed in his Super Hornet's wake. Smoke billowed forth over a wide swath of desert. Like his section leader, his gun brought the Chosen One's end to enormous numbers this day.

His subjugating task completed, Worm rushed to his partner's side.

Both pilots viewed the scene upon the unforgiving landscape. There wasn't an attacker alive within a mile of the oasis. Vast throngs of Mourad's adherents breathed no more.

"Okay, Worm, looks like we've eliminated the immediate threat. The Cobras should be here in fifteen minutes. Ready to buy the Marines some time with your cluster bombs?"

"More than ready, Blackjack."

"Let's split up again. Head west and pick out the biggest groupings you can find. Hit them with your cluster bombs and we'll turn for home."

The destructive pair soared high above the tumultuous display.

Six miles southwest, Mitchell found a surging formation of buses and trucks filled beyond their limits. He thought about saving his bombs for a target closer to the Marines. But the pickings were too good to ignore. He released the first of his bombs.

The vengeance-seeking assailant dropped from the Hornet's left wing. It spun toward the beckoning earth. While it did, the cluster bomb released its load of malignant bomblets. Two hundred and two solemn killers, each containing a half-pound explosive charge, would soon be striking a football field–size area of the withering world below. When it did, the desert would erupt in a riotous display of unspeakable proportions. Caught in the maelstrom, absolutely nothing, neither man nor machine, would survive.

Moments later, Mitchell released the cluster bomb resting beneath his right wing on a nearby gathering of Pan-Arab vehicles. The plunging killer spewed its deadly cargo. Hundreds of slaying serpents sailed toward Mourad's hapless reserves. The maligned ground was ripped apart by the power of the impacting ordnance. Not an inch was left unscathed. The effect of the strike was predictably certain. The caravan exploded. In every corner, assailed figures dropped upon the waiting sands. Their anguished screams were carried immeasurable distances on the afternoon's winds. Their agonizing cries, however, would soon end.

Sweeney found similar elements, not quite as large as his section leader's, a few miles from the oasis. He too released his munitions to destroy and dispatch. The scourging bomblets tumbled toward the flowing dunes. The ardent desert erupted once again. Hellfire consumed those it found on the unyielding landscape. Like his section leader's, the results of his attack were breathlessly final.

Death had come once more from beneath a Hornet's wings.

Their actions completed, Blackjack Section re-formed. They flew over the scarred trees, tipping their wings in triumph as they passed.

The F/A-18Es headed for home. Behind them, the Sahara was on fire.

Blackjack Section lined up their landings. Darkness was falling full upon the Middle East. It was going to be a busy night for every Hornet crew. During the black hours, Mitchell and Sweeney would make three additional incursions to assist scattered Marine positions. Using their cannons and cluster bombs, they'd continue to deliver the hapless reinforcements to the Chosen One's magnificent next world.

The exhausted pilots wouldn't find their beds until four in the morning. This time Mitchell was too tired to care how many e-mails his wife had sent. His family problems could wait.

Both were asleep within minutes of crawling into their bunks. By eight the next morning, after three short hours of sleep and a hurried breakfast, they'd be back in their cockpits.

It was going to be a hectic few days for the carrier-based aircraft. So far, the Super Hornet pilots had averaged four missions per day. In the coming week that number would nearly double.

Bradley Mitchell would have little time to worry about Brooke. In his busy cockpit he would be safe and secure from her intrusions.

52

They'd reached another minefield.

Erickson signaled for his haggard men to halt. Frustration was scrawled across the platoon leader's face. It was the same dejected look every member of the battalion was wearing. Even the tireless James Fife's resolve was starting to waver. For four days, they'd struggled toward Cairo. On the first, confident and cocky, they'd covered a significant distance. In the past three, however, they'd barely made five miles each day. They were sixty tough miles from their goal. And they were bogged down once more. To a man, they suspected it would be many sunrises before they'd see the towering pyramids rising in the distance.

Erickson looked at the men of his platoon. After four days of combat, their numbers had fallen by six. Four wounded and two dead were all his point unit had suffered. It was a remarkable number after so many hours in the line. Still, it reflected more than anything the Pan-Arabs' unwillingness to slug it out with the Allies.

The Chosen One's tactics were painfully apparent. Harass and delay in the north, consuming precious time while waiting to see if the suffocating seven million he'd called forward would arrive in great numbers. The satellites confirmed that with or without those elements, the Mahdi was preparing for a massive attack upon the city.

With another minefield in front of them, there was nothing the Allies could do but stop until the path had been cleared.

"Platoon Sergeant," Erickson said, "have the men set up a defensive perimeter until the minesweepers arrive. Tell them to dig in."

The entire platoon groaned. They'd received the same order a dozen times since leaving the beach. Stop and dig in. Another morning, another foxhole. Most were convinced they were going to end up digging their way to Cairo.

By midmorning, the latest crippling field had been cleared and they were once again on the move. With each tired step, they drew a few feet closer to the end of the war. The British battalion's thirty-four surviving tanks continued to plod along. On their right, similar advances were being made by countless units. The Allies pressed on.

There'd been no significant battles in northern Egypt. Occasionally, somewhere along the stretching line, the Pan-Arabs would stand and briefly fight. Yet such contests had been rare and uneven. The Allies had brushed their opponent aside with a modicum of effort. To a man, however, the Marines recognized things couldn't stay this way forever.

Sooner or later, the enemy would have to hold their ground. And when they did, the British Challengers, along with American airpower, would finally get a chance to finish things. Even with their halting progress, there was little doubt they'd emerge victorious. They were certain they'd crush the Mahdi's forces. They knew on a yet-to-be-determined day they'd reach the streets of the historic city.

It was all a matter of time.

After breaching the minefield, they'd been heading south for nearly thirty minutes. Captain Richards hurried up to walk beside Erickson.

"How's your platoon doing, Sam?"

"About as well as could be expected, sir. They're definitely discouraged by the bastards' unwillingness to take us on."

"That's what I came to tell you," Richards said. "Your men won't be disappointed for much longer."

"How's that, sir?"

"Appears Mourad's finally decided to face us. Three miles ahead, just over the next rise, two divisions of armor are waiting. There are seven hundred T-72s, with an equal number of BMPs in support. Lots of air defense weapons, artillery, and mortars too. Word is they're not playing around this time. This'll be no hit-and-run raid by his pathetic followers. It's going to be one hell of a fight. I guess once we got within a hundred kilometers, Mourad decided he'd no other choice. Scout drones took a good look around as they passed over the Pan-Arabs. The enemy's heavily fortified his defensive positions. Our opponent isn't going to retreat this time. There's little doubt there will be significant suffering on both sides before this one's over. Even with air superiority, it could take a day, possibly longer, to defeat the massive force in front of us."

"Doesn't matter, sir, because we will defeat them. Sooner we kill every last one of the sorry excuses, the sooner we get this over with."

"And the sooner Sam Erickson gets back to a certain beautiful reporter we all know." Richards smiled.

"I'd be lying if I said that wasn't part of it, sir."

"Can't blame you, Sam. I'd be in a hurry too if Lauren Wells was waiting on the beach for me. We're going to halt to get resupplied. Got a couple of King Stallions filled with Javelins, LAWs, and TOWs headed this way. The helicopters should be here any minute. As soon as they're unloaded, the battalion commander's issuing each of your guys all the LAWs they can carry. He wants them to go after the initial line of BMPs. That will allow the Challengers to focus on the T-72s."

"Yes, sir. Sergeant Fife and I will organize the fire teams. We'll get the men set to concentrate our part of the attack on the personnel carriers."

"Sam, you need to take the enemy out. Each of the BMPs is armed with Spandrel missiles. We're reasonably certain the Challengers' frontal armor will hold against a Spandrel attack. But we don't want to test that theory any more than we have to. So eliminate as many as you can before they're able to launch against the British."

"Understood, sir. This platoon will do everything possible to keep the BMPs off them."

"Over ten percent of Mourad's remaining armor is waiting in the desert in front of us. That's a significant chunk of what he has left. Command element's convinced this is one of the key moments of the war. They've decided to concentrate everything we have on it. Two additional British battalions are within striking distance. They, and their Marine supporters, are headed this way. They should be here in under two hours. Twelve Hornets are in the air. All twenty-four F/A-18Es from the *John F. Kennedy* are being allocated to this one. The second twelve will launch the minute the first dozen complete their runs. The *Lincoln* released a handful of Super Hornets to handle any bandits the Mahdi might send this way. Division commander's freeing up every remaining Cobra. That's twenty-nine angry tank killers. We're also launching a significant force of Reaper drones. So there'll be lots of support for our attack. And in a couple of hours, another seventy Challengers will arrive to reinforce our positions. That should even the odds a bit. Even so, it could take quite a determined effort to finish off the enemy."

Erickson took off his helmet and swiped his shirtsleeve across his face. "Sir, we're sick of Mourad's games. I don't think my guys care if we have to fight until the end of time, just as long as we're fighting. Because until those misguided fools stand and face us, we're never going to finish this."

The large King Stallion transport helicopters appeared in the hazy sky behind them.

"All right, Sam, resupply's here. Halt your platoon and let's get set for the attack."

"Yes, sir. Platoon Sergeant, stop the men and send out scouts to defend the perimeter. It's time to get serious."

The lead elements crested the final rise. The swarming desert unfolded in front of them. Two Pan-Arab divisions, nearly fourteen hundred armored vehicles and thirty thousand men, were waiting.

The reconnaissance drones had been right. Mourad's armor was heavily dug in, attempting to hide their weaknesses and equalize their chances against the more mobile Challengers. Their defensive strategy was sound. With only their turrets rising above the sands, the waiting tanks and personnel carriers were going to make for difficult targets.

Erickson looked to his left. The platoon leader watched as a dozen Hinds rose from the Nile's bountiful grasses and headed toward the battlefield.

The Allied forces spread out along the small rise. Three miles away, the enemy's positions began. The time for the first of the great clashes to determine the outcome of the war had appeared. The cruel vista would soon run deep in the blood of vanquished and victor alike. When the carnage would end was anybody's guess.

Armageddon was upon them.

The Allies were outnumbered in armored vehicles forty to one. And in men by nearly one hundred to one. But with stout reinforcements approaching and their significant air superiority, they were a heavy favorite to prevail.

Erickson turned to see the menacing Cobras approaching. When the Hinds arrived, they'd find the ruinous Marine helicopters waiting with fangs bared. A first set of Hornets appeared above the battleground. Staying above the three-mile limit of the Pan-Arabs' older Stinger missiles, they lined up their spirit-rendering runs. It didn't take long for the pilots to identify inviting targets. The leading fighter dropped a long string of five-hundred-pound bombs toward the waiting T-72s.

The second Hornet soon followed. The death-filled loads dropped toward their fanatical foe. A section in the center of the Pan-Arab defenses erupted in thunderous sound. For thousands, their austere death's discordant lyric was poised to begin.

A dozen Pan-Arab tanks responded with a volley from their T-72s' mammoth cannons. The huge shells screamed toward the surging Marines. Scores of artillery soon joined in.

The battle was joined.

53

Next to him, Sanders felt Reena stir. He relit the candle. For two days, he'd lain in the basement with heaven in his arms. Since she'd come to his side of the cellar, she'd seldom left his sheltering embrace. Her strength was much improved. Her wounds were healing nicely. She could get up without assistance. And could walk across the room with comparative ease. She appeared immeasurably more comfortable with her situation. For someone who hadn't eaten in almost a week, the boyish sergeant couldn't have been happier. He'd gotten his wish. Despite the obstacles standing in the way of his wildest fantasies, the woman he wished to spend his life with had come around.

She opened her dark eyes.

"Reena, after two days without food I'll bet you're real hungry. Probably hungry enough for me to start catching the dinner waiting in the kitchen. In four hours it'll be dark. Then I'll sneak up these stairs and get us something to eat. Even uncooked rat meat sounds real good right now."

She looked at him, unable to understand a word he was saying. Even so, her eyes said it all. There was something magical in those dark eyes of hers. Her look showed a sincere appreciation on her be-half. He recognized Reena's expression couldn't be called love. Not yet anyway. Her stunning eyes, however, were filled with affection. And for now, he was willing to settle for that. He was certain the rest would come. As far as he was concerned, food or no food, these wonderful days could go on forever.

He held her tight. She snuggled even closer.

"We're about out of candles, Reena. So we'd better not waste any more of this one."

Sanders blew it out. The darkness returned to swallow them.

An hour passed. Another ticked by. She fell asleep once again. The artful Green Beret continued planning his attack to catch tonight's dinner. There was nothing else to do but wait for evening to arrive. Boredom overcame him. His head slowly drooped. Despite his best efforts, his tired eyes closed. He was soon deep within his wayward dreams.

He'd never be certain how long he'd been unconscious before it happened. It could have been as little as a handful of minutes or as long as sixty. Yet suddenly the idyllic afternoon's peace was shattered. He awoke with a start. Reena had roused a brief moment earlier. Above him, he could hear the squealing rodents scampering in every direc-tion. For the moment, his muddled mind couldn't comprehend why.

The answer soon came. Without warning, there were footsteps. Muffled voices accompanied the telling sounds. There were people overhead. But the conversation was much too suppressed for Sanders to determine what was being said or how many were present.

Reena hesitated, trying to decide what to do. Her hatred for the American had greatly lessened in the past days. Because of his kind-ness, she'd actually begun to care for him. Nevertheless, at her core she was still a Pan-Arab soldier, and the infidel next to her remained a sworn enemy. It was her responsibility to her God, and to the Mahdi, that came before all else. And her august duty called for her to alert those above of the rival soldier's presence.

She pulled away, leaping to her feet. The girl yelled something in Arabic.

"Reena, don't!"

He attempted to grab her leg. In the absolute darkness his aim was off ever so slightly. She broke free and ran toward the stairs. As she did she screamed again, long and loud. If she continued, there was no way those in the kitchen wouldn't hear her.

Sanders scrambled to his feet. He hurried toward the sound of her plaintive voice. "Reena, stop," he whispered.

She shouted something in Arabic once more. He blindly swung a powerful arm, knocking her to the floor. He leaped upon her, desperate to keep her from calling out. She struggled beneath him, striving to set herself free. While she fought, she continued to shriek. Sanders placed his hand over her mouth. She bit him as violently as she could. He instinctively pulled back. He could feel the warm, sticky liquid oozing from the nasty wound she'd opened beneath his thumb. The frantic girl furiously kicked and punched her captor. This time, she wasn't going to be denied.

"Reena, stop!" he whispered again. "You're going to give us away."

She screamed over and over. She wouldn't relent until those above came to kill the interloper and rescue her from this prison.

Sanders's survival was on the line. He knew he had to silence her. Without realizing he'd done so, he instinctively felt for his knife. The lethal weapon was soon in his hand. She continued to strain against his actions.

"Reena, you've got to stop! Please, Reena, I'm begging you."

She sensed the long knife inches from her throat. Still, that wasn't going to keep her from completing her reverent task. She was going to alert her compatriots of the heathen's presence or die trying. She raked her fingernails across his face, tearing chunks of flesh from beneath his left eye. A trail of red ran down his cheek. She cried out, an endless stream of indecipherable words escaping her mouth.

He couldn't let her continue. It was his life or hers. He was out of options. Without conscious thought, he slit her throat.

Reena's screams stopped in mid-sentence. Her head slumped to the side, blood gushing from the wound. Sanders drew back. In stunned silence he knelt over her, unwilling to accept the despicable act she'd forced upon him. In one startling moment, his idyllic dreams were forever lost. Her life had ended. And he'd soon be joining her if he didn't move quickly.

He raced over, scooped up his rifle, and ducked behind the wine rack farthest from the slender door. Covered in Reena's blood, he crouched in the dirt, waiting and praying those above hadn't heard her pleas.

The doorway opened. A flashlight's seeking beam shined into the foul-smelling basement. Whoever was behind the shimmering glare was being extremely cautious. The light pierced the blackness, exploring the cramped room without placing its holder in a position where he'd be exposed to anyone within the space. The person at the top of the stairs knew what he was doing.

Sanders raised his rifle. He'd no idea how many there were, but he wouldn't go down without a fight.

"I'm telling you, Sarge," an American murmured, "this is the place. There's a body lying on the floor. And I'm certain the yelling we heard was coming from here."

Sanders knew that voice. It was one he would've recognized anywhere. "Porter? Is that you?" he called out.

"Charlie?" Porter said. "You down there, man?"

"Hell yes, I'm here."

Porter turned to the figure standing behind him in the kitchen. "You're not going to believe this, but it's Sanders."

Porter and Abernathy started down the short steps. At the bottom of the rotting stairs, they stepped over the lifeless girl.

"Man, Charlie, you're one lucky son of a bitch," Porter said. "All this time stuck in this hole and you're still alive."

"How'd you get down here?" Abernathy asked. "How the hell are you still breathing?"

"It's a long story."

"We figured they lopped your head off long ago," Porter said.

"You know better than that," Sanders answered. "Gonna take a whole lot more than a few million of Mourad's crazies to take me down."

"Same old Charlie," Porter added. "Still thinking he's invincible."

"Hey, wait a minute," Sanders said. "What are you two doing here? Did you get cut off behind enemy lines too?"

"What are you talking about?" Abernathy said. "We retook all of Cairo a while ago. You're two miles inside your own defenses. Have been for the past four days."

"Four days? I've been within my own lines for four days? How could that be? I don't remember hearing any fighting around here."

"There wasn't much in this neighborhood. The minute the French tanks hit them, the Mahdi's forces collapsed. By the time we got back into this part of the city, they were in full retreat. And they didn't stop running until they were dead or had swum to the other side. Probably wasn't a shot fired within a mile of this creepy old hotel."

"French tanks? What French tanks? Hell, I'm so out of it I've no clue what's going on. Either of you happen to have any food? I haven't eaten in six days."

Abernathy and Porter looked at each other. "Nope," Porter said. "No food, but there's plenty at the team's base camp. There are five of us left in the detachment—us two, Captain Morrow, Master Sergeant Terry, and Staff Sergeant Donovan. With you, that'll make six out of the original ten. Would you believe it, we're back on Rhoda Island. British engineers rebuilt that little bridge you blew up between there and Old Cairo. Had to do it to get the Leclercs onto the island. We're getting ready for the big counterattack everyone knows the Chosen One's going to launch."

"Don't know how I feel about a counterattack, yet food, any kind of food, sounds great. But I still don't understand one thing—what are you two doing here?"

"We came to the wonderful Hotel Louraine to see if there was any chance of finding your body," Abernathy said.

"Or what was left of it," Porter replied.

"We've been begging the captain to let us check around. Didn't want you to be permanently listed as an MIA. Hate seeing what that does to someone's family, waiting year after year for word that's never going to come."

"We knew your mother would want to bury you," Porter said. "So we kept pushing Captain Morrow to give us permission to come looking. Finally, he couldn't take it anymore. So he allowed us to come back to make a quick search, upon the condition that after we failed to find your body, we'd never mention it again. Gave us an hour to check around and return to Rhoda Island."

"A whole hour," Sanders said. "God, I knew the captain really cared about me. Giving you guys one hour to travel this far and search for me. Could he have been more generous?"

Abernathy glanced at his watch. "Speaking of which, our time's almost up and we're still two miles from home. Sanders, are you hurt? Can you walk?"

"I'm fine. Very hungry and a bit weak, but I can make it, no sweat. Especially when there's food waiting on the other end. Let's get out of here. I can't wait to see blue sky again and get some fresh air after what I've been through."

"Then pick up your stuff and let's go before it gets any later," Abernathy said. "Otherwise, the captain's going to hang our asses out to dry."

Sanders reached down, gathering his gear and rucksack. The trio turned and headed toward the feeble stairs. Porter led the way, with Sanders trailing.

As he stepped over her, Porter looked at Reena lying in a pool of blood on the dirt floor.

"Hey, Charlie. Who was the girl?"

54

The Iranians had no idea three new American divisions had arrived. The descendants of the once-magnificent Persian Empire had gathered in the squalid desert twenty miles inside Saudi Arabia. Thirty-three divisions were ready to pounce. Half a million men and thousands of armored vehicles had come together for the overwhelming assault. They were supremely confident of victory. At sunrise, two days from now, they'd launch a brutal surprise attack against the Americans, intent on slaughtering the Great Satan's spawn. Not one would be spared.

Yet, as they'd soon learn, the deadly surprise was going to belong to the Allies.

Seven a.m. Normally the fighter aircraft, attack helicopters, and artillery would have hit the enemy well in advance of the main assault, softening him up for the dagger thrust to the heart in the form of crushing American ground forces. But the Allies didn't want to tip their hand. So they waited until the last possible instant to strike. With the monumental day's first light shining down upon them, a dozen 1st Cavalry Apaches slammed into the thin Iraqi lines holding the left flank.

Hellfire and TOW missiles went forth to seek and destroy. An Iraqi T-72 burst into flames. A second soon followed.

The American attack had begun.

The tank-killing Apaches' goal was to wreak havoc upon the Iraqis' frontline armor. In the east, a similar foray by the 25th Infantry was intended to do the same. A handful of minutes after the Apaches' assault, carrier-based F/A-18Fs swooped in from the Arabian Sea to hammer both flanks. The confused defenders attempted to answer back with their air defense missiles.

Phase two began. From their bases in Saudi Arabia, Air Force F-35s roared into the center of the Iranian lines to disrupt and confound the waiting divisions. Their primary targets were the communication systems and air defense radars. They performed scores of bomb runs throughout their stunned foe's defenses. After an hour of intense raids, Iranian communications were no more. And the enemy's radars were smoldering in the sands.

The Persians were blind. They'd no way of knowing what was coming.

Eight a.m. Explosions rocked the unmerciful Saudi desert as Super Hornets and Apaches continued to rip apart the Iraqi armor. It was obvious the F/A-18s and attacking helicopters were having their way. The time had come to let loose American armor.

Lead elements of the 1st Cavalry had hidden in the desert a scant eight miles from the lean Iraqi force. The command was given to move out. Darren Walton's three Bradleys, accompanying a four-tank Abrams platoon, would show the way.

On Walton's orders, the Bradleys headed north toward the Iraqi point elements. With their hatches open, Walton and Sanchez viewed the staid world. Both knew it wouldn't be long before they reached their astonished opponent's lines. Walton looked back. The platoon's remaining Bradleys and the four M-1s were nipping at their heels. Behind them was a limitless line of armored vehicles.

The battle-hardened platoon sergeant was assuming the lead position for the entire division. His Bradley would be out front throughout the long day.

"Wally," he said into the intercom, "it'll be no problem finding the enemy—just follow the smoke from the burning T-72s. That'll take you right to them."

If they wanted to ensnare their gargantuan prey, they had to move fast.

Nine a.m. Breakout. The cavalry division smashed the meager Iraqi defenses and moved on. They rushed across the sands to close the trap on the Iranians. As they reached their assigned locations, the rear units began dropping from the endless formation. Each began setting up its defenses. An ever-tightening noose was being placed around their adversary's neck.

"Okay, Wally, head north for another hour. That should put us a few miles from the Saudi-Iraqi border."

The Bradley raced across the ponderous desert at thirty miles per hour. Fifteen minutes after piercing the faltering enemy, the platoon crested a high dune. As they did, they ran headlong into an Iraqi armored battalion racing toward the front.

Both sides were caught unaware. Even so, the Americans' response was quick and proficient. Within seconds, Miguel unleashed a TOW with devastating effect. A BMP was ripped apart. A thundering explosion rocked the bitter morning. The remaining Bradleys of Walton's platoon joined in. Two T-72s fell. The American M-1s discharged their mighty cannons. The approaching armor fell. The staggered enemy battalion ground to a halt. The unanticipated battle was over as precipitously as it had begun. Leaving seven burning pyres, the Iraqis turned and ran.

Ten a.m. Walton checked their location. The information from the global positioning satellite indicated they were six miles from the Iraqi border.

"Okay, Wally, we're right where we should be. Make a ninety-degree turn to the east."

The Bradley driver did as he'd been instructed. The huge formation changed direction.

"Keep going until I tell you to stop," Walton said. "It's time to encircle the Iranians."

The Bradley headed toward the midmorning sun. Hundreds of combat vehicles followed.

Noon. The lead platoon was on the move through the unending desert. The trailing column of armored vehicles was growing shorter as every few minutes units reached their designated locations. The 1st Cavalry soldiers had encountered only token resistance since the fleeting combat three hours earlier. It was obvious the Iraqis were in full retreat. The bewildered Iranians were on their own. The cavalry division was five miles north of where intelligence placed the last of their ruinous opponent's forces. It wouldn't be long before they slammed the door shut. They rushed to surround their immense adversary.

Walton and Sanchez sat in the Bradley's open hatches. To their left and right, the wide steel treads of the platoon's remaining fighting vehicles plowed forward. Behind them, the M-1s rolled through the barren lands. They continued on for nearly an hour. In that time they saw neither friend nor foe. Without warning, however, that was about to change.

"Hey, Sarge, we've got company!"

"Where?"

"Big dirt cloud to the southeast. Got to be armored vehicles. Lots of armored vehicles. Looks like they're headed this way in one hell of a hurry."

"I've got them, Miguel. Iranians must've figured out what we're up to and are trying to escape. Let's see what battalion wants us to do." The time had come to break radio silence. Walton picked up his handset. "Two-Six, this is Alpha-Four-Five. Two-Six, this is Alpha-Four-Five."

"Roger, Alpha-Four-Five, this is Two-Six, go ahead."

"Two-Six, we've got a large formation in front of us, approximately four miles east. They're headed this way. How do you want us to proceed?"

"Wait one, Alpha-Four-Five," the battalion radio operator said.

While he waited for a response, Walton's Bradley moved toward the billowing sand. The voice soon returned. "Alpha-Four-Five, you're to continue on your present course. Engage the target head-on. Remainder of Alpha and Delta troops are to follow on Alpha-Four-Five's lead and attack the approaching formation. The rest of the regiment is to swing farther north to cut them off. The division commander doesn't want any of those pathetic bastards to escape."

"Roger, Two-Six. Will head straight for the enemy and make a frontal assault."

"Attacking forces will open fire on Alpha-Four-Five's cue."

It would be up to Darren Walton to determine when and where to commence the developing fray. Once he engaged the retreating Iranians, the remaining ten Bradleys of Alpha Troop and the sixteen M-1s of Delta Troop would follow his lead.

Walton watched the mountains of dust and sand drawing near. It was painfully apparent the grouping they were racing to meet was considerable. At their present speed, the platoon would reach the attack point in three minutes.

"Looks like we've got our hands full," he said. The concern in his voice couldn't be masked. "Miguel, drop into the compartment, slide behind those TOWs of yours, and get ready."

The lead Bradley flew across the banal desert. The impending on-slaught was near. A few insignificant dunes and an immense battle would be joined.

"Get ready, Miguel, they're almost here. Fire on my order."

Walton readied his Bradley's Bushmaster cannon.

Using his periscope, Sanchez searched the barren world. He soon located the summoning arrangement's foremost armor. He aligned his initial shot. There was no way he was going to miss the massive quarry. In a few seconds, there'd be one less Iranian tank to worry about. It was then he realized what it was he'd acquired.

"Sarge, whatever you do, don't fire. Did you hear what I said? Don't fire!"

"Why the hell not, Miguel?"

"Look at the silhouette of the lead tank. That's no T-72, it's an M-1. And there are Bradleys behind it. Those aren't Iranians, they're our guys! It's the 25th."

"Are you sure?"

"Hell yes, I'm sure. Those are Americans coming this way."

One p.m. The encirclement was complete. The Iranian army was sur-rounded. Now the division's job was to keep their opponent from es-caping the rearing slaughter. The final 1st Cavalry battalions began selecting defensive positions throughout the expansive desert. They needed to ensure they'd left no weaknesses their monstrous adversary could exploit. To their left, the 25th Infantry's forward elements did the same.

Walton quickly identified firing locations for his foot soldiers and Bradleys. The platoon started digging in. The M-1s did the same. The beginnings of individual foxholes and armored fighting holes soon appeared. Sandbagged walls rose. By shortly after nightfall, their Bradleys would be in their comforting burrows with only their turrets visible.

Once they were in place, the word would go out. In the night's dreadful darkness, the two French divisions and the Americans' 1st Armor would hit the cocksure invaders with everything they had. A thousand Allied tanks would roar across the frightening sweep. They'd signal the waiting air forces, attack helicopters, and Multiple Launch Rocket Systems. America's great armored killers would be unleashed to annihilate and destroy. The trap would be sprung.

Eight p.m. Walton's men were set. The 25th Infantry's forces indicated they also were ready.

The final strands of the deadly spider's web had been strung. The platoon sergeant picked up his radio handset. He sent out the coded signal to the waiting attackers. The time had come to finish their abhorrent rival.

A half million were about to die in a single, decisive battle.

The Allied armored divisions edged forward.

55

S am Erickson had never been so tired, or so thirsty, in his life. As he stood in the chest-deep trench, he shook his canteen. It was empty. He reached down, unfastening the canteen from the waist of one of the Pan-Arab soldiers he'd killed moments earlier. The overcome enemy's half-full metal flask was soon poised near his face. His mouth was so parched he had to pry his bloodied lips apart. The tepid water had an unpleasant smell. Yet he no longer cared. In two long swallows, the lieutenant consumed the life-sustaining liquid. He dropped the depleted canteen. A stray bullet stung the horrid ground a few yards in front of the man-made trench. A second whizzed past his ear. The exhausted Marine made no effort to protect himself from the random rounds. Unable to see more than a few arms' lengths, the spent platoon leader didn't bother searching for the source of the gunfire.

There wasn't a cloud in the heavens. Yet the battlefield was as black as the darkest night. The noxious smoke from two thousand raging fires billowed forth over an immense area, masking the sickening scene. Blazing armored vehicles stretched to the horizon, overwhelming the sunlight and blotting out the death-tinged sky. Explosion after explosion rocked the ominous landscape.

After a second day of fighting, the siege was nearly over. In a handful of distant venues, the malignant struggle continued. Nevertheless, the Allied victory was assured. It had taken a massive effort, but eventually they'd prevailed over their tenacious adversary. Even though the results were certain, it didn't matter to the scattered Pan-Arab survivors. They knew they had no chance, but the Mahdi's followers would continue fighting to the last tank and final soldier. That time was drawing near. The end would soon be upon all of Allah's warriors involved in the wretched battle.

They'd been scarcely more than sheep to the slaughter.

They'd opened Pandora's box, and the suffering they'd released had consumed them. It had been a clash of historic proportions. It had started the previous afternoon with one battalion of Challenger tanks, supported by three hundred Marines, facing two divisions of Pan-Arab armored vehicles and thirty thousand of the Chosen One's devoted. Throughout the first day and into the present one, the clash had grown. With the significance of the contest obvious, the Mahdi had ordered a third division to rush to the killing ground. They'd arrived shortly before midnight. The Allies had responded in kind, continually sending fresh combatants to join their determined brothers. At its end, seven battalions of British tanks, accompanied by their supporting Marines, had joined the furious fight.

Forty-five thousand Pan-Arabs had succumbed. As if tossed by a vengeful deity, shattered T-72s and BMPs were strewn across thirty square miles of desolate landscape. The dead and dying were everywhere.

Two hundred and fifty Challengers had been engaged in the furious struggle. Their losses had been severe. Barely half had survived. By its conclusion, three thousand Marines had fought in the feverish conflict. And while the totals weren't yet in, less than one-third had escaped unharmed from the ravenous tornado. Marine dead and wounded were nearing twenty-one hundred. Even those in the sky had felt Thor's wrath. The unending fight had devoured six Hornets. And eleven Cobras had fallen beneath the Mahdi's determined air defenses. Pan-Arab helicopter losses were above three score.

Yet so monstrous a result as had occurred in the Egyptian desert would be dwarfed many times over in the coming hours. Five hundred thousand Iranians were soon to suffer the same hideous fate. And a titanic struggle double that was poised to begin in and around Cairo. Under Mourad's direction one million obsessed souls were preparing for a final push to destroy those guarding the Nile.

For the previous sixty minutes, the surviving Americans had been involved in fierce hand-to-hand combat with the flailing defenders. In the end it had taken a classic Marine charge, evoking distant memories of Tarawa and Iwo Jima, to subdue the unrelenting enemy.

The front of Erickson's uniform was covered in fresh blood. None of it, however, was his. He picked up his M-4. His bayonet was flowing red. To his right, the mangled bodies of two additional Pan-Arabs were sprawled in the ditch. Both had multiple stab wounds, the results of their futile attempt to defend themselves against the rock-hard lieutenant.

Despite the three-to-one odds against him, Erickson had leaped into the trench to battle the Algerians without giving it a second thought. Though outnumbered, his unchecked rage and superior fighting skills had carried the day. It had been a violent struggle, lightning quick and filled with desperation. Just minutes after its end, it was hardly more than a blur to the spent American. But somehow he'd overwhelmed his opponents. And he'd survived.

The fear and anguish of his beaten foes were frozen upon their faces. The dead soldiers' features were imprinted on Erickson's brain. On trembling arms, he struggled from the ditch. After horrendous hours of abject carnage, the sounds of battle were dwindling. Even so, the macabre battlefield was far from secure. Sporadic gunfire continued. As voracious flames consumed the devastated tanks and personnel carriers, secondary explosions surrounded the platoon leader, assailing his frayed senses. The angst-filled screams of both sides' wounded carried to every corner of the horrific venue.

The shock of it all was too much to bear. The innumerable fires' poisonous residue threatened to devour the staggered lieutenant. Nausea overwhelmed him. Erickson bent over, hands resting on quivering thighs. He fought to keep from vomiting. Still it was no use. He dropped to the ground, his stomach heaving.

He'd no idea what had happened to the platoon. In the addled melee of the past hour, he'd become separated from the rest. Not that there was much of a platoon left. Of the seventeen men who'd arrived on the small rise overlooking the agonizing tract, six were still in the fight.

In the immense contest's swirling confusion, shortly after yesterday's sunset, Sergeant Merker's Humvee had strayed too near a defeated T-72. The tank's munitions had chosen that moment to erupt. A violent blast had reached out to claim the exposed Humvee. The American combat vehicle had been demolished.

Somehow its four passengers had survived their brush with eternity. None, however, was unscathed. Their wounds ran the gamut from moderate to severe. Merker's injured team had been plucked from the fight. Placed on board a medevac helicopter, they'd been rushed to the beach and its waiting hospital. Throughout the night that followed and well into the present day, one by one the members of the platoon had perished or, cradling their gaping wounds, been carried away.

Fifty-three Marines had taken part in the platoon's initial battle on the beach. Thirteen days later, only six remained. Along with their platoon leader, Gunnery Sergeant Fife and Sergeant Joyce's fire team were all that were left. Joyce's Humvee had more dents and bullet holes than any of them could count. Yet it, and its men, continued battling the enemy.

Unable to regain his footing, Erickson painfully raised himself onto one knee. The revulsion of the tortured hours failed to subside. His stomach continued to expel its scant holdings. He was powerless to stop his body's response to the disgust he felt.

An unidentified figure appeared out of the black swirls. The furtive image headed toward the heaving Marine. Rifle in hand, the shadowy form moved toward the ditch.

James Fife stood over the kneeling lieutenant. "You okay, sir?"

Erickson looked up at his platoon sergeant, unable to speak. He nodded affirmatively.

"We've been looking all over for you," Fife said. "Got to tell you I was starting to get more than a bit concerned." He stared at the platoon leader. "Are you sure you're all right, sir?"

Sam Erickson could barely form the words. "After living through this, I've no idea what 'all right' means. I'm still breathing, if that's what you're asking."

"For the moment, still breathing will do, sir."

Fife reached out a strong hand to help him up. Erickson stumbled to his feet.

"Where's the rest of the platoon?" the lieutenant asked.

"If you mean Sergeant Joyce's Humvee, they're searching the ground to the west of us in hopes of finding you. They were to meet me in twenty minutes about a quarter mile from here."

The grizzled sergeant tugged at his sleeve and stared at the iridescent glow of his watch, straining in the swirling void. "That was seventeen minutes ago. Which means if we're going to rendezvous at the scheduled time, I need to head over there right now."

"Go ahead, Gunny. I'll be okay until you get back."

"You sure, sir?" He looked at Erickson, measuring whether to momentarily abandon him. "I've got to let Joyce know I've located you so they don't continue searching and eventually get themselves killed. I'll be back in less than ten." He paused. "Are you certain I should leave you?"

"I'll be fine. Go meet up with Joyce's team."

"All right, sir." Fife started to walk away. He looked back. "I'll be back before you know it."

The platoon sergeant vanished into the wall of smoke. In the middle of the surreal scene, once again Erickson was alone. Beyond exhaustion, his mind as worn as his battered frame, he could stand no longer. His trembling legs collapsed. As night's impending arrival further darkened the haggard scene, Erickson slid back into the trench. He curled up between the dead Pan-Arabs. Their bodies were still warm. Within minutes, he fell asleep.

Fife returned shortly thereafter with Joyce's team. It didn't take long to find the ditch where he'd left the platoon's leader. The bone-weary group walked over to the tortured furrow. They looked at the sleeping lieutenant nestled in the middle of those he'd killed.

Fife jumped in the hole and held his hand in front of Erickson's face.

"Is he okay?" Joyce asked.

"He's fine. Sound asleep from what I can tell."

"What should we do now?"

Fife looked around, unable to see more than a few feet. With the constant explosions, it was difficult to determine what fighting was still ongoing and what was nothing more than the aftereffects of acidic efforts past. But as usual, the veteran sergeant's judgment was sound.

"Despite everything, it looks like the battle's starting to settle down. I know it doesn't sound like it, but there's not much fighting going on. And from the feel of things, none of it's within a mile of here. It doesn't make sense to stagger around in the dark looking for another fight. The lieutenant's got it right. We ought to stay where we are for the night. Let's get these stinking bodies out of the trench and grab some sleep."

The members of the platoon's surviving fire team leaped into the ditch. They tossed the dead Pan-Arabs onto the pillaged ground. There was one thing remaining before they could consider closing their eyes. They needed to set up a guard rotation.

"Two on, two off, just like usual," Fife said. "We'll let the lieutenant sleep. Pitzer, you and I will take the first two hours. Joyce, Benson, and Lewis will handle the next two."

They settled in for their first tentative rest in quite some time.

That's where Captain Richards found them late the next morning.

"Sorry I took so long getting out here, Sam," Richards said. "But it couldn't be helped. Been busy loading the wounded onto medevacs and identifying as many of the dead as I can."

"How many left in the company, sir?" Erickson asked.

"Counting the six of you, I've located thirty-four. If we're lucky, there might be a straggler or two out there somewhere, but probably not many more than that. Except for you and Gunnery Sergeant Fife, none of the platoon leaders or platoon sergeants survived."

"When's the battalion heading out again?" Erickson asked.

"Battalion? What battalion? There are so few of us left it's less than company size. Division's decided we've had enough. For the moment, our combat role's over. The British tanks are re-forming. If all goes as planned, they'll depart this afternoon. But we're not going with them. A battalion from the 1st Division will be taking over for us. We're staying here to locate any remaining wounded, and tag American and British dead."

"Then what, sir?" Erickson asked.

"Then comes the fun part. They're bringing in bulldozers. Once our casualties are removed, we're going to dig mass graves for the Pan-Arabs. With this many dead in so concentrated an area, health concerns will become quite real if we don't do something. So our job's to get them underground."

"You've got to be kidding."

"I wish I were, Sam. Battalion's set up its command post a half mile southwest of here. Have your men gather their equipment and head over to receive your assignments."

Pitzer eased the Humvee across the seeping crimson ground. Fife walked in front of the vehicle, his rifle at the ready. In two hours of searching for the dead and wounded, they'd encountered more than one Pan-Arab with fight left in him. The last had been a political officer whose aim was no straighter than his twisted beliefs. The platoon sergeant quickly dispatched him to the exalted existence he desperately craved.

Gunny was also there to ensure in the smoke and confusion they didn't run over a dead or wounded Marine or British tanker. Every few feet, another Pan-Arab corpse waited. For now they'd ignore the unending carcasses, concentrating on their own losses. The time would come soon enough to deal with the massive numbers of Algerian and Libyan dead.

Erickson and Joyce walked on one side of the Humvee, Benson and Lewis on the other. To this point, they'd found few Allied wounded, and far too many dead. As they discovered another lifeless American they'd pick up the shattered body and place it in the Humvee. When they reached another defeated Challenger, they'd enter its smoldering hull to retrieve the charred remains of its crew. With the aggrieved Humvee piled high with those who'd failed to survive, they'd return to the battalion command post to await the next King Stallion to land and receive its grisly cargo. That task completed, the scarred vehicle and its dazed attendants would return to the distorted circus to retrieve another gut-wrenching load.

In another day, with the Allied casualties collected, the bulldozers would arrive and the truly horrendous portion of their efforts would begin. Forty-five thousand remains would have to be gathered and dumped into the mass graves being dug throughout the unforgiving terrain.

With the desecrated battleground still filled with smoke, the enormity of what had happened hadn't fully sunk in. It would take three days for the final banishing fires to conclude.

When they did, and the lingering shadows cleared, the ruinous sands would reveal their gruesome secret. And the hideous scene mankind would find was beyond description.

Yet in the end, none of what had happened in this place would matter, for the appalling slaughter would go on.

56

General el-Saeed entered the King's Burial Chamber. Having returned from his sunset walk along the crumbling wall next to the ancient cemetery on the western side of the Great Pyramid, Muhammad Mourad was sitting in the center of the archaic kingdom's most sacred room.

"Well?" Mourad said, his words echoing throughout the enclosed space.

"Chosen One," General el-Saeed said, "the great battle in the north has reached its end. Our divisions fought bravely. Not one of our warriors retreated from his post. Each died honoring Allah. The exalted voyages to their honored place are assured. For many hours the fighting raged. But it was no use. Our enemies were too powerful. We've suffered defeat. The infidels will soon be on the march again across a wide area. Their advance elements will be within eighty kilometers of Cairo by morning."

"Are we preparing further defensive positions?"

"Our forces are gathering. They're digging in and readying to engage the nonbelievers in many more battles in the coming days. That should slow their progress and buy us time."

"How much longer before those in the north reach us?"

General el-Saeed hesitated, reluctant to admit the war might soon be over. He understood his army's destiny had been decreed the moment the Mahdi refused to bypass the Egyptian capital and attack Israel. Only a miracle, or a swift and decisive victory in the coming assault upon Cairo, could save the day. With the venerable city conquered, the general might still be able to rush his tanks across the Sinai, drawing Israel into the war. Even so, there wasn't much time remaining.

"A week, ten days at most," the bearded el-Saeed said.

"A week . . . What's the word on our reinforcements?"

"It's as projected. The Sudanese are making solid progress up the Nile. Many should be in a position to join us in a matter of days. But the American defenses on the Libyan border have proven too strong for our forces coming from the west."

"We cannot wait for our reserves to arrive. If we do so, we'll be too late."

"Your assessment is correct, Chosen One. Even without the additional soldiers, we've devised a plan giving us a reasonable opportunity for a successful attack. Our units have been briefed on their missions. We've seized every piece of usable wood within Giza. Thousands upon thousands of rafts have been constructed and our bridging equipment is ready. We have a million men, with ample artillery and armored vehicles poised near the river. We'll begin the moment you give the word."

"We've little choice. Launch the attack without delay."

"It will be done. Our artillery will strike in a few hours. Lead elements will begin crossing the river at first light."

57

At midnight, the well-orchestrated prelude began. An intense artillery barrage hammered the eastern banks of the Nile and far beyond. Much of the spreading city fell beneath the colossal power of a thousand long-range cannons. Howitzers and heavy artillery pounded the anguished Egyptian capital. The French tanks answered with salvos of their own, fervently searching for the Pan-Arab weapons. Countless innocents on both sides of the contested waters were destined to die before a new day would encroach upon North Africa. Nonetheless, the French had no choice but to respond. If they didn't, and the Pan-Arabs were allowed to assault Cairo with impunity, the result would be catastrophic.

Before the attack, the night had been eerily silent. Now, without pause, man's odious handiwork lit up the skyline once again. Brilliant colors stormed across the heavens to cripple and destroy. The riotous timbre was deafening. On Rhoda Island, the struggling Allies waited. The men of Alpha 6333, a dozen Leclercs, a few British armored personnel carriers, units from the 82nd Airborne, and a battalion of Egyptian infantry were well dug in. The island's burrowing defenders crawled deep within their sheltering dens and waited for Mourad's battering to end. Once it did, they knew his forces would undertake the onslaught to crush them.

As the unrelenting hours passed and the bombardment continued, the A Team's survivors peered out at the malevolent landscape. Little had been standing on the isle before the attack. Now all that remained was unrecognizable rubble.

Always careful to avoid the city's mosques, the unyielding Pan-Arab bombardment went on without respite. At shortly before two, the Hotel Louraine was struck by a thundering howitzer's shell. Beneath the savage impact, the decrepit building burst apart. It tumbled to the ground in a whimpering roar of protest, the weight of its six stories crushing the wine cellar below. Reena's body was buried beneath thirty feet of debris. Her sullen tomb was forever sealed.

Along with the detachment's other five survivors, Sanders hid within the protective womb they'd hollowed out beneath the island's shattered remains. In the two days since he'd returned, the once-affable sergeant had been a recluse. A dark mist hung over him. They all saw it. Something was wrong with the team's youngest member. Each recognized the person in front of them wasn't the one who'd disappeared behind Pan-Arab lines on an ill-disposed October evening. Yet they were far too preoccupied preparing for the coming assault to explore the situation further. So they'd left him to sulk and suffer while continuing with their endless tasks.

At first, he'd denied the horrific reality of the wine cellar. He'd done his best to pretend it was nothing but a reviled dream. But he'd failed miserably. The enormity of his life-taking actions gripped his soul, tearing at the fabric of his being. Reena's death was on his hands. And no matter how hard he tried to wash the blood away, he could sense its cruel presence upon his skin. The appalling event weighed heavy upon him. He thought of little else. He shunned his comrades, keeping to himself and wallowing in self-pity.

The Green Berets had drawn an exceptionally dangerous assignment. They'd expected no less. They knew Mourad's hordes would have to traverse the wide river in innumerable locations. In overwhelming numbers, the Chosen One's supporters needed to ford the Nile if they were going to claim their prize.

Just how this was to be accomplished was uncertain. All the Allies could do was wait and wonder. Once the Mahdi's plan became clear, the determined defenders would respond with every measure of fire and fury they could muster. One thing was certain: the Pan-Arabs had to get great quantities of tanks onto the eastern side if they were going to stand any chance against the proficient French crews and their superior Leclercs. And the only way to do so was by erecting huge sums of makeshift bridges across the challenging waters. The attackers' assault would undoubtedly call for a significant attempt to build and hold scores of temporary spans. That's where the Green Berets came in. From Alpha 6333 in the southern reaches, to Special Forces stretching to Cairo's northernmost limits, they waited. Each would move to the consecrated river's edge to destroy the Mahdi's hastily constructed crossings the moment they touched the eastern bank.

The detachment would split into two teams. Morrow and Terry would accompany Donovan. They'd attempt to protect him as he hurriedly prepared each new passageway for destruction before the Chosen One's armor could rumble to the eastern side. Abernathy and Porter would do the same for Charlie Sanders. With the battle raging, each member of the team would be exposed to enemy fire for extended periods. They'd be extremely vulnerable. Still there was no other choice. Someone had to stop the fanatics. And even in his present state, Sanders was still as good as there was at destroying things.

The cannons' contest went on without end. For over six hours, without the briefest pause, the big guns laid waste. It felt like forever, crouching in the gloom waiting for an explosive round to find you or the artillery duel to cease. The dawn was near. The faintest signs of the coming morning were tugging at the horizon. As suddenly as the artillery assault had begun, the shelling stopped. The Leclercs responded in kind, saving their ammunition and waiting for the next element of the assault to begin. The world went quiet. The Green Berets understood what the silence meant. It signaled the next overture in Mourad's murderous symphony was about to begin. They scrambled from their holes and moved toward the water's edge. Sanders trailed as they slipped in and out of the murky rubble. Throughout Cairo, their counterparts were doing the same.

In incalculable numbers, the Mahdi's tanks roared to life. The furtive morning's momentary lull was shattered. From inside Giza, the T-72s and M-60s started toward the ancient Nile. A mile from the contested river, they stopped and waited. Pan-Arab infantry edged forward, ready to support the tanks. Among the disintegrating buildings they settled in, preparing for the daybreak offensive to begin. The time for the armored invasion wasn't yet here. The building of the bridges would have to come first.

The initial wave was about to attack. The trucks carrying the cumbersome bridging equipment struggled through Giza's splintered remains. The going was, by necessity, slow. Many streets, blocked by fractured mortar and tumbling stone, were impossible to traverse. The detours were unpredictable and frequent. Each vehicle, however, eventually found its way. They halted a few blocks from the great flow.

The launching of the rafts would be the signal for the first of the bridging components to move to the river's edge. Once those on the crudely created watercraft reached the far bank and began battling the defenders, the construction of the spanning equipment would commence. If all went well, in a few hours Mourad's tanks would roll into Cairo. Yet before that could happen, they had to get soldiers onto the other side to protect the engineers as they bolted together the floating pontoons. To reach the distant shore, they needed to let loose thousands of primitive watercraft. Four to ten men struggled through the decaying streets carrying each of the strange objects over their heads.

Their construction had been a unique effort, filled with ingenuity and resolve. There was scarcely any wood in Giza. The rafts, varying in size, shape, and composition, had been fastened together using any-thing that would float. Not a single door remained on the widespread suburb's houses. Not a tabletop or scattered tree had been left un-touched. Wooden headboards, empty oil drums, and pieces of Styro-foam were strung together in haphazard fashion. Running behind those carrying the floats, others cradled armloads of table legs and hefty tree limbs. These would be used as makeshift paddles during the hurried crossing.

As they passed through the chaotic streets, thousands joined the extended procession. They'd be the initial force ferried to the distant shore.

The raft carriers would launch their rudimentary dories. Paddling furiously, loaded with Allah's holy, they'd cross the hundreds of yards of water separating them from the far bank. Their human cargo un-loaded, they'd turn and head back to gather more of their federation's anxious men. They'd go on without reprieve, paddling from shoreline to shoreline until either exhaustion or the next world found them. Gunfire from the infidels' defenses would be severe. They knew their losses would be extreme. They'd be in the open for expansive periods and highly susceptible to their antagonists' actions. The paddlers understood most wouldn't survive even a single journey.

If their desperate effort was to succeed, they needed to launch the rafts in so massive a quantity the heretics couldn't contain them all.

Their plan was to overwhelm the unbelievers with sheer numbers.

58

An initial raft tumbled down the Nile's western bank, splashing into the waters across from Rhoda Island. Chasing after it, a dozen Pan-Arab soldiers slid down to the river's edge. They clambered on board the wallowing craft, loading it to overflowing. Their human cargo in place, the determined paddlers began the precarious trek. A second strange raft appeared. And behind it another . . . and another . . . and another . . . without end. Like the first, the odd creations struggled into the languishing flow.

The Chosen One's plan was evident. Throughout the length of the city, the Leclercs, supported by the 82nd Airborne, along with British and Egyptian infantry, were waiting on the eastern side. The entrenched defenders opened up with everything they had upon the crude vessels. The searing battle was joined. The crackling sounds of small-arms fire turned into a thundering crescendo.

Mortar rounds, machine-gun fire, automatic rifles, and cannon shells poured down upon the perilous souls caught upon the brutal currents. Those on the dubious rafts attempted to answer back. Their comrades on the western end also responded, determined to pin down their outmanned opponent.

Initially, it was little more than a slaughter. One at a time, or in hulking handfuls, the Mahdi's followers were ripped apart. With each passing minute, death came to claim them by the hundreds. Their trifling floats were torn to pieces, or grossly overweight, floundered and sank in the stretching river. Few in the first wave would survive the grievous crossing. Even so, the Pan-Arabs saw no reason to panic. They'd anticipated such losses. Replacements for those who'd fallen in the bold venture would keep coming, hour after hour, day after day.

The momentous strife wore on throughout the morning. A regal sun rose high over the bloated battleground. The Nile's burgundy waters shone, its blood-streaked currents the color of the reddest wines. The unsated brutality refused to abate. Incalculable numbers were dying with every hour. Yet more and more of the persistent rafts were succeeding in their quest to reach the eastern bank. Mourad's immense force was beginning to take its toll. Nine out of ten disjointed barrages never experienced a single successful journey. Yet through sheer determination and unconquerable vision, the Pan-Arabs were finding ways to deposit significant amounts of armed men upon the far shore. And that force was growing.

The roving marauders were starting to have an impact. So far they'd had limited success in protecting the engineers piecing together the transient bridges. Nonetheless, as the horrid day lengthened, those who'd beaten the immeasurable odds were beginning to turn the Allies away from attacking their cohorts working on the critical paths.

Under withering fire, the Chosen One's builders continued spanning the Nile in hundreds of locations. So far, few of the floating causeways had survived for long. The desperate defenders had seen to that. Only handfuls of T-72s had reached Cairo's streets. And the Leclercs, along with the 82nd Airborne's Javelins and TOWs, had dispatched most who'd breached the river.

Sanders had been extremely busy. For the first time, Reena had left him. If he wished to see tomorrow there'd be no time on this day to mourn. The lethal gunfire had been profound, but the adept demolitions expert had destroyed a handful of bridges before the tanks attempting to use them reached Rhoda Island. Still, for each span lost, another appeared through the battle's thickening curtain.

Another floating form had touched the island's soil. The Green Berets had to stop its construction before the Pan-Arabs gained a foothold and the armor started across. They'd five minutes, no more, to destroy the structure.

"Okay, Sanders, let's go," Abernathy said. The three of them leaped to their feet. In a well-practiced crouch, they ran toward the river.

Behind them, a British armored personnel carrier provided covering fire. Shooting their weapons as they went, Abernathy, Porter, and Sanders scrambled across the island's lurid landscape toward the nearly completed causeway. Four of the Mahdi's engineers were feverishly working on connecting the final piece. Porter eliminated them with two lightning bursts from his M-4. The mortally wounded Arabs tumbled from the modest bridge. Facedown, their motionless bodies floated upon the horrifying currents, slowly drifting toward the inviting sea. They'd soon join the countless souls already there.

Abernathy and Porter took up defensive positions, using the unfinished bridge for protection. While his partners fired at the western bank, Sanders reached into his rucksack and withdrew the explosive charge. Enemy fire was intense. The striking bullets came from every direction. Scores ricocheted off the bobbing bridge. They stung the ground around him. The demolition expert attached the explosives. The job, by necessity, was hurried. There'd be no need to perform the precise work of which the talented sergeant was so proud. All that was required was to destroy the floating structure to the extent its twisted pieces would be of no further use.

The explosives were ready. He motioned for Porter and Abernathy to head for cover. The moment they were clear, he set the timer and raced away. The scurrying team ran for safe ground. Fifty yards from the soiled water's edge, they dove behind a pair of mangled automobiles. As they did, and the explosives went off, destroying the causeway, they tumbled onto two terrified Pan-Arab soldiers hiding within the wreckage.

The deft Americans instantly reacted to the unexpected encounter. Porter pointed his M-4 at the enemy, ready to pull the trigger without a second thought. Abernathy kicked their rifles away. They looked at the cowering Tunisians. Both were in their teens. The younger couldn't have been more than fifteen, with the other three or four years older. Each was frightened beyond comprehension.

"Well, look at what we've got here," a grinning Abernathy said.

Sanders stared at the cringing twosome. He was in no mood to do anything but exact revenge for what had occurred throughout the past two weeks. There was disgust in his words. "Pull the goddamn trigger already and get it over with."

"Negative," Abernathy said. "If you'd have paid attention during the ops briefing, you'd know we're under orders to get our hands on a few prisoners."

Captain Morrow was quite pleased when Abernathy presented the detainees.

Each of the detachment commanders had been directed to capture and interrogate any prisoners they could find. The purpose of the interrogation was twofold—to determine the precise details of the attack, and to see if they could locate Mourad's hiding place.

They dragged the pathetic pair into the hole where the Green Berets had waited during the artillery bombardment. Both Morrow and Terry had received months of intense language training and were fluent in Arabic. Nevertheless, they suspected the process would go better if conducted by someone who'd recognize the nuances and inconsistencies in the teenagers' words. The Alpha 6333 leader sent his senior sergeant to locate an Egyptian company commander to act as translator.

"What do you want us to do, sir?" Abernathy asked.

"I've got orders to get whatever information I can from whoever we get our hands on. But we've got to continue knocking out those bridges or we're going to be in deep trouble. I can handle these two until Master Sergeant Terry returns. The rest of you head back to the Nile. Abernathy, you go with Donovan. Porter, stay with Sanders."

Terry arrived with an Egyptian captain.

Special Forces officers spent long hours learning how to coax information out of reluctant prisoners. Their skills in judging what would get a captive to talk were well developed. Captain Lawrence Morrow was no exception. He stared at the twosome. He'd use some well-practiced interrogation techniques to see what he could obtain from the anxious teenagers. He held out cigarettes. Both shook their heads, refusing the infidel's gesture. Morrow smiled.

He'd start with, "What're your names?"

The Egyptian company commander translated his words. Neither Morrow, nor Terry, let on they understood what was being said.

Either too dismayed, or simply unwilling to talk, neither prisoner uttered a sound.

"Okay," Morrow said to the Egyptian, "tell them we can make this easy or we can make this hard. It's up to them."

With the horrid battle raging, the process continued for forty-five minutes without success. The Pan-Arabs said little, and what they did say was of no use. Critical time was passing and Morrow was growing impatient.

After failing to get a response to yet another question, the Egyptian looked up and shrugged. "Looks like they either won't tell us what's going on, or they're just so stupid they don't know."

"Shit," the frustrated Morrow said, "tell the little bastards they've got one minute to make up their minds. If they don't give us what we want, I'm going to slit their throats. And when I'm through, I'm going to find the Mahdi and slit his too."

The Egyptian translated. It was clear from the teenagers' reactions they were startled by his comments. Both looked into Morrow's eyes. They could tell from the American's expression he meant every word. He'd finally gotten to them. He was convinced his threat of imminent death had done the trick. Yet it wasn't that portion of his statement that disturbed the pair.

The younger started talking. The Egyptian commander began translating the endless stream.

"You're a fool," the teenager said while looking at Morrow. There was defiance in the boy's tone. "Your threats are worthless. No nonbeliever will ever harm the Chosen One. Such is impossible. It will never happen."

"Shut up," the older one urged.

Yet the fifteen-year-old, his bravado building, ignored his comrade. "Allah will not allow it. The Mahdi's invincible. No harm will ever befall him. He's beyond your reach. You could put your rifle to his chest and pull the trigger and nothing would happen. What makes you think you could end his life? You've already dropped a bomb that fell right on his head and he walked away without a scratch. Try all you might, but you'll never succeed in killing the great man."

"If such is true, I guess it won't matter whether we know where he is or not," Morrow said. The Egyptian interpreted.

"It's true," the boy said. "With Allah protecting him, who cares what you know?"

"And you want us to believe someone as insignificant as you knows his location?"

"Of course I do. Every Pan-Arab soldier knows where he is."

"Then tell us, where's Muhammad Mourad?"

A grin came to the teenager's face. He'd prove to the disgusting infidel that even a lowly peasant had knowledge of where Allah's holy messenger was. "Right under your noses. He's not more than ten kilometers from here. He's in the King's Burial Chamber of the Great Pyramid of Khufu."

Morrow stopped and looked at Terry. A smile came to both their faces. The Americans had found the Chosen One.

Sanders attached the explosive charges to yet another pontoon and ran for cover.

Forty-five seconds later, the floating bridge exploded. It collapsed into the riotous currents.

The day of reckoning droned on. With a long night nearing, and neither side gaining a significant advantage, the relentless attack continued.

With each fleeting hour, Mourad's chances of winning were slipping away.

59

L ike Sam Erickson, Lauren Wells had felt a growing confidence on the day the Marines departed to support the British tanks. Conquest was close at hand, of that she was certain. She'd surrounded herself in that positive glow as she watched Sam disappearing in the distance. She was unequivocal. They'd quickly be reunited to celebrate the Allied victory.

Yet within the hour, her resolve began to fade. With him gone, his handsome face little more than a memory, the first doubts appeared. She tried to shake those loathsome emotions, but they overcame her. She longed to touch the man she adored. She craved the comfort of his enveloping presence. She needed reassurance that things were going to turn out exactly as they'd planned. In painful silence as the hours passed, she'd stood on the dust-choked spot where she'd last seen him, clinging to his dwindling essence.

Throughout the sweltering afternoon she'd remained where she was, observing one unit after another head into the unyielding desert in support of the Challengers. As sunset approached, and the final elements of the second British armored division departed, she'd little choice but to return to Press City. As she walked between the rows of tents, she felt totally alone.

The moment Wells lifted the flap and saw the wondrous place where life's love had found her, the day's events rose to consume her. Teardrops trickled down her cheeks for well into the night. Her anguish flowed until she could cry no more. Having rested little in the past days, she lay down and was soon fast asleep. Shortly before dawn she awoke with a start and was forced back into the here and now.

In the days that followed, the agonizing time without him refused to pass. At first, she'd nothing to do but wait. And then the medevacs started arriving. In the beginning, they were only a trickle. Every few hours a handful of wounded would reach the beach. At unpredictable moments, the dead's spectral images were solemnly unloaded and placed in body bags for the journey home. Wells met each arriving helicopter. Her heart in her throat, she searched the wounded's bloody faces. She forced herself to examine the staid dead, hoping against hope not to find her love. And her pleas had been answered. Sam hadn't been among them. Yet she understood the next flight could forever change that. Her life became an appalling routine of endless hours of boredom punctuated by stark panic at the sound of a nearing medevac.

At least that was the way her wayward reality had been until two days earlier. Quite unexpectedly, everything changed. In a matter of hours, the unmerciful arrivals exploded. The King Stallions' and Ospreys' appearances increased tenfold. So did Wells's torment. She watched as one after another reached the beach, unloaded its human cargo, and took to the air to pluck additional casualties from the distant field. She'd seen the hospital tents fill to overflowing. She'd viewed the constant jaunts of the landing craft as they ferried the most difficult cases to the hospital ship anchored offshore. She'd witnessed the terrifying helicopters filled beyond capacity with American and British dead. And by the hour, her misery swelled.

No one in the press corps could coax a word out of the command element. Nevertheless, something of grave consequence was evolving in the distant deserts. Try as she might, she couldn't get confirmation from any official source. Even so, there was no denying the truth. A battle of immense proportions was occurring somewhere between here and Cairo. A demanding conflict taking many lives. She found a handful of wounded Marines willing to tell their tale in exchange for a few minutes with a pretty face and comforting smile. They confirmed her worst fears. Sam's battalion had been the first to enter the horrific fray. And casualties on both sides were severe.

The lethargic early days without him had been anguished. Yet she'd gladly have returned to those monotonous hours in exchange for what she now faced. Her heart stopped with every arriving medevac. The landings became so frequent she couldn't keep up. Afraid to ask, and then afraid not to, she checked with the hospital incessantly. She roamed the beach like a specter, examining the remains of those who'd fallen. Sam, however, was nowhere to be found. In stark terror, a prayer poised on her lips, she'd gone over the rolls of American dead and wounded. She'd wondered if she'd ever again see her splendid lieutenant.

Wells was beside herself as the body bags mounted on the Mediterranean's sands. With every quarter hour, more dead and wounded appeared. Day and night, dread filled her heart as the whirling blades neared.

She searched the tents of the swelling hospital complex in hopes of finding an answer to his whereabouts. Maybe, just maybe, she'd find someone who could tell her about Sam.

Her fruitless investigation dragged on for hours. Her inquiries entered a second frantic day.

And the exacting toll kept coming. It was nearing noon. Even though she hadn't eaten in twenty hours, she never considered stopping her decided mission.

Wells slowly walked through one of the hospital's many tents examining the wounded. Suddenly she stopped. One of the faces looked vaguely familiar. She hesitated in front of a small cot holding a badly injured Marine. His chest and stomach were covered in bandages.

His left arm was in a sling. Tubes ran into his stomach and down his shattered arm. The anguished Marine looked at her and attempted a feeble smile.

"Haven't I seen you before?" she asked.

"Yes, ma'am," the Marine, his pain evident, answered. "We spoke just over a week ago in this very tent."

An all-consuming joy came to her face. "You're one of Sam's men, aren't you?"

"Yes, ma'am. I'm Brian Merker, one of Lieutenant Erickson's squad leaders. Or at least I was until last night."

"Looks like you're badly hurt. If you don't mind my asking, what happened to you? Where's Sam's platoon? I've got to know what's going on. I've got to know everything."

After her conversation with the struggling sergeant, Wells knew what she had to do.

The time for decisive action had come. She couldn't take the waiting any longer. She had to see for herself what was occurring on the Sahara's stained sands. She had to find Sam.

Once again, her request to leave the beach had been denied. For a moment, rage filled her, storming into her worried eyes. Her anger was soon replaced with overwhelming frustration. Despite everything she'd tried, she couldn't find a way off the beach. She couldn't figure out how to do her job. And she hadn't discovered an approach that would allow her to reach Sam.

In her mind's ever-expanding fog, she walked toward Press City. Darkness was about to fall.

Another dissolving sunset had arrived without her being allowed to report on the greatest story of the millennium. Another day had passed without her knowing Sam was okay. Head bowed, she moved down the beach.

That's when, to her surprise, she found it.

The answer to her prayers had appeared. In disbelief, she stared at her salvation. Sitting twenty yards from the central mess tent was an unguarded Humvee. Its engine was idling. From where it had come and to whom it belonged, she hadn't a clue. She looked around. There wasn't a soul in sight. Obviously, a Marine had left the vehicle and hurried inside to grab some hot food for the men in his unit.

A smile came to her face. The solution had presented itself.

They could lock her away for a long time for what she was about to do. Yet she no longer cared. She jumped into the front seat and put the Humvee into gear.

The vehicle screeched to a stop in front of her tent. Wells left the engine running. She had to hurry if she was going to make her escape. She leaped out and raced inside. Grabbing anything and everything, she shoved articles of clothing into an oversize bag. She was soon back behind the wheel. One more stop and she'd be on her way.

The stolen Humvee pulled up in front of a tent farther down the lengthy row. The flap was open. She peered inside. To her relief, her cameraman was sitting there cleaning his equipment.

"Chuck, get your stuff and let's go," she said.

He gave her a confused stare. "Where the hell'd you get that? Were we finally released to go to the front? I thought they said when they let us go, they'd be sending a military escort?"

"Never mind that. If you want to keep your job, grab your gear and let's get out of here."

A few minutes later, a lone vehicle headed into the suffocating desert. Lauren Wells was behind the wheel. Where exactly she and her cameraman were going she hadn't a clue.

But it no longer mattered.

60

They'd been on the move for seven confusing hours. The going had been extremely slow and painful. They'd averaged less than ten miles per hour on their poorly thought-out odyssey. Having had no time to plan, they'd brought neither food nor water. Both were beyond thirsty. Wells hadn't eaten in over a day. Each had searched for a road, yet none appeared.

With no map or compass, they'd roamed the trackless distances. Just past midnight, they'd stopped and emptied the contents of the Humvee's lone five-gallon gas can into its bone-dry tank. Even so, it was once again critically low. They continued making their way south. On the distant horizon, a gleaming artillery duel lit up the bleak horizon. Lost and discouraged, Wells drove through the night in search of who knew what.

Her cameraman peered into the darkness. "Where the hell are we?" he said. It was the thirteenth time he'd asked during the tortured drive.

Her frustrations burst forth. "How do I know?" she said. "We're somewhere between the beach and Cairo. We're headed south. That's all I can determine for the moment. Now shut up and stop asking me the same stupid question every five minutes."

Chuck looked at the dashboard. The gas gauge was touching empty. "We're about out of gas. Why don't we find a good place to hole up for the night? Maybe we can locate a nice gully where we'll be out of sight. The war'll still be there in the morning."

But she was determined. "We'll stop when we've reached the front lines and not before."

They drove for another half hour with no change in their predicament. Wells glanced at the Humvee's gauges. There could be no denying their fuel was spent. Whether she wanted it or not, stopping would soon be forced upon them.

Their fortunes, however, were about to change. Even though neither knew it, they were in fact quite near the battle zone. Much to their surprise, the Humvee's headlights picked up the outline of a figure standing on a crest a hundred yards ahead. The moment the bouncing beam fell upon him, the unidentified image dropped into the sands. The duo spotted the reaction a football field away. The movement was obviously human.

Wells looked over and smiled. "See, I told you we'd find someone." Just then, the engine faltered. There was nothing remaining in the tank but the faintest of fumes. She patted the dash. "Come on, baby, we're almost there."

The vehicle lurched forward, sputtering again while struggling through the dubious terrain. She pumped the pedal over and again, coaxing just a little more out of the reluctant transport.

Ahead, the vague form got to his feet. More soldiers appeared behind him. The small rise was near. There were a handful of trucks and a few tents nearby. They were heading toward a small encampment. In the middle of the combat zone, the bivouac was pitch-black.

Neither Lauren nor her cameraman could determine its exact size or composition. The Humvee took a final gasp and died thirty yards short of the location. Wells turned off the headlights. A dozen figures walked toward them, their rifles at the ready. Others were silhouetted behind them.

If she wanted to avoid a hasty return to the beach, she knew her story had to be convincing. Yet she wasn't overly concerned. She was immensely talented at bluffing her way out of difficult situations. She'd done it many times, and in much tighter spots than this one. She'd smile a generous smile and tell the nearing Marines that the press had been given vehicles and left the beach under armed escort in the afternoon.

She'd explain that somehow she and her cameraman had gotten separated from the rest. She'd depend upon them being too tired, or too preoccupied, to check her story further. Hopefully, she'd driven up to a platoon-size unit, commanded by no one higher than a 2nd lieutenant who'd be more interested in a pretty face than a believable story. The approaching soldiers were a few feet away.

"Boy, am I glad we found you guys," Wells said. "After getting separated from the main convoy, we've been wandering around for hours. I don't think I've ever been this lost in my entire life. We could use as much gas as you can spare and some directions, if you don't mind."

The next thing she knew, an AK-47 rifle barrel was being shoved against her cheek. She could feel the weapon's cold steel upon her face. And the terror leaping into her heart.

In the confusion of the chaos-filled battlefield, she'd inadvertently skirted her own lines and driven into an enemy outpost. She looked up, instantly recognizing the soldier's Pan-Arab uniform.

His companions moved forward, surrounding the vehicle. There were animated shouts and excited talk among her captors. Having spent the previous five years in the Middle East, she'd become fluent in Arabic. The group's dialect was different from what she was used to, but she understood every word. Even so, she made no attempt to indicate she was aware of what was being said. The Americans were dragged from the front seats. Their arms were pulled behind them. Their hands were bound together. Wells's captors began searching the vehicle's contents. They picked up the cameras and satellite equipment, admiring the expensive electronics gear. They knew it would bring a hefty price on the black market. They opened her bag. With a hearty laugh and a few obscene gestures, they threw its contents onto the ground. The clothing was scattered across the blowing sands. The leader of the group motioned for the stunned captives to walk toward the camp.

She knew the Mahdi's standing order was to execute infidel prisoners. She didn't for a second believe the Chosen One's edict excluded members of the press.

They'd already taken Chuck's watch and wedding band. They'd wait until the executions were complete to remove the woman's jewelry. Those who'd been involved in the capture would draw lots to see who'd receive which part of the unexpected bounty.

The camp's political officer took out his sword. These would be the young mullah's first beheadings. He tried to hide his nervousness. In the dim light, he hoped no one would notice his shaking hands. He needed to perform well if his men were going to continue obeying his edicts.

"The woman first," he said.

They dragged Wells's struggling figure in front of him. The soldiers bent her over, exposing her neck. She continued to rebel against their efforts.

"Hold her still," the mullah said.

He raised his curved sword into the air. He was moments away from bringing it forward. With a single blow he'd separate her head from her shoulders.

"The Mahdi's going to be quite disappointed when he finds out what you've done to me," she said in perfect Arabic.

The mullah hesitated. He brought the sword down. "What did you say?" he asked.

"I said the Mahdi's going to be extremely unhappy when he finds out you've executed us."

"And why would that be?"

"Because he knows me, and I believe he considers me a friend. He's gone so far as to ask me into his home. I'm Lauren Wells. Do you know who that is? I'm the only television reporter to have ever been invited to hear his words. Three months ago, I spent an entire evening sitting at the feet of Muhammad Mourad recording his thoughts for the world to hear. During our time he made it clear he thought highly of me and my work. And he indicated he'd enjoy meeting again."

The mullah motioned for the soldiers to release her. She stood up, looking the straggly-bearded stranger in the eye. She'd always been bold, and now wasn't the time to lose her nerve.

"You've met the Chosen One?" he said.

"That's what I said. Three months ago, at his headquarters in the mountains of Algeria, I sat with him and his closest advisers. We spoke for a broadcast on worldwide television. This man"—she motioned toward Chuck—"he held the cameras for the interview. He used the very ones your men are holding. He and I have both spent a number of hours in Muhammad Mourad's presence. The Mahdi told me he and his advisers had personally chosen me for the interview. I think after what he said that night, he'd definitely be upset if you put us to the sword."

The mullah seemed perplexed. His orders were to execute any heretic, male or female, adult or child, who fell into his hands. But if the woman was telling the truth, and she was an acquaintance of the Chosen One, he would be risking his immortal soul by carrying out such an act.

He couldn't chance offending the one Allah had placed on this earth to lead the way. To slay someone who was a friend of the Mahdi, someone who'd been in his presence, was beyond comprehension. His sin could never be forgiven. And paradise forever lost. The confused political officer stood frozen, uncertain of what to do.

Wells saw her opening. "Look, if you don't believe what I'm telling you, there's an easy way to find out. Take me to the Mahdi. He'll verify who I am. I'm confident he'll tell you he wishes my head remain upon my shoulders. Take me to him personally. You've got nothing to lose. If I'm lying you can end my life in the Chosen One's presence. But if I'm telling the truth, you'll have gotten to meet him face-to-face. And I'm certain he'll be pleased with your wise judgment in sparing my life. He'll tell you how happy he is with your decision."

"Meet the Chosen One?" the abashed figure said.

He envisioned himself standing in the Mahdi's presence. He could see the federation's leader smiling as he greeted him and praised his judgment. So astonishing an opportunity was one he could have never imagined in his wildest dreams. It would be the highlight of his humble life. For the rest of his days, there'd be nothing to compare with so glorious an event.

"Yeah, meet the Mahdi," Wells said. "I'll ensure when we get to his headquarters you get to meet him."

A broad smile replaced the puzzlement upon the mullah's face. The wish of a thousand lifetimes would soon be fulfilled. He turned to the soldiers. "Put them in the back of my truck," he said. "Bring their equipment. I'll need a few of you to come along as guards. I'm taking them to Muhammad Mourad."

They'd been driving for hours. The decrepit truck had been through untold checkpoints, Wells fearing each time the present stop would be her last. They'd come under close scrutiny. The nearer they'd gotten to the pyramids, the more difficult the interrogations had become. Yet her story had remained constant, and none had dared deny her passage for fear she really was a friend of the Chosen One. At a final checkpoint the sentries radioed ahead, alerting the Pan-Arab leadership of the group's arrival.

A sultry dawn was breaking. In front of them, only a few hundred yards away, the three majestic pyramids rose. There were armed warriors everywhere she looked.

The struggle to take Cairo had reached its twenty-fourth hour. As the truck reached the Giza Plateau, the sounds of the far-flung conflict overwhelmed its occupants. Sitting in the back, she had an unrestricted view of the Nile's waters. She could see the battle raging six miles away. Even from this distance, she could identify the newly constructed bridges. It took her some time, however, to determine what the hundreds and hundreds of specks on the flowing river were. Yet finally she realized each of the far-off shapes was carrying human cargo.

"Chuck, do you see what's going on down there? It's the story I've been dying for. What I wouldn't give to use that camera of yours right now."

They drove onto the plateau and slowed to a stop in front of the Great Pyramid's northern face. The anxious mullah got out and stood by the tailgate. Wells stared at the weatherworn monument. It was her turn to be confused.

"Why are we stopping here?" she asked.

"You wanted to be taken to the Mahdi, so we've taken you to him."

She looked at the millennia-old shrine rising in front of her.

"Here?" she said. "Muhammad Mourad's here?"

He untied their hands. The small party began climbing up the pyramid's stone blocks until they reached an opening in the northern face. Two of Mourad's bodyguards were waiting outside the majestic structure's entrance. Each carried an automatic weapon and a jewel-encrusted sword whose blade flashed in the gathering sun. With the flowing robes covering their uniforms and their distinctive headdress, both appeared as if they'd stepped out of an *Arabian Nights* tale. Without a word, the menacing forms turned and entered the opening into the pyramid itself. Wells looked at the mullah, her bewilderment unabated. He motioned for her to follow the mujahideen. She soon found herself in a low, narrow passageway. She'd no choice but to assume an uncomfortable, stooped position as they started down the initial tunnel within the immense structure. The constricted path was less than four feet high and scarcely three and a half feet wide. It wouldn't end until it was below ground level. Chuck, half carrying, half dragging his equipment, was right behind. The wide-eyed mullah brought up the rear. They continued down the restrictive hallway for nearly a hundred feet. It felt endlessly longer. If they'd have stayed on this course, they'd have eventually reached a subterranean room beneath the massive composition whose original purpose had been lost in the passing eons.

The group traversing the pyramid's inner structure wasn't going nearly so far on this track. As they neared what would be ground level, a second shaft split off toward the middle of the imposing framework. This one was as confining as the first. The guards turned and headed in the new direction.

The small party struggled up toward the center of the pyramid. Wells was beginning to feel more than a bit claustrophobic. Her tormented back was aching. Much to her surprise, straight ahead the passage inexplicitly opened upon an area fifty yards long. They had reached the "Grand Gallery." The ancient walls within the space were narrow, but the ceiling was thirty feet high. Able to move freely, the guards straightened up and increased their pace. The relieved Wells, the pressure on her spine abated, followed the mujahideen as they continued their ascent. At the stretching gallery's end they reached the three-foot-high "Grand Step" that would bring them to the level of the antechamber and tomb beyond. One of the mujahideen turned and gave the Americans a hand as they labored to conquer the impediment.

Another constricted area, similar in width and size to the earlier tunnels, awaited. But much to her surprise, this one was only a few feet long. They entered a modest room with a high ceiling. Sitting on the floor inside the unassuming space were a half dozen of the Chosen One's advisers. She recognized a few of their faces from her earlier meeting with Muhammad Mourad. One got up and approached the new arrivals. In hushed tones he spoke with the young mullah. The brief conversation completed, the uneasy individual returned to stand by Lauren Wells. The man he'd spoken with disappeared through a small opening on the far side. He was gone for an extended period. The wary newswoman could do nothing but await what destiny would bring. She understood far too well that her final breaths could soon arrive.

Muhammad Mourad saw them entering the rectangular King's Chamber. As she stood, free from a final modest shaft, Mourad instantly recognized her. He got up, motioning for his advisers to stay where they were. He headed toward the new arrivals. "Miss Wells, it's so nice to see you," he said in English.

She looked around, taking in the scene. This room was twice the size of the one she'd just left and the ceiling was once again quite high. Even with the empty, lidless sarcophagus toward its western end, there was sufficient space for the Mahdi and a dozen of his closest followers. Some were dressed in military uniforms, but most wore peasant clothing similar to their leader. From their expressions, it was apparent many were less than pleased with her presence.

"It's nice to see you too, Mr. Mourad. I told you we'd meet again."

"So you did." He paused for a moment. "What in the world are you doing here?"

"It's a long story, sir. We took a wrong turn in the middle of the night and somehow ended up behind your lines. One of your outposts captured us. This man"—she motioned toward the trembling mullah—"was about to place his sword on my neck when I convinced him you might not be pleased if he did so. So I asked him to bring us here to let you decide what to do with us."

Mourad paused. "You're an infidel, Miss Wells. And my orders are for all infidels to be placed under the sword. But you've also been a guest in my home. And it would be ungracious of me to end your life. Still I cannot have you running around with all that's going on. I hope you understand."

"Yes, sir, I certainly do."

"Good. Then why don't you and your cameraman go back into the room you were just in—it's called the antechamber. For the time being you can stay there." He signaled and the two mujahideen stepped forward. "These men will escort you and see to your needs."

There wasn't much she could say. He'd spared their lives, even if it meant she would be his prisoner for the indefinite future. "Thank you, sir, for your hospitality," she said with a forced smile.

The guards gestured for them to return to the brief passage that would return them to the adjoining room.

61

The blistering winds unexpectedly changed. After blowing from the south for the previous week, they did a complete reversal. With the welcoming sunrise, they were gusting from the north at thirty miles an hour. For the first time since the colossal conflict's birth, there was nothing but blue skies above Walton's position. The platoon sergeant opened his hatch. A passing grin appeared on his face. The wind's sudden shift was a blessing to them all. On this morning, his Bradley commanders wouldn't need their thermal imaging to find the enemy. His exhausted men in the foxholes wouldn't struggle beneath the consuming smoke.

Since shortly after the historic conflict's beginning, they'd been unable to see more than a few precious yards. Now, with the wind's shift, they could see for miles. And what they beheld astounded them. The enormity of the battle came into view. Burning Iranian armor stretched far beyond where they could witness. The nearest of the smoldering tanks was less than a quarter mile distant. Miguel had defeated it with a well-placed TOW late on the previous evening. It was one of many the cavalry platoon had ravaged during the long hours.

Black plumes spewed forth from the uncountable fires. Hundreds of thousands of lifeless forms littered Saudi Arabia's sands. Some of the Iranian dead were within fifty yards of the platoon's firing holes.

Behind Walton's position, one of the Multiple Launch Rocket Systems fired. He turned and watched as the world's most lethal tank killers commenced the attack. The rockets surged skyward, intent on adding to the merciless scene. Their target was one of the few surviving enemy armored brigades. Twelve miles away, an Iranian commander had gathered his men and equipment in a desperate attempt to escape the deadly entanglement. But the massing of so large a force attracted the Americans' attention. The Iranian's decision had been a terrible mistake. It forever sealed his floundering brigade's destiny. Not one of his men would survive the ruthless assault reaching for them from across the skies.

Inside each soaring rocket were five hundred and eighteen armor-piercing bomblets. Once the rockets reached the targeted area, they'd burst open, releasing the little assassins to search out and destroy. Each of the falling killers would bore through the upper armor on a personnel carrier or tank and explode inside. Two hundred armored vehicles soon would be nothing but pockmarked hulls upon the unforgiving desert. Five thousand Persians were minutes away from reaching an unspeakable end. And they didn't even know it.

For the most part, the uneven clash had been this way. The stunned invaders were surrounded and overmatched. The anguished slaughter had been without compromise. Fifteen thousand had died with each passing hour. Yet to the relief of all, the morose spectacle was nearing its end. Few of the half million were still alive.

It had been an arduous struggle. For thirty-six hours, the 25th Infantry and 1st Cavalry had felt the brunt of the Iranians' furious attempt to escape their hopeless lot. Once the enemy figured out what had happened, they headed north at a high rate of speed. They'd run headlong into the entrenched American divisions. The prolonged fighting had been fierce and brutal. Nevertheless, with the Allies' domination of the airspace and their superior command and control, their foe's frantic efforts had failed.

Not that victory was without cost. Allied casualties had been severe. The cavalry division's medics had been stretched to the limit treating their wounded countrymen. Yet the victors' loss of life had been reasonably contained when compared with the enemy dead.

Walton's platoon was down to two Bradleys, the result of a barbarous clash with an Iranian division the previous morning. The Abrams platoon supporting their position had lost an M-1 during the same battle. And the platoon's infantrymen had suffered grievously throughout the lengthy strife. Few had escaped unharmed. For a short while, as an incalculable force rushed toward them, it had been the embattled cavalrymen who'd grown desperate. Still they hadn't panicked. And scores of helicopters filled with reinforcements from the 101st Airborne Division had arrived. With the welcome relief, the relentless combat had ended in unqualified triumph.

The Airborne Division's soldiers had been exceptionally useful at yesterday's sunset when a significant Iraqi force appeared in the withering desert behind Walton's men. The onrushing Iraqis had arrived intent on freeing their confederates from the life-taking snare.

They'd gathered five of their best divisions to smash the encircling lines. Yet the battle never materialized. The fighting dissipated before it had begun. Despite the impressive arrangement of men and equipment, the Iraqi soldiers demonstrated fleeting interest in further bloodshed. Like most in this war, they'd grown disillusioned by the killing. Their counterattack had been halfhearted and piecemeal. They'd withdrawn at the initial sign of American resistance.

Walton dropped into the command compartment. He looked at his Bradley's gunner. Sanchez peered through his periscope, searching for signs of approaching Iranian armor. For the moment, however, nothing of interest was within his sights.

"How we fixed for TOWs, Miguel?"

"We're fine, Sarge. I haven't used but half the ones from the last resupply."

"Why don't you relax a bit?" Walton said. "We're safe for the moment. There's nothing out there but the dead and dying. Open your hatch and grab some fresh air."

"Sarge, I'll relax when the last Iranian's taken his final breath," Sanchez replied. "Until then, I'm going to stay right here, ready and waiting to kill any I see."

It was late afternoon. Throughout the day the cavalry platoon had done little more than watch and wait. They could hear the conflict continuing in faraway venues. Yet none was occurring within twenty miles of their position. The sounds had been decreasing with every passing hour. Each hoped it signaled the end would soon be upon them.

The unpredictable winds changed once again. They swirled in every direction, unable to settle upon a steady course. One moment the platoon's survivors were staring at a bright, inviting day, and the next they could see nothing in a choking ebony world.

Night would soon be upon the Arabian desert. The billowing smoke had engulfed the cavalry platoon's frustrated soldiers once more. For the past minutes, however, the black plumes had been the least of their sergeant's worries. In the Bradley's command compartment, both cavalry soldiers were picking up notable movement. A steady advance was headed in their direction and wasn't far away. The images were too small, and too slow, to be vehicles.

After blowing into their faces for nearly an hour, the desert gale picked that instant to shift again. The gloomy blanket rolled away. The barren world cleared. Carrying white flags, three lines of wavering forms were walking toward them. There had to be at least two thousand in their number. Some carried weapons over their heads. Most had none at all. Many were wounded. The injured hobbled across the sands with the aid of their dejected comrades. Of the half million, only a piteous few had found their way out of the abyss. Walton and Sanchez popped their hatches. Each stared at the wretched assemblage. The Iranians' foremost elements were half a mile away.

"Jesus Christ," Sanchez said. "Will you take a look at that?"

Walton peered at the oncoming lines. The columns stumbling toward them could only vaguely be recognized as human. "I see them, Miguel." He paused, pondering the situation. "What in the world are we going to do with them all?"

There was a bitterness in his voice Walton had never before heard from the typically cheerful specialist. "After Sakakah the answer's easy. Show no mercy. Kill them, and keep killing until every last one's dead."

"Miguel, you know we can't do that."

"Why the hell not? Either you get behind the machine gun and shoot the sons-of-bitches, or move out of the way, and let me do it."

"I'll tell you what, let's find out how battalion wants to proceed. If they direct us to eliminate them, I'll gladly let you take over." Walton didn't wait for a response. Instead he spoke into the radio. "Two-Six, this is Alpha-Four-Five. Two-Six, this is Alpha-Four-Five."

"Go ahead, Alpha-Four-Five."

"Two-Six, we have at least two thousand Iranians walking toward our position. They're carrying white flags. What do you want us to do?"

"Wait one, Alpha-Four-Five."

As Walton waited for the radio operator to return, their subdued rival continued pressing toward the American guns. Five minutes passed. The humbled enemy was growing near.

"Alpha-Four-Five?"

"Roger, Two-Six," Walton answered.

"Supreme Command's got something special planned requiring the capture of a number of Iranians. The battalion commander wants you to take them prisoner. Do you understand? Do not engage. Disarm and take prisoner. Relieve them of their weapons but don't fire unless fired upon. The platoons from the 101st supporting your position will assist in controlling them until reinforcements arrive."

"Roger, Two-Six."

The orders were clear. The bested Iranians were going to survive. Walton glanced at Sanchez. His Bradley's gunner didn't hide his unhappiness.

The water trucks came first. The captives were allowed to fill their canteens and return to the trucks as often as they wished. Medics appeared minutes later. They began treating the wounded. Within the hour, food arrived to fill the detainees' bellies. At dawn, a Special Forces captain used a bullhorn to speak to the dispirited mob in Farsi. He made sure they understood it was the Iraqi failure to support them that had resulted in their defeat. He left no doubt in the pummeled prisoners' minds that the blood of their countrymen had been spilled because of the cowardice of their coconspirators.

More food was passed out. The Iranians were allowed to refill their canteens a final time. The Americans released those who could walk. The defeated figures started shuffling across the sands toward the Iraqi border.

Evening had fallen and the scorching desert was beginning to cool. Not one in the platoon had fired a shot on this day. Yet it wasn't calm everywhere. To the north, many miles distant, the sounds of another battle reached their ears. The initial clash inside Iraq was getting under way. It would be the first of many.

As the Americans had anticipated, after their forceful expulsion from Saudi Arabia, the Iranians and Iraqis, enemies for untold millennia, had turned on each other. A new war was beginning. It would involve many years of useless struggle and the wasting of hundreds of thousands of lives.

Saudi Arabia and Kuwait were safe. This decisive portion of the war was over.

Walton's brigade had been the original force to reach the desperate conflict. Once it was certain they wouldn't be needed in Egypt, they'd be the first to go home.

In a few weeks, he would arrive. His joyous family would be waiting on the docks in Galveston.

62

A few hundred feet off the ground, Blackjack Section's Hornets roared up the Nile. Both pilots were alert for Stinger firings. The fighters had reached the northern tip of Rhoda Island. As the unremitting assault went deeper into its second day, the gunfire from both sides was extremely heavy. Mitchell had expended his rocket pods on a trio of recently constructed bridges. In front of him, innumerable Pan-Arabs were visible upon the quarrelsome waters. Those on the makeshift rafts could see them coming. Many raised their rifles and fired long bursts. A few panicked at the sight of the marauding Americans. They leaped into the harrowing river.

Mitchell squeezed his cannon's trigger. A line of rebellious rounds spewed from the F/A-18E's nose. Their life-taking ordnance reached out for those upon the spreading swells. Once more, death and suffering poured forth to claim those caught by the powerful attack. The rounds tore into one pathetic craft after another. Countless bodies tumbled into the flowing waters.

"All right, Worm, that about does it for me. My Vulcan's nearly empty."

"Same here, Blackjack."

"Let's head back to the boat."

Their first mission in days directed toward anything but the desperate battles on the Libyan border was at its end.

The decisive duo hurried below to grab a hasty lunch. Sated, they headed for their room. There'd been few opportunities to catch their breath in the past days and both were planning on savoring each precious minute.

Mitchell was soon lying on his bunk while Sweeney played on the computer. They hadn't been there long when the squadron commander appeared.

"Brad, the wing commander wants to see you."

"Did he say what he wanted, sir?" Mitchell asked.

"Nope. Just said to tell you he needed to speak with you right away."

"All right, sir. I'll head to his office immediately."

"Thanks, Brad. Stop by on your way back and fill me in on what he has to say."

"I'll do that, sir."

The squadron commander disappeared. Mitchell looked at Sweeney. From the expressions on their faces, each suspected whatever the wing commander wanted wasn't good.

Mitchell knocked on the open door. "You wanted to see me, Admiral?"

The wing commander was a legendary flier whose exploits were known by every pilot in the Navy. His rank and age had pushed him behind a desk. He didn't like it one bit.

"Yeah, Brad, come in and take a seat. It'd be best if you closed the door behind you."

Mitchell did as he'd been told. He settled into the chair, the worry on his face evident. "What's up, sir?"

"I'll come right to the point. I sure hate losing a damn fine pilot in the middle of this, but I've been ordered to send you home. You're to catch the next transport to Naples. From there you're to take the first available commercial flight back to the States, pick up your kids, and drive them to California. Then get back here as soon as you can. You've ten days, no more, to take care of your family situation and return to the *Lincoln*. Is that understood? Until you're back I'll assign Lieutenant Sweeney to fly with one of the sections who've lost a pilot."

Brooke and her father had gotten their way. The Pentagon had folded beneath the unrelenting pressure.

"But, sir, in ten days this'll be over," Mitchell said. "And until it is, Norm Sweeney belongs on my wing not somebody else's."

"I know that but it can't be helped. This directive came from high up, and neither of us is in a position to question the reasons behind it."

"Sir, we both know where it came from."

"Yeah, Brad, but that doesn't change anything."

"You may be right, sir. But I've got another mission in an hour. I can't just walk away and force some other section to pick up the slack in my absence. I'd never forgive myself if someone got killed while completing a job assigned to me. Can't you at least let me complete that one before I go?"

The admiral paused, weighing his options. He liked Mitchell and thought highly of his skills. In many ways, he reminded him of himself when he was younger. "I certainly understand how you feel. I'd feel the same way if I were in your shoes. Hell, what's the Pentagon going to do if I let you take another assignment? As cantankerous as I am, with as many enemies as I've made, I'm sure as hell not going to get any more stars on my collar. To tell you the truth, I don't know how I got this high. They're probably going to force me into retirement when this is over. Take that last mission before you go."

"Thank you, sir."

"Don't worry about it. Just come back in one piece so I don't have to explain why I let you fly."

"If that happens, sir, tell them you got the message after I left for the mission. In all the confusion, you could probably say you never received it at all."

"You're right about that. With everything going on, half my stuff's getting lost in transmission or routed to the wrong place. Some things are showing up days after they should."

There was a lull in the conversation. A slow smile came to Mitchell's face. The admiral had given him a possible way out of his dilemma. If he could get his superior to go along, he'd figured out how to stay in the war.

"You know, sir, if that's the case, why don't we act like this message got lost? With the way things look, in three or four days the war could end and I can leave in good conscience."

Mitchell could tell his superior wasn't thrilled.

"And you'd not have to sweat it one bit, sir," Mitchell added. "I'll make sure your backside's covered. Worse comes to worst we tell them you gave me the order but the transport aircraft to Naples were full and we've been waiting for a seat to open up."

The wing commander sat taking in his words. He hated the thought of one of his best pilots leaving before the fighting was over. His answer contained a hint of reluctance, but nevertheless he acquiesced. "All right. Like I said, even if we're caught, what the hell are they going to do to a used-up old fighter pilot like me? They're not going to courts-martial me and let it become public some money-hungry senator put the squeeze on the Pentagon in the middle of the war to satisfy a wealthy donor. The worst they're going to do is quietly end my career."

"Thank you, sir. You won't regret it."

"Hell, I already regret it. Three or four days, no more. And you've got to agree if the pressure becomes too great, you'll get on the next transport and leave without hesitation."

"Yes, sir, that's fair enough. You tell me to go and I'm gone."

63

The usual group had gathered. It was obvious from their relaxed movements and upbeat tone that the dark clouds of the previous weeks had disappeared.

"The casualties were heavy, Mr. President, but Saudi Arabia and Kuwait are secure," the secretary of defense said. "And it looks like they're going to stay that way. The Iranian army's been defeated and the Iraqis have run back inside their own border. Nearly half a million dead litter the sands of northern Saudi Arabia. At least we're fairly certain there are that many. The fires from the burning armor are masking the battlefield. It's impossible to know what it actually looks like on the ground. Even so, one thing's for certain. The fighting's stopped."

"Fantastic, Mr. Secretary. I can't think of anything better than knowing the Saudi and Kuwaiti oil fields are safe."

"And according to our radio intercepts, they're going to stay that way."

"How so?"

"The Iranians had a huge relief column rushing our way in a desperate attempt to save their army. That force ran into the fleeing Iraqis.

An Iraqi retreat when thirty-three of their elite divisions were being slaughtered didn't sit well. To say they were upset is putting it mildly. Skirmishes had begun when the Iranian prisoners we'd released arrived on the scene. When they did, and their countrymen got word of the Iraqi treachery, the fighting began in earnest. At this moment, there's an immense battle going on in southeastern Iraq between the two countries. It's spreading along the border between them. It could blossom into a full-scale war before the week's out. The last struggle between the two took ten years and ravaged both countries with neither side gaining a thing from their misguided efforts. This one shows the potential to be as devastating. So while they're killing each other, they'll be too preoccupied to bother either Saudi Arabia or Kuwait. Even so, we'll need to keep a decent-size force at the Iraqi border for the foreseeable future. But we figure all our guys will need to do is sit back and watch the Iranians and Iraqis go at it."

"That's wonderful news. I can't wait to tell the press at my three o'clock briefing. I'll bet after I announce the oil fields are safe, gas prices drop five dollars within the first hour."

"That's not the only thing, Mr. President," the chairman of the Joint Chiefs said. "While we're still fighting in Egypt, things are going well there, also. In the north, the Marines and the British armored divisions have won significant battles in the past twenty-four hours. Our advance elements are within forty miles of Cairo and getting closer each day."

"When do you estimate they'll reach the Egyptian capital?" the president asked.

"Four or five days at the latest."

"What's the word within Cairo itself, General Greer?"

"Not much different than yesterday. The Pan-Arab assault's in its fourth day and neither side's given an inch. Hour after hour, the fighting has raged. A conservative estimate is the Mahdi's losses in this battle alone are over one hundred thousand dead with three times as many wounded. There have been a few successful crossings by the fanatics followed by tank engagements. But we've beaten each one back. Every time the enemy gets a toehold we've been able to respond."

"So can I tell the press Mourad's attack has been a total failure?"

"I wouldn't call it a failure yet, sir. But it hasn't been a success. And unless something unanticipated happens, it won't be. Don't get me wrong, the Chosen One could still wear us down and win this thing. But at this point it's not likely. He's running out of time. If he doesn't take Cairo in the next day or two, he never will. There've been rumors his army's about to break. Desertions, surrenders, and retreats are becoming commonplace. The prisoners we've taken are quite dejected. They're sick of all this, and the Mahdi's fanciful promises are losing their rapturous appeal. And it's only going to get worse from here."

"In what way?"

"The 4th Infantry and 10th Mountain arrived in Egypt this morning. Both have off-loaded. The minute they did, they took off across the desert. As of an hour ago, the 10th Mountain had reached the Nile about seventy-five miles below Cairo. With night approaching, we thought it would be prudent to keep our forces where they are until morning. They're consolidating their positions. Bridging equipment is moving forward. By morning we'll have half a dozen spans over the river and both divisions will cross in force."

"Once they're across, Mr. President," the secretary of defense said, "we'll put into action the plan we talked about a few days ago. The two divisions will cut off the Sudanese. After that the 10th will turn south, destroy everything in their path, and secure Egypt's border. The 4th will head up the western bank of the Nile to attack Mourad's forces in Giza. With the British and our Marines hammering him from the north, and the 4th Infantry's M-1s and Bradleys coming at him from the south, he won't know which way to turn. Unless massive Pan-Arab reinforcements reach the battlefield, which isn't going to happen, I wouldn't be surprised if his army collapses in the next few days."

"What's the latest word on his reserves?" the president asked.

"Sudanese have arrived in fairly significant numbers," General

Greer said. "But we'll put an end to that tomorrow. We won't have to worry about further reinforcements from the south. The Marines on the Libyan border continue to be hit by waves of conscripts. We've suffered significant losses. But our Hornets have been great in providing support. Our guys are holding on and only a handful of the enemy's gotten through. We estimate less than five percent have been successful in breaching our lines. And that's certainly a number we can live with."

"Excellent, General." The president was all smiles, but there was one item with which to deal before concluding the meeting. He turned to the director of the CIA. "Well," he said, "what's the word on Mourad?"

"It's confirmed, Mr. President. As unbelievable as it sounded when the initial reports came in, the information's true. Mourad's headquarters are in the Great Pyramid."

"Are you certain, Chet?"

"Yes, sir. We were skeptical at the time, but further prisoner interrogations supported the intelligence we received from our Special Forces. Once we had that information, we started pinpointing radio transmissions to see what we could find. Apparently, a few days earlier we'd eliminated Mourad's main communication center on the Giza Plateau. But the Pan-Arabs quickly replaced everything we'd destroyed. That alone was sufficient evidence to investigate further. There was enough high-level radio traffic going into and out of the pyramid complex to heighten our suspicions. So we slipped a covert team into western Giza. They spent last night watching what was going on at the plateau. They didn't see the Chosen One, but signs of his presence were everywhere. Mourad's personal armored division surrounds the hilltop. And when our team spotted his mujahideen patrolling outside, they knew we'd found the right place."

"Too bad they didn't spot him. They could have taken care of things then and there."

"Yes, sir. That's what we had in mind. But no such luck. And it wasn't like they could stay around hoping for a shot at the old bastard. Still, they did provide valuable information."

"No chance Mourad's set up an elaborate ruse and he's really somewhere else?"

"We don't think so. His mujahideen are never far from him. And they were crawling all over the place."

"Are you sending your team back in to get him?"

"No, sir," the director of the CIA said. "Once was enough. They came close to being discovered more than once last night. We don't think we can press our luck any further."

"If his army is near collapse, we need to be working on getting our hands on him. I don't want to chance him escaping in the confusion that will follow when the war ends."

"We're working on it, Mr. President," the secretary of defense said. "But as long as he's got his best armored division securing the area, I don't know how much luck we'll have in killing him without one hell of a fight."

The president looked at them. "Find a way, gentlemen. You've got two days to come up with a plan to eliminate him once and for all."

64

Muhammad Mourad sat in the burial chamber along with his closest advisers. A pall was on nearly every face. There was little doubt in his followers' minds that the war was lost. Only their leader seemed unaffected by the battle's recent days.

"Chosen One," General el-Saeed said, "one of the American divisions in the south is drawing near."

"How far away are they?"

"No more than sixty kilometers. They've defeated the units you diverted from the attack upon Cairo and are marching toward Giza as we speak. There's nothing standing in their way. They could be here in a few hours if something's not done."

"What about our Sudanese reinforcements? Can we use them to slow the infidels?"

"No, Chosen One, they're cut off. The other American division has pushed them back toward Egypt's southern border."

Mourad looked at General el-Saeed. The threat was unmistakable. There was only one thing he could do. He'd send his best division to face the 4th Infantry.

"Order my personal armored division to head south to meet the Americans. They're to leave within the hour. The communication complex and a few of the air defenses are to remain behind, but everyone else in the division is to go."

"But, Chosen One, if we do that there'll be almost no one guarding this place. You'll be vulnerable to an attack."

"Nonsense, General. I'll be fine. No harm will befall me. Allah will see to that. Until Islam rules and the world reaches its final days, I will live." He could tell from el-Saeed's face his general wasn't happy with his decision. "And my mujahideen will watch over me."

"Your bodyguards are great warriors. But two hundred men, no matter how fierce, no matter how loyal, cannot stop a determined opponent. All I'm asking is to give your directive some thought before sending your division to face the Americans."

"What choice do we have? No one stands in the heretics' way. We cannot allow them to advance unfettered. We've got to do something to give us time to capture Cairo and turn the tide."

El-Saeed measured his words before speaking. "Chosen One, even if we were to capture the city, I'm not sure it would make any difference. Not with the enemy closing in on nearly every side. The American Marines and British tanks in the north are a mere forty kilometers away. We have viable defenses in their path, so we should be able to hold a little longer. But I cannot see what we'll gain by taking Cairo. It's too late to cross the Sinai and reach Israel even if we're somehow victorious in the present battle."

"Nonetheless, you are to keep attacking with everything we've got. For Allah's plan to be realized, we must unite Islam. And the first step in doing so is to overthrow the Egyptian government. It's been five days since our attack began. Are we any closer to capturing the capital than we were yesterday?"

"I'm sorry to report we are not," el-Saeed answered. "It appears we've failed. What forces we've placed in the city are falling back. And while our attempts to get more of our soldiers across the river continue, we're meeting with little success."

"We must keep trying, General el-Saeed. The building of the bridges and fording of the river will continue until our enemies lie dead at our feet."

The commander of the Pan-Arab army once more vacillated, weighing his options. His reluctance to follow the order to continue the assault on Cairo was unmistakable. The time had arrived to disclose the military reality. "Chosen One, it's no use. We should cease our attack and withdraw from Egypt. We've no chance of taking Cairo. Our army's beaten. Our men demoralized. Despite everything the mullahs have tried, many are discarding their weapons and beginning the long walk home. We're shooting any deserters we find, but it's not stopping them from trying. And it's growing worse with each passing hour."

El-Saeed expected a lengthy tirade from his leader. Yet Mourad just looked at him in eerie silence. It seemed an eternity before the Mahdi spoke again. "The assault will continue. But tell the political officers and our field commanders to allow those who wish to go to do so in peace. I will no longer judge those who turn away from our sacred mission. Make sure, however, those who leave understand that even though I'm not stopping them, Allah will be measuring their every action."

"It will be done, Chosen One," el-Saeed said.

Mourad looked at those assembled. He was far from ready to concede defeat. "Despite all that's happened we won't give up. We'll persist in our holy venture. We'll fight to the last man. We might falter in our righteous endeavor, but it won't be because we've lost faith. If we fail it will be because Allah didn't find our sacrifices befitting of his honor."

"We all know why we've failed," Kadar Jethwa, the high cleric of Algiers, said. "We've spoken of it many times in the past days. Allah's displeased with your allowing the heretic woman and her companion to keep their heads. The signs are all there. To tolerate debased infidels in his Chosen One's presence at such a crucial time has led to our downfall. They must forfeit their lives if we're going to return to his favor."

"Nonsense," Mourad said. "I've heard too many discussions regarding my permitting the woman to live. And I've grown quite weary. I'll hear no more talk of it. It was my decision to spare her life, and mine alone. To try to blame our shortcomings on her is without merit. We cannot place the responsibility onto anyone but ourselves. We've so far failed because Allah did not find our efforts worthy of his blessing. The woman has nothing to do with this. It's we who must examine our piety before God."

"But, Chosen One . . ." the high cleric said.

The Mahdi held up his hand. "The discussion of the woman is over."

The sunset was drawing near. The time had come to honor his mother. With a pair of mujahideen to watch over him, he headed for the passage through the interior walls that would take him to the pyramid's opening.

On his way through the antechamber he spotted Lauren Wells sitting in a corner. She appeared to be staring at nothing in particular. He wondered what it was she was thinking. She looked up and half-heartedly smiled. Other than Sharif, he'd never felt anything but uneasiness when dealing with women. He'd shunned female contact after his wife's death, and until this moment had no desire for that to change. Yet for some unexplained reason, he didn't feel that way about the engaging American. He wasn't sure why, but he'd liked her from the moment they'd met.

He hesitated, trying to form the words. "Would you like to accompany me on my evening walk, Miss Wells?"

He seemed perfectly relaxed. She would have never suspected his world was in near collapse.

Her initial response to his invitation was astonishment. He'd barely acknowledged her presence in the past days. She soon recovered. Her smile became genuine. "I think I'd like that very much, Mr. Mourad. After being in this room for so long, I'm starting to feel more than a bit cooped up. I'd enjoy the opportunity for some fresh air. Are you certain I won't be intruding?"

"Not at all. In fact, I think I'd rather enjoy the company."

Wells got to her feet. She was at least half a foot taller than the diminutive Algerian. "All right, then. I'd be honored to join you, sir."

He turned toward the low entrance into the Grand Gallery. She followed close behind.

They were soon at the pyramid's exit. She poked her head out, peering at the fading light upon the western desert. The late afternoon's warmth was a welcome relief. They headed down the archaic stones toward ground level. When they reached the firm sands, she stopped to look upon the Nile. The sounds of fighting were still there. The battle was raging. Yet it wasn't nearly as intense as it had been on the morning she'd arrived at the foot of the pyramids. To her surprise, the armored division guarding the plateau was nowhere to be found. She'd no idea where the tanks had gone.

The Mahdi started walking north, away from the Great Pyramid. He continued in that direction until he was even with the northernmost edge of the ancient western cemetery. Without a word, he turned and headed across the mesa toward the setting sun. One hundred meters silently passed. He'd reached the eons-old remnants of the deteriorating rock wall on the northern edge of the aboveground necropolis. He'd found the crumbling aperture during his earliest days on the plateau. He began walking next to the venerable limestone, out of sight of those at the pyramid. With the constant activity on the hilltop, it was the one place he could find a modicum of peace. His thoughts were on the distant past and the unassuming home where his mother had waited at the end of each day. Calmness gathered in his soul. His bodyguards kept their distance, giving him the space he craved. Nevertheless, they stayed vigilant, their rifles at the ready.

Wells hurried to catch up. As he moved along the disintegrating wall she remained a few feet behind, unsure of what his reaction would be to a woman attempting to walk next to him.

Even more, she didn't know how the mujahideen would respond to any presumptuous actions she might take. At first, lost in pleasing memories of long past years, the Chosen One didn't notice her attempt to lag. Yet it wasn't long before the demure little man figured it out.

"Miss Wells, please. Why don't you come up next to me? It'll make it so much easier to talk."

"I didn't know if it was permitted, Mr. Mourad. And with these guys carrying rather nasty swords, I figured it was better to be safe than sorry. I've had a blade on my neck once this week. I wouldn't want that to happen again. Are you certain it's okay for me to walk with you? What are your followers going to think about a woman appearing to act as your equal?"

"The nice thing is in my position it doesn't matter what anyone thinks. I do what I want, when I want. No man can judge. Only Allah can do so. If I wish a woman to walk at my side and speak with me, then that's what I'll do."

"But won't it make many of them angry?"

"They're already quite upset about your being here. So our walking together won't change that. To be frank, they've pleaded with me often to remove your head, so what difference will this evening make?"

She stopped and looked at him, her worry evident. "It's clear from how they stare, some of them resent my presence. There's hatred in many pairs of eyes passing through the antechamber in the past few days. But I'd no idea they wanted you to take my life."

"So many lives have been lost. In many ways what's one more? But for some reason yours does matter to me. And you've nothing to fear as long as you're under my protection."

"Are you sure, Mr. Mourad?"

"Like I said, I do what I want, when I want."

"And for some reason you want me to live?"

"Yes, I wish that to happen. I didn't know why until just a few minutes ago. And it's become even clearer as we've walked together. It's obvious what I saw in you that fascinated me so. I should have realized it well before this moment."

"What's obvious? What should you have realized?"

"That in many ways you remind me of my wife."

"Your wife?"

"Yes, my wife. You're extremely different from her, but you're also remarkably similar. Sharif was so exceptionally smart, and so stubbornly determined. Just as you are. She was a woman who spoke her mind."

"And as the Mahdi that didn't bother you?"

"At first it bothered me a great deal. I was thoroughly confused by her approach, but after a while I began to see the benefits of loving a woman who'd tell me the things I needed to hear. And Sharif would definitely do that. She knew her place, but she also understood it was her counsel I cherished above all others. She was a remarkable woman and I was so fortunate to have her in my life." He paused. Lauren could see the pain in his eyes as his memories took him back to the woman he'd loved.

"You must miss her very much."

"More than you'll ever know. But please don't concern yourself. It won't be too much longer before we spend forever in each other's arms. The years will pass, and my life's burden will be complete. When it does, Sharif will be with me once again."

Wells smiled, her expression genuine. She didn't know what to say, so she walked along in silence.

"I sense there's more about you reminding me of her," he said. "But I'm not certain what it is. Like Sharif you're quite beautiful, but no one would ever mistake you for her. Her hair was long and shimmering black. Yours is short and an attractive shade of reddish brown. Both of you have brown eyes, but hers were much darker. Your smiles are similar, but hers was a smile of love for me . . ."

He stopped his reminiscing, his face turning a bright shade of red. He'd let his guard down, and for the life of him couldn't understand why. His embarrassment was unmistakable. He couldn't imagine how the conversation had gone so far down this path.

"I'm so sorry, Miss Wells, I don't know what got into me. I'd no right to say such things in your presence. It was highly inappropriate. Other than when I was with Sharif, I've never spoken in such a manner to a woman."

"It's perfectly all right, Mr. Mourad. To tell you the truth I rather enjoyed hearing what you had to say." She smiled again, trying to reassure him.

He looked toward the horizon, doing his best to hide his discomfort. "It's a pleasant evening, isn't it?" he said.

"Yes, sir, it is."

"I wish all could be so."

"I've seen you leaving every day about now. Is this what you do each time?"

"It is. At sunset, since I was a boy, I've gone outside to honor my mother's memory. I do so again tonight. I'll do so again tomorrow night, and for every night remaining within my years."

The daunting day had nearly disappeared, with only the faintest orange wisp upon its edges.

He grew quiet as he recalled those long-ago moments. Serenity overcame him, the tranquillity of the distant evenings returning as if they were yesterday. He'd performed his duty to his mother.

He turned to look at Lauren Wells. "Well, I guess we need to be heading back. Evening prayers will soon be upon us."

65

Beneath the burning North African sun a week was far too long to leave the thousands of corpses unburied. Hour after hideous hour, long night and unyielding day, the Marines stoically moved about the disagreeable ground collecting the enemy dead and depositing them in enormous communal craters. In response to their grievous task, the taxed Americans had long ago shut down their minds. It was the only defense they had from the horror and revulsion closing in from every side. They were in a loathsome nightmare from which they couldn't awaken. They felt like unearthly creatures as they stumbled through this surreal world. It was as if they could no longer separate themselves from the dead. The wretched smell of decaying flesh clung to their skin, overwhelming their agonized senses. Sam Erickson was convinced no matter what he did the vile sensation would never leave his battered psyche. The malodorous smells and gruesome images would walk with him for the remainder of his years.

With James Fife's assistance, he tossed the fractured pieces of a mangled Pan-Arab into a deep hole where hundreds of others waited. That was the last of them, a final body, a final pit. With the coming of the stark morning's first offensive glare, their unutterable task was over. The vexed platoon leader signaled and the bulldozers started pushing dirt onto the immense gravesite. The spiritless Marines looked around. For days, they'd done nothing but fill one fissure after another with once-living forms. Their onerous undertaking was at an end.

The helicopters were waiting to take off. Their engines were running, their blades spinning. The numb survivors shuffled across the sands. They were soon heading toward the beach. Not a word passed among them as they rushed toward the Mediterranean shore. In twenty minutes they'd return to the place where it had all begun. Erickson was too exhausted to think about where they'd been and where they were going. The only thing keeping him sane was the thought of holding Lauren. Within the hour, he'd do so once again. After a lengthy shower in an ineffectual attempt to wash away the corruption, he'd find the woman he loved.

The formation churned north. The fateful shore came into view.

Sam lifted the flap on Lauren's tent. He was anxious to see the surprise on her face. Yet it was the spent lieutenant who was surprised. She wasn't there. He searched for her among the row of tents. Still, she was nowhere to be found. He was confused by her absence, yet saw no reason to be concerned. He glanced at his watch. It was the first he'd done so in forever. For a horrid eternity, time had had no meaning. For hideous days without end, there'd been only a sickening present. No past. No future.

It was nearing eight. A smile appeared on his rugged features. The explanation for her absence was apparent. He knew she was a creature of habit. At this moment, she was probably in the mess tent having breakfast. He turned to join her. After enjoying a hot meal, something he hadn't experienced in uncounted days, he'd return with her to her tent.

Erickson hadn't gone more than a few steps when he spotted his company commander approaching. He could tell from Richards's face something was amiss.

"Figured you'd be here, Sam," the captain said as he neared.

"Yes, sir, I came to find Lauren."

"That's the reason I was looking for you. She's not here."

"What do you mean she's not here? Where is she? Did she get another assignment?"

Richards hesitated. "Not exactly, Sam. I don't have all the details, but it seems nearly a week ago she stole a Humvee and took off with her cameraman for the front lines."

Erickson's heart sank. "I warned her not to try anything so stupid."

"Well, obviously she didn't listen."

"Is she all right?" Erickson asked. "Was she wounded?"

"Nobody knows. Three days ago, our guys overran a Pan-Arab outpost sixty miles north of here. They found the Humvee she'd taken. It was out of gas."

"Was there any sign of her, sir?"

"Not exactly. They spotted women's clothing scattered about near the abandoned vehicle. And a watch and wedding band the outpost's dead political officer was wearing were identified as belonging to her cameraman. But there was no sign of either of them."

Erickson stared at Richards in disbelief. His mind was racing as the implications set in. He couldn't form the words to respond.

It was late afternoon. Erickson sat on the shoreline staring at the swelling tide. He'd been there for hours, alone and motionless. The emptiness within him wouldn't abate. His grief was all-consuming. He'd only known her for a handful of days. Even so, he felt her loss more deeply than anything he'd ever experienced. In a passing moment, the woman he loved had been taken from him. The irony was overwhelming. He felt cheated by life's cruelties. A torment was growing that couldn't be put into words.

Her death had served no purpose. Once this was over, he wouldn't rest until he found her remains. If he didn't, he'd never find peace. He continued staring through unfocused eyes at the mocking waters. That's where Richards and Fife found him as night fell. They walked up to where he was sitting. There was a bizarre sort of smirk on both their faces. He looked at them, his pain immeasurable.

"I know we thought we were out of this, but if the opportunity arises, do you think you're up for another mission?" Richards asked.

Erickson knew revenge wouldn't bring Lauren back. But it no longer mattered. "Sir, if it gives me a chance to kill a few more Pan-Arabs, I'm definitely up for it. The more of those sons-a-bitches we eliminate the better off this world's going to be."

"Like a chance to go after the biggest son of a bitch of them all?"

"What are you talking about, sir?" There was confusion in his response.

"Ever seen the pyramids, Sam?"

The question struck him as strange, even in this rather peculiar conversation. Still it was obvious Richards was waiting for an answer. "No, sir, only on television and in pictures."

"Well, in thirty hours you'll see them firsthand."

"What? I still don't understand. What are you talking about?"

"What I'm talking about is the killing's not over for us yet. They located the Chosen One hiding in the pyramids. We're going to support an attack on the Giza Plateau to eliminate the sorry bastard. We're going to take out Muhammad Mourad. Battalion commander's at division right now getting the details."

66

Night was settling around them. Sanders, Porter, and Abernathy hid in the sheltering rubble near the isle's southern tip as they observed the final piece of another lengthy crossing being bolted into place. In days past, the deadly trio had rushed forward at precisely this moment to destroy each nearly finished span. This time, however, they stayed where they were, watching their adversaries work. They made no effort to eliminate the enemy structure. Within the hour, their orders to do so had changed.

"Okay, Sanders," Abernathy said, "couple minutes and the bridge will be ready. Tell Captain Morrow to have the French bring their tanks forward. As soon as Porter and I get on the other side and secure the far end, the Leclercs can start across."

"All right, Sarge, I'm on my way."

Sanders scrambled to his feet and headed across the tumbled landscape. He soon disappeared.

Four of the Mahdi's engineers rushed about, finishing the final portion of the hazardous task. A pontoon bridge soon floated uninterrupted from the Nile's western bank to Rhoda Island.

"Okay," Abernathy said, "it's our turn."

The duo attached silencers to their sniper rifles. Each raised his malignant weapon and took aim. Both squeezed the trigger. Two of the Pan-Arabs went down. They tumbled into the waters on the northern side of the bridge. Their bodies slowly floated away. The kills had been so exact neither victim uttered a sound. Their startled companions searched the island, trying without success to locate the aggressors' position. The surviving Pan-Arabs turned and ran toward the distant shore. A new round loaded, the long rifles appeared on the Green Berets' shoulders. They had the running figures in their sights. A second squeeze and the last of the engineers fell from the structure.

The time had come for Abernathy and Porter to complete the harrowing assignment. It was a mission neither was anxious to initiate. But if the counterattack was to commence, someone had to cross and establish a defensive position on the western bank. Abernathy signaled the 82nd Airborne squad lurking nearby to provide covering fire. Both Americans got to their feet and edged toward the Nile. After a careful look around, they started running across the endless expanse. Five hundred yards away waited Giza's shore. They'd be exposed and vulnerable the entire time. Fortunately, after six days of fighting with nothing gained and far too many lives lost, their antagonist was confused and dispirited. And the 82nd's burgundy-bereted soldiers did a masterful job of pinning their scattered foes' noses in the dirt. No real resistance rose up to meet the sprinting team. Only a handful of haphazard shots were fired in their direction.

Despite the Mahdi's orders to fight on, the intensity of the Pan-Arab assault had dissipated hours earlier. By a sweltering midafternoon's arrival, all of the grappling rafts had vanished or been destroyed. For the first time since the siege began, the Nile's vivid red was beginning to fade. Nothing more than an occasional mortar round screamed toward the battered island. Only scattered gunfire continued from the distant shore. To a man, the Chosen One's followers recognized they were beaten. Throughout the day, uncountable thousands had walked away without giving it a second thought. More were doing so each hour.

They'd survived the battlefield, but considerable numbers wouldn't live through the undertaking they now faced. The cruel desert stretched for hundreds of miles before the demoralized deserters. Yet it no longer mattered. Most were willing to take their chances with the blinding Sahara. At least they no longer feared the political officers' swords. With Mourad's edict, the mullahs were making no attempt to dissuade the deserters from leaving.

It would be a difficult journey filled with misery and suffering. The wounded especially stood scant prospects of success. Still, despite what they'd face, all were determined to endure the steadfast exodus.

Those who stayed did so reluctantly. With the outcome certain, none was anxious to forfeit his life in the waning struggle. To die now seemed almost senseless. Their agony-filled passing needed to serve a greater purpose if they were going to serve their God. Paradise could wait until their death would contain notable meaning in Islam's future conquests of the nonbelievers.

Even with his army crumbling, their leader continued to cling to the hope that an all-powerful deity would intercede and grant the pious a miraculous result. As Allah had accomplished untold times throughout history's annals, he would smite Satan's followers and show his chosen the way.

Still unwilling to accept defeat, Mourad continued to insist upon building the bridges for a fanciful conquest that would never arrive. It was a huge mistake. One the Allies would use to their advantage.

With the day's end near, the Americans allowed the Pan-Arabs to complete a dozen bridges across the wide river. It was a gamble they were willing to take. Even if their counterattack into Giza failed, they suspected the enemy was too weak to take advantage of the opportunity.

The first of the Leclercs started over the troubled waters. Others moved forward along the Nile. Across the wide river the Allies poured.

The determined advance had been timed to coincide with major pushes in the north and south. They would close in on the laboring defenders from three sides at once. Thirty miles from the Egyptian coastline, Hornets roared from the carriers to bolster the attacks. At the same moment, the British Challengers and their Marine supporters struck with renewed fury.

The 4th Infantry slammed into Mourad's personal armored division. They'd use their superior night-fighting capabilities to turn the contest in their favor. They recognized it would be an arduous clash. These were the most fervent of the fanatics. It mattered not that they were losing on all fronts. The elite warriors would fight to their final breath.

The rancorous night had reached its midpoint. The battle for Giza had been fierce as the cornered Pan-Arabs rallied their remaining units in a desperate attempt to hold off the advance. The fighting had been of the nastiest kind—house to house, street by street.

The combatants' lines were quite fluid. In some places the Pan-Arabs were still within reach of the river. In others they'd lost two or three miles. No portion of Giza was safe. Pockets of resistance remained throughout the stretching suburb.

Near a wide boulevard, five members of Alpha 6333 assumed defensive positions in an abandoned house. They were a mile west of Rhoda Island. Heavy gunfire and life-devouring explosions were everywhere. Like every humble home around it, this one had no doors. The Pan-Arab raft builders had seen to that. His rifle at the ready, Sanders peered out a tiny window whose shattered panes had long ago disappeared.

Ever observant, the detachment's soldiers waited for their leader to appear. Captain Morrow had been recalled to receive an urgent directive from the 6th Special Forces Group commander. He'd been gone for two hours. It felt far longer.

"Looks like the captain might not be coming back," Donovan said. "What do you think we should do?"

"We stay right here and wait," Terry replied. "And we'll keep waiting until someone tells us otherwise. The captain had to cross a mile of unsettled territory to return to the river, and three miles more to get to group headquarters. That doesn't count the time he'll have to spend going over the assignment. He's only been gone a couple of hours. If he runs into trouble, it's going to take a hell of a lot longer than that to get back. So we're staying put and waiting for him to return."

It would be 3:00 a.m. before Morrow arrived. As he stood in the meager room catching his breath, he didn't bother putting down his gear. The detachment leader knew they had to hurry.

"All right, guys," he said, "we've no time to lose. We've got to cover five miles behind enemy lines before sunrise. Pick up your stuff. We're moving out."

Every member of the team looked at him in puzzlement.

It was Sanders who asked the question poised on their lips. "Five miles behind Pan-Arab lines. What in hell's the assignment, sir?"

"Start getting ready," Morrow said. "I'll brief you while you do." He didn't speak again until he was satisfied the detachment's soldiers were gathering their gear. It was obvious from his tone he was pleased with the orders they'd received. "Okay, here's the deal. This team's been chosen for the mission of a lifetime. We're going to infiltrate the Pan-Arab defenses and make our way to the western outskirts of Giza. Once there, we'll hole up until night. At one a.m. tomorrow, we're to attack and eliminate the Chosen One. Intelligence has verified his location. Despite how they scoffed at our report, those prisoners we captured were telling the truth. The sorry bastard's hiding inside the Great Pyramid. But with his forces falling back he won't be for much longer. We've got a day, two at most. It's our responsibility to get to him before he has a chance to escape. We're to work our way inside his defenses, go into the pyramid, corner and kill him. Let me be clear about that. We're to kill him. Under no circumstances will he be allowed to surrender."

"What kind of defenses are we facing, sir?" Terry asked.

"He's protected by two hundred bodyguards, some air defense personnel, and a hundred or so support troops."

"The six of us are expected to take out over three hundred of the enemy and then kill Mourad?" Sanders said. "Sir, you've got to be kidding."

"Sanders, it could be a hell of a lot worse. His finest armored division was guarding the Giza Plateau. But he sent them south in response to the 4th Infantry's arrival. So we could've been facing fifteen thousand of his best soldiers instead of three hundred. And we're not going in alone. It'll be a fully coordinated effort. The carriers will provide air support. And the Marines are sending some of their best men. Their job will be to engage the bodyguards while we enter the Great Pyramid. There's only one way in. So you know what that means— there's only one way out. With us there, there'll be no way to escape. I'll go over the details once we've found a safe place near the target to hide until tomorrow night."

"But why us, sir?" Sanders asked as he loaded a fresh magazine into his M-4.

Morrow smiled. "Sanders, that's the funny part. Remember the bridge you blew up during that huge Pan-Arab attack the day after we got here? The big one running from Rhoda Island to Giza?"

"Yes, sir. How could I forget?"

"Guess what the name of the road was leading onto that bridge."

"I've no idea, sir."

"The Pyramids Road. All this time we've been fighting on the road leading straight to the pyramids. It's real easy to figure out why we were chosen. This detachment's the closest to the pyramids. So we're the logical unit to draw the assignment."

Next to Sanders, Porter stood sharpening his knife. He'd likely use it on many an occasion this night. A sadistic grin came to his face. "That and the fact we're the meanest bastards on the planet."

Porter and Abernathy took the point. The infiltrators needed to cover significant ground in less than four hours. If they failed to do so, the dawning light would give them away and all would be lost. Yet to traverse so precarious a distance behind enemy lines in so little time would call for a tremendous amount of ability. And more than a bit of luck. The simplest mistake would prove fatal.

Sanders knew if anybody could do this, it was the practiced apparitions at their head.

They reached the eastern edge of the Giza Plateau mere minutes before sunrise. In their wake, the dead ran for five miles.

Every home in the area had long ago been abandoned. They picked one giving them an unrestricted view of the Great Pyramid's northern face.

There they watched the goings on during the unending hours of a long and dangerous day. The activity into and out of the opening in Khufu's monument occurred with regularity. Some who entered were in uniform. Others wore civilian dress. The Chosen One's mujahideen were everywhere. That alone was enough to assure the Green Berets the Mahdi was still there.

In the north, south, and east, the Americans kept the pressure on throughout the morning and into the afternoon.

At 5:00 p.m. on the 6th of November, the Pan-Arab lines began to collapse. Neither side had expected events to change so rapidly. The end was near. If, however, the Americans couldn't kill Muhammad Mourad, their triumph would have a hollow ring.

67

W hy are all of you so glum?" Mourad asked.

"Chosen One," General el-Saeed said, "how can we not feel this way? Our army's beaten. In the north the infidels are twenty kilometers away. To the south the Americans have defeated your personal armored division in fighting as determined as any in our righteous quest. We inflicted great casualties upon them. Their blood is like a flowing stream. Even so, they have reached Giza's outskirts. And that's not the worst of it. The enemy's counterattack across the Nile has succeeded. More than half the city's been lost since the assault began. We're running out of time. I've directed the support elements on the plateau to begin packing up and moving out. They are filling the trucks as we speak. If we wait until all are ready and leave in a large convoy, we'll have no chance. The infidels will have no choice but to destroy so tempting a target. So as each truck is filled it will depart on its own. Please understand, our situation is growing desperate."

"I understand quite well. But each of you must realize one thing. Despite appearances, this is not the end. We've suffered a setback. It is, however, nothing more than a stumble in Allah's grand plan. You mustn't lose faith. We'll rise once more. We'll emerge victorious. In my lifetime Islam will conquer, and once it has, I will guide the world through its final days. Of that you can be assured. The prophecy has foretold of these glorious events, and as certainly as I stand before you, it will come to pass. The one true God has so decreed. For now, we'll withdraw into the mountains and deserts from which we came. There we'll rebuild our forces until we're strong enough to venture forth upon the final triumph."

"To do so, Chosen One, what remains of our army must survive," el-Saeed said.

"General, I agree with your assessment. We need to save our army. Weapons can be obtained, but brave men willing to serve as Allah's sentinels are growing precious."

"The infidels have a history of sparing their vanquished adversaries. We certainly wouldn't do so in their place. Your advisers are confident if our men throw down their weapons, the heretics will allow them to withdraw without significant retribution. They'll show us mercy and let what remains of the devout escape. We're just as certain, nonetheless, that they've no intention of permitting you to live. Their ire toward you knows no bounds. Your death will be the prize they'll pursue with boundless vigor. We've informed your loyal commanders it will be two hours before you can safely depart this place under cover of darkness. They've promised to hold our enemies for at least that long. Once night is fully upon us, we'll escort you to freedom."

"Inform my bodyguards, General," Mourad said. "When we leave, they're to remove their robes and headdresses so they cannot be identified. We'll then begin our journey home to prepare for the glorious time when the world will be ours."

68

While Abernathy kept watch, Aaron Porter rushed to the back of the small dwelling where the other four members of the team were sleeping. He grabbed Morrow's shoulder and shook him. "Sir . . . sir, you'd better come right away!"

The detachment commander, more asleep than awake, answered, "What's the problem, Sergeant?"

"You need to see for yourself."

The members of the A Team opened their eyes, each wondering what the urgency was. Porter headed back into the area in the front of the house where they could see what was occurring on the wide mesa without being seen. It wasn't long until the others joined him. None had the slightest idea that the war's end was occurring faster than any had planned.

"What's the emergency?" Morrow asked while rubbing the sleep from his eyes.

"Half-dozen trucks are spread across the plateau, sir," Abernathy said. "The Pan-Arabs are loading them in one hell of a hurry."

"Couple of others already have taken off, heading for the desert," Porter added. "They're bugging out."

"Aw shit," Morrow replied while taking a long look out the shaded window. It didn't take long for him to realize the Americans' efforts to kill the Chosen One were in peril. "They're definitely packing up and leaving. The mujahideen don't appear to be involved yet. So it's likely Mourad's still here. But given what I'm seeing, he won't be for long. Sticking with the original plan, we'll have no chance of eliminating him. Attack's still seven hours away. The Chosen One will be halfway to Libya by then. We've got an hour, no more, to hit the hilltop before we're too late. If we don't, once it's dark, they'll sneak him out of there and head west as fast as they can. Sanders, get me the radio."

69

With the assault moved up, and occurring during daylight hours, the scrambling Marines were going to be extremely vulnerable. They'd planned on the darkness concealing their sudden appearance and catching the majority of the enemy sleeping. Yet it couldn't be helped. They had to go now.

Their engines running, the transport helicopters waited. Twelve MV-22 Ospreys, with the capability to act as both helicopters for vertical landings and takeoffs, and conventional aircraft for faster flight, were committed to the battle. The final mission of the war, its timeline altered, had begun. Erickson's battalion would be the first of the swarming raiders to get under way. When they touched upon the Giza Plateau, they'd be outnumbered nearly two-to-one. With the daunting odds, all one hundred and sixty-eight of the proud unit's survivors would take part in the foray.

They had to reach the target at precisely 6:48 p.m. if the attack was going to succeed. The timing would be crucial. If they arrived too soon, their appearance would alert Muhammad Mourad. Before the

Green Berets could seal the escape route, he might make it to ground level and flee. To make matters worse, if they were early American air support would be minutes from the hilltop, leaving the Marines alone to face a furious counterattack.

If, however, the Ospreys were late, the Green Berets would be on their own as they attempted to move toward the objective. Exposed and isolated, they'd stand no chance against the meaningful force on the sacred elevation. And with the plateau bristling with Stingers, the fighter aircraft providing close-in support would be at risk. Without the Marines to address the majority of the Pan-Arab air defenses, the Hornets would be vulnerable to a deadly assault.

The incursion had called for the Ospreys to be accompanied by Cobras. Unfortunately, with so many of the attack helicopters lost in the endless battles, the few that remained presently were involved in the British and American onslaught pushing toward the Egyptian capital. With the sudden change of plans, none would reach the beach in time to rearm, refuel, and join in on the assault. The formation would be on its own. They'd have to depend on the Ospreys' weapons—a machine gun mounted on the open ramp that could only fire to the rear, and a three-barrel Gatling gun nestled in its belly capable of addressing targets in every direction. Neither weapon was intended for anything more than self-defense. Without the night to shield them, they were going to be quite exposed. For that reason, while the transports were capable of carrying twenty-two Marines, each would contain only fourteen.

Their faces covered by their forearms, the battalion shuffled through the swirling sands toward the spinning blades. They began to enter their assigned craft.

Erickson walked up the rear ramp and into the lead Osprey. He selected a spot near the helicopter crewmember who would handle the belly gun. As they neared the landing zone he'd use the gunner's television screen to view what was occurring around the Great Pyramid.

One by one, thirteen additional Marines entered the windowless hold. Carrying ample arms and munitions, they clambered down the narrow aisle. Each aircraft soon filled.

The loading completed, the strange-looking transports rose. The wide formation was soon rushing south with Erickson's Osprey slightly ahead of the rest. The battalion staff and a handful of riflemen rode in the helicopter to his left. The company commander to his right. The plan was straightforward. Richards's thirty-four men, accompanied by the command element, would handle the most critical element of the endeavor. They would touch down directly in front of the Great Pyramid. It would be up to them to gain control of the northern portion of the spanning vista and the area in front of the ageless edifice. They'd eliminate those guarding the towering form, opening the way for the Green Berets to enter within its venerable walls.

The remaining Osprey trios would land on the eastern, southern, and western edges of the mesa. While the Green Berets were entering the pyramid, the arriving Marines would eliminate the mujahideen on all four sides of the plateau. They knew the staunch bodyguards were fearsome fighters whose loyalty went beyond anything they could comprehend. Each of the two hundred would have to be dispatched if the attack was going to succeed.

The droning Ospreys continued on. As the relentless miles passed, Erickson's Marines sat in self-imposed silence. None could hide his growing apprehension. They knew they faced an immense challenge. And all had seen far too much of death to question his mortality. They'd been promised this would be the final battle, but they couldn't afford to look beyond the here and now. To do so would prove fatal.

With the lingering sun edging toward the horizon, they rushed south. The historic moment would soon be upon them. On the television screen, Erickson could see their destination drawing near. In the distance, the pyramids were rising in front of them. It wouldn't be long now. They'd soon attempt to settle in the midst of the ferocious stronghold.

The platoon leader stared at the timeless relics as they grew larger with every disappearing second. The fleeting strands were ticking on an immutable clock. A few miles more and the landing zones would be reached. The war's concluding struggle was about to begin. The copilot relayed the information to both crew chiefs.

The belly gunner turned toward Erickson. "Sixty seconds, sir."

70

Twenty minutes after the Marines left the beach, as the catapult's power increased, Bradley Mitchell sat in his cockpit wearing a satisfied grin. To his right, Norm Sweeney's aircraft rested on the one next to his. This was it, Blackjack's final mission before returning home. The Pentagon had made it clear—get on the next transport or forfeit his career. Even so, Mitchell was pleased with what had occurred in the past days. He'd done well on the unending assignments. He'd made a difference in the perverse conflict. And despite the problems Brooke had caused, he'd been selected as the lead pilot for the most important mission of the war. He was going to play a significant role in ridding the world of the Chosen One.

Things had gone exactly as he'd hoped. In a few hours, the Americans would declare victory. And he'd been able to withstand his wife's incessant pressure, holding on until the bitter end. His plan had succeeded. With the wing commander's help, he'd gotten away with it for a few extra days. Yet once Brooke had figured out her husband wasn't on his way, her wails had become so shrill no one could ignore them.

There'd be hell to pay when he reached Virginia. He could hear her screaming, the ireful tirades more than he was willing to endure. He'd grab the kids and get out of there. Nonetheless, there was no doubt his transgressions would cost him. His shrew of a mate wouldn't allow him to forget his trespasses for the remainder of his days.

In his way of looking at it, what he'd face when he got home would be worth the anguish. For the rest of his years he could hold his head high, knowing he'd done his part in this horrid contest. He could proudly smile, secure in the knowledge he'd done what was right.

Fortunately, the next transport aircraft wasn't departing for Italy until morning. So there was time for a last sortie before leaving. One crowning achievement and he'd be on his way.

The catapult fired.

The first of the climactic operation's six Super Hornets leaped from the carrier's deck. Sweeney's aircraft soon rose to join him in the southern Mediterranean sky. The F/A-18Es rapidly headed inland. In ten minutes, they'd reach the target. Once there, the skillful pilots would use their bomb loads to destroy Mourad's communication center and remove the possibility of significant reinforcements arriving. They'd then use their lethal cannons to provide close-in support for the Marines and Green Berets.

Two additional Hornet sections would trail at five-minute intervals.

High in the heavens, Blackjack Section's aircraft reached the bright waters' end. They roared across the coastline.

The precious minutes slid by. With each one's end, they'd sped fifteen miles closer to the target.

"Blackjack," Sweeney said, "I'm picking up the Marine helicopter formation on my radar. They're nearing the hilltop."

"Roger, Worm, I've got them. Looks like we're both going to arrive right on schedule. We should be there within seconds of the Marines touching down."

They continued to watch their countrymen's progress as they grew closer to the prize.

71

On all sides of the monument-laden ground mujahideen were stationed one hundred meters apart. In front of the northern face of the Great Pyramid a dozen stood vigilant.

The Special Forces detachment was ready. Sanders crammed his cherished beret into his pocket. He put on the soiled cap he'd liberated from a dead Pan-Arab while making his way through Giza. The ragtag headgear was two sizes too large, but it didn't matter. It would serve its purpose. And for once Sanders didn't care how he looked. There'd be no fetching women to impress on this trip. The members of the detachment did the same, each shoving an enemy cap down around his ears.

With silencers attached, the long black barrels of Porter and Abernathy's sniper rifles eased out an open window. The skilled marksmen took aim.

Throughout the day, a constant stream of humbled Pan-Arabs had been withdrawing from Giza. Vast thousands had moved through the area on their way toward the mighty desert beyond. Some had been alone when passing the hiding Americans. Others had been in motley groups of varying sizes and descriptions. Many were unarmed, but a few still carried weapons.

The Green Berets would use the faltering day's muddled events to their advantage. At a distance, in the twilight their uniforms wouldn't look notably different from those of the enemy. They were depending upon the vague similarity, and a bit of trickery, to get them close. They'd wait for the next bone-tired file to wander by and fall in a short distance behind. If things went as planned, to the watchful eyes upon the mesa they'd look like little more than stragglers from the gathering they followed. They hoped the ruse would get the team within striking distance.

Morrow checked his watch. In six minutes Alpha 6333 needed to reach the northeast corner of the plateau. He'd timed the various collections as they'd struggled past to determine how long the average one needed to reach the rise. He'd calculated the typical formation required four minutes to make it to that point.

The detachment's six men needed to arrive at the exact moment the Ospreys touched down. With the Marines engaging the mujahideen, it would take his soldiers another four minutes to cross the plateau and battle their way up the pyramid's ancient stones. If things went as planned, eight minutes after stepping from their hideout they'd be standing at the massive structure's entrance.

From watching the activity into and out of the timeworn monument, Morrow knew many who entered weren't armed. Whether or not there were additional weapons inside its sacrosanct walls he'd been unable to ascertain. He also knew from the Pan-Arabs' movements that the overwhelming majority of the mujahideen were stationed outside. Throughout the day he'd identified less than a handful entering and exiting the portal into the immense tomb. Nevertheless, he didn't have an exact count of who or what they'd face once the detachment breached the opening. And despite their planning, there would be events none could anticipate.

There were also important political considerations. They were

under strict orders to keep the damage to the pyramid's internal structure to an absolute minimum. There'd be no using anything beyond
their M-4s and a few stun grenades while within its rugged walls. In
place of explosives, Sanders's rucksack contained the grenades along
with sight and hearing protection for the team.

Morrow and his men had examined the maps of the ancient pathway to the King's Chamber. The timeless route was imprinted on every
brain. He knew the tunnels would be somewhat restrictive, with
scarcely enough room for one person to move through at a time. The
detachment commander was unsure of the difficulties they'd find
within the narrow confines. Even so, he suspected it wouldn't take
long to reach the spot where the Chosen One was hiding.

Twenty minutes from now Muhammad Mourad would be dead.

Morrow glanced at his watch. The time had arrived to initiate the
operation. They'd received the signal—the Marines and Hornets were
in the air.

A short distance away, more deserters were approaching. Another
line of haggard Algerians was nearing the sheltering house. There were
nearly forty in their number. A dozen carried rifles. Lagging behind
the plodding group would soon be six new individuals.

The beaten-down gathering was a minute away from passing their
hiding place. Morrow signaled. Abernathy and Porter fired. Each was
a long, difficult shot. Silhouetted in the blinding sun, their objectives
were a quarter mile away. Yet the bullets ran true.

Both mujahideen guarding the northeast corner went down. The
Green Berets grabbed their weapons. One after another, they stepped
out moments after the disjointed stragglers passed. None in the struggling band noticed the added presence at their rear.

They headed toward the plateau.

Inside the King's Chamber, the harried departure's preparations continued.

In response to a comment, the Mahdi said, "Thank you, General. While you do so, I'll make my sunset walk."

"Please, Chosen One, I beg you not to attempt such a perilous act," el-Saeed replied. "Things are quite unstable. To venture outside at this moment could be extremely dangerous."

"Nonsense. I'll be fine."

At 6:44, as the Green Berets stepped from their hiding place, Muhammad Mourad entered the first of the modest passageways that would take him to the outside world.

Moments after he left, Kadar Jethwa turned to his closest lieutenants. "I know what the Mahdi's commanded, but each of you is to listen," he said in whispered tones. "In another hour, when he's made his escape from this place, you're to take the nonbelievers outside and remove their heads. If we're to avoid Allah's wrath, before we leave, the presumptuous infidel woman and her companion must forfeit their lives."

"Why don't we do so now, while the Chosen One's momentarily away?" the junior of the mullahs asked. "We can slay them in the antechamber. It will take a minute, no more. Their heads will be removed and placed on display long before he returns."

"No, we cannot disobey his decrees, even one as misguided as this, for fear of losing Allah's favor. But once he's gone, it's my interpretation of our laws that his order sparing the pair no longer stands. So we'll wait. The moment the Mahdi leaves, kill them both."

"It will be done," the three said in unison.

Lauren Wells sat in a quiet corner of the antechamber attempting to be as unobtrusive as possible. She looked up as Muhammad Mourad appeared, giving him a huge smile. He attempted a meek one in return, but didn't make a sound as he passed through the room.

Through the Grand Gallery and into the narrow tunnel beyond he went. It wasn't long before he reached the opening in the pyramid's northern face. A dying November sun rested upon the western horizon. He started toward ground level.

Once there, he turned to survey the world around him. The sounds of battle reached out for him. There could be no mistaking the threat closing in from each of three sides. Yet nothing saddened him as much as the view to the west. There, on the open desert, hundreds of thousands were walking away.

Dusk was nearly here. The time had come to surround himself in his mother's warming memory. He started toward the disappearing sunlight, walking on the far side of the decaying wall along the northern edge of the western cemetery. Behind him two of his bodyguards kept their distance.

It was 6:47 p.m.

72

A n initial burst of ground fire ripped through the dying day. Others soon followed. It was nothing more than scattered rifle volleys from the Pan-Arabs' outermost sentries. As the Marines drew closer, additional assault rifles burst forth. Lengthy lines of searching tracers soared skyward. Silhouetted by the fading sunlight, their dazzling display danced on the harsh winds. The belly gunners' Gatlings responded in kind.

Despite their surprise at the precipitous attack, on the plateau the Pan-Arabs instantly responded. Across the wide hilltop, Stingers appeared on a dozen shoulders. The air defenders fought to acquire the onrushing infidels in their sights. They pleaded for the firing tone to sound.

Hugging the frail earth, the surging American formation split into fourths. Each headed for its designated landing zone upon the historic mesa. Three of the onrushing craft continued forward, aiming for the northern edge. The foremost Osprey, carrying Erickson and his men, skimmed across the incensed desert toward the Great Pyramid. They were almost there. In seconds, they'd deposit the remnants of the beset battalion upon every side of the Giza Plateau's sands.

The two mujahideen protecting the Mahdi saw the Americans coming. The threat was unmistakable. Near the hoary wall northwest of Khufu's colossal shrine, the bodyguards trailing the Chosen One rushed forward and dragged him from harm's way. They threw their leader into a weatherworn depression in the venerable barrier and stood over him. Both began firing their weapons at the oncoming aggressors. Three meters from their position, a pair of Stinger gunners took aim. The high-pitched tones went off at nearly the same instant, screaming in their ears. They'd each locked on to one of the invaders. Without hesitation, both fired.

The little killers leaped from the air defenders' shoulders and raced skyward. There was hardly any distance between hunter and prey. Those in the advancing Ospreys never had a chance. There was nothing the condemned pilots could do to avoid the inevitable. Their destiny was sealed the instant the slender assassins were launched. In a fleeting moment, the lives of everyone on board both would reach their end.

The deadly missiles were soon upon them. The aircraft on each side of the leading one erupted. Flaming pieces of the smashed craft poured from a fiery sky.

In an instant, the battalion staff and Bravo Company commander were gone. The conflict's leadership, along with two-thirds of the force assigned to attack the northern perimeter, had disappeared. A sole invader carrying fourteen riflemen was all that remained.

Erickson and the belly gunner had spotted the Stingers the instant they were launched. Each had seen the malicious shadows streaking across the lengthening landscape. The battle-scarred lieutenant stared in disbelieving silence as the missiles reached out for their blighted objectives. Two simultaneous explosions rocked the world around them.

With the abhorrent sounds still echoing, the stunned gunner pivoted his camera to the left and right to verify what they already knew. On each side of them, their speeding brothers had disappeared. "They're gone, sir. We're all that's left," the gunner said.

It took little more than an instant for Erickson to realize the horrible truth. He was the sole officer remaining. Whether he wanted it or not, he was now in charge of the attack on the northern face. Yet his hush didn't last long. As the defeated Ospreys' wreckage fell upon the unforgiving sands Erickson instantly responded.

"Did you see where the Stingers came from?" he asked the belly gunner.

"Yes, sir. Both were fired from the area near that crumbling wall on the west side of the pyramid. I can see the guys who launched them on my screen. Not too far from them, there are also a couple of figures in bright robes firing assault rifles."

"As long as the Stinger gunners are there, they're a threat. Take them out before they rearm and get off another shot. Nail the other two guys while you're at it."

Without another word, the belly gunner aimed his Gatling toward the meager wall. He opened fire, sweeping the soft limestone. He hurled burst after burst toward the four figures.

Both Stinger gunners had bent over to pick up a replacement missile. Each went down beneath the Osprey's frenetic attack. A few tortured breaths were all either could muster before their end arrived. The danger posed by the air defenders had been eliminated. They'd have no opportunity to reload their tubes and let loose another slayer. But the belly gunner wasn't finished.

A first of the mujahideen followed the slaughtered soldiers into the next existence. The devoted bodyguard had taken half a dozen shells in the center of his chest. He was dead before his shattered body fell in front of Muhammad Mourad. All around the Mahdi, bullets smashed into the decomposing wall. The surviving bodyguard continued firing at the rapidly approaching helicopter.

Even so, his flailing rifle was no match for the Osprey's daunting gun. A second mortally wounded escort dropped at the Chosen One's feet. His silken dress was flowing red. His death rattle was the final sound he'd ever make.

The gunner momentarily stopped. He scanned the area, looking for another threat to his craft's survival. Yet none appeared. The immense danger emanating from the outcropping had been eliminated. He turned his focus elsewhere.

Hidden behind his bodyguards' tattered bodies, Mourad remained concealed in a crumbling crevice west of the Americans. Once more, he'd survived a brush with death.

The Osprey was nearing the hilltop's northern face. The pilots queried their crewmen.

"Pilots want to know if you wish to abort the mission, sir," the belly gunner said.

"Negative. Nothing's changed. Get us onto that plateau."

"But there's only fourteen of you. With what I see gathering in front of the pyramid, you won't have a chance," the belly gunner responded.

"Doesn't matter. The mission's too critical. Tell the pilots to put her down."

The platoon leader looked at the screen. In significant numbers, the mujahideen were gathering in front of the harsh monolith. With each moment, more running figures were arriving.

The belly gunner relayed Erickson's message. He turned to the lieutenant once again. "I'll do what I can to pin them down, sir. But with as low as we are and my gun's positioning, once we descend farther I won't be able to do so any longer." He fired a lengthy burst toward the pyramid.

At ten thousand feet, Blackjack Section roared over the mesa.

Mitchell headed for the center of the ancient burial ground. Sweeney was tight to his wing.

The target, its many antennas reaching skyward, was unmistakable.

Blackjack lined up his run. At precisely the right moment, he released a radar-guided bomb. Worm did the same. Whistling death plunged toward the remorseless planet. Neither pilot wavered. Each stayed with the quarry until their munitions arrived at the impact point. The communication center was struck by the plummeting armaments. The complex's metal framework and sophisticated electronics were torn into a million shattered pieces. When the F/Λ-18Es were through, little more than a smoldering pile remained. A dozen soldiers had been working within its structure. None had survived. The Pan-Arabs' ability to call for help was gone. The Hornets sped off a short distance.

"All right, Worm, scratch one communication center. Let's find a secure piece of sky to wait for our guys to call us in."

Both knew that soon would arrive the real test of their abilities. They flew west over the open wastelands.

In front of the descending helicopter, Erickson watched as frantic figures ran in every direction. Among them, the striking outfits reserved for the mujahideen were unmistakable. Unaware that Muhammad Mourad was not within its massive structure, most of the arriving defenders were assuming positions in front of the pyramid and on the levels of stone leading to the entranceway.

Erickson's platoon was outnumbered three to one and the daunting odds were growing. To make matters worse, the Pan-Arabs had seized the superior fighting positions.

Touchdown was moments away. The platoon leader rushed to the rear of the craft, motioning for his Marines to stand and get ready. Each leaped to his feet and crowded around their leader. As they did, the Pan-Arab rifles opened fire in earnest.

Erickson's Osprey was settling onto a modest roadway near the rim of the history-laden hill. The helicopter was little more than one hundred and fifty yards from the spectacular crypt.

The Americans hovered inches above the ribbon of asphalt. Before the landing gear touched, its determined passengers leaped from the open rear ramp. The moment their feet reached the contested ground the Marines opened fire. The mujahideen answered back, the intensity of their efforts steadily increasing. The first of the Marines went down. A second followed. Neither moved further. The survivors dove for cover. A handful dropped into a modest depression in front of the road. Erickson and the remainder found themselves in the one behind it. Each attempted to take advantage of the modicum of protection provided by the shallow ditches. Having deposited its human cargo, the Osprey rose. It pirouetted and rushed away with its rear gunner firing long bursts from his machine gun.

Morrow's timing had been perfect. The ploy had worked. Without being detected, they found themselves walking across the northeast portion of the plateau at the exact moment Erickson's Marines appeared. The grim helicopter was landing three hundred yards away. In front of the Special Forces detachment the stragglers they'd followed onto the sacred sands froze. A rearing inferno was roaring to life in front of them. None was prepared for the ferocious firefight erupting before their eyes.

The ragtag gathering wanted no part of the fearsome struggle. All they wished was to escape into the limitless Sahara to begin the lengthy journey home. Yet the way west was blocked. If they hoped to see the smothering sunset, movement forward was impossible. Panic seized them. They'd no choice. Before the startling onslaught reached out to claim them, they needed a place to hide. Their only chance was to rush back into Giza's slums.

Almost as one, all forty reversed direction, intent on scurrying toward the sheltering houses.

Blocking their path were six strangers. It took a single retreating step for the frightened group to realize pieces of the scene were dreadfully amiss. Something didn't fit. And then it hit them—they were wearing Pan-Arab headgear, but the interlopers weren't their country-men. The Pan-Arabs were staring into the camouflage-painted faces of a half-dozen well-armed infidels.

The Green Berets had their rifles ready. Those with weapons in the fleeing party attempted to react. But they'd been caught off guard. They'd no chance against so accomplished an adversary. Their reaction was far too slow and much too splintered.

Morrow's force opened fire. They mowed down the disorganized collection. The astonished assembly got off no more than a few belated rounds before the last succumbed. None of their hasty shots came near its intended mark. It was over in a handful of terrifying seconds.

Forty dead lay on the blood-soaked ground. Not one in the be-draggled mob had survived.

The brilliantly quick skirmish attracted the attention of those upon the broad vista. Before the smoke cleared, the victorious Berets were diving into the rock-hard ground beneath a withering assault from dozens of angry mujahideen firing from the pyramid's heights. The Americans were out in the open. Each was pinned down. They pulled the bleeding bodies of those they'd vanquished in front of them, hopelessly attempting to use the conquered flesh as makeshift protection.

For one, however, luck had run out. A first of the Green Berets went down.

73

The stringent enemy response continued to expand with every frightening moment. It was far too great for twelve desperate Marines to suppress. Like the Green Berets, they had scant cover. Those in the forward ditch were especially vulnerable. Scorching bullets struck all around. Confusion reigned. A life-stealing rifle-propelled grenade fell within a few feet of a newly arriving American.

Erickson's small force was outgunned. The survivors' numbers were dwindling. They were severely outnumbered by their growing foe. And those continuing to appear in front of the pyramid didn't stop. It wouldn't be long before the Americans would be overwhelmed.

"We need to consolidate our position. Everyone fall back to the ditch on the north side of the road," Erickson ordered.

Three of the four surviving Marines in the forward depression began withdrawing to the far side of the pavement. Fife remained, intent on providing as much covering fire as he could while waiting for the others to clear.

Satisfied that the beleaguered men had safely reached the far ditch, the platoon sergeant leaped to his feet to run across the narrow asphalt. As he attempted a first hurried step, a well-placed bullet struck high upon his right leg. It smashed his thighbone, severing it and sending splintering pieces in every direction. Sharp slivers pierced his skin in a dozen locations. He dropped to the ground beneath the excruciating pain. Blood poured upon the sweltering blacktop.

"Gunny!" Erickson yelled. "Sergeant Joyce, give me a hand. We've got to get him out of the line of fire."

With relentless rounds slamming into the desolate ground, the lieutenant and team leader crawled forward. They grabbed James Fife's arms and dragged him into the northern ditch. Joyce didn't hesitate. He tore away the frayed uniform. Blood continued to spurt from the vicious wound. He ripped off his belt. In seconds, he was fashioning a makeshift tourniquet and applying it above the bullet's entry point. The bleeding slowed to a manageable trickle. Satisfied with the belt's positioning, he pulled a bandage from his first-aid pouch and applied it to the entry wound on the back of the mangled leg. When he was finished, he retrieved an identical bandage from the wounded platoon sergeant's pouch and did the same at the bullet's exit point. There was nothing he could do about the horrid bone fragments. Those would have to wait until they got Gunny to the beach.

"You all right, Gunnery Sergeant?" Erickson asked.

"I'm fine, sir," Fife said through clenched teeth.

Yet each understood the grizzled platoon sergeant wasn't okay. The injury was severe. Still, if they could contain the bleeding, it likely wouldn't end his life.

Erickson searched the disconcerting scene, looking for the glimmer of hope. Yet nothing appeared. Forced to attack in daylight, they'd known this wasn't going to be easy. None, however, could have predicted the dire circumstances they now faced. The Americans were struggling throughout the hilltop. On the northern end of the plateau, Erickson's men were trapped.

If they were going to avoid swift annihilation they needed help. Erickson glanced over to see another of the Green Berets perish. He

signaled for the company radioman. In a low crouch, the corporal
raced through the modest trench to the lieutenant's position. A blanket of seeking gunfire followed in his wake. He dove for cover next to
the platoon leader.

"Give me the handset!" Erickson ordered. The radioman complied.
"What's the Hornet Section's call sign?"

"Blackjack-One, sir."

"Blackjack-One, Blackjack-One, this is Bravo-Three-Six."

"Roger, Bravo-Three-Six," Mitchell answered. "This is Blackjack-
One."

"Blackjack-One, we're in serious trouble. We're pinned down in a
small ditch on the other side of the road north of the Great Pyramid.
We're taking heavy fire. Our losses are mounting. The Green Berets
are three hundred yards east of my position. They're out in the open
and totally exposed. They've already suffered casualties and probably
won't be able to hold on much longer. There are sixty to seventy mujahideen defending the pyramid. They've taken positions on the ground
in front of, and the stones leading up to, the opening. You've got to
eliminate them if we're going to have any chance."

"Roger, Bravo-Three-Six," Mitchell said. "We're on the way. Pop
smoke and hunker down. We'll take out anything that moves between
your location and the northern face."

"Understood, Blackjack-One."

"Hold tight. We'll be there in fifteen seconds."

The Hornets raced toward the plateau. Their plan was to come in
wing tip to wing tip across the front of Khufu's enormous shrine.
Mitchell's aircraft would be closest to the age-old edifice. With an
ounce of luck and an immeasurable amount of talent, all they'd need
was a single pass to complete the intrepid task. They'd little doubt
there would be few Pan-Arabs alive once they finished the overriding
assault. That, however, wouldn't be the end of Blackjack's mission.
With the next pair of F/A-18Es still three minutes out, it would be up

to them to do what they could for the remainder of the floundering Marines upon the expansive plateau. The moment they dispatched those in front of the grand monument, they'd make a sweeping turn and strafe any mujahideen they found. As they neared the plateau's northwest corner, the Hornets were barely two hundred feet above the barren desert. They continued to descend.

"Worm, I've got smoke."

"Roger, Blackjack. I see it. And I think I've spotted the rest of our guys. That's got to be the Green Berets lying out there firing toward the pyramid. We'll need to be real precise with our cannon fire. If our Vulcans are the least bit long, we'll hit them along with the fanatics."

"I concur, Worm. But we've been in tighter spots than this in the past few days. You take those on the ground. I'll eliminate the ones firing from the pyramid. Just keep a light touch on the trigger and we'll be fine."

"Roger, Blackjack. I'm right with ya."

The pair dropped their death-tinged noses until they were hugging the frantic scene. The Hornets surged across the complex. Even in the day's failing half-light, in their vivid outfits the mujahideen were unmistakable.

The F/A-18Fs were nearly there. Straight and steady they rocketed toward their goal.

Mitchell gave his trigger a quick pull. Two dozen 20mm shells poured forth. It was followed by another light squeeze. And a third . . . An assured mortality screamed across the hilltop. The rabid munitions reached out for the pyramid's imposing stones. As the deadly ordnance worked its way across the huge structure's timeworn features, the rounds began striking everywhere. The ravishing cannon had an instant effect. As Erickson watched, one after another of Mourad's disciples was crushed beneath the hellish fury that befell them. The conscious-consuming shells were ripping the defenders apart. With nowhere to hide, none would be unscathed.

Sweeney did the same, spewing a certain end upon those caught on the chronicled ground.

The pressure on the junior pilot was even greater than that on his section's leader. In firing at those on the intemperate sands he had to avoid hitting the Americans.

Mitchell fired again. And a fraction of a second later, he squeezed his Vulcan's trigger a fifth time. The result was startlingly predictable and exceedingly certain.

Sweeney's firing pattern was nearly identical. The Hornets were so close Erickson could feel the heat from their engines as they ripped across the mesa. As the F/A-18Es passed, the gunfire from the substantial stones ceased. There had been at least three score fighting to protect the Great Pyramid. Only five or six were still alive. Each was hopelessly struggling to overcome his horrific wounds. The rest lay scattered and unmoving. Crimson flowed in every direction, scarring the sacred stones and seeping into the pitiful landscape.

Blackjack Section had opened the way.

The instant they reached the pyramid's eastern end, the Hornets banked right. Each attempted to put some air beneath his wings. They wanted the added altitude in order to identify where they were needed next.

Since the battle's beginning, a Stinger gunner had been standing in the evolving darkness on the Great Pyramid's southern face. As they raced past, neither Mitchell nor Sweeney spotted the stealthy figure. The air defender raised his missile and pointed it toward the soaring fighters. He soon had the leader in his sights. The fatal tone sounded. With a victorious smile, he fired. A five-foot, guiltless executioner screamed into the dimming skies.

The threat was unmistakable. Mitchell's screeching aircraft begged its pilot to take severe evasive action. Yet he was much too low, and the purposeful Stinger far too swift for him to ever hope to escape.

"Break it off! Break it off!" Mitchell screamed. "I'm picking up a missile firing."

Sweeney instantly reacted. He banked left toward Giza.

"It's right on top of me, Worm!"

"Blackjack, bail out!" Sweeney pleaded. "Bail out while you still can."

Mitchell hit his afterburners and rocketed across the hilltop with the resolute missile on his tail. The Stinger was rapidly closing. In another second, no more, death would come to claim him. There was no time to release flares to fool the primitive heat-seeker. He'd one chance. He'd have to eject from his aircraft. He knew at so low an altitude, if he survived at all, the drastic action would likely cripple him. It was his final, fading gambit. He reached for the canopy release. Yet for some ill-defined reason, he hesitated. The stark, suicidal thoughts he'd encountered over the Libyan air base returned to tug at his mind. He'd no desire to live as an invalid. And he'd been given a second opportunity to avoid an anguished existence with Brooke. Unlike during the frightening events over the enemy airfield, the corrupting sensation didn't pass. He started to pull the handle. Yet without conscious thought he'd made his choice.

He relaxed his grip. His innate need to live dissipated. A final crooked smile found its way to the corners of his face.

At that moment, the Stinger found him.

It smashed into the Hornet. The massive explosion destroyed the right engine and blew off its wing. The doomed fighter's shattered shell spun out of control, plunging for the muted ground. Ravenous flames roared toward the cockpit.

Strapped in his seat, Mitchell was very much alive. Still, he knew his last moments were an instant away. There was no chance he could control the mangled aircraft. And no time to bail out. He couldn't avoid the inevitable. All that remained was the crowning finish. He prayed he'd perish before the uncontrollable fires found him. The plane, its burning fuselage and remaining wing fully engulfed, twisted over and again as it headed toward an enraged earth.

His F/A-18 was nearing its impact point. Yet much to his surprise, his wounded Hornet was no longer reaching out for the center of the plateau. The missile's impact had redirected his fiery tomb. He was hurtling toward an area southeast of the Great Pyramid. He couldn't believe what his eyes beheld. To his astonishment, his passing was going to be far more memorable than he could have ever imagined. His ill-fated aircraft was on an uninterrupted course toward the Sphinx. The spectacular stone structure was right in front of him. Closer and closer the disabled fighter approached its inevitable end.

Mitchell's mangled Super Hornet smashed into the eroding wonder. Porous limestone and shattered metal flew in every direction. When the dust settled, and the determined fires died, the Sphinx's time-honored image was gone. What had taken ancient man eons of creativity and backbreaking labor had been destroyed by his descendants in a single, vehement act.

Erickson surveyed the damage the Hornets had wrought. Lifeless mujahideen were sprawled across the death-spattered framework. While the torrid battles in every corner of the hilltop raged, rifle fire from those guarding the entrance into the Great Pyramid had ceased.

The Marines had their opening, but they needed to move fast. Others might soon appear to take the deposed defenders' places. The lieutenant leaped to his feet. "Now's our chance. Get out of this ditch and let's go!"

He started running toward the towering artifact. His men were right behind. Firing at anything that moved, they scurried toward the rising stones. A handful of severely wounded mujahideen tried to answer back. But it was no use. With ruthless intensity, they were dispatched without further losses among the Americans. Erickson was soon clambering up the rows of stones to claim them as his own. With Benson and Pitzer's assistance, the wounded platoon sergeant brought up the rear. Every hobbling step on his remaining good leg was sheer agony.

Morrow watched the Marines charging across the contested ground. He could tell his team's survivors were anxious to join in. Much to their displeasure, he motioned for them to stay where they were. Having sacrificed two of his men, he couldn't afford getting involved in the attack for fear of losing any more. If the detachment's numbers declined further, their assault upon the King's Chamber would be in peril. He'd no choice. Until the perimeter was secured, they would wait.

He turned to the soldier lying next to him on the unyielding sands. "Sanders, before we head out, crawl over and check on Terry and Donovan."

"What's the point, sir? Neither has moved since the Pan-Arabs nailed them. We all know they're dead."

"Do it anyway."

Erickson stood at the profound shrine's opening. He turned to survey the field. The area in front of the northern face was under American control. Nonetheless, with the unrelenting sounds of battle assailing him, he'd no way of deciphering what was occurring throughout the plateau. For all he knew, the mujahideen were preparing a massive counterattack. He had to get a perimeter established.

He yelled down to ground level. "Sergeant Joyce, how many men do we have?"

"Not sure, sir." He began to count.

"Nine if you include me," Fife said as he struggled toward where Joyce was standing.

Erickson looked toward his grimacing platoon sergeant. "Gunny, are you out of your freakin' mind? You're going to kill yourself if you don't knock it off."

"Sir, the only thing I'm planning on killing are a few more

mujahideen if they're stupid enough to show their faces. So why don't we stop worrying about me and start getting our defenses set up?"

"Okay, it's your funeral. Sergeant Joyce, I want two men up here to guard this entranceway. You're to take two more and handle the lower levels of stone. The remainder will defend the area in front of the pyramid. Now let's get to it."

In seconds, the Marines were in place. Erickson looked around. He'd done his best with what he had. He signaled for the Green Berets to move up. As the depleted Special Forces detachment's soldiers ran toward them, a second Hornet section appeared.

It wasn't long before Alpha 6333's soldiers reached the pyramid and climbed to its entry point. Morrow was all business. "Lieutenant, did you see anyone in peasant clothing exit the pyramid during the battle?"

"No, sir. From what we saw, no one went in or came out."

"Good. Then the bastard's still in there." He turned to his remaining men. "Let's go get him."

74

On his belly, Porter slipped inside the downward-sloping passage. A solemn-faced Abernathy was right behind. Sanders and Morrow followed them into the narrow space. Even though there was sufficient room for a stooped walk, they'd be far too inviting a target if they elected to do so. They'd no choice but to crawl, cradling their rifles, to the distant prize. Their faces would be pressed against the clammy floor throughout the journey.

Ever on the alert, Porter started down the sinister path. The team's survivors were on edge, uncertain of what awaited. They were ready to repel an attack from any source. Yet as they made their way into the ghostly structure, no one appeared to contest their presence. They moved through the constrained interior unopposed. When he reached the point where the pathway split, Porter breathed a sigh of relief. There was still a long way to go, but so far things were progressing exactly as planned. A few minutes more and the Chosen One would be dead.

At the spot where the tunnel separated, Morrow motioned for Sanders to break from the group. They had to ensure no one was hiding in the shaft to the underground chamber. If the enemy was lurking below, they could easily come in behind the Americans. If the mujahideen did so, the plan to reach Mourad would be doomed. They'd never make it to the King's Chamber before forfeiting their lives. If anyone was waiting belowground, they had to be eliminated.

As the group headed up into the center of the pyramid, Sanders continued down within the severe walls leading to the hidden space. He was quite uneasy with the assignment. He'd no idea what he might encounter. A dozen enraged warriors could be waiting, intent on trapping the invaders. Whether he could handle such determined opposition, he hadn't a clue. He wasn't supposed to be doing this alone. The plan had called for Donovan to accompany him. But Donovan was dead and Sanders knew the detachment's primary responsibility was to get to the Chosen One's hiding place. If they were going to succeed, they couldn't afford to send a second person to scour the belowground portion of the pyramid. It would be up to the team's junior sergeant to handle the task on his own. Once he'd completed his search of the sloping shaft and the distant room at its end, he'd head back to assist his countrymen.

The distance to the subterranean area was quite far. Sanders would only be halfway to the unimpressive enclosure by the time the remainder of the team reached the Grand Gallery.

Inside the King's Chamber it was apparent a notable assault was under way. Who and what was involved in the attack the Pan-Arab leadership had no way of knowing.

In the past minutes, the sounds of the fierce fighting in front of the pyramid had abruptly ended. What had happened beyond the austere enclosure none could guess. Hopefully, if Allah was with them, the mujahideen had triumphed over their reviled foe. Yet each suspected the truth lay elsewhere. In all likelihood, the enemy had defeated the loyal bodyguards.

If that were the case, their tenuous position within the restraining walls would place them in severe peril. Their lives would likely end this day. Each was certain the nonbelievers wouldn't rest until they killed the Chosen One and his advisers. They were convinced the Americans would enter the pyramid intent on slaughtering anyone they found. Their only chance was to defeat the aggressors. Once they had, they'd attempt to slip outside and escape into the infinite desert.

General el-Saeed grabbed his AK-47 and headed toward the antechamber. He stopped at the edge of the burial room, looking at those within its confines. "The infidels will soon come looking for us. We must destroy them if we wish to live. General Akhtar, organize those within the King's Chamber. Distribute the weapons and set up your defenses on the far side of the pharaoh's sarcophagus."

"It will be done," Akhtar said.

"I'm going to make my stand in the Grand Gallery. I'll take the two mujahideen stationed in the antechamber with me. If we don't prevail, it'll be up to you to save your lives."

"What about the Chosen One?" Akhtar asked. "Our efforts mean nothing if he doesn't see tomorrow's sunrise. His survival has to be our first priority."

"For the moment, there's nothing we can do. We've no idea where he is. And from the sounds of battle, the fighting outside has been intense. The defiled ones may have already spilled his blood. If Allah has decreed, the Chosen One's journey to join the honored martyrs may have begun. In our present situation we've no way of helping him. We must first save ourselves."

Those present stared at the federation's military commander. None was particularly pleased, but each understood the general's impressions were sound.

"I'll need someone to guard those in the antechamber until I'm able to eliminate whoever comes in search of us," el-Saeed said.

"Set up your defenses, General," Kadar Jethwa said. "I'll have one of my lieutenants assist me. We'll take charge of the woman and her associate."

El-Saeed and the bodyguards moved to the upper edge of the Grand Gallery. The general's plan was to wait on the Grand Step. They would lie prone within the narrow space and use the superior elevation to their advantage. With any luck, it would also mask their presence, allowing them to surprise their adversary. They'd no idea who was coming, or how many they'd face, but it no longer mattered. If they were going to endure they had to stop the attackers, find the Chosen One, and escape into the night.

Each took his position. Three rifles were leveled at the small opening on the far end. The moment the first of the raiders poked his head into the room, el-Saeed planned on firing.

The Green Berets slithered up the passageway. Porter gave a hand signal. They'd reached the Grand Gallery. In their discussions, the team had been unified in the belief that this was the most likely spot for an ambush. The lethal trio stopped, lying motionless in the cramped tunnel just short of the opening. Their breathing was shallow and slow. Not a muscle moved. They'd stay this way for however long it took to confirm what, if anything, waited inside the pyramid's most expansive area. Porter was inches from where the upward-leading room began. He could see partway into the gallery, but couldn't be seen by anyone waiting inside. He lay there letting his senses examine the scene.

Forever passed—although it was barely a minute on the clock.

Something was there. He was certain of it. Where, he hadn't yet determined. He continued to take it in. He soon identified a prone presence waiting on the distant side. He was positive someone was near the far wall. It wasn't long before his well-sharpened abilities told him a second person was hiding close to the stretching room's end.

He wasn't, however, completely confident in his findings. So he waited still longer.

Because the third defender was between the others, he nearly missed him. The first two's presence masked his position. Yet eventually Porter picked him up. This time he was beginning to feel comfortable with his assessment. There were three people hidden within the gabled expanse. The existence of more was unlikely. Even so, now wasn't the time to make a mistake. So Aaron Porter continued his keen observations.

Finally, he was ready. He held up three fingers, followed by further signs indicating where in the room their quarry would be. Without a sound, the Green Berets edged closer to the gallery's opening. Porter had gone as far as he could go without being detected. He pressed against the left wall, making room for Abernathy to slide up next to him.

The mujahideen were great warriors. And General el-Saeed had earned his exalted position by his unquestioned bravery in many a barbarous battle. They were formidable adversaries.

But the Americans had no intention of underestimating their determined foe. Two rifle barrels slid ever so slowly out of the narrow opening. Even to their combat-savvy opponents, the movements were imperceptible. Porter and Abernathy aimed at the enclosed end of the hallway. The enemy was fifty yards away, shielded by the high step and the room's upward angle. It would be a difficult shot, even for the world-class marksmen.

"Now," Abernathy whispered.

Both fired. The bullets ripped through the lengthy space. On the left and right, the mujahideen were dead before the sound of the shot reached their ears.

General el-Saeed reacted with blinding speed. He opened fire upon the slender aperture at the far end of the gallery, releasing a long burst from his automatic weapon. He couldn't see those hidden within, but it didn't matter. The general's bullets struck all around the opening.

More than a few found their way into the restricting tunnel. Morrow yelped as a ricocheting round passed through the flesh on his left arm and continued on its way. Blood trickled onto the squalid stones.

El-Saeed fired another extended blast from his AK-47.

Porter and Abernathy unloaded their magazines into the remaining Pan-Arab. Round after round tore through the contested room. El-Saeed's rifle dropped onto the floor below. He moved no more.

With a fresh magazine, the Green Berets lay where they were, making certain no one attempted to enter the space and challenge their presence.

"You all right, sir?" Abernathy whispered.

The captain didn't respond. Abernathy looked behind him. To his surprise their commander was lying facedown upon the soiled floor. The concerned sergeant turned him over. Morrow grimaced from the girding pain of the careening bullet that had ripped through his chest. Every tortured breath was a wretched struggle. There was no question his injuries were critical. He needed immediate medical attention.

"We've got to get you out of here, sir," Abernathy said. He reached for Morrow.

The detachment leader pushed him away. "Never mind me. Get Mourad." Morrow dug at his side, taking out his Beretta and handing it to Abernathy. "Finish the mission, Sergeant. Kill the Chosen One, then we'll take care of my wounds."

Abernathy propped the anguished captain against the wall. With wounds this extensive, there was nothing he could do to help. They needed to eliminate the Mahdi without delay to have any chance of saving Morrow. Abernathy and Porter recognized, nonetheless, that the worst thing they could do was to rush the assignment and make a mistake. The immensely skilled soldiers begrudgingly accepted the need to stick with the original plan.

"Should we stay here?" Porter asked as he looked at Abernathy. "Or head over to the other side to wait for Sanders?"

"Let's hold where we are," his partner said. "We're going to be most vulnerable while making the crossing. If we run into trouble, a third rifle will help."

Sanders had heard the gunfire moments earlier. He'd instinctively frozen, waiting and listening. It had taken everything he had to resist the urge to go to his countrymen's aid.

The shooting quickly stopped. He hesitated, uncertain of what to do. If his comrades were dead and their vanquishers came looking, his life would soon end. He knew the Marines were under orders to do nothing to assist the Special Forces detachment once they'd entered the tomb. This wasn't their fight. And they weren't prepared for such an operation.

Sanders threw off the impulse to deviate from his role. He was already too far underground to escape if anyone came looking. If the others had been killed and the Pan-Arabs pressed their advantage, he'd be trapped no matter what he did. So he set aside his fears and returned to crawling toward the pyramid's underground reaches.

To his relief, he arrived at the staid room dug deep within the bedrock. The downward tunnel was empty. And the space at its end was hiding no one. He turned to rejoin the team.

Without incident, one at a time, the deft trio crossed the Grand Gallery. Porter stood next to the tunnel into the antechamber. The demure room at its end was a few feet away. With so short a distance, it would serve no purpose to attempt to move through undetected. If anyone was in the modest enclosure, the team's best bet was to stand up the moment they could and dash inside with their rifles ready. And from Porter's observations, there was no question someone was within the summoning space.

"How many?" Abernathy whispered.

"Two," he replied. "They're standing a few feet apart against the opposite wall. No . . . wait . . . there's three, probably four of them. They threw me for a minute. They're in two groups, extremely close together." He got on his hands and knees, peering into the plaintive room.

"Do you see any weapons?"

Porter looked again. "No, but I can't be certain."

He listened for the telltale signs of a rifle's safety being released or a round being chambered. Yet no such sounds appeared.

"All right," Abernathy said. "Get set. With the way this place is configured we'll have to rush them. But don't fire unless you have to. I'd like to see if we can find out from whoever's in there what we're facing in the King's Chamber."

The able aggressors prepared to move. They'd enter single file with their backs bent, heads pressed against the low ceiling. As the tallest among them, Sanders would have the most difficulty.

For that reason, he'd trail his partners. Each knew he'd have to make a lightning-fast decision whether to shoot the instant he breached the room.

Porter led the mad scramble into the harboring niche.

The deadly group was soon standing inside the antechamber with their rifles raised. Against the far wall waited the final surprise of the mission. Lauren Wells and her cameraman were standing near the entryway leading into the burial tomb. Behind Wells, using her as a shield, was Kadar Jethwa. The sneering cleric was holding a long knife to her throat. One of Jethwa's lieutenants was doing the same to her cameraman.

She frantically held out her hand. "Don't shoot! Don't shoot! We're Americans."

The Green Berets hesitated. They could see the terror in the woman's eyes. In the back of Sanders's mind something told him she looked vaguely familiar. The Americans kept their rifles poised, but didn't fire.

"Tell them to let us through, Miss Wells," Jethwa said in Arabic. He peeked out with only the slightest portion of his face showing. "Once we're given free passage, we'll let you and your cameraman go."

She repeated his demand in English. Until the threatening cleric had used her name, none of the soldiers had recognized who the prisoners were.

"Let us through or we'll kill them here and now." Jethwa brought the knife closer to her exposed jugular. There was no doubt the mullah meant what he said. Once again she translated.

"Is either of them the Chosen One?" Abernathy asked. She shook her head ever so slightly, indicating the answer was no. "Do they understand English?"

Wells took a chance and spoke. Her words were hurried and filled with angst. She knew they easily could be her last. "Not that I know of. Of all those inside the pyramid I've only heard Muhammad Mourad speak English. Listen, whatever you do, don't release these two. If you let them go they'll kill us for sure."

"We've no intention of letting them go."

Jethwa clearly didn't like the ongoing discussion he couldn't understand. He pulled the infidel woman closer, obviously upset at the conversation in the incomprehensible foreign tongue. He pressed the knife against her throat. A gaunt, red trail trickled down her neck.

"Release them if you wish to live," Abernathy said. She repeated his words in Arabic.

The indignant mullahs stared at him, their ire all-encompassing.

"Porter, you got him?" Abernathy said without taking his eyes from the hostages.

"Yep."

"I'll take the other one. Sanders, get ready to grab both Americans the moment we fire."

Only the smallest part of the Pan-Arabs was exposed. There was no margin for the slightest miscalculation. Porter knew his kill would have to be perfect. If it wasn't, the mullah would slit her throat before Sanders could get to her.

"Now," Abernathy said.

Both fired at the same instant. The bullets whizzed by, passing no more than a millimeter from the captives' ears. The raucous gunfire consumed the resonating space. Behind the slain forms, the seasoned stone was splattered with exploding brain cells. Each was dead before the knife fell from his hand. They slumped against the stained wall and slid onto the floor.

Wells let out a terrifying scream.

Sanders rushed forward, grabbing the pair. He hurried them to the opposite wall. Porter and Abernathy trained their M-4s on the slender opening at the end of the space.

"How many are in the final room?" Abernathy asked.

"Aw . . . I'm not certain," the visibly unnerved Wells said, trying to regain her composure. "People are constantly coming and going. What do you think, Chuck, probably about six or eight?"

"That sounds about right," her cameraman said.

"Do they have any weapons?"

"Yes . . . maybe . . . I don't know!" she said. "We were only in there once, and at the time I wasn't in a position to notice."

"Okay. I sure hate to lose a rifle, but we can't take a chance with either of your lives. Sanders, give us your rucksack then get them to safety," Abernathy said. "Collect Captain Morrow on the way and get him medical attention as fast as you can. If we don't come out in the next twenty minutes, seal the entrance and wait for orders from the group commander."

Sanders nodded, pulled the canvas bag up over his head, and handed it to Porter. He motioned for the hostages to follow as he headed toward the way out.

"What about my equipment?" Chuck said. "If I leave it, I'll probably never see it again."

Abernathy glanced at the cameras and satellite equipment. "All right, gather it up real fast and take whatever you can carry."

Sanders was soon escorting the captives toward the distant entrance-way. As they started into the Grand Gallery they stepped over the bodies of General el-Saeed and the dead mujahideen. When they reached the far side and entered the restrictive tunnel, Captain Morrow awaited. His unseeing eyes were set in a fixed stare. After verifying his commander was dead, Sanders decided that for the moment he'd no choice but to leave the body where it lay and lead his charges to safety.

75

P orter and Abernathy had reached the far edge of the final, short
passage. The King's Chamber was inches away. One more room
to conquer and the war would end.

Despite everything he tried, with those in the burial vault hidden by
the large sarcophagus near the opposite end, Porter couldn't identify how
many were present. He did, however, recognize the sounds of ammunition magazines being loaded, rounds chambered, and safeties released.
The unidentified force within the eternal crypt definitely had weapons.

Upon the contested plateau, the fractious fighting was nearing its end.
The swarming fighter aircraft and unyielding Marines had seen to that.

Crouching inside the wind-crusted barrier's weatherworn crevice,
Muhammad Mourad stared at the lifeless mujahideen lying in front of
him. A few feet away, the misshapen bodies of the dead Stinger gunners were tossed in a brutal heap. The singular purpose for the infidels'
frenetic raid was unmistakable. He knew they'd come for him. He
realized what the result would be if they discovered his presence.

Even so, his faith wasn't shaken in the slightest. Allah would protect him, of that he was certain. He was also just as convinced his God would expect him to use the infinite gifts he'd been given to find a way to save himself.

He looked at the silent images in front of him. The Americans would be after a diminutive man dressed in peasant clothing. He had to fool his determined pursuers in order to have any opportunity to escape. His sole chance was to somehow change how he looked. There weren't many options. He couldn't put on one of the mujahideen uniforms. The infidels would shoot, without question, anyone so dressed. That left a single choice. He crawled over and started stripping the blood-drenched clothing from the smaller of the two air defenders.

Much to Erickson's relief, with the arrival of the third pair of Hornets, the swaying battle turned toward the Americans. The bullish counterattack the small band of Marines in front of the Great Pyramid had anticipated never materialized. A few groups of disorganized defenders arrived to tangle with his men. Despite their efforts, they proved to be little more than an annoyance.

It didn't take long for the platoon leader to realize the hilltop was nearly secure. The crimson-stained robes of the slain mujahideen were everywhere he surveyed. Nothing arose to threaten the tenacious Marines. The worst was past. Other than an occasional burst of gunfire, the onrushing night was almost serene.

When they reached the spot where the compressed passageway dead-ended into the original tunnel, Sanders stopped. It wouldn't be much farther now. They were almost home.

It would be a relief to leave behind these spectral walls. Still he wasn't about to let down his guard. Before heading up to the entranceway, he needed to alert those waiting outside of his presence. "Hey, guys . . . hey,

Marines, don't shoot, it's Americans coming up the tunnel," he called out. He peered up at the opening. "Did you hear me? We're Americans."

"We heard you just fine," Erickson said. "Come on up."

Wells couldn't believe her ears. But there was no mistaking whose voice she had heard. Lauren would recognize it anywhere. For the first time in many days, she knew Sam was alive. The gritty reporter would soon exit the ancient gravesite with an unending smile upon her face.

Lying inside the short tunnel, out of sight of those within the final chamber, Porter and Abernathy reached into the rucksack and took out the shielding gear. They needed to shelter their eyes and ears from what was about to happen. The protective equipment in place, each soon gripped a stun grenade. Given the direction of the toss, both would have to use their left hands. Neither, however, was concerned about the added challenge. To bounce the cascading grenades off the wall behind the cowering Pan-Arabs they would only need to lob them a modest distance. And there was no need for the throws to be perfect. With the grenades' ability to disable, especially in the encased space, all that was required was getting them close.

Unlike a fragmentation grenade, the ordnance they gripped wouldn't explode in the conventional manner. Nor would it kill. Instead, each would send out a brilliant flash of light to blind for five to ten seconds and leave an "afterimage" that would keep the victim from focusing. Along with that would come a one-hundred-and-seventy-decibel soundwave creating hearing loss and damaging the middle ear. The resulting loss of equilibrium would temporarily incapacitate the enemy, allowing the Green Berets to dispatch them all.

Porter and Abernathy grasped their grenades and pulled the first ring. With the grenade's short fuse, the moment they pulled the secondary pin they had to toss them or risk losing a hand. They glanced at each other. Both were ready. Each made a second pull.

The final pins were out. They tossed the sailing ordnance toward the far wall. The moment it left their hands, they scooted toward the safety of the antechamber. With mere seconds remaining, each dove into the sheltering room. Both arching throws ran true. As the grenades hit the consecrated stones a few feet above their prey, the timers expired. Unimaginable levels of disconcerting sound and crippling light overwhelmed those inside. Behind the sarcophagus, their dazed forms were sprawled across the timeless granite.

The scrambling Green Berets rushed back into the passage. Abernathy had Morrow's Beretta. Porter held a razor-edged knife. They clambered into the still-echoing room and headed toward the west wall. Abernathy placed the barrel against a skull and fired. He moved on. The next victim awaited. He quickly worked his way through the melee. One by one, he put a bullet into every brain. To ensure none survived, Porter walked through the devastating scene, methodically slitting each throat. In seconds, the gruesome task was over.

Both, covered in blood, looked at their handiwork. "Now all we've got to do is figure out which one's the Chosen One," Abernathy said. "Then we'll take his sorry ass outside for the entire world to see."

Most were badly chewed up by Abernathy and Porter's efforts. After checking three or four, Porter said, "What'd the captain tell us he looked like?"

"Little man in his early seventies with sunken cheeks and a scraggly beard."

"Hell, that describes almost everyone in here. Got anything else we can go on?"

"He's supposed to be wearing peasant clothing," Abernathy said.

"Thanks, Sarge. Except for the one in uniform, they're all wearing peasant clothing."

"Well, keep looking. He's got to be one of these dead bastards."

Sam was standing ten feet to Lauren's left as she exited the pyramid. The sounds of the explosions from deep within the hallowed structure were still ringing in her ears. He saw her the moment she stepped from the cramped corridor. The stunned platoon leader's jaw dropped. In disbelief he watched her coming toward him. She ran into his arms, smothering him with kisses.

"Sam. Oh my God, Sam. I thought you were dead."

He stared at her, struggling to form the words. "Lauren, it's you who's dead. How the hell did you get here?" He was certain he'd awaken at any moment and the memory of this unreal embrace would forever dissipate.

She smiled at him, the love in her eyes as striking as anything he'd ever seen. "I assure you, Sam Erickson, I'm very much alive. I'll tell you all about it later. For now, let's just say it's a long story and leave it for another day."

Sanders exited the pyramid. He pulled his well-worn green beret from his pocket and positioned it on his head. He walked up with a wide grin to where the loving couple stood. "I see you two have met before." He held out his hand. "Sergeant Charlie Sanders, Detachment Alpha 6333, 6th Special Forces, sir," he said while shaking the lieutenant's hand.

Erickson responded without letting go of Lauren. "Sam Erickson, 2nd Marine Division. Glad to meet you, Sanders."

"Chuck," she said, "we're missing it. Remember my promise to record the story when the first Green Beret and Marine met. And we're missing it."

"We're not missing a thing, Miss Wells."

She turned to look at him. He was standing with his camera running.

In a few hours, the scene would play over and again as the war's end was joyously proclaimed in every American home.

On the hilltop, the firing had stopped. Only the cries of the wounded disturbed the coming evening. The medevac helicopters would be busy on this night.

A beaming Sam held Lauren so tight he nearly crushed her. But he was still in charge and there were a few more actions to undertake.

"Sergeant Joyce, take half the men and comb the area around the pyramid. While you're at it, check real close in the cemeteries on both sides of this place and anywhere the enemy might be hiding. Orders still stand. If they look like they're not going to surrender, kill every Pan-Arab you find."

"Will do, sir," Joyce said. "Okay, you guys, the war's not over quite yet. Let's go clean this place out."

Pressed against the northern side of the crumbling rocks, the Mahdi watched as the Marines moved about checking the dead and wounded. A couple of wary Americans, their rifles ready, were starting to move in his direction. He knew if he stayed where he was, he'd soon be discovered. Yet despite his perilous position he was certain Allah would intervene. His God would allow him to emerge unscathed, but only if he showed the courage expected from a true believer. He looked about, unsure of what to do. The pair was coming toward the eroding barricade. To the west, a scant twenty meters away, the decrepit wall all but disappeared. Still, he had no choice.

He'd show how much faith he had.

His conviction growing, Muhammad Mourad stood and started toward the sheltering desert. The primitive bulwark he walked next to was at least a foot taller than he was. No one on its southern side could see him as he moved along its rough exterior. He was so confident of his salvation he was almost strolling as he tramped next to the masking obstruction. From the look on his face and the ease in his stride, he didn't appear to have a care in the world. The twenty meters was soon covered. He didn't hesitate when he reached the wall's end. Walking on, he headed for the open sands.

Erickson spotted the furtive figure in the deepening twilight. He pushed Lauren aside and picked up his rifle. He had the Pan-Arab in his sights. For some reason he'd never be able to explain, at that moment Mourad sensed the danger. He stopped and turned to face his tormentors. Even in the fading gloom, the Marine platoon leader could see that the pitiful person in the bloody, ill-fitting uniform had to be quite elderly. The insignificant enemy was almost comical in his appearance. Erickson put his finger on the trigger.

Despite his change of clothing, Wells instantly recognized the fleeing figure.

She knew what she had to do. The Mahdi had spared her life. Now it would be her turn to save his. She couldn't tell Sam at whom he was aiming. If she did, the man she loved would have no choice but to finish him. "Sam, don't. For my sake, please don't," she begged. "There's no reason to take another life if you don't have to."

Erickson stood there frozen. The bedraggled shape was certainly not a member of the mujahideen. From his dress, the weaponless old man couldn't have been more than an ordinary soldier. With as blood-soaked as he was, he probably wouldn't last much longer before his wounds ended his life.

"Let him go, Sam."

The exhausted lieutenant hesitated, taking in her haunting words. Ever so slowly, he dropped the weapon from his shoulder.

The Chosen One looked at Lauren Wells. Their eyes met for the briefest of moments. Even so, she didn't let the growing satisfaction appear on her face. She didn't want to do anything that would give away her secret. The aging Algerian shifted his gaze to the American Marine. He stood motionless, staring at Erickson. A hint of an ironic smile appeared on the Mahdi's lips. The little man did something resembling an ill-practiced bow, turned, and headed toward the desert.

The smothering night would soon hide him from those who would do him harm.

EPILOGUE

NOVEMBER, TWO YEARS LATER

As they'd always done, the moment the shooting stopped the Americans packed up and returned home. The sordid conflict was over and the time for celebration had come. They'd leave a token force in Egypt to act as a trip wire. And with the Iraqis and Iranians continuing to battle, they'd bolster their defenses in Kuwait and Saudi Arabia.

At least for the time being.

Sam and Lauren hurried off to renew the fervent romance they'd begun in a dour place called "Press City." They spent an incredible month visiting London, Amsterdam, and Paris. They had a marvelous time touring Europe. It further reinforced the beguiling feelings they held for each other. Their month filled with unrepressed desire soon passed.

When it was over, there was no doubt this was a once-in-a-lifetime love. Each accepted it without the slightest hesitation. Yet in the end, neither was capable of relinquishing their first love. Their parting in Paris had been memorable. It was filled with gut-wrenching emotion and unending tears.

She remained at her post in the Middle East. He returned to the 2nd Marine Division in North Carolina. Lauren did everything she could to create reasons to travel to the States. When she did, she'd find a way to return to Sam's arms. Sometimes they'd be together for a few fantastic hours. Occasionally, they'd hold each other for a whirlwind day. Once, they'd developed an elaborate scheme to spend an entire week addressing their longing. Each missed the other terribly in the spanning stretches apart. Nevertheless, both continued to cling to their life's goals.

Wells's ever-expanding fame was heightened by the war. Her book on the days spent with the Chosen One inside the Great Pyramid was a runaway best seller. It failed, of course, to mention the circumstances surrounding Mourad's miraculous escape. She'd become a household name. In another few years, if her career stayed on this course, she'd be sitting behind the anchor desk at a major television network.

Within six months of the war's end, Erickson was promoted to captain. With the Marines' losses, the need for combat-experienced officers was great. He'd taken command of a 2nd Marine Division Infantry Company and was excelling at his new duties. Recently, however, he'd received orders to leave for a two-year stint in Okinawa. During that unending time, the stolen moments with the woman he loved would nearly disappear.

Yet they'd chosen their paths, and neither was willing to turn back.

James Fife, his pronounced limp permanent, reached the maximum number of years the Marines would allow him to serve his country. He could put off retirement no longer. Forced into civilian clothing, he felt out of place. Yet he soon found a way back to where he was most comfortable. He moved to Oceanside, California, just outside the huge Marine base at Camp Pendleton. A buddy owned a company that provided security guards to roam the ocean-swept encampment's distant reaches. The old platoon sergeant eagerly took the job his friend offered. Even though his uniform looked quite different from theirs, he was among his own kind as he watched the next generation of Marines prepare for desperate battles to come.

He found a sweet widow whose children were grown. Having lived through a Marine's torments with her first husband, she understood what his previous life had been like. She demanded little, accepting whatever companionship he could provide. He kept a modest apartment a few miles away, but seldom went there. Neither was in love, and they likely never would be. Still, as they headed into their middle years, each was happy with what the quiet relationship provided. Although they'd never spoken of it, both planned on making this a long-term partnership with the potential to last for the remainder of their days.

Having recently celebrated his twenty-fifth birthday, Charlie Sanders remained a member of a reconstructed Detachment Alpha 6333. His engineering skills were even more practiced than before. The Pan-Arab War had been his initiating taste of combat, but he knew in this troubled world it wouldn't be his last.

Within weeks of returning to Fort Bragg he'd wed one of his fiancées. The misguided marriage hadn't lasted more than a few acrimonious months. The couple's divorce had become final within the year. Since then, his relationships with women had grown even more transitory. His attempts to hide from his past through these shallow encounters had failed miserably. Not a day went by when Charlie didn't think of Reena and the tragic events in the wine cellar. Those who knew the gregarious sergeant prior to the Pan-Arab War barely recognized the melancholy loner who'd taken his place.

The recently promoted Aaron Porter was still single. And still one of the best at his trade in any army in the world. He was also an enduring member of Alpha 6333, working to rebuild the decimated team into a viable fighting force. Despite Sanders's efforts to rebuff him, Porter remained his one close friend.

After twenty-four years of service, Matthew Abernathy retired a few months after returning from Cairo. His latest wife pressured him into opening a small business in a town near Fort Bragg. He turned out to be an inept shopkeeper. After the excitement of his prior years he fared poorly in this mundane existence. Without telling her, within the past week he'd accepted a highly dangerous assignment with the CIA. It would be the end of his struggling endeavor and his failing third marriage.

Bradley Mitchell's funeral was by necessity a closed casket. After his burial at Arlington National Cemetery his folks took the children to California. They remained with their grandparents, and would continue to do so for the indefinite future. Given their tender ages at the time of his death, even two years after his passing their memories of him were growing hazy and a bit distorted.

Far into the future his children would inherit their mother's immense fortune. Despite what her wealth would bring, they'd have traded every cent to see their father a final time.

Their mother they missed little. Neither had seen her since their father's funeral. Even so, she made sure to call and send presents on birthdays and at Christmas. Brooke had spent the majority of the previous two years in the Hamptons. With so busy a social schedule, she'd little time to grieve her husband's death.

Norm Sweeney made good on his threat to leave the Navy. Since then, he'd had a number of offers for work as a commercial pilot. He knew he'd someday accept one, but he wasn't ready to return to the skies.

For now, he eked out a living dealing blackjack at the Desert Inn. He'd gone back to Las Vegas to find the vivacious Lisa and the solace she could bring. She continued to work as the lead dancer at the Riviera. Norm shared a cozy apartment and her enticing bed for the sixteen hours of the day they weren't on the job. He'd never been happier in his life.

Darren Walton got his wish. His third child was a healthy baby boy. Between his father and older sisters, the inquisitive toddler was terribly spoiled. The sixteen-month-old towheaded infant carried a tiny football with him wherever he went. His father continued to coach Pee Wee football and wait for the day when his son would express a desire to join the team. Walton had recently received transfer orders to Germany. While they'd miss the friendships they'd made at Fort Hood, the family was excited about the change of scenery.

Despite his threats to never again speak to his platoon sergeant, Miguel Sanchez stayed fast friends with the Walton family. He'd burst with pride when he was named the new child's godfather.

Prior to the Pan-Arab War, Miguel had considered making the Army a career. But with the events at Sakakah, he forever changed his plans. Eight months after the unit's return to Texas his enlistment ended. Until the day he was discharged, he remained one of the best sources of information in the 1st Cavalry Division.

He'd headed home to Phoenix. He was presently two months into his sophomore year at Arizona State University and through his diligence and determination was doing well in school. The maturity he'd developed in the Army was evident in his approach to campus life. He'd found a pretty coed who was interested in understanding what he'd gone through, but never pushed him to tell more than he was willing to convey. Marriage was a real possibility.

With constant e-mails and occasional phone calls, he kept in contact with the Walton family. He'd remain close to them for the rest of his life.

There was more than enough turmoil at the war's end for Muhammad Mourad to slip away.

For five days, worldwide television proclaimed his demise. Still it wasn't long thereafter that the Americans figured out their mistake.

The Chosen One survived the blighted journey home. Despite his devotees' pleas, the Mahdi refused to accept any special privileges during the tortured trek back to the mountains of southern Algeria. It took many weeks for the survivors to cover the thousand miles of barren landscape. A notable host failed to make it. Yet eventually the end had come. And once more, by Allah's grace, the Mahdi was building a union strong enough to strike out and destroy those whose beliefs didn't conform to his.

The Allies had placed severe economic and military restrictions upon his federation. And its citizens were suffering beneath the sanctions' stifling yoke. Yet their brilliant leader was finding ways to reestablish his power.

The Americans were certain they'd won the war. But the Chosen One understood they were mistaken. The heretics had prevailed in the opening battle of the holy struggle, yet they'd accomplished no more. It was just the initial clash of many to come.

He was growing old and it would take years to overcome his failures in Egypt. Yet it didn't matter. For he understood he'd been placed in this world for a specific purpose. And nothing occurring in his futile struggle with the nonbelievers had changed that. He knew the prophecy would come to pass.

By his hand, Islam would rule the world.

Of that he had no doubt.